# Summer of Rain,
# Summer of Fire

*a novel*

## BILL MEISSNER

STEPHEN F. AUSTIN STATE UNIVERSITY PRESS

Sections of this novel previously appeared in the short story "Freddie and the Dreamers," published by *Missouri Review* and reprinted in the story collection *The Road to Cosmos* by Bill Meissner, University of Notre Dame Press, Notre Dame, Indiana 2004.

The italicized quote in Chapter 11 is taken from "Water," a short story by Bill Meissner, included in *Hitting into the Wind*, published by Random House Publishers and reprinted in paperback by SMU Press, Dallas, Texas.

The paraphrased sections in Chapter 7 regarding the Native American legends are based on the article "The Legends and Archaeology of Devil's Lake: A Place of Ancient Power in Wisconsin" by Jason Jarrell and Sara Farmer in *Ancient Origins: Reconstructing the Story of Humanity's Past*.

The quote from "America," by Allen Ginsberg, from COLLECTED POEMS: 1947-1997 by Allen Ginsberg. Copyright 2006 by the Allen Ginsberg Trust. Courtesy of HarperCollins Publishers. The quotes from "The Road Not Taken" and "Nothing Gold Can Stay" by Robert Frost, from *Collected Poems of Robert Frost*, Henry Holt and Company 1930, New York, N.Y.

The italicized quote at the end of Chapter 11 is from "Water," a short story by Bill Meissner, from the collection Hitting into the Wind, Random House Publishers, 1994 New York, N.Y.

The mixed-media painting, "Peace Sign," used in connection with this novel is by Laura Barbosa. The author thanks her for permission to use it.

For more information:

Stephen F. Austin State University Press

P.O. Box 13007 SFA Station

Nacogdoches, Texas 75962

sfapress@sfasu.edu
www.sfasu.edu/sfapress


Managing Editor: Kimberly Verhines

Editorial Assistants: Katt Noble and Meredith Janning

Distributed by Texas A&M Consortium

www.tamupress.com


ISBN: 978-1-62288-936-5

FIRST EDITION

*Also by Bill Meissner*

## PROSE

*Hitting into the Wind*
*Spirits in the Grass*
*Light at the Edge of the Field*
*The Road to Cosmos*

## POETRY

*The Mapmaker's Dream*
*American Compass*
*Learning to Breathe Underwater*
*The Sleepwalker's Son*
*Twin Sons of Different Mirrors*
*The Glass Carnival*

# Acknowledgments

I'd like to extend my sincere thanks to the following people:

To my mother and father, who provided me with my first Royal Quiet DeLuxe typewriter, a stack of paper and a stack of memories, and then encouraged me, saying *Yes, write!*

To my son, Nate, for his love and for believing in my writing as I typed my way through the decades.

To my friends, colleagues (especially Shannon Olson), and former and current St. Cloud State University students who have supported my writing over the years.

To Jack Driscoll, long-time friend and extraordinary writer.

To Tim O'Brien, for writing the brilliant book, *The Things They Carried.*

To my literary agent, Felicia Eth, for her support of my writing and this novel.

To Kimberly Verhines, for bringing this novel to light.

To Verlyn Mueller, Curator/Archivist of the Badger History Group, for valuable research information regarding the Badger Ordnance Plant in central Wisconsin, which supplied gunpowder for use in Vietnam.

I'd also like to thank Jack O'Keefe for his friendship and his detailed information about the Badger Ordnance Plant, and in particular about a catastrophic explosion at that factory.

This book is in memory Clayton Luther and Bob Crawley, the first young men from my small hometown to lose their lives in Vietnam. I am grateful to those men and women who served nobly and came back to tell about it.

With fond memories of Bill Kehoe, lost friend, gone too soon.

And most of all, thanks to my wife Chris for her love, her ongoing belief in my writing, and her expert editorial suggestions regarding this book. Without her, this novel would not exist. I'm also grateful to her for teaching me how to swim one evening in a lovely starlit pool in Acapulco, Mexico on our honeymoon.

# Author's Note

*December 31, 1969, members of the radical antiwar New Year's Gang stole a Cessna 150 airplane outside Madison, Wisconsin and attempted to drop firebombs on the Badger Army Ammunition Plant, located in rural central Wisconsin. This little-publicized but true incident became an incentive behind the writing of this book. The bombing scene is included in this story, but compared to the actual event, it is highly exaggerated.*

*This novel is a work of fiction. Although it includes several actual central Wisconsin settings, the events in this book are fictional, as are the characters, and any similarity to persons, living or dead, is purely coincidental.*

—Bill Meissner, July 21, 2022

# CHAPTER 1
*Summer, 1968*

The first explosion erupted, opening like an orange flower surrounded by a ring of angry gray smoke. Leaning over a copper bin of gunpowder, Phil Keyhoe felt the shock wave, like a fist pummeling him from the inside of his chest.

He ran to the open doorway of Powder House 121, and what he saw made him stop there, frozen, unable to move in or out, his legs and arms stiffening like concrete. Panic rushed through him as he spotted a low-flying Cessna, its wings wobbling as if it were balancing precariously on the updrafts. Phil had heard that a plane might fly over the Strongs Ammunition Plant one of these days, dropping hundreds of anti-war leaflets to the workers below, or pulling a fluttering banner that might read **STOP THE WAR! CLOSE THE STRONGS!** In a fleeting dream last night, Phil saw the plane dropping yellow flowers from the sky like tiny spiraling suns.

But this plane, its whirring propeller shredding the morning air like a buzz-saw, had no banner or fliers, and contained no cargo of peaceful flowers. Instead, a solid object—ablaze like a meteor—plummeted from it. The object tumbled in slow motion until it struck a storage building and detonated in a blinding flash of red.

"What the hell?" one man screamed, "Someone's bombin' the plant!"

Phil felt himself being shoved against the frame of the doorway as frantic workers—all familiar men from his home town, their faces etched with terror—dashed toward the open grassy areas between the buildings. Pieces of burning wood rained down around them.

Phil still couldn't move.

He felt as though his feet were rooted in the insulated floor. A numbness rose in him, the sensation climbing from his feet inside his steel-toed boots to his forehead. All he could do was stare, open-mouthed, as smoke from the explosion rose in a mushroom cloud.

"Run," he remembered his girlfriend saying to him one night when they swam at the lake. "If something happens out there," she had cautioned, "don't hesitate. Just run." He understood why. After all, the place manufactured gunpowder, and some buildings were stockpiled with hundreds of thousands of pounds of it.

Phil finally broke from his trance and sprinted toward the asphalt path that led to the exit gates. He merged with the other workers who stampeded alongside him, bumping each other's shoulders, their mouths frozen into Os.

Absurd thoughts flashed through Phil's mind. He could have been doing wind sprints with his best friend Tommy during football practice. He could have been with a platoon under attack on a battlefield in the middle of Vietnam. But this was no game. This was no war, here in the middle of rural Wisconsin.

The smoke intertwined with the shouts and curses of the workers, the rising and falling of sirens, the rapid popping of gunshots as plant guards fired at the circling plane.

Reaching the entrance gate and jogging into the parking lot, Phil coughed out the bitter taste of sulfuric smoke that clawed deep into his lungs.

The plane went into a sudden dive, dropped its cargo, and another explosion erupted. Phil crouched down and pulled his knees up to his chest to protect himself. Then something hit him hard, making him shudder. Not a fragment of wood or a chunk of asphalt, but the realization that he, Phil Keyhoe, the Security Supervisor's son, might have something—not just something, but a lot—to do with this.

# CHAPTER 2
*Sixteen Months Earlier*

Phil Keyhoe knew nothing of explosions.

What made him shudder this morning was the cool air whirring from the vent of his father's Chrysler at seven a.m. and the whining country song on the radio. Phil didn't know what this job at the Strongs Ammunition Plant would hold for him; he only knew that he'd find out in a few minutes. As he rode along with his father, passing the dark wood frame Bluff Lake houses that huddled shoulder to shoulder, he noticed, above the hills ahead of them, the splintered yellow beams of the sun spoking through the low clouds. The beams pierced the windshield and burned his tired eyes.

With the country music station playing on low volume, Karl rattled off a few instructions. His usual way. His Standard Operating Procedure.

"So, you'll go into the office and get an ID badge. You know—name, ID number." Karl checked his rear-view mirror as they passed the slightly bent city limits sign; he veered into the left lane as Main Street seemed to flex its muscles and expand into the broad asphalt Highway 12, a four-lane road that led the three miles to the plant.

Ahead, Phil noticed a few pigeons perched on a telephone wire. One of them, startled by the muffler of a passing truck, left its perch and swooped low over the highway, directly in their path. With a dull thump, the bird bounced off the thick glass of the windshield, sending out a burst of iridescent purple feathers.

"Jeeze, Dad," Phil uttered.

"Damn," Karl exclaimed. "Stupid bird. Couldn't avoid it."

Phil glanced behind the Chrysler to see the carcass of the bird, its wings splayed, rolling a couple of times in the middle of the road.

"So, like I was saying," Karl continued, unfazed, "They'll issue you a locker. Some safety equipment. You know, helmet, safety glasses, work gloves, all that. Don't lose that stuff either," he added, "Like you do at home." He glanced at Phil, who was still peering at the bird in the rear-view mirror, and asked "You listening, or what?"

Phil nodded. *Or what,* he thought, but he didn't dare say it. He couldn't help but notice his father's enthusiasm as he discussed the protocol of the day. After all, with his pull as a supervisor, he'd gotten Phil this job at the plant—a high-paying job for a eighteen-year-old. He'd be earning more than any part-time job watching the tikes splashing each other at the Bluff Lake municipal pool or slinging root beer floats onto the countertop of Eddie's Drive-In. But Phil, tired as he was from getting up at 6:15, didn't share his dad's excitement. He felt, more than anything else, a kind of numbness. On a typical Saturday morning he'd still be sleeping, wrapped in a quilt of dreams until almost noon. Then he'd untangle himself from the covers, place the Beatle's *Rubber Soul* on the turntable and dress slowly as "Here, There and Everywhere" sifted through the small speaker of the Sears record player on his dresser.

Now, as they crested the hill and the car picked up speed, Phil noticed the Strongs Plant seeming to grow from the dark earth in the valley below as if it were filmed in time-lapse photography: gray clapboard buildings rising, some of them partly covered with sod, like huge turtles embedded in the earth. Dreary rows of beige barrack-like buildings skulked off into the distance. Refinery buildings lifted their broad metal shoulders. Utility poles held up clusters of transformers. Black wires cut the horizon into pieces. Dark smokestacks coughed out yellowish smoke and poked holes in the morning sky.

Phil rubbed the crusted sleep from the corner of one eye. He had passed the plant dozens of times, of course, while driving this highway to Madison with his buddies enroute to a concert or to hang out at Lake Mendota, but he never thought much about the plant's ever-expanding acres. "Look at that goddamn place!" his buddy Tommy once declared as they passed the entry gates where armed guards stood. "It's a frickin' concentration camp." Phil had heard that the federal government—which was the plant's contractor—forced farmers to sell their land so they could add extra square miles to the place for powder storage.

"So, um, what'll I do there?" Phil questioned.

Karl adjusted his hands on the leather-covered steering wheel, steadying it. "Whatever they tell you. Just report to the riggers building. There's lots to get done out there." He nodded as if agreeing with himself. "Lots."

Phil speculated about what his assignment might be. A couple of weeks ago, he had talked to some guys from town who worked there. They told him about the shitty jobs they were assigned to, like shoveling gravel for eight hours in the heat, or unloading fifteen-hundred-pound rolls of pulp paper from rusty boxcars. Jimmy Moore related that a full-time worker once lifted him on a forklift in a warehouse so he could change light bulbs thirty feet above a concrete floor. "He gave me a handful of bulbs, then told me to put one foot on each frickin' fork," he explained, "then he hoisted me up."

"Thirty feet up?" Phil questioned.

"Hell yeah," Jimmy nodded. "You learn to balance pretty damn quick. Otherwise, you bust your head on the concrete like a goddamn melon." He patted the top of his crew cut. "Not to mention that one of the bulbs broke. It snapped off right in my bare hand as I tried to untwist it."

"Huh," Phil responded.

"I kid you not. Foreman said it must have been an old bulb or something. Probably from the Korean War days."

Jimmy also told him about the explosion last year, one that killed three men. Phil recalled reading about the incident in the *Bluff Lake Freedom*, and his dad—who began working out there at that time—was really upset about it. "Yep," Moore said callously, "Blew 'em right through the third-floor wall of a goddamn refinery building. Guess it happened when some yokel fiddled with a light switch, flipping it off and on to be funny." When Phil gave him a puzzled look, he added "You know—a damn little spark. That's all it took."

That night, at two-thirty a.m., Phil jolted awake, seeing that flicker of yellow static in his sleep. He lay there, winding himself in the covers; he couldn't stop thinking about what kind of dangers lurked in a place that used flammable chemicals to make gunpowder. Two hours later, he was still awake, trying to stop imagining the incident—a man flipping a light switch, a sudden bright flash filling the room, the unsuspecting workers being blown sideways. He hoped he wouldn't work anywhere near that building, or near the gunpowder.

As they continued the last miles to the plant, Phil yawned.

"You out late again?" Karl quizzed, giving Phil a squinting look that always meant disapproval. Guilty as charged.

"Not that late," Phil replied to Karl's interrogation.

What's *not that late*?" Karl pried.

He had no comeback except to turn his head and look out the window. The question was a rhetorical one, and had its own answer: *Too damn late*. Karl didn't even have to say it.

Last night Phil hung out with his best friend since grade school, Tommy Laudermilk, who cruised the town square, revving his dented powder blue Ford Falcon. Phil would have preferred to be out late with some girl, parked behind the woolen mills where they'd be staring at the distant night sky and whispering amorously to each other until their lips met in a steamy kiss.

But no such luck.

The fact was, it was just he and Tommy, with their usual Friday night routine—chugging a couple lukewarm cans of Hamms in the alley behind the theatre, then hopping in Tommy's car with the windows rolled down and the radio turned up so loud the tinny speakers buzzed. Last night, Tommy slapped his palm on the dash, keeping time to the Rolling Stones "Satisfaction" and embarrassed Phil by honking at girls. "Hey!" Tommy hollered as they passed two girls, "Phil Keyhoe's in love with you!" Phil slunk down in the seat and barked "Shut up, dork!"

As Karl and Phil followed the gradual one-mile descent to the plant, they noticed a man ahead on the side of the road, facing oncoming traffic. The man was bearded and wore a tattered jean jacket; he stood in silence and held a handwritten sign that read **Stop the War in Vietnam!** As Karl passed, he flashed his bright lights into the man's face.

"Idiot," Karl barked. The word filled the car, lingering for a few seconds before it was absorbed by the dark blue cloth interior.

Karl slowed the car as they approached the newly installed blinking caution lights at the intersection. A few feet away, on the ten-foot cyclone fence topped by barbed wire, a white sign with bold red letters:

**Warning, Government Property**
**No Trespassing Under Penalty of Law**
**Unauthorized Persons Are Subject to Arrest.**

Those commands were his father's. A few months ago, Karl pleased the plant's Supervisor-in-Chief, Colonel Digby, by posting a new set of warning signs along the perimeter of the twenty-five square mile plant.

Karl veered into the parking stall marked **Reserved for Security Supervisor,** lifted his big wing-tip shoe and pressed on the power brake. Phil, sunken into the extra-cushioned velour seat, rocked slightly. "Well, here we are," Karl announced, as a droning Hank Williams song faded.

Karl took a pack of cigarettes from the breast pocket of his white shirt, tossed them to the dash. He smoked a pack of Lucky Strikes a day, but only at home, since all cigarettes and flammable materials were banned from the plant. Everyone knew that bringing in matches, cigs, or anything flammable would get you fired.

"So how do you feel?" Karl asked, pulling his aluminum dome top lunchbox from the seat between them.

Phil didn't have an answer to that, unless it was a mildly sarcastic one. *Not the greatest. I'd rather be on the beach at the lake, drinking an Old Style I smuggled from your case in the basement.*

"Ready for work?" Karl pulled the keys from the ignition.

"Um-hum." Phil was always agreeing with his father lately, it seemed, whether he meant to or not.

"It's not just a job, you know," Karl said with a little surge of pride. "We're out here for a reason."

"Yeah," Phil agreed again, though he wasn't exactly sure what that reason was.

Stepping in front of the car, Phil noticed a few small feathers from the pigeon, still stuck to the windshield. As he strode past, Karl reached over and, with a quick back-handed motion, brushed them off.

They made their way to the Security Administration office. Phil noticed the vague scents of sulfur, and tar, and something else, which he couldn't quite identify.

Phil watched the workers walking past—working-class middle aged men and women from Bluff Lake. No one greeted each other. To Phil, they looked tired, expressionless, as they shuffled, round-shouldered, toward the check-in-gates.

The two-story Safety Administration building was sided with mouse brown clapboards. Karl used a pass card to unlock a dull metal door, then strode up to a guard who stood at the entry to the main hallway. Phil wasn't sure, but it looked like the man kept a holster and pistol beneath his jacket. The man greeted Karl by name and tossed him a grin.

"Whatta you got?" the man asked, nodding to Phil, who trailed behind Karl. "Discipline problem?"

"Hell, no," Karl let out a wheezy laugh. "It's my son. Works here now."

"Oh." The man chuckled. "Sure. You bet."

Phil followed behind his father as they climbed the stairway to the second floor. Karl, balding and putting on the weight, walked with a lumbering, swaying gait, his right leg limping slightly. Glancing at the smudge marks on the tan plaster walls, Phil couldn't imagine his dad coming to this place every day.

Karl led Phil to a barred window and a brass tray below it, like the kind you see at a bank. There, a man issued Phil's badge and equipment. Karl continued down the hall to his office to check the safety reports that came in overnight. As Karl well knew, the plant was operating twenty-four hours a day with three eight-hour shifts.

"Keyhoe, eh?" the middle-aged man behind the window said with a crooked-toothed grin as he scanned Phil's papers. "You Karl's boy, then?"

Phil gave a curt nod.

"Well then, great."

"I won't be working near any of those refinery buildings, will I?" Phil questioned.

The man, chawing on a wad of gum, gazed blankly at him like a cow chewing cud. "Shit, ya never know. Depends on where they need ya, I s'pose."

Phil grabbed his badge, glasses, and coveralls. Then he pulled on an ill-fitting yellow hardhat and tried to adjust it. It kept tilting to the right, then to the left. As he passed the open doorway of the office, he saw Karl, sitting at his large metal desk, his eyes already fixed on the stack of work orders.

"Do me proud," Karl said without looking up. "I know a lot of people out here."

# CHAPTER 3

Phil tipped his head back and gasped, coughing out a mouthful of water, and that's when he saw her—that girl from English class. She climbed from the railroad track bed down the steep, hard-packed dirt path that led to the lake, a couple other girls trailing behind her. He couldn't stop staring. He kept paddling his arms and legs frantically in the lake water, since that's all he could do to stay afloat on this, or any Sunday afternoon.

He had never really learned to swim, though he never admitted that to his buddies. He'd become adept at treading water, and that was about it. He always agreed to join his friends and jump off the rocks into the deep water of Bluff Lake where the lake bottom dropped quickly to fifty, then one hundred feet. The purplish quartzite rocks had— thousands of years ago—been pushed by the shoulders of a glacier to become the lake's towering five-hundred foot tall east and west shores. Or so his high school science teacher lectured to the half-dozing class. Phil was adept at doing a steady dogpaddle, keeping his head slightly above the surface. Sometimes the dark green water water felt so deep beneath him that he believed the lake bottom was a thousand feet below. He always tried to fake it, laughing to hide his inevitable sensation of panic as his buddies horsed around, doing cannonballs near him and sometimes dunking him and each other under.

"Hey, Aqua Man!" a voice called. It was Tommy, who stood on shore. A class comedian, and a buffed 200-pound all-conference fullback on the football team, Tommy Laudermilk wasn't afraid to whip his shirt off and flex his muscles, just to show off. Tommy could hop into the lake and do the breaststroke a hundred yards out and then return without even being winded. Phil, on the other hand, was a tall and slim 175-pound wide receiver. He excelled in most sports, especially football and baseball, but swimming was his one weak zone. "You drownin' out there, or what?" Tommy questioned.

"Yes and no," Phil sputtered, trying to be funny. He was surviving, some ten feet out from the nearest large rock.

"Aw, Christ," Tommy mocked, hands on his hips. "Don't make me have to rescue you, doofus."

Phil's eyes were fixed beyond Tommy, where the girls, laughing and talking, casually made their way to the lake.

Following Phil's gaze, Tommy muttered, "Oh, I get it. Babes."

Phil focused on just one of the girls in particular, the new girl who caused quite a stir in his lit class last Friday. The scene replayed in his head.

That Friday morning in American Lit, Phil hadn't seen the newcomer enter the classroom and slip into a desk in the back row. And when he heard her clear voice striking a resonant, melodic note, it woke him from his trance of apathy and boredom.

"I don't agree," she had said. She had countered Miss Abigail Tuttle, which, at BLHS, was heresy. Tuttle was single, age fifty-something going on seventy, and she wore high-waisted stretch slacks and a boxy navy suit jacket that disguised her stocky torso. She was advisor for the Tri-Hi-Y Girls club for twenty years, and after her summer trip to England, proudly showed the unimpressed class her charcoal tombstone rubbings of the gravestones of Chaucer and Dunn. That morning, Miss Tuttle had announced that Robert Frost's poem, "The Road Not Taken," was analyzed too much. "It's simply about a man walking through the woods and choosing a path. A rather ordinary poem by Frost, actually. Not much of a message here," she proclaimed as she anchored herself behind her oak desk which, it was rumored, was quarried from a chunk of Stonehenge during the dark ages. Behind her back, kids called her *The Turtle*.

"I think Frost had a message," the girl in the back continued. "I mean, it's a message we should all think about." Phil turned to look at her and was taken by shimmering blue eyes as she focused on Miss Tuttle. The girl thoughtfully twirled one lock of her long hair that, to Phil, looked like blonde fire.

Tuttle peered over her half-shell glasses. Showing she did not approve of this contradiction, this little rebellion, she lobbed a leaden stare like a shot-put toward the back row. "And who might *you* be?" she asked wryly, her puzzled, creased face glancing down at her class list, then back at the girl. "You're not on the list."

"Mariah. Mariah Stiller. I'm new."

"Well. Of course," The Turtle said, pronouncing each word with her low-pitched voice as though it had two syllables. "And, I take it, you had something to say...?" she questioned.

"Yes. Frost was talking about being an individual. About nonconformity." Then she added, "It's really a poem about making a difference in the world."

The Turtle stood, then planted herself beside her desk. "It's much more simplistic than that." What I suggest...," she uttered, "is that you read the poem again." She jabbed the air in front of her as if giving someone a shot in the arm. Phil knew that with that, most students at BLHS would have backed down, would have lowered their gaze to their maple desks, where initials and obscenities were carved and re-carved, their sharp edges smoothed over with varnish.

"Yes, I've read it," Mariah countered, "A couple of times." At that moment, the air in the classroom seemed to hold still and even the most sluggish students' heads turned to stare at the source of the insurrection. Phil understood, as did the other students, the protocol of American Lit 300. You didn't cross The Turtle. Everyone understood that The Turtle's interpretation was not just the correct one, or the best one, but it was the *only* one; you learned that from the first day of class. You followed that principle if you wanted to get any kind of a decent grade in the class—a B minus, perhaps, or a B. An A was a coveted trophy, handed out only occasionally to the meek but attractive girl who sat in the front row, taking notes fastidiously and highlighting them in pink and yellow in her notebook. Phil knew you regurgitated the flowery interpretations or opinions The Turtle wanted to hear, and you wrote them down in your blue-covered paper essay booklet. He knew that you basically shut up and paid attention, unless you focused on the vent at the top corner of the room, from which a couple of spiderwebs constantly spiraled.

So in the hushed air of Room 201, this new girl and The Turtle reached a stalemate, as surely as the gridlock of desks that were bolted to the floor so there'd be no crowding of students, as if, given any chance, they would suffocate each other.

The Turtle, her eyes narrowed at this little mutiny, chortled. "Well," she said, "this poem is clearly about making choices, and nothing more. You'd best read the ending again." Miss T. gave a nod, as if the discussion was over, the door closed, as if the safe was locked and she had swallowed the key down the crepey turkey-neck of her throat. Phil glanced up at the wall clock, with the thin black second hand that never revolved. It was just one minute until dismissal. Then Mariah suddenly said "The ending?" Her voice rose, bright crimson in the colorless room. She proceeded to start to quote the final section of the poem. "I shall be telling this with...with...," she said, stumbling a little at first. Flustered, and blushing, she closed her eyes a few seconds, her eyelashes fluttering, as if she was looking inside for the rest of the words, or to gather some strength. Then she opened them and continued:

> I shall be telling this with a sigh
> Somewhere ages and ages hence:
> Two roads diverged in a wood, and I—
> I took the one less traveled by,
> And that has made all the difference.

Phil glanced at the girl's desk. He figured she was reading straight from the text, but was amazed to see that her 1,421 page *Masters of Literature* anthology, resting on her desk, was closed.

"Those are the *exact* lines I'm referring to," the Turtle countered, trying to acquire some ownership. Just then, the 4th hour bell rang, like a clanging between rounds at a boxing match. Its tinny decibels that told students that fourth hour was now ancient history, and they could lumber out the door. The students approached their mouse-brown lockers, numbly grabbed books, slammed the wobbly tin doors shut, and hurried to their next class. As Mariah passed him, Phil blurted, "Wow, you sure know a lot about Frost."

She smiled modestly. "Not really. Maybe just that one poem."

Phil stood by his locker and gazed beyond the herd, focusing on her as she continued to the far end of the hallway where two stairways led to the second floor. In the mid-day glare of the row of windows, she became a silhouette, then disappeared up the left stairway.

Now, as Phil treaded water, he watched Mariah reach the base of the path near the lake. She took lithe, graceful steps time as she navigated between two jagged rocks. Her legs were long and delicate, like Phil imagined the stems of fine crystal glasses to be. Still, they seemed strong, like two bronze shafts of light. Her blue and white towel, draped over one tanned shoulder, fluttered like a wing in the wind. Her hair was tied back in a thick ponytail that swayed, grazing her bare shoulders with each stride.

The three girls shed their blue jean cutoffs and gauze tops. The two dark-haired girls, clad in two-piece swimsuits, lowered themselves to their beach towels and leaned back on their elbows. Mariah, taller, with medium-length wavy blonde hair, and wearing an aqua swimsuit, padded barefoot toward the water.

"Wow," Tommy exclaimed, "Quite the extraordinary bod on blondie."

"She's a brain, too, buddy," Phil was quick to add.

"Who cares?" Tommy flipped back.

She lingered there, gazing out over the lake, contemplating it, and the bobbing waves seemed to calm themselves for her. Without hesitation, she slid the towel off her shoulders, scaled a fifteen-foot-high rock platform, and stepped to the narrow edge that jutted out over the water. She quickly untied her hair from the ponytail. At that moment, to Phil, she seemed perfect, the way the afternoon sunlight seemed to bend around her. But he realized he was just doing his usual romanticizing again; everything that seemed perfect was always flawed. Maybe good ol' Robert Frost had it right in his poem when he claimed "Nothing gold can stay." As Mariah poised at the edge, Phil wondered if she might be a little too fearless, and maybe too confident. And those things, Phil always believed, eventually got you in trouble.

"Hey! Careful!" Phil called out. "Lake's pretty deep." It was against his usual shy nature, but he heard himself blurt it anyway. Though he hoped the words sounded authoritative, they came out flattened, like the air was let out of them.

With a quick turn of her head, she tossed him a flickering smile, a few strands of wavy hair falling over one eye. "Thanks for the warning," was all she said, followed by a laugh that skimmed like light across the water.

He felt embarrassed that he had decided to call out to her, and he shrugged, though he knew his shoulders were under water, so she wouldn't even be able to see them. *Brilliant lifeguard advice,* he thought. *Yeah, a lake occasionally has a habit of being deep.*

But before he could chide himself anymore, he watched Mariah raising her arms gracefully above her head, then clasping her hands together as if she were praying. She held that pose, toes curled over the sharp edge of the quartzite.

Her sudden, strong leap surprised Phil.

She arched into the humid air that held her for a second. It was a motion that seemed to say to the world: *plunge in.* As if in slow motion, her shoulders, then her waist, her smooth hips and legs parted the water, and she slipped easily into the lake. Her arched feet and toes were the last to disappear.

He was astonished that she left barely a splash.

Phil blinked in expectation, waiting for her to appear again, but she didn't come up for a few long seconds. He hoped there were no hidden rocks just beneath the surface.

As he waited, he held his breath. Finally, twenty yards farther out from where she dove in, she burst through the surface, her head tipped back, hair flowing in golden tendrils onto her slim, long neck, her eyes opening wide to the sky. It was like the sunlight was threading through her.

"C'mon, Key!" Tommy called, breaking Phil's trance. Standing on the gravel near the railroad tracks, Tommy circled his Bluff Lake Thunderbirds T-shirt over his head and then slipped it on. "I gotta get back, man."

Phil paddled to shore, grabbed his beach towel, retrieved his watch and brown leather wallet with the usual two dollars stuffed inside it. Not one, not three, but two dollars—exactly enough for a chocolate malt at Arnie's Dairy Queen with change left over.

He and Tommy began the half-mile walk along the tracks that led toward the south shore beach. There, little kids dug holes with yellow and red plastic shovels.

"So what's the big hurry?" Phil asked. He brushed back his brown hair that was growing a little longer into a Beatle style, much to the disapproval of his father.

"Gotta clean up and vacuum the damn garage. Then fix up the disaster of my room." The breeze ruffled Tommy's ash blonde beach-boy style hair. "Or my old man won't let me use the car next weekend. He wants the garage floor spit-shined so he can see his face in it." Tommy fiddled with the dial of a small transistor radio, the first chords of *The Lovin Spoonful's* "What a Day for a Daydream" played, and he sang along with the chorus.

Spreading his arms like a tightrope walker, Tommy hopped on a shiny rail and balanced on it. "Hey, do you know how Jumbo, the world's largest elephant, died?"

Phil scratched the top of his head and squinted one eye. "No. Please enlighten me. I'm not up to date on my elephant facts."

"I read about it yesterday. In *Life Magazine*, even."

"Since when do you read, Milk?" Phil quipped.

"Hey, I can recite the alphabet. Wanna hear me?"

"Spare me."

"So anyway, Jumbo weighed something like five thousand pounds. Twenty feet high. The Ringling Brothers toured him all over the country. But then the big lug got hit by a train."

"A train?"

"Yep. Stands to reason. When you think of it, that's the only thing it that could kill something that huge. I mean, imagine if a Volkswagen ran into it, the little Volks beetle would get crushed under one of its big feet. And Jumbo would just keep walking."

"Wow, Milk. You're the purveyor of the most useful information."

Tommy smirked and hopped off the rail.

"Guess what?" Phil said, shifting the conversation. "My dad got me a job."

"Job? You mean real work?"

"Yeah. At the plant."

Tommy stopped abruptly, scraping his scuffed Converse tennies on the gravel. "The powder plant?"

"Yup. The one and only famous powder plant. It's only weekends, though, until summer. Then it's full time. Until fall."

"Jesus. I hear it's a shitty place to work."

"Me, too. But my dad's all proud about it."

Tommy spit toward the weeds. "That's dads for you. Mine's the same way about his job at the post office. I think he recites the damn Bluff Lake zip code in his sleep."

The two followed the railroad ties, sticky with melted creosote in the magnified afternoon sun. Tommy spun his wet towel around in the air like a propeller, making a fluttering sound. Phil kept glancing back toward the rock outcrop.

Noticing Phil's distraction, Tommy said "That girl still on your mind?"

Phil lifted his eyebrows in a *Yeah, maybe* expression.

Tommy set the transistor radio on a rail, dropped to the gravel, and did a few quick pushups. "Wanna join me, Key? Might do you some good. You know—release that sexual tension, and all."

"I think I'll pass," Phil chuckled.

Tommy jumped up and said, "Man, half the senior girls are salivating to go on a date with you. So what's the big deal with blondie?

"Dunno. Just something different about her." Phil couldn't exactly say what it was. Unlike the other girls at the high school, when he was near her, she made him feel attracted to her and nervous at the same time. Maybe she made him feel more alive. Just something.

"Hey, I know what you're thinking," Tommy said. "I've seen your girl in the lunchroom." He shook his head, his curling locks bobbing on his forehead. "Sure, she's pretty cool. But kinda aloof. Forget it, man. I mean, new girls are like Campbell's soup cans without the label. You never know what you'll get."

"Profound, Tommy."

"It's true, kinda. New girls are *always* trouble."

"Yeah, maybe," Phil said, picking up a rock from between the ties and tossing it to the boulders alongside the tracks. With a click, it skipped and bounced into the darkness. "Or maybe not."

As he lay in bed that evening, unable to fall asleep, Phil pictured her sleek form, arcing in the air like a slice of light. He knew that split second would stay in his memory for a long time. He couldn't stop admiring the ease with which she dove from that high rock into the dark green drop-off with fearlessness and abandon, even as he called out his feeble warning. *Who was she?* he wondered—this mystery girl who seemed to be part rebel, part poet, and not to mention queen of the mysterious glacial lake? *And how could he—ordinary, cautious, non-swimmer Phil Keyhoe—possibly get to know her?*

He knew he'd replay that dive again and again in his dreams. It amazed him, the way she could stay underwater for so long. As he waited for her to come up, his heart sped up, and his own lungs seemed to constrict, crushing the air from them, as if he was there, deep under the water with her.

He envisioned her breaking the surface. He could still feel the concentric ripples that glided out from her, moving steadily toward him, calming his panic, and buoying him up.

# CHAPTER 4

Nervous about where he'd be assigned to work, Phil stood with a group of newly hired summer crew guys in the riggers building. He was surrounded by the scents of oil and a faint burnt aroma from some workers welding in the side room. There was a third scent, too—something he couldn't quite identify as he walked through the entry gate earlier this Saturday morning.

The walls of the riggers building were decorated with rubber fan belts circling metal hooks, buckets of sawdust for smothering chemical spills, loops of rusted chains and heavy-duty yellow extension cords dangling from posts. Tacked to a wall were a couple of signs with red letters—his father's doing. One said **Safety Is No Accident** and another proclaimed **Safety Rules Are Your Best Tools.** *Extremely catchy slogans*, Phil thought. Along the entire back wall of the building were racks and racks of shovels of all sizes—some narrow and square, some with pointed tips, others flat and wide, like the kind you'd use to scoop up grain. Why would they possibly need so many shovels? he wondered. Were they burying things out there, or what?

"Keyhoe, you're on haircut crew," a foreman with a clipboard barked as he doled out assignments to the new workers.

"Haircut?"

"Yeah. You know, the mowing crew."

"Oh. Sure." The detail sounded harmless enough. He was relieved to hear he wasn't going to be pushing boulders up hillsides for eight hours a day.

In the doorway of the building, an assistant foreman presented a less-than-enlightening orientation about the beauties of a government-issue Briggs and Stratton lawn mower, saying things like "this here's your throttle" and "don't mess with the oil plug unless you need to," and "try not to spill gas from the gas cans or nothing. We don't need no goddamn fires around here."

Phil hopped into the back of a rickety, 1940s Army-green truck filled with a dozen lawnmowers, sat on the floor next to one. Someone had scratched *screw you* into the side panel. The bed of the truck, covered by a sagging khaki canvas canopy top, was thick with the scent of stale gasoline. *Don't light a match,* he thought, though he already knew the cardinal rule that all smoking materials were outlawed on the plant grounds. He waited as the rest of the part-timers—a crew of ten eighteen-and-nineteen-year-olds—climbed in one by one and sat down.

"Greetings, dumbshit," a voice called.

Phil looked up to see Tommy Laudermilk climbing in with a sly grin.

"That makes two of us, now that you're here," Phil quipped.

"Or, four thousand of us," Tommy added, "If you count the rest of the shmucks working in this crazy joint."

"So what are *you* doing here, Milk?"

"Hey—didn't you hear? President Lyndon Johnson requested my official presence. So I signed on," Tommy said with a snicker, giving a mock salute.

"Because I support truth, justice, and the American way."

The truck, bouncing on the uneven road, made its way to the mowing site a couple of miles from the administration offices. Jostling left and right, Phil gazed out the back of the truck. He saw a corroded three-story acid refinery building, its smokestack belching yellow sulfuric smoke. The rusted narrow-gauge railroad tracks paralleled the road and a few tram cars, transporting piles of material, trundled along it. Beyond them, the rows of powder storage buildings seemed to march into the distance. Beige-suited workers pushed canvas carts into the open doorways like insects lured into ant traps. Everything he saw seemed to be dull, flat, and one dimensional: mono, not stereo. Beyond the plant, just over hills in the distance, he knew, were the glimmering blue waters of Bluff Lake. He wondered if the new girl, Mariah, would be swimming out there today. He pictured her diving in, her fingertips touching the water and setting fire to the lake. She was stereo, definitely stereo.

As the brakes hissed and squeaked, the truck lurched to a stop, and the guys' heads snapped back. They all piled out and gathered around Ray Duke, the lawn crew foreman. Compared to his gangly, mostly skinny teen-age crew, Duke was the epitome of manhood: muscular, late thirties, with a shadow of a beard, a bristly crew cut, and a black T-shirt beneath the unbuttoned neck of his coveralls. He had worked in the plant years ago, when it reopened briefly during the Korean Conflict. A tattoo on the muscle of his right arm bulged with the scarlet words *Freedom Battalion*, which, Phil figured, was from his stint in the Army. Rumor was that he got in fights in the local taverns after he drank too much.

"Looks like I got the freshman follies here," he began sarcastically as he scanned the crew. "So lemmie tell you something," he barked. "You work for me, and we'll get along." He folded his arms. "You *don't* work for me, and I'll kick your goddamn ass." He rubbed his tattoo with his knuckles. "Just like America, boys. Love it or frickin' leave it."

"Hey, this is gonna be a shitload of fun," Tommy said under his breath, and he did a little tap dance with his leather work boots. A couple of the guys snickered.

Duke shot Tommy a steely stare. "What'd you say?"

"Nothin'," Tommy smirked.

Duke took a step toward Tommy. "I said *what* did you say, kid?"

"I said, um, I *love* this job," Tommy said, his voice intentionally high-pitched to be comical. "Can't wait to get started."

Another guy let out a muffled laugh, and Duke gave him a glare. He then corrected Tommy, saying, "You mean I can't wait to get started, *sir*."

Tommy rolled his eyes.

Duke leaned close to Tommy, so they were almost touching nose to nose. "Don't just stand there, shit for brains," Duke commanded. "Say it." Phil could see Tommy take a quick gulp, and he felt nervous for him.

"Um, can't wait to get started. *Sir*." Tommy repeated in his normal voice.

"That's more like it. So we have an understanding then, don't we?"

Tommy nodded.

"And if you screw around on this job, you're not just off the lawn crew. I'll have your goddamn ass fired. Do you read me, Mister Comedian?"

"Yes, sir," Tommy acquiesced, blinking a little as he said the words.

Duke spun around. "And which one of you is Keyhoe?"

Phil raised his hand reluctantly.

"So your ol' man, the bigshot, got you this job, eh?"

Phil didn't answer. He could feel the other guys looking at him. He didn't want anyone to think he was privileged, which Duke was implying.

"Whatever," Duke spat. "Just know I'll be keeping an eye on you, too."

Then Duke turned to the others, folded his arms in front of his muscular chest. "Okay enough jawing. Let's get our asses in gear." He pointed to the overgrown field between two buildings. "We're mowing this quadrant. I want two guys on each perimeter, mowing your way to the middle." He checked his watch on a black leather band. "Your deadline is eleven-hundred hours, sharp."

"So…" Tommy said in a hushed but satirical tone. "We have eleven hundred hours to finish mowing? That's quite a long time."

Phil elbowed him in the ribs as if to say *knock it off.*

"Got another wisecrack, buster?" Duke barked from behind.

"I said I've been waiting to do this for a long time," Tommy replied, trying not to sound sarcastic.

"I forgot to mention, boys," Duke announced, "that break time is at ten o'clock. You'll have fifteen minutes, and no more. You can sit in the grass or the truck, have a snack from your lunch pail, fantasize about your girlfriends' asses, whatever. Except for Bozo the Clown here." He pointed at Tommy. "He'll be working right through the break."

When Duke turned his back, Tommy mocked a frown and pretended to wipe a tear from his cheek with his pinkie finger.

As Phil rolled his mower down the ramp, he gazed between the buildings where a large section of grass rippled in the wind. Beyond that was the next quadrant, and the next. The grass out there seemed endless, an ocean of green and sharp weeds. Twenty-five square miles of land in this plant, his father had told him. *Damn*, Phil thought. He tried to compute how many acres of grass that would be, but it was too much for his brain. The past few summers, without a job, he'd hitchhike to Bluff Lake each afternoon with his buddies, or sometimes catch a ride with Tommy. There, they'd jump off the rocks on the west shore, toss a football back and forth on the beach, or drop quarters into the jukebox of the Chateau, the 1940s dance hall that served as a concession center. They'd bob their heads to "The House of the Rising Sun" or "She's Not There" by the Zombies. But in a few weeks, as soon as school let out, he'd be full time, mowing the expanses of grass that seemed to lead all the way to the horizon. *But for now, it's just a part-time job*, he assured himself. *Just eight to four on weekends. I'll survive, won't I?*

Tommy slapped the enameled green carburetor of his mower, and announced, as though this was the beginning of the Indy 500, "Gentlemen, start your freakin' engines. Let the brain surgery begin!"

One by one, the grass-stained mowers chugged to a start, their sharpened blades whirling, motors rising to a deafening roar. Phil leaned over and pulled the taut starter cord on his stocky mower. A bluish-white globe of exhaust rose from the muffler, drifted above his head and then toward the field, where it separated, torn apart by the wind.

He grabbed the hollow push bar, felt it vibrating in his hands, and took a step into his first day of work. Inhaling a slow, deep breath, he tasted dust, and smelled exhaust, and the third scent, which he had noticed when he first entered the plant. Now he could finally identify it. It was the scent of gunpowder, wafting from one of the nearby production houses.

At 11:35, with a wave of his arm, Duke rounded up the crew for the twenty-five-minute lunch break.

Phil grabbed his lunchbox from the truck. He had only mowed for three hours, but it seemed like three days. His T-shirt was sweat stained from the mid-day heat. "Um, where should we eat?" he asked.

"Usually in the nearest magazine building," Duke answered.

Tommy, standing next to Phil, burst out with "Magazine? What's inside?" he questioned. *"Man's World? Playboys,* maybe?"

"Are you being stupid on purpose, numbskull?" Duke scoffed. "There's gunpowder in those buildings."

Duke pointed across the road, to a squat wooden structure with a small porch in front and sprigs of grass sprouting between the timbers of the roof. "That one looks real cozy."

As the crew approached, a couple of pigeons, cooing on the beam above the entryway, fluttered away. Phil read the red letters of the warning sign nailed above the doorway:

### Danger: 100,000 Lbs. of Explosives.

"Hell, I'm not going in there," Tommy said, narrowing his eyes at the sign. "No way are you gonna get me in there."

"You'll get used to it," Duke sneered from behind. "We all do."

Phil was the first to venture through the open front doorway of the building. But he didn't see any explosives. Inside, it was just a hollow thirty by thirty-foot square room with a pyramid-shaped ceiling and a dull black floor. He figured the powder must have been stored beneath the floor, or behind the creosote-coated beams and tarpaper walls. The place smelled sort of like a freshly tarred road, but not as sweet. The floor was coated with a layer of black, rubberized material. So there wouldn't be any sparks, Phil figured. Out here, friction was a bad thing.

The rest of the crew followed Phil, not because they were daredevils, not because they wanted to tempt fate, but for a simple reason. The sunny day was hot and humid, and the building was cool and moist and dark inside. Insulated by three-foot thick walls, it was a quiet place that seemed to absorb the guys' words, making their conversations sound muted, as if they were telling hushed secrets to each other.

After he finished his lunch, Tommy, as a gag, clicked his lunchbox fastener back and forth with his index finger. "Sparks," he said with a laugh. "Hey guys, I'm making sparks."

"Shut up, lame brain," Phil replied, with a nervous chuckle.

With a few minutes still left in the lunch break, Phil lay back, resting his head on the cushioned floor. Having finished their lunches, the rest of the guys lay down on their backs, too. One of them yawned. For some odd reason, Phil felt like he could doze off here, even with all that gunpowder around him. With his head resting on his leather work gloves, he closed his eyes, felt himself sink into a blue pool of sleep. Deep. Deeper. Then someone dove into it, waking him.

Startled, he opened his eyes, sat up, and looked around at the other guys from the crew, who were napping. It was eerie, the way they were all lying on their backs and lined up in a row. Their eyes were closed, mouths slack, arms crossed over their chests. "Rise and shine, ladies!" Duke barked at the end of the lunch break, and one by one they finally came back to life.

Phil dragged himself to his feet. He'd get used to having lunch and sleeping in a powder house, wouldn't he? After all, he was out here for a reason. He was Karl's boy. The smell of the tarpaper still clinging to his skin, he squinted as he and the crew marched slowly toward the shafts of bright light that seemed to be waiting for them, slanting through the open doorway.

# CHAPTER 5

After the dance, Phil and Tommy and the football quarterback, Schmitty, sat in the parking lot in Phil's dad's Chrysler. They were chugging cans of Miller High Life Tommy had pilfered from his basement. "Okay, beer number two extinguished. We have lift-off," Tommy proclaimed as he held the can up, then crushed it between his palms. "Gotta go. Shirelle's hot to trot tonight. I think she's ovulating, or something," he laughed. "That's the one thing I learned in bio class."

Tommy and Schmitty hopped from the car to meet up with their girlfriends. "See ya tomorrow, Key!" Tommy called, and he jogged across the lot to his Falcon with nearly ninety thousand miles on it. It was a Memorial Day Special at Bluff Lake Auto that Tommy had nicknamed The Makeout Mobile.

Phil noticed three girls exiting through the glass doors and into the semi-darkness of the gravel lot. He recognized the taller girl's slim shape. It definitely *was* Mariah. Out of sheer luck, he got paired with her last week in biology class to dissect a frog.

They hadn't talked much as they injected the amphibian with adrenaline to see what effect it had on its tiny heart. "Nice looking innards," Phil had said about the frog, splayed in front of them in the biology lab. The comment caused Mariah to tip her face toward him and laugh.

When the girls reached the corner, two of them branched off from Mariah with a wave and she continued walking alone.

Tonight's weekly BluffTeen dance had progressed with its usual predictability: Phil, talking to his buddies between dances with their girlfriends. Couples dancing—doing the pony or the mashed potato—or else draping over each other like syrup during the slow songs. The blue and gold streamers of crepe paper, taped onto the high school lunchroom ceiling, rose and fell, rose and fell as if they were breathing. Phil had noticed Mariah, who arrived late. She stood on the far side of the room, talking with a group of girls.

Phil had dated a few girls during the last couple years, and Tommy always remarked that several girls had crushes on him, but he always seemed oblivious. The dates he had were unspectacular, usually involving going to the weekend movie at the Bluff Lake theatre. His worst date was freshman year, when he went out with a girl named Wanda. When a couple on the big screen tipped onto the couch during a passionate make-out scene and then glided, hand in hand, into the bedroom, both Phil and his date shifted uncomfortably in their red velvet seats. During that steamy scene, Phil—regretting it later—nervously asked Wanda, "Um, so, want some *Jujubes?*" He held the big seventy-five cent box toward her. Wanda declined, saying "No thanks," and then added "Braces." Later that night, he kissed her under a glowing front porch light. Her shoulders seemed to stiffen a little, and he felt nothing. That was the clue. There was no rush of adrenaline, no burning fuse igniting inside himself. Instead, all he felt was the hard metal fence of the braces on her teeth as her lips parted slightly. "You've got to brace yourself for a date like that, Key," Tommy quipped later. Phil went to junior prom with a reasonably attractive girl named Vanessa, but it was more of a case of both of them wanting to go to prom rather than an actual boyfriend-girlfriend relationship. Unlike the other couples, who seemed to melt into each other as they danced or made out in the dark hallways, the conversations between them were pleasant, but always a little formal and stiff. Though they remained friends, he never dated her after prom night.

Tonight, as the last few songs played just before the eleven o'clock closing time, Phil considered making his way across the murky sea of dancers to ask Mariah to dance, but he hesitated. He had a bad habit of second-guessing himself. He might stall halfway, he rationalized. His shoes might get stuck to the floor on Doublemint gum or something. Gum was definitely a dancing hazard. So he just sat there on the cool metal of the card table chair, feeling as if he was marooned on a small, dry island.

But now, fueled by the effect of a can of Miller, Phil felt a sudden burst of confidence. When a light rain shower began, he saw Mariah pulling the hood of her pink windbreaker over her head. *Perfect timing,* he thought, *Go.* And the next thing he knew, he started the car and steered toward her.

Veering next to her, he pressed the silver button and rolled down the Chrysler's power window, then asked, "So, you walking?" He felt stupid as soon as the words slipped out, his invitation not quite coming off like he intended. Normally, he had some confidence, but for some reason, she made him feel so damn self-conscious. "Home, I mean."

She turned and looked at him, pushing back strands of blonde hair that cascaded across the side of her face. Her subtle smile told him that she recognized him through the sheet of rain. "No, I thought I'd swim," she replied wryly.

"How about a ride? It's dry in here," Phil returned. He had no idea where she lived, so he didn't know exactly where he might be taking her. For all he knew, it might be miles out of town, halfway to Wisconsin Dells or Baraboo. But he didn't care.

When she didn't answer, he thought she might refuse. In that case, he'd have to blurt something humiliating and awkward like "Oh. Sure. I get it." He felt his pulse speed up, keeping time with the windshield wipers that thumped left, then right, then left.

But when she angled toward the car, Phil felt relieved. He put the car in park, jogged around to the passenger's side and opened the door for her with a flourish. Trying to be witty, he brushed his brown hair back from his eyes and said "Madam, may I?"

Climbing in and pulling the hood of her jacket down, Mariah glanced at the car's high-tech dashboard, lit up with an orange glow: the AM/FM radio when most cars came with a standard AM, the cushy velour seats, the oval clock face embedded in the front of the navy-blue padded dash.

"Nice looking innards," she said, and he knew she remembered his joke from last week.

"My dad's," he replied. "The car, I mean. It's a Chrysler Imperial. When it comes to cars, he only likes the luxury stuff." Karl had agreed to let him use the car this evening because he was in a rare, good mood after Phil helped out with the yard work.

"What's that?" she asked, pointing to the small plastic globe mounted in the middle of the dash. The silver needle, pointing north, bobbed in a tiny pool of thick liquid.

"That's his dashboard compass. Always needs to know where he's going, I guess," he chuckled.

"Well, that's not a bad idea."

"Sometimes I prefer to be lost. More of an adventure."

Catching Phil's humor, Mariah smiled.

She pulled a cigarette from her purse. "Do you have a light, by any chance?"

"Um, no. Don't smoke."

"I don't either, really. I just have one once in a while. Nervous energy. Got it from my mom, I guess. She's hooked."

"My dad would be furious if he smelled smoke in the car. He's really particular about his cars. Even though he smokes about a pack a day. But only on the back porch, not in the house. Better for the lungs, he claims."

"I get it," she said, dropping the cigarette back into her purse. "So, you always get to use your dad's car?"

"Um, just for tonight." He checked the clock, then admitted "But I have to have it back. Like right after the dance, I mean." He regretted the words as soon as he uttered them. He knew how it sounded: A kid with dad's car has to be home early.

"Oh? So your dad has lots of rules?"

"Only about a million," he said wryly. The brief rain shower let up as quickly as it had started, and Phil switched off the wipers. "How about you? Your dad doesn't have a curfew?" he questioned as he pulled up at a corner, a bent stop sign igniting in the car's headlights.

With that, her expression changed, and she shifted uncomfortably in her seat. She turned her head, looked out the window where the rain trickled off the sheet metal roof of an older house. "He's not around." Her voice cracked a little, and Phil sensed something fragile about her.

Guessing that she didn't want to say more about it, Phil asked, "So, where's home?"

"On the south side. But now that the rain's stopped, you can take me as far as downtown. That would be fine."

Obliging, Phil turned left on Ash street. Hoping to add some music to the drive, he clicked on the radio, but then realized his dad had tuned it to some awful country station. Annoyed, he spun the dial, trying to get rock and roll. He tuned in a faraway Madison station, and for a few seconds, The Beatles "Do You Want to Know a Secret?" played through the speakers. Then the song faded to a steady fizz. He spun the dial to find Bluff Lake's one station, WBLW, but there was just static. "Local station's off the air already, I guess," he apologized.

Phil drove through the darkened neighborhoods. They passed the 1940s houses, the shades pulled behind the eyes of the rectangular windows. No cars on the street, still shiny from the rain. A dog on a leash that had tramped a dirt circle in the yard lunged at the car and barked.

Recalling Mariah's adventurous dive at the lake, and hoping to initiate a conversation, Phil asked, "You're a swimmer, then?"

Mariah tucked one leg under her. "I *was* on the swim team. At my old high school." Then she added, "But your school doesn't have a pool."

"Nope. Kids here don't need to learn to swim," he said with a smirk.

She shook her head at this. "So they prefer to let you sink?"

"More or less."

As they continued toward the center of town, Mariah put him at ease, filling up the pauses as she chatted about everyday topics: her high school classes, taking her ACT test, and colleges where she planned to apply.

"I noticed that you're an expert in poetry," Phil said. When she gave him a questioning look, he added, "I mean, the way you countered The Turtle about that poem."

"So, what do you know about poetry?" she asked.

Phil squinted one eye. "It's made up of words, right?" He saw her slight smile, then added "And there's always something hidden beneath the surface. But, that's about all I know." He was exaggerating, of course. Actually, freshman year, inspired by his literature teacher, he had secretly tried writing a few poems.

At the next stop sign, Phil glanced over at Mariah and noticed again how really pretty she was. Her shoulder-length hair curved like a wild blonde ocean wave and when she turned her head toward him, her intense blue eyes seemed to look right into him. Her lips were poised in a half-smile, as if she was almost flirting. As Phil studied her, he was convinced that if she were a poem, she would be a beautiful and deep one.

In two blocks, the big stone courthouse on the town square rose into view. The large, yellowed clock face on the tower always seemed to be caught in the crooked limbs of the one large oak tree. "Approaching the square," Phil announced, as if he were an airplane pilot, zeroing in on a destination. "Hang on, in case of turbulence or something."

"Bring on the turbulence," Mariah said, propping one hand on the dashboard in jest.

They drove past the red brick Kluge's soda fountain where, after the dance, high school kids hung out, dropping quarters into the juke box or leaning on parking meters. Phil spotted Tommy, who was pressing himself against his girlfriend Shirelle in a dark doorway. Noticing Phil's car, Tommy called out "Hey, Dude! Can we borrow your back seat?" Phil gave him a condescending look and shook his head. On the next block, in the furniture store window, a pair of 1950s-style mannequins held empty stenciled glasses in one hand, while the other hand waved at passersby. Next door was the Main Café's storefront display, where hundreds of green olives were arranged symmetrically in two five-gallon glass jars, the red pimentos facing outward. The display had been there for since fifth grade, when Phil was sure the olives were staring at him each time he walked past.

"There you have it," Phil said. "The town square. Quite a spectacle, isn't it?"

"Not much going on, it seems. So," she quizzed, "do you like it here?"

"Yes. And no."

"I mean, all everyone talks about is the football team," she said. "And that Strongs Plant. Pardon me for saying it, but, this place doesn't seem all that exciting."

"We make the best of it," Phil offered as he took a left on Main by Carrigan's Standard Station with the two rounded pumps and the used tires stacked in even columns on opposite sides of the building. "Everybody pretty much tries to blend in, I guess."

"You think that's a good idea?"

"Sometimes. So where are you from that's so exciting?"

"Madison. We just moved from there. It's a great city. The UW campus, and everything. There's so much going on there."

"Well, we manage to find a few things to do around here, too."

"Such as?"

Groping for a follow-up to his claim, he added, facetiously, "A couple nights before Halloween, some kids smashed some pumpkins in the lot of the A & P."

"Hmmm… Sounds like quite a night."

"Yes, it was. It certainly was," he smirked. "Earth-shattering, actually." His eyes shifted to the clock, which read 11:30. "So where to now?" he asked.

"I thought you had to be back. Aren't you past your curfew?"

"Yeah, I am. But it doesn't matter." Phil knew he'd break his curfew for her. He'd break a lot of rules, if he had to.

Her expression changed. "Maybe you can just drop me off. At the next block would be okay."

Phil wondered what was behind her request. Maybe she was embarrassed to be with him when he'd pull up in front of her house. Or had he said something wrong? Insecurity rushed through him.

"Okay. If that's what you want." He pulled the car to the curb.

"Thanks for the lift, then." she said pleasantly, then stepped to the sidewalk and started down the street.

This wasn't how Phil pictured the night to work out—him sitting in his car, and her, walking home alone in the dark. He felt bad that his time with her, which seemed so perfect for the past few minutes, had suddenly started to spiral away from him, leaving him frustrated, alone at a dead end. Instead of feeling buoyed up by this night, he felt like he was about to drown in it.

He pressed on the gas pedal and, two blocks further, caught up to her. He knew he'd feel better if he drove her all the way home. He veered sharply to the curb alongside her.

"Um, hey," he called through the open window. "Sure you don't want a lift the rest of way?"

"I'm sure," she said. She walked over to the open passenger side window and leaned in. "Don't get me wrong. I *did* like talking to you. Until tonight, I didn't realize any boys in Bluff Lake had a sense of wit."

"Okay then," he replied, "just get back in."

"I can't," she said illusively. Phil noticed that the assured, confident girl he'd seen diving into the lake suddenly seemed uncertain. He sensed a hesitancy, or maybe a hurt behind her voice.

"But why?" he questioned, flustered.

"See you in bio on Monday," was all she said.

Phil watched her graceful strides as her silhouette shrunk smaller and smaller. She reached the next block, turned left at the corner of Division Street and was out of sight.

He pressed the button on the armrest and, like clear water rising in a tank, the window glass slid up with a smooth sigh.

He knew he needed to head home soon. He pictured his father, snoring on the couch in front of the snowy-screened television set, pictured the way, when Phil opened the latch to the back door, Karl would always wake, his eyes darting directly to the western wagon-wheel style clock on the wall.

Remembering the empty beer cans on the floor of the back seat, Phil quickly gathered them up and tossed them into an open trash bin behind someone's garage. Incriminating evidence disposed of.

He glanced at his face in the rearview mirror. He looked flushed from the adrenaline, and the emotions he was feeling. He ran his fingers through his mussed-up hair, straightening it, then fished a Clorets mint from his shirt pocket and popped it into his mouth to disguise the alcohol on his breath.

He put the car in gear and it lurched forward. It was then that he felt it wobbling, the right fender dipping up and down. Hopping out and stepping through a puddle, he saw that the tire was flat. When he had pulled next to Mariah, he'd hit the curb, popping the heavy-duty Firestone. "Shit!" Phil spat. "Damn it all!" He knew there was no spare in the trunk; his father had moved it to the garage last week to make room for a work bench. Phil winced at the thought of his father, having to call Bud's Towing. Or worse, his dad would, by himself, slowly maneuver the car the two and a half miles back. He'd be silently seething as the tire flopped on the pavement, the steel hub cutting into the vulcanized rubber.

Phil pictured Karl giving him the third degree. "How'd you pop that tire?" he'd demand, rubbing the heel of his hand on the sidewall of the tire. "There's a big scrape on it where it blew."

"Bumped a curb, I guess," Phil would reply.

"What curb?"

"Dunno. Just a curb."

He pictured Karl, giving him a suspicious shake of his head. "And what were you doing with the Chrysler way over on the south side, anyway?"

"Nothing," Phil would answer, though right now he hoped it was a lot more than nothing. It was something. For him, the time with Mariah really *was* something. A start, he hoped, a lit fuse.

But then there was that unsettling moment as they parted. Why, he wondered, did she choose to walk the rest of the way home?

# CHAPTER 6

"Hon? You awake?" a voice called through Mariah's slightly-opened door, startling her. It was her Mom, Janelle, making sure she was getting ready for school.

Mariah quickly slid her personal journal beneath a stack of school notebooks, the weight of science, math and econ holding it still and silent. "Of course," she replied.

"Then what are you doing?" Janelle asked, peering in and seeing the pen on the desk and Mariah, still dressed in her plaid flannel pajama bottoms and a plain, baggy pink T-shirt.

"Solving the problems of the universe."

"As usual." Janelle pushed the door open and leaned her thin body against the doorframe. She looked sharp in her work outfit: dark blue dress, white pearls, light makeup. "So what were you writing?"

"Not much. Just working on the next Pulitzer Prize book." She flashed a grin.

"And when will it be published?" Janelle said with a laugh.

"By next week."

"Wonderful. I'll buy the first copy. Will you sign it for me?"

"Definitely."

Mariah had already been awake for an hour, writing an entry in her journal, which she'd entitled, on the inside cover, **Poems and Dreams in Invisible Ink.** The outside cover had a different, dull label to disguise it so no one would know it was a journal: **Homework Assignments.**

It was the place where she scribbled her doubts, her worries, her daily ramblings, her innermost feelings, her poetic musings. This morning's entry was entitled **Transfer Student.** *Sometimes I feel like I'm caught under a glass jar,* she had written. *Like some kind of butterfly. A monarch that should be migrating south for the winter. Lately my life just feels stalled. Like I'm in-between things. I'm waiting, but for what? Something? A gentle touch, maybe. Or a hammer to break the glass. Yes, something...*

*Something.* Mariah had concluded her journal entry with that word, that one all-encompassing word. It was one of those words—a word that seemed bigger than it was, a word that spiraled outward across the calm water of the blank page. She made it a point of ending each entry on a word or two that carried her through the day, a word that, once she scrolled it with her blue Bic pen, left her hanging or pushed her forward into another thought the following day when she reopened the journal.

Then there was the other topic that intrigued her. Not a word, but a person: *Phil.* Who was he, and why had she been thinking so much about him since that night after the dance? It was the look on his face when he followed her with his dad's car. Phil seemed so honest, so authentic, so intriguing. His sweet shyness was attractive to her, and she wondered what was beneath the surface. But then there was the fear of diving in too quickly. The fear of a rock hidden beneath the surface. And, after what her father did, there was always a gloomy cloud of distrust hanging over her relationships with the opposite sex. Besides, having grown up in a city like Madison, she harbored some stereotypes about small town boys and their limited view of the world. Most of the boys she had met were interested in only a few primal things: sports, souped-up cars, hanging out on Saturday nights, and, of course, sex.

"Better get going, honey," Janelle said, checking a silver watch on her wrist. "You don't want to be late."

"Heaven help me if I was late for Bluff Lake High," Mariah sighed. It came out a little more sarcastic than she intended, so she winked at her mom and added "My grade for perfect attendance would go straight to you-know-where."

Her mother made a *tisk tisk* sound.

"You want decaffeinated or regular today?" Mariah asked. Part of her morning routine was making coffee for her mom before she left for work. Janelle had been working as a temp since they got to Bluff Lake.

"Regular. *Definitely* regular, and strong. I'm at Industrial Coils today. With that charming boss in the front office."

"Oh. You mean *Mister Handy?*"

"Yes, that's him," Janelle said, referring to the boss who didn't mind brushing a little too close to his office assistants whenever he walked past. Sometimes his hand wasn't on his clipboard, and it would find its way to a woman's rear end.

"Why don't you just smack him? I would."

"I'd love to. But he'd never have me back there. And we could use a little cash here and there, right? It beats being on welfare and picking your clothes out of dumpsters."

"Oh Mom, don't be so dramatic." Still, Mariah knew Janelle had a point. Her mom didn't always work as a temp at places like the Industrial Coils, where workers boxed small and large rolls of wire. She had a couple of almost-careers back when they lived in Madison, where she was part-time with the City Attorney's office and worked with the downtown arts council.

As Mariah dressed herself and tossed her books into a backpack, she thought about her time so far at what she called **The Latest School.** At Bluff Lake High, the kids were basically divided into three groups that didn't really interact with each other. First were the cliques of girls who wore Bobbie Brooks and were snooty because they lived on mortgage hill, which was, in reality, just an average middle-class area of town that was built on a gradual slope. They went out with the conceited guys who were on the football or basketball teams. Then there were the blue collar kids who brought saggy bag lunches and lived in the old part of town in the run-down houses with tin roofs. Those kids went through the motions of high school like drones in a hive. Finally, there was a contingent of rural kids. They wore FFA farm jackets and planned, after serving their four-year high school sentences, to jump onto their daddy's John Deere tractors. Mariah, on the other hand, the new girl, didn't fit into any particular group. Some days she felt like she was cut from paper and pasted to the wall above her school locker. Like she wrote in her journal last week, some mornings she felt like Alice—not in wonderland, but in some strange, claustrophobic place that she described as "less-than-wonderland."

Mariah poured some water into the coffee pot, added a few extra tablespoons of Folgers grounds, and then plugged in the cord, a frayed brown snake. A half minute later, it began to perk, the brown liquid bubbling into the clear plastic cap. Meanwhile, her mother poured some cereal for both of them. Her mom always smelled of the heavy scent of Chanel No. 5. Janelle believed it would carry her, like a cloud of sweetness, through the day. They crossed near each other gracefully as Janelle glided over to grab the milk from the refrigerator and Mariah waltzed to the toaster.

It was just the two of them in the silver and purple aluminum trailer, so they had to lean on each other. No Dad in the picture. It was just Mariah and her mother, trying to make a go of it in Camelot Acres, this too-near-the-train-tracks park where, late at night, the trailer vibrated ever so slightly when a train passed. Their trailer was not exactly a Frank Lloyd Wright house, Mariah sometimes mused. But it was just temporary, they assured each other.

Each morning at 7 a.m., Mariah would hear that yippy little dog outside the narrow window of her bedroom. And then, exactly ten seconds later, overweight Mrs. Fenske would step out in a blousy faded nightgown, give it a smack with a rolled-up newspaper, then waddle back into her trailer, letting the screen door clack shut behind her. Each night at six o'clock, a patrolling squad car crawls through the place, as if someone was about the break the law. *Everything's predictable here*, Mariah thought. *Nothing changes.*

The trailer court was a place where, in the morning, the exhaust billowed into their window as the battered low-slung Pontiacs started with a grinding wheeze and then rumbled past. A lot of the residents were on their way to the Strongs Plant— that factory everyone in town seemed so proud of. Mariah couldn't help but notice that here, at this trailer court, there were too many cars with duct-taped bumpers and rust spots the size of open mouths, too many seedy drivers, dressed in yellowed tank tops, who leered at her when she stepped from the trailer on her way to school.

Mariah preferred not to admit that she lived in Camelot Acres. That's why, the night after the dance, she didn't want Phil to drop her off here. She wasn't trying to be coy, or illusive. She was just plain embarrassed. Camelot Acres: there was no utopia here, no romance. It was just a place that could flatten anyone's dreams like a tin can.

Sometimes, when Mariah pictured her life, it appeared in her mind as a series of frames in a black and white film that should be moving forward. But for the time being, everything was held still. There seemed to be all these obstacles in front of her. Like the grease-stained cardboard box, pushed by the wind, that tumbled and woke her as it clunked the side of the trailer this morning. Like the row of garbage bins—a stout midnight blue regiment—that lined the entryway to the lot. Like Camelot Acres itself, all its promises false as the Medieval castle archway at the entry gate. Like herself, her own doubts, those big holes she could fall through daily.

For the time being, it was just present, *the here,* and *the now.* It was just Mariah and her mother, eating breakfast across from each other at the small red Formica table. It was Mariah, trying to chat optimistically about school or the weekend each morning before her mom left for work at another job—a short-term secretarial stint at Bluff Lake Office Supply or somewhere. Just Mariah, with no makeup or perfume, leaving for school, almost bumping her head on the frame of the doorway like some too-tall Alice. She and her mom always said goodbye to each other, calling out the word *love* as they parted. It was a word that carried them through the day.

"How's the coffee?" Mariah inquired as she watched her mom take a sip and leaving a faint pink imprint of lipstick on the pale china cup.

"Strong," Janelle answered. "Your usual."

Mariah rolled up the sleeve of her blouse and flexed her muscle.

"So, are you seeing that boy at school today?" Janelle asked.

"Not sure." She spooned some Shredded Wheat from her bowl, held it in front of her and stared at the small biscuit in the shallow puddle of milk. She thought about him, giving her a warm half-smile and a nod as she passed him on the way to homeroom.

"Think he'll ask you out on a date?"

"Dunno." She felt herself blushing a little.

Janelle blinked at Mariah. "You genuinely *like* this boy, don't you?"

"Oh mom," she chided as she lowered her eyes to the cereal box and focused on the ingredients on the side. *100% whole grain wheat. No Artificial Additives.*

"I can tell," Janelle insisted. "By your expression. That night when you talked about him there was a light about you."

Mariah shrugged her shoulders. This observation by her mom made her feel self-conscious. "Maybe I just had a fever that day or something," she explained, downplaying her feelings. "Or maybe I was getting my period."

Janelle leaned her elbows on the table, which wobbled a little. "So tell me. Is he real?"

The question caught Mariah off guard. "What do you mean?"

Janelle set her spoon on the table. "Does he seem *real?* You know—honest. No deceptions? You need to know that. It's important."

"Mooomm," she stretched the word into three syllables. "I hardly know him." She took a sip from her glass of milk. "He's just a boy. In my lit and bio classes. Let's just leave it at that, okay?"

"Whatever you say."

Though she ended the conversation that way, Mariah knew exactly where her mom was coming from.

Six years ago, when her mother's divorce began to become a reality, Janelle confided in Mariah, who was twelve at that time.

"Your father wasn't who I thought he was," Janelle had said.

That year, the truth came to them in a progression of painful realizations. First there was an emptied bank account, then rumors of a lover in the suburbs of Madison, a changed identity, airline ticket charges, a looming foreclosure on their comfortable house on the north shore of Lake Mendota. Her mother explained to her that because he worked in real estate, his career could take him anywhere.

And as it turned out, it did. They just didn't know where that *anywhere* was. It was one of those words. A detective had looked for him for a while the first year after he left, but only found a few leads. Only something about a condo in the Bahamas, where he and his girlfriend had stayed for a while. "Shacked up," was the phrase her mother used to describe it, the words bitter on her tongue. Mariah tried not to let the painful image enter her head, but still, it did: It was an imaginary photograph of her father, standing on some white sandy beach with another woman, the azure waves in the background held mid-break as they turned to foam. In Mariah's mind, John Harlan Stiller stared toward the camera, his head tipped to one side, blonde hair slicked down slightly except for a few ruffled strands poking upward like some arrogant teenager who just pulled up in a convertible. *I guess I didn't care a damn about you, after all. Not a damn,* he could be saying from that photograph, his voice dry as bleached sand.

She always thought he could have at least said goodbye to her—something he never bothered to do. He was just gone, out of her life. Like she wrote in her journal last week, *Some days I feel like I'm in a cave, and someone rolled a huge stone in front of the entrance, leaving me there in the dark, slowly suffocating.*

As the time passed, the father Mariah once idolized became hazier and more out-of-focus. Mariah began describing her feelings in a section of her journal entitled **The Non-Father**. *Dear Daddy,* she would begin each entry, *Where are you, exactly?* His running off didn't just reject Janelle; he rejected Mariah, too, making her feel worthless, disposable. *I feel like a piece of paper squeezed into a ball by your fist,* she wrote, then ended the passage with *Sincerely, Your Crumpled Daughter.*

The divorce documents arrived by express mail, and Janelle signed. Then she and Mariah moved out of the house, a For Sale sign wavering in the wind on the lawn.

Somehow, her father—a white-collar con man—finagled the funds from the sale of their house in Madison and siphoned off much of their bank account. He was good at that—finagling and making deals—since he was a big-time realtor in a major realty company in Madison with clients who were state senators at the capitol. And the woman he ran off with worked there, too, in the Attorney General's office. All that was six years ago. After that day, there was no father. No father at all. And yet his shadow seemed to press on Mariah's shoulders year after year, and she wished she could get out from under it.

"This is all just temporary, you know," her mom told Mariah when they moved to Bluff Lake and into this trailer court. Janelle assured her that they'd stay there until they could get their feet back on the ground and Janelle could get decent full-time work and find a permanent place. "Soon," her mom assured her. *Soon.* It was one of those words.

Five years ago, when Mariah was in junior high and they were about to relocate again, Janelle had told Mariah, "When we move to the next town, I'm telling people that he died." That spring, the two of them sat on an old burgundy couch in the top level of a rental bungalow in Madison. The couch always smelled like something strange to Mariah—dead flowers, or stale wine, or cat urine, she wasn't sure—so she rarely sat on it. "I'm saying that he had a car accident one day and was killed," Janelle had said, continuing her fabrication.

"Where?" Mariah had asked. "*Where* did it happen, mom?" she asked again, breathlessly. It was as if this story—through the magic of saying it—was becoming real, and Mariah wanted to see the whole scene, visualize the place, to believe it all. She wanted to touch the place on a map with her fingertip, to make this fictional story real. To erase the pain of what really happened.

"Say it was on a county highway. Between Madison and the Dells," Janelle had said, continuing the fabrication. "Say he was driving home at night from a real estate conference, taking a short-cut so he could get home sooner. Because he loved us so much." Her mother released a kind of muffled half-laugh. Mariah had heard that sound before, and knew exactly what it meant. Her mother—laughing a little, but, at the same time, crying and bleeding inside.

"Okay, but *then* what?" Mariah asked.

"Then, then…" Janelle thought for a moment and wrung her hands, too bony and pale for an attractive 33-year-old. "Say he tried to take a curve." Janelle said, fighting back a sob. "Say he tried to take a curve too damn fast."

"Okay," Mariah agreed, grabbing her mother's hand to comfort her as Janelle took a deep, uneven breath. "That's good enough, Mom. That story will work." At that moment, it was as if a pact was made, a pact that somehow turned her father into a someone she could talk about more openly. Now he was gone, faded into the past. She didn't have to call him, in her mind, a *damn son of a bitch*—those words she heard her mother utter under her breath dozens of times.

"That's what I'll say, then," Mariah agreed. "That's just what I'll tell the other kids, if they ask. We'll keep our stories straight. A car accident. On a curve. Trying to get home sooner. Right?"

Her mother didn't answer, just nodded, and Mariah thought she could see glittering crescents of bitter tears form beneath her eyes. Janelle finally said, "Because he loved us so damn much." Mariah leaned over and gave her a hug, felt her shoulders quaking.

During those junior high years, rumors still followed Mariah to the other schools where she enrolled, the way scraps of paper and candy wrappers followed the dust devils that glided across the school lot on windy days. Those lightly whispered comments grew heavier and heavier some days until Mariah felt like they might suffocate her. Feeling more and more alienated from the kids who had fathers, and whole families, she poured herself into her books: history, sociology, classical poetry, literature. She identified with the character in *The Scarlett Letter*. And she loved *Alice in Wonderland* for its magic and the levels beneath its surface. Alice always seemed to fall through rabbit holes but still survived. In ninth grade, she re-read the dog-eared copy of the book she'd had since sixth grade, and she adopted Alice as her personal heroine. After all, Alice beat the odds, despite the jacks and aces and the queen, and she came out of the experience with her head still on her shoulders. Mariah vowed— like Alice—to be strong, to be independent, no matter how much she might be trembling inside.

Freshman year in a Madison school, when Mariah interpreted a poem by Longfellow, her English teacher told her that she had the sensitive soul of a 60-year-old woman. Though she wasn't sure, at first, if that was a compliment or not, she liked the idea of being so much more mature than the other kids, who, in the hallway, threw spitballs and swatted each other with wide-ruled notebooks, the covers filled with doodles. She felt a core of brightness within her, a light that she kept to herself, like a glimmering jewel somewhere deep inside, and she cherished it and vowed to protect it. She had her dreams, her goals, and no one—especially not her father, or even his lingering shadow—was going to steal them from her.

This morning, after finishing breakfast and stacking the dishes on the counter, Mariah and Janelle headed toward the trailer's narrow front door, her mother with her heavy vinyl purse, Mariah following behind, her canvas backpack stuffed with books.

Mariah stepped to the hard-packed dirt and passed the trailer next door, its roof partially covered by a blue plastic tarp to stop the rain from seeping through. Waiting at the school bus stop, she pictured her journal, safely sandwiched between the textbooks, and the section simply entitled **That Boy**. This morning, before breakfast she'd written this entry: *Yesterday, I dropped my pen in the hallway. When Phil picked it up and handed it to me, the look in his eye made me think about him the rest of the day. His face lit with a handsome grin, and he said, with a whimsical voice, "Lost something, Ma'am?"*

*"Maybe," I replied, caught a little off guard.*

*So…am I falling for him? I'm not sure.*

# CHAPTER 7

Phil tossed his work gloves to the back of his locker, where they made a hollow *thump*. He then picked them up again and pulled them on. The gloves, made of rough leather, always felt scratchy and too tight on his hands. Another Saturday of work at the plant, and he wished he were anywhere but here. He was tired and listless, and the grueling workday of mowing lawns for eight hours hadn't even started. The only glimmer in his early morning fog was Mariah.

As of last night, he and Mariah had been dating for two months. After seeing a movie at the art-deco Bluff Lake Theatre, he had driven them to the county park overlooking the Bluff River. Phil left the ignition on as "Ferry 'Cross the Mercy" played low on the radio and a curtain of cricket sounds draped itself over the car. He gazed at the river; its slate-colored surface seemed hard and unmoving in the darkness, a blank, meandering chalkboard with no words written on it yet.

"This place brings back a memory," Phil mused.

"Of what?" Mariah responded.

"Well," he continued, "when I was a kid, I used to put notes in bottles and toss them in the river."

"Oh?" Mariah encouraged, "Tell me more." She had heard a little about his childhood, but not all that much.

"Yeah. Tommy and I thought up the idea." He tipped his head back against the headrest. "We were about eight or nine. We'd write our names and addresses and phone numbers at the bottom of the notes. Then we'd stuff them in empty bottles and fling them into the river. I remember how fast the current whisked them away." He closed his eyes a second. "Seems like our childhood went that fast, too."

"I feel the same sometimes," she agreed. "So what did you write on those notes?"

"Don't remember, exactly. Probably something profound, like, 'Hello, my name is Phil Keyhoe and I live in Bluff Lake, Wisconsin. I am eight years old. I have a dog. His name is Spot. Please let me know if you find this. Yours very truly, Phil Keyhoe, Bluff Lake, Wisconsin, USA. Planet earth. By the way, I can be reached at EL-356-6133.'"

"Cute."

"Yeah, I was quite the budding author."

"One day at school," he continued, "I had opened a U.S. map, and saw that the Bluff River fed into the Wisconsin River, which fed into the Mississippi. I got really excited, picturing that bottle floating all the way down to New Orleans and into the ocean. Thought it might get picked up by a fisherman in the gulf." He turned his head toward Mariah. "Dumb, eh?"

"No," she countered, "Not dumb. Just a dreamer." She added "And you still are."

"Yeah, but to think that bottle would float downstream for two thousand miles.

38

And somebody would *actually* find it? And then get in touch with me?"

"Maybe somebody already did," she said tenderly. Her arms circled him, pulling him closer, and she pressed her soft lips against his.

In that instant, Phil felt a rush rising inside him. He had kissed other girls in the past, but those were just kisses; he was never moved by them like he was at this moment. He felt his emotions swirling—a mixture of passion and wonder and longing, and something else, too. He gazed at Mariah, her iridescent blue eyes just an inch from his. He took a quick breath, wanting to express it, to say whatever it was he was suddenly experiencing.

"I think..." he began, but then faltered. The right words were always deep inside him, and always so hard to retrieve. "I think...."

"You think what?" she asked, encouraging him.

"Maybe we should head back," he finally said. "Before something happens, I mean." He lifted his hand from her shoulder and placed it on the steering wheel.

"Before *what* happens?" When he didn't reply, she asked, more insistently, "What's going to happen, Phil? Say what you're feeling."

He broke the pause, his words like pebbles tossed into a smooth pond. "I don't know," he said under his breath. "Just something."

"You mean *we're* going to happen. Is that what you mean?"

"Maybe." He felt embarrassed now that he had said anything. The radio station began to fade, and he reached over, fumbled with the dial, trying to find another one. Mariah put her hand on his, lifted it away from the dial and placed it on her waist. His fingers touched her warm skin, exposed between her tank top and her cut off jean shorts.

"So tell me," she persisted, "why are you so afraid of *us* happening?"

"I'm not. I mean, I am. I mean....,' he stammered. "Okay, you're right. All this scares me a little, I guess."

"All this?"

"You know—you. Me." He chuckled. "Guess I get a little nervous when I'm not on solid ground."

"Maybe that's a good place to be. It means anything can happen." She leaned over and kissed him again. This time it was a longer, deeper kiss.

With that kiss, Phil felt everything drop away: the car, the faint shimmer of the Milky Way overhead, the curving river. The whole world seemed to drop away, leaving just the two of them. He felt an exhilarating, out-of-control sensation. For once, he wasn't neutral or hesitant. A part of him that had been asleep was suddenly waking, and he felt himself rushing downstream along some strange, unfamiliar shores. Their lips, their fingertips, were touching in the darkness, their bodies rising and falling with the current. They pressed into each other until they both exhaled a gasp. He was filled with a deep-down emotion he'd never experienced before in his life. And he liked that feeling. Not just liked it—*loved* it.

"Wake up, moron!" a voice barked. Reality, in the form of Tommy's manic voice, smacked Phil in the face. "Welcome to another day at the world's largest munitions plant!" Tommy announced, smirking as he strode to the varnished bench in front of his locker. He twirled his car keys that hung from a plastic keychain shaped like a girl in a bikini with the word *Chevy* stamped on her midriff. "So much grass, and so little time. We got ten thousand acres of it out there waiting."

Phil ignored him, though he knew that wouldn't be possible for long. He braced himself, knowing that Tommy, after pounding down a few cans of Mountain Dew with breakfast, was always much too awake early in the morning.

"So," Tommy said, juggling a couple of oranges from his lunch bucket, "Did ya breathe the delightful aroma of hydrogen sulfide on the way in? My favorite scent. Quite refreshing, I must say. My second favorite is cut ragweed, which we shall inhale later." Tommy dropped one of the oranges, picked it up and tossed it with a basketball jump-shot to the garbage bin next to the lockers. "Three-pointer!" he called. "And the T-Birds win at the buzzer!" He cupped his hands on either side of his mouth imitating the sound of a roaring crowd. Bending over, he played with the combination lock, finally got it open, and yanked on the locker door. "Okay, Key. Here's the plan for the day." He peeled the wrapper of a Baby Ruth candy bar half-way down, then chawed on the end.

"Plan? Please, not another plan," Phil held up one hand like a stop sign, though he knew Tommy wasn't about to be deterred.

"Yep. Here's the deal," he said in a hushed, fake-confidential voice. "At 0900 hours, we go AWOL from the lawn crew. We ditch our mowers out by some remote building, cover them with sticks and brush. Then we'll disguise ourselves by putting on Lone Ranger masks. We'll rub creosote on our arms to camouflage them." He took another bite of the Baby Ruth. "Comprendo?" he inquired, the word emerging through a mouthful of chocolate and nougat.

"Wonderful idea."

"Then we hop a ride on one of those stupid tram cars and ride it to a storage house way back in a corner of the plant." He spread his arms to his sides triumphantly. "There, we shall sleep away the rest of the day until punch-out. Another successful day of work, under our belts. Just think of it—another twenty-two dollars and fifty-six cents, gross. With that kind of money, we'll be a fraction closer to a million." Tommy finished the candy bar, balled up the wrapper, then jumped in the air and dunked it into the space behind his locker.

"Great, Milk. Perfectly logical. You're full of shit, as usual." Phil pulled his required gear from the locker: heavy gray coveralls, steel toed boots, an absurd yellow safety helmet that wobbled on his head, thick-framed government-issue safety glasses, making him look like Buddy Holly.

"Okay, okay," said Tommy. "I see you're not all that keen on my master scheme." He rummaged through his locker, the inside of the door plastered with a couple of pictures of The Beach Boys with surfer girls and surfboards, and a sign that proclaimed **Kilroy Was Here**. The bottom of the locker was coated with *Payday* and *Sugar Babies* candy wrappers, empty *Milk Duds* boxes, rumpled *Teen Beat* magazines, and what appeared to be a couple of balled-up socks the color of soot. "But shit, at least we're only here for the summer, Key. We'll survive. We'll find a way, right?"

"I suppose. You heard back from Blackhawk Community yet?" Phil quizzed. Tommy had applied to smaller community colleges because, with his average-to-below grades, he'd never get into the U. in Madison, or the larger state schools. He heard Blackhawk admitted students on a probationary basis and was holding out for that.

"Nope," said Tommy. "But hey—any day, I'm guessing. They'll recognize the scholar in me and beg me to enroll."

"You say that every damn day."

A wince crawled across Tommy's face. "Yeah, I know. But if that doesn't work out, maybe Vince Lombardi will draft me for the Packers. "Right, Key? Right, Keyman?" Phil couldn't get himself to muster a response.

That morning, Ray Duke drove the lawn crew out to the far north quadrant of the plant and laid out the morning detail. The crew was told to mow the area that was, back in the 1800s, a pioneer settlement. Powder storage buildings took over the land where log cabins once stood and crops flourished.

One member of the crew, Bob Ramsey, was a college senior, a six-foot-four tackle on the U. of Wisconsin football team. He was muscular, and conceited, and often pushed up his sleeve and flexed his biceps to show off to the less bulked up guys on the crew.

At midday, when they mowed near an old stone well, Ramsey peered over the rim into it. Shutting off his mower, he called "Hey, Keyhoe, look at this!"

Phil couldn't hear his words due to the roar of his mower, but he saw Ramsey's lips move and his astonished expression. Phil shut off his mower and leaned over the well. There, he saw what Ramsey was gawking at.

It was a huge rattlesnake at the bottom of the fifteen-foot well. Curled in a circular shape in the mud, the rattler was about eight feet long, its body thick. Its back was covered with a symmetrical pattern of gold and black diamonds.

"Shit! It's a diamondback. That sucker's big enough to kill both of us," Ramsey said with a nod of his head. "Imagine if we stepped on the damn thing in the grass." Then he turned to Phil and said "Only one thing to do."

"What's that?" Phil asked.

"This." Ramsey pulled a chunk of stone from the wall of the dilapidated well. He held it up, then dropped it, hitting the tail of the snake. With the impact, the snake curled and slithered.

The rest of the mowing crew, seeing Phil and Ramsey at the well, gathered around the opening.

Ramsey threw another stone, this one striking the snake in the middle of its body. The snake coiled rapidly, seeming to wind itself into a knot, and then went still again, its tongue flickering. Its rattle echoed all the way up the well.

Damn," one of the guys said. "That thing's tough."

Ramsey dropped a bigger stone, and the result was the same.

"That does it," Ramsey sneered. "I'll show the son of a bitch." He reached into the side of the well, pulled hard at a large thirty pound boulder. The clay mortar crumbled, and he pulled it free. Then, as the guys around him cheered, he hefted the boulder above his head, held it there a few seconds. He yelled "Bombs away!" and flung it hard into the well.

The stone landed directly on the rattlesnake's head with an echoing *thud.*

"Yeah!" one of the guys shouted, pumping his arm in the air. "You got him!"

The rattler was motionless and silent for a few seconds as Ramsey stood there, victoriously dusting off his hands. But then, to everyone's amazement, the snake began to move. It writhed, then crawled slowly out from under the rock, its rattle hissing again. Somehow, its body, with soft mud below it, had absorbed the impact.

"Damn!" Ramsey spat. "It won't die. The goddamn thing *won't die!*"

As the snake circled itself, Phil could see its red tongue flickering menacingly.

In the afternoon, Phil and Ramsey were assigned to mow the grass in the cemetery.

"Cemetery?" Phil questioned.

"Yeah," replied Duke. "There's some old cemetery out here. We got orders to maintain it. The dead prefer short grass, I guess," Duke said sardonically.

Phil heard the pioneer cemetery had been there long before the government took over the land and built the plant during World War II. The stretch of land in the valley was once home to dozens of farms, three schools, three churches and three cemeteries. Landowners received official government notice in January 1942 to get off their property by March 1, and construction of hundreds of buildings started immediately.

While searching for information about the region at the local library, Phil was fascinated to discover a Native American legend about the formation of Bluff Lake:

*A quarrel once arose between the water spirits, who had a den in the underworld depths of Bluff Lake, and the Thunderbirds—the great birds, flying high above the lake's surface—hurled their arrows or thunderbolts into the waters. The water serpents threw up great rocks and water-spouts from the bottom of the lake.*

*The Ho-Chunk tradition claims the battle resulted in the cracked and jagged rocky surfaces of the bluffs surrounding the lake. The lake was considered to be so deep that it was a bottomless pit. Although the Thunderbirds were ultimately victorious, it was believed that "The water spirits were not all killed, and some are in Bluff Lake to this day." The lake was always considered to be a spiritual and sacred place by the Native Americans, who originally named the lake Holy Water.*

Phil also learned that, before the European settlers arrived, the plant's ten-thousand acres were Native American land. The Ho-Chunk tribe once thrived in a large village close to the Prairie du Sac River. The Native Americans used this broad, fertile valley, west of the bluffs, for hunting and gathering until the Black Hawk Wars of 1832 and the Battle of Wisconsin Heights. The white militia, under the command of General Henry Atkinson, outnumbering Black Hawk's contingent by 1300 to 100, decimated the natives.

Pushing a lawn mower for eight hours a day gave him a lot of time to think, and Phil often mulled over how the inhabitants of this land changed over the centuries: first, the indigenous people, then the pioneers and farmers. Now, the place was taken over by a squadron of production buildings and storage houses, and each day, the chemical waste from the refineries seeped into what used to be rich farming soil. It was sad, Phil thought, that when it came down to it, this land was always tied to violent conflict and war—first with the Native Americans, then World War II, then the Korean War, and now Vietnam.

For the next hour, Phil mowed around the small tombstones, tasting the pungent scent of the freshly cut weeds that had overgrown the place. Some stones from the 1860s and 1870s were readable. He felt empathy for the settlers that were buried here, their graves no longer tended by survivors. No flowers here, no memorials. Just the remains of husbands who died in war or from disease, wives who died young from the harsh living conditions, and infants who survived only a few days. Some headstones were toppled, and others were worn from the years of rain and snow and heat so that the names and dates of the deceased were nothing but slight indentations that were unreadable.

A few stones—the small rectangular ones that marked the infants' graves—were loose in the soil. Phil lifted one headstone from its socket like a loose tooth, mowed the grass, then bent down to replace it. As he did, his Bob Ramsey lunged past with his mower. Phil heard a loud, low-pitched *clunk*.

The next instant, an object struck him in hard the face. "Ahhh!" he gasped, recoiling and falling onto his back in the grass.

# CHAPTER 8

"Okay, fellas." Karl Keyhoe surveyed the room as he called the meeting to order in the Riggers Building at 7:30 a.m. sharp, "Listen up." The group of almost fifty recently-hired workers sat on folding chairs in front of him.

Dressed in a shirt and navy-blue tie, ready to deliver the day's safety talk, Karl waited for the chatter to die down. His front-office blue suit jacket hung stiffly from his shoulders as he stood next to a metal podium. His black and red ID badge clung to the right-side of his white shirt, a shirt crisply ironed by Frances the night before.

"I'm Karl Keyhoe. Your security supervisor," he began. "Today's talk is about your safety glasses." He paced a few steps to the side of the podium, then returned to it, and held up a pair of black-framed safety glasses. "Now, some of you grumble about wearing these. I've heard my share of complaints. Some of you say they're a nuisance, that they just get in the way. Or that they steam up in the afternoon heat. Some fellas keep them in the pocket of their coveralls and don't wear them at all." His voice, a low baritone, was informative and practical, but still with an authoritative edge to it. Just the way he wanted to project himself. "Well, I've got something for you to think about."

Karl looked out at the group, nodded at Phil, who was sitting in the second row, and commanded, "Okay, Phil. Stand up."

Phil complied, rising slowly from his chair. "This fellow…" Karl said, pointing to his son.

Out of the corner of his eye, Phil got a glimpse of Tommy's shoulders shaking, and he was trying to hold back a laugh. Phil felt stupid, standing there and tried not to look around as heads turned toward him and stared. He glanced down at his scuffed work boots. Not knowing what to do with his hands, he self-consciously stuffed one into his pocket and scratched the side of his head with the other.

Karl continued. "This fellow, he was on a mowing detail yesterday. Abiding by all the rules." Karl held another pair of glasses in the air with white cracks spidering out from the center of one lens. "You see these? These glasses were hit by a flying projectile. A small rock, to be exact. But," he added, "small as it was, that rock, tossed by a lawn mower's blade, struck the glasses at a terrific rate of speed." He paused for dramatic effect, nodded. "So, if it wasn't for these required safety glasses, that rock, flying at that speed, well, it could have gone right into that worker's eye. Like a bullet." He lifted the glasses higher in the air, pointed with his thick index finger at the opaque lens. "Like a bullet, almost."

Phil started to sit down again, figuring his dad's point was made, but Karl noticed and said, "No, stay standing." As everyone continued to stare at him, Phil felt tingling blood rush to his face and bloom there. He tipped his head back and stared at the corrugated metal ceiling where hooks hung from the beams.

"So you can see," Karl continued, "the tempered glass stopped it. These glasses…" he cleared his throat, then continued "these glasses saved his eyesight. They might have saved him from being blind. Even better, they might have saved his life."

Assuming the speech was over, Phil lowered himself to the chair. Tommy initiated an exaggerated applause, clapping his cupped hands together. "Let's hear it for the star, folks!" Tommy called. The fellow teenage summer workers in the crowd joined in, clapping and guffawing. Tommy hooted. "Yay, Phil!" somebody called out. In an attempt to cover his embarrassment, Phil waved weakly at the guys. The scene reminded him of the time he dropped his plastic lunch tray in the school cafeteria, the kids cheering as his glass of milk shattered and the hamburger-noodle casserole splattered across the tiled floor.

Irritated, Karl scowled, his eyes hardening like BBs. He arched his back, waiting for the raucousness to die down, then strode over to Phil. "I'm not done here yet," he chided. "Stand up again," he commanded. Karl held the broken glasses toward Phil. "Hold these." Phil reluctantly took them from him, held them waist high.

"Higher," Karl said. "Hold 'em higher. So the fellows can see them."

Humiliated, Phil pinched his lips together and held the glasses over his head—one lens clear, the other looking like it was covered with milk.

"So, fellas," Karl concluded, pointing at the workers. "We're all about safety here. Safety is number one." Phil knew his father constantly used these phrases, clichéd as they were. He had seen similar wording in the plant's new safety brochure Karl had written. "If you follow the rules," Karl continued, "the rules will be good to you. This goes to show…," he grasped for some final words that would end the talk with something powerful, something the workers would remember. Something that might register with the teens who were still chuckling and elbowing each other. "All this just goes to show…" He faltered again, then just barked out the words: "Just wear the damn glasses. Any questions?"

"Good job, Phil. You're quite the hero," Tommy said to Phil, patting him on the back as they shuffled out of the riggers building. "A frickin' poster boy for wearing these goony things."

"Yep, that's me."

"Hey, I think I'll even wear *two* safety glasses today," Tommy mocked, patting his coverall pockets. "I can only find my extra pair…" They paused by the tailgate of the truck. Inside the flatbed, dark green mowers waited, lined up wheel to wheel. "So, is your old man gonna put those glasses on display? In a Strongs display case, maybe? Shit, he could charge admission, just to walk by and look at 'em."

"No doubt," Phil nodded. "Now, if you don't mind, would you please just shut the hell up?"

"Yes, sir," Tommy gave him a salute. "Anything you say, sergeant safety."

Phil just grimaced and adjusted the new safety glasses his dad had pulled out of his shirt pocket and handed to him this morning.

"You could at least say thanks," Karl had grumbled. "These are the newer style. With the amber frames, even."

"Um, yeah," Phil said under his breath. "Thanks."

That evening, after work, as they sat on the front step of Mariah's trailer, Phil relayed in detail his dad's embarrassing safety lecture.

"Sorry you had to go through that," she said sympathetically. "Your dad always seems to put you on the spot, doesn't he?"

"I guess."

"But the fact remains," she added, "that plant is an awful place to work. The more I hear about it, the more disturbing it sounds. All that gunpowder production."

"Hey," Phil replied, trying to minimize things. "I survived, didn't I? And the job earns tuition money. Besides, I'm just mowing lawns and shoveling gravel out there."

"That doesn't change anything," Mariah persisted, shaking her head somberly. "It's still a dangerous place. And you're still a part of it."

# CHAPTER 9

Wearing a charcoal suit, he stands sideways in the doorway of her bedroom. She's lying on her back, covers pulled up to her neck, staring at the pink ceiling. Then she shifts her gaze and stares at him.

The hall light is on behind him, making him just a silhouette, though she knows it's him. It's her father. It's her father in the doorway, in the middle of the night.

He doesn't move for a few seconds; he just seems to be staring at her, though she can't really see his features. His face is an oval blur. No smile, no frown.

*He's stopping to say goodbye,* she thinks, and she sits up in bed in anticipation.

But he doesn't say anything; he just backs slowly out of the doorway without a word. He's gone, but he leaves behind his elongated shadow, still lying flat on the floor. Suddenly, a gray color bleeds outward from the center of the ceiling to the corners of the room. As the pink ceiling disappears, a sad and anxious feeling rises inside her. She wants to open her mouth to call to him, but it feels like her lips are sealed shut, and she can't breathe.

Mariah woke in the middle of the night, startled. Glancing around, she realized that she was in her bedroom in the trailer, the pale thin strips from the Camelot Acres security lamp sliding through the blinds. She was filled with emotions. Regret, anger, guilt, sadness—they all wrapped around her like a net. Her cheeks were wet from tears, and she realized she'd been crying in her sleep. *That dream,* she thought. *That damn dream again.* It was a dream she'd written about in her journal, pressing down hard, so hard on the pen that it almost punctured the paper. She hated it that he never said goodbye, or gave *her* a chance to say goodbye, not in the dream, and not in real life, either. Everything just stayed like it was—unresolved, in neutral. She hated it that, at the end of the dream, though he had walked away, his shadow always lingered there in the room, just to remind her.

She climbed out of bed, padded to the kitchen on bare feet. Lifting a glass from the cupboard, she opened the rounded refrigerator that was steadily humming. His shadow would not keep her down, she told herself. She would not allow it to remind her, to drag behind her, to make her weak. She would be strong. *Strong.* But how could she do that? Could she roll up his flat shadow like an old rag rug and toss it in a dumpster?

She poured a glass of milk from the carton, took a slow drink.

"You're up?" a voice asked, startling her. It was her mother. Janelle, wearing a green satin nightgown, moved closer. "What's the matter? Bad dream?"

"I guess." She hesitated. She pulled at the sleeve of her oversized T-shirt, then finally said "It was about dad."

"Oh?" Janelle lowered her eyes to the square tiles of the floor. "Oh."

"I've been having it for a while. And it always wakes me."

"Want to talk about it?"

"No, not really," she said, not wanting to dredge up the hurtful topic at three a.m.. "It doesn't have a point. Doesn't have an ending, really. It's just sort of a neutral scene, a few seconds long, but it always wakes me." She took another sip of milk.

"So why are *you* up, Mom?"

"My usual." Janelle lifted the carton of milk and poured some into a glass. "Happens almost every night about this time. Goes with the territory, I guess." She glanced at the carton. "I got whole milk this time. They were out of two-percent."

"So, what's waking *you*?" Mariah inquired. Janelle didn't answer at first, just turned her head toward Mariah in the dim light. Her features looked grainy.

"Just nothing," she said. "And maybe everything." She lowered herself onto the red vinyl kitchen chair, rested her elbows on the table. "But morning's on its way, right? We better get ready to face the day. It'll be here sooner than either of us think."

Mariah nodded, smiled weakly. "Mornings have a way of doing that."

Janelle held up her glass toward the window, where the light from the trailer park security light angled through. The glass cast a silhouette on the table. "Hmmm. My glass is half empty. Though you can look at it one way or the other."

"You sure do love your clichés, Mom."

"I guess." Janelle glanced at Mariah's glass. "I think I know which way you see yours."

"Half full, of course," Mariah said without hesitation.

"You *should* always look at things that way. Even if I don't."

There was an awkward pause. Mariah wanted to pour out her emotions to her mother. Her anger at her father, her frustration, her feelings of abandonment, of hatred, of love. The feeling that everything about her life was unresolved. The way colors seemed to turn ashen. But she knew that three in the morning, in a dark kitchen, was not the time or place.

"Sooo," Janelle finally said, and let the word hang there. She stood from the chair, her nightgown swaying at her knees like a soft wave. "Let's hope this will help us both get back to sleep." Janelle raised her glass and toasted Mariah, their glasses clinking.

"To whole milk," Janelle said with a faint smile. "Not skim, or two percent."

"To whole milk," Mariah chimed in, "making us whole again."

"And to sweet dreams," Janelle added. "Or should I say *sweeter* dreams?"

"Yes. Sweeter dreams."

## CHAPTER 10

*It's not just a place to work, like it is for Phil,* he thought. *It's more than that. A lot more.*

The day began like this: five forty-five in the morning, Karl Keyhoe was already moving through the darkness of the kitchen, opening the Philco refrigerator. Bathed in the glow of the yellow light, he scanned at the shelves, lifted a package of bologna. He set it on the counter, then flipped on the overhead fluorescent light and the room woke.

He glanced at the plaster ceiling.

Phil was still asleep up there, he knew. The boy always slept as late as he could, and relied on Karl to get things going in the morning. He'd wake him in due time.

He tugged at the handle of the cupboard, and the hinge he was meaning to fix creaked open. Lifting a loaf of bread, he set it on the countertop: *Wonderbread. White.* The kind he liked. None of this whole wheat or grain, he reasoned, which is always too dry. He placed two pieces of bread on a plate and buttered them. He then layered three round bologna slices, a piece of iceberg lettuce, a heaping spoonful of mayonnaise, and placed the second piece of bread on top. He cut off a square of Saran Wrap, wrapping the sandwich tightly, so no air could get in. Then he folded the loose edges into sharp, V-shaped corners on both ends, as if he were wrapping a Christmas present, and it was done: the little rectangular world of the sandwich, just the way he liked it, preserved until his lunch break. It was an orderly lunch, just as it would be—he hoped—an orderly day at the plant, and more importantly, an orderly day in the world.

It'll be a darn good lunch, he thought, and he'll wash it down at noon today with coffee—black, no sugar—poured from his stainless-steel thermos. Then he and the other supervisors will talk about the new production lines that just opened up, and the latest about the war effort in East Asia.

Frances, his wife, was up early, too. She'd make Phil's sandwich in a few minutes; she knew Karl always preferred to make his own.

At six-thirty, after he watched some of the early news on TV, the flickering Motorola's volume turned low, he checked his watch. Time moved forward, as always. Never stopping. Karl always believed it was your job to keep up with it.

"I'll wake him in five minutes," he said to Frances, and she nodded. She knew the routine, the protocol. A woman needed to know that, Karl believed, to support her husband, and Frances never faltered. She was always there, always where a woman needed to be. She always stood behind him.

Not like Phil. Sometimes he wondered what the boy was thinking, like last weekend, when Karl had asked him to wash and wax the Chrysler.

"Why?" Phil had questioned. Phil was getting ready to drive out in his '59 Rambler and meet the girl. The girl was getting to be his main priority lately, rather than his duties around the house. He seemed to be getting dreamy, distracted, listless.

"A car doesn't wash and wax itself, you know," Karl had stated.

"Guess not," Phil uttered.

"You couldn't find the time to do it yesterday. So I guess you're going to do it now."

Phil had given him a perturbed look, then shuffled to the garage to pick up the plastic bucket and sponge. He took the down the cardboard box, labeled **Waxing Kit**, where Karl had neatly stored a tin of Turtle Wax, application rags, and a folded buffing cloth. No excuses.

At six thirty-five Karl lumbered up the creaking steps to wake Phil. He made a crisp right turn through the doorway of Phil's bedroom. He leaned against doorway's molding, which he had painted white. Enamel, oil paint. So it wouldn't chip.

He entered the room with the faded eggshell walls that didn't quite meet evenly in the corners. On one wall, a slightly off-kilter poster of the Rolling Stones. Karl always disliked that poster: the long-haired band members, the rumpled clothes. That lead singer with his tongue sticking out. Phil's idea of decorating a room.

On Phil's desk—a cluster of pencils, all sizes, some sharpened down to nubs. They should be held together with a rubber band, Karl always thought. Instead, they sprawl across the desk like a game of Pick-up Sticks.

*The kid should clean this place up,* Karl thought, *he's got no sense of organization here.* He angled his gaze to the single bed without a headboard where Phil was asleep, his face half-buried in a pillow. He was wrapped in a swirl of blankets.

"Okay, Phil," Karl announced. "It's time."

Phil didn't roll over, or even move. It was like he was in a coma, so Karl repeated, louder: "*Okay*, Phil." Phil stirred a little, dragging an arm across the dusky covers, his eyes still half shut.

*He could sleep all day, if I let him,* Karl thought with a wag of his head. *Counts on me to be his damn alarm clock.*

"You got twenty minutes to get out the door," Karl finally barked, "or the Chrysler leaves without you."

Phil's eyelids opened, blinked, then blinked again, as if a bright light shined in them. "Yeah," he finally said, his sleepy voice ragged and raspy like a smoker's, though he'd never taken up smoking. Phil rolled to his side, the bed creaking; his eyes closed again as though they were weights he just couldn't lift. Still, he managed to sigh, "I'm up. I'm up."

"Well you don't look *up*." Karl reached over and flipped the light switch, and the 100-watt bulb in the middle of the ceiling flooded through the frosted glass of the fixture. Karl liked the 100-watt bulbs, not the 75-watt ones; you could see where you were, and where you were going.

"I've got a safety meeting this morning at seven-thirty sharp," Karl stated as Phil finally sat up in bed, his shoulders hunched. "Colonel's stopping in. Got to get there early. Things need to be ready."

Phil didn't respond. *His usual,* Karl thought.

As he and Phil lingered in the half-opened doorway, Karl turned toward

50

Frances, who stood in the dim light. A kind of vacuum always pulled air through that doorway, and her stylish auburn medium-length hair lifted slightly off her forehead. Her attractive features softened, and she gave him a sad look, because leaving was always sad for her, even if the leaving meant her husband going to a workplace he enjoyed. Karl gave her a quick kiss. Karl noticed that lately, whenever he leaned to kiss her, she seemed to stiffen her small frame and turn her cheek, just so, before his lips were about to touch. Thirty years of marriage. No bumps in the road. Lately, her smooth and flawless cheek tasted cool, but sort of sweet, a mix of soft baby powder and Noxzema. She gave the two of them a wave with her pale hand, and called, as she always did, her voice lilting, "Good luck at work, you boys."

It began like this: At 7:10, Karl Keyhoe clicked the ignition in the pre-dawn, the engine turning over quickly and then humming as it warmed up. Karl switched on the headlights, and they illuminated the tan panels of the garage door. "Remind me to turn off my lights when I get there," he said, and Phil mumbled "Um-hum." Karl backed out of the driveway, and the small sticks, fallen from the oak tree, crackled beneath the tires. Not Goodyears, which didn't last as long, but solid Firestones. He stopped abruptly at the edge of 5th Street, and the keys jingled on the key chain. He silenced the swaying keys with his hand, looked both ways.

He waited at the stoplight at Main, though there was no traffic yet this morning. None of the town square businesses opened until nine. The turn signal pinged, a small right arrow on the dashboard flashing. The curling exhaust turned red in the glow of the taillights behind him. When the light changed, he turned the corner at Main methodically, hand over hand on the steering wheel, and accelerated down the street that led toward the plant. Though he could go a lot faster, given the horsepower of his full-sized American car, he kept his speed at twenty-five, the legal limit. He kept the radio off. Not so the two of them could talk, because they didn't, but just because today he wanted it off.

Glancing in his rearview mirror, Karl saw a couple of cars turn the corner. They formed a line behind him, a line he felt like he was leading. Courteous drivers, they kept a steady distance between bumpers and their lights on low beam. They knew their purpose this morning was to drive at an even pace through town and toward the plant, to make a right turn at the main entrance gate, and to park in orderly rows on the expansive lot that stretched all the way to the base of the rising bluffs.

Karl knew his purpose, also: to report to work each day, to make things safer for the employees of the Strongs Army Ammunition Plant. It wasn't just a job for him. Far from it. His duty was to report early, if he was asked to, and to prepare his lecture for the foremen of the acid refinery area. The lecture—to be delivered at 0830 hours sharp—would address the subjects of refinery safety: the necessity of wearing coveralls and a long-sleeved shirt, the mandatory use of heavy-duty rubber gloves, the hazards of sulfuric acid, and the correct procedure in the event of an acid spill on your exposed skin.

"Got your safety boots on, I hope," Karl cautioned.

51

"Um-hum," Phil gazed idly through his faint reflection in the glass.

"I heard there were rattlesnakes out where you're mowing." This was the same thing he said to him last week, and just so it would sink in, Karl said it again.

Phil nodded.

As he headed downhill, the twenty-five square mile plant expanded to fill the broad windshield. Karl scanned the 7,500 acres. From that angle, the 1400 buildings of the plant appeared symmetrical. A series of grids within grids. Each asphalt pedestrian path was far enough away from the production houses to keep the workers safe. Each powder storage building was separated from the next one by a hundred yards, so there'd be no chain reactions. No fires. No explosions. And the entire place was sealed tightly by 75,000 feet of cyclone fencing. No gaps in it.

As they neared the parking lot, Karl was happy that the ragged bearded man who stood there some mornings with a protest sign wasn't there. *Maybe the bum finally got arrested*, he thought.

Those types knew nothing about serving their country, Karl thought. Karl served in the infantry in WWII, and then on the rugged winding Burma Road, delivering supplies, and he'd seen the worst of it.

Karl flashed back to that day: His truck was strafed with machine gun bullets by a dive-bombing Ki-30 Jap plane. Tiny McKenzie from Texas always rode with him. Tiny, at 275 pounds, was no small man. Karl had ducked down below the dash, but Tiny, riding on the passenger's side, was hit in the shoulder as the window imploded. Karl felt a sharp pain in his right heel as a bullet struck it. Everything was chaos for the next few minutes—the rat-tat-tat of the strafing, Tiny's voice shouting in pain, the snarl of the dive-bombing planes. The next thing Karl knew, he was dragging Tiny from the smoking, stalled vehicle to the roadside beneath a canopy of trees. Minutes later, the Ki-30 circled, dropped a bomb, and their truck blew to kingdom come. Luckily, with the help of a medic, Tiny survived his deep shoulder wound.

Later, though Karl didn't feel like he deserved it, and he hardly remembered carrying Tiny to safety, he was awarded a Bronze Star. "It was nothing," he had told his commanding officers, "It's just what you do." He was a hero. Plain and simple.

That's why these protesting kids bothered him so much. They didn't know a thing about bravery, or loyalty, or sacrifice. They were spoiled. Whiners. They knew nothing about America's history, and what made it strong; they hardly thought about the Japs bombing Pearl Harbor, the drowned bodies trapped inside the hulls of the Arizona and the Oklahoma. They were all about dissent, and dissent, he knew, only led to weakness.

Wheeling the car into his designated parking stall, Karl glanced up at the **Reserved for Security Supervisor** sign. On the top edge of the sign, a decal of an American flag Karl pasted there one morning.

He pushed open the car door and grabbed his silver lunch box with the initials K.J.K. printed on it. Important items were labeled with a Magic Marker. The garage shelves were lined with boxes, each with its contents clearly labeled: **Wrenches, Engine Coolant, Work Gloves, Washer Fluid, Duct Tape, Waxing Kit**. Better that way, he told himself; things don't get lost. It seemed like Phil was always losing things when he was a kid—his school lunch box, ice skates, a ball glove. Scatterbrained.

Karl took a few strides toward the check-in gate, walking with that slight but ever-lingering limp from the World War II injury in his Achilles tendon. Sometimes, when he walked, he felt as if the world was uphill, and he was constantly climbing it. And maybe he was.

He glanced back at Phil who was still lounging in the car, listening to the radio, his eyes closed like he was sleeping. Karl stopped and returned to the car. He opened the driver's side door, reached in, punched a chrome button on the dash with his palm. "Damn it, why didn't you tell me the lights were still on?" he chided.

"Oh," Phil uttered. "Didn't know,"

Karl just gave him a stare, figuring the boy was daydreaming about that girl again. He was all wrapped up about her.

The morning continued like this: Karl Keyhoe, pivoting and marching toward the plant entryway. At the same time, other workers filtered from their cars and converged, each tributary merging to form a moving stream, then a broad artery that led to the check-in booths. It was all part of a necessary chain: The workers made the chemicals that created the powder that fired the bullets that would, eventually, win the battle against the communists in North Vietnam. He felt pride swell up inside him like clear water rising in a well. As he strutted, his lunch box swung from his right hand with a pendulum motion. Never his left, always his right hand. It felt better there.

He pictured himself, at 12:01, unwrapping his sandwich. Yes, he'll think as he admires it and brings it to his lips. The perfect sandwich, the perfect lunch.

And the perfect job. An important job, one that had to be done.

But then he winced as one thought marred the perfection: How, he wondered, could he convince the kid—his own son, who always seemed to lack focus—to feel the same way?

53

# CHAPTER 11

That night at eleven o'clock, Phil tipped backward in the water, his head slightly raised.

Phil had insisted he and Mariah should stop at the lake tonight to unwind, after what he considered his worst day ever at the plant. This morning at nine a.m., with ropes tied to a harness on his waist, Phil was lowered through the circular opening of an empty twelve-foot-tall iron boiler. He had to clamp his arms to his sides just to squeeze through the narrow opening. Inside, it was dark and stuffy, and the hot air tasted like soot. Claustrophobia squeezed its fist in his chest. Once he reached the base of the boiler, the foreman, on a grated walkway above, lowered a jack hammer by its hose, and Phil began jack hammering the walls of the boiler. The hammer shook Phil's arms like a machine gun as it rattled against the rings of calcium deposits. The stuttering sound assaulted his ears; sweat trickled from his brow and the billowing dust stuck to his face. By lunch break, he was certain that he looked like those West Virginia coal miners who emerged from deep within the mines, their faces painted with dark, haunted expressions. He never felt more like he was in hell than during that morning. When he paused for a moment to rest his arms and gazed upward, all he could see of the world was a pale circle of light, one small opening that seemed so out of reach.

Tonight, at the lake, the pale-yellow full moon, high overhead, was a welcome sight.

Mariah had told him she'd teach him the back float some time, and tonight was the night. Standing on a rock slab in four feet of water, she instructed him to lie back in the water, feet extended, arms at his sides. When he did, she slid her arms beneath him, one under the small of his back, just above his swim trunks, one supporting his thighs. Her fingers touching his skin seemed to transfer warmth as though they were embers.

"I take it you never took swimming lessons as a kid," Mariah said.

"No such luck," Phil replied, feeling a growing anxiety.

"What about your parents? Didn't they teach you?"

"Nope. Neither can swim. They're both afraid of the water. Like me."

"Okay, just try it," she coached. "The way I showed you."

"And if I sink," he joked, "will you write my obituary?"

"Come on, Phil." Her breasts, cupped in her aqua bikini top, grazed softly against his chest as she leaned close. When Phil tipped to one side and struggled a little, she encouraged him, saying "If you learn the back float, swimming will be breeze. Confidence. That's all you need."

"Whatever you say."

"Think of yourself as something in flight," she coaxed. "The lake water is like thick air. Be aerodynamic. Arch your body. But relax. Don't gasp, or hold your breath." Then her voice became softer, her words almost hypnotic. "Let the lake carry you," she continued. "Let it inspire you. Try to become one with the water."

"Yeah," Phil quipped, "when I drown, I'll definitely be one with it."

"Shut up," she said playfully.

Phil looked at her face that was so close to his, her intent but caring expression. Beyond her, the moon tossed down its layer of soft, massaging light. Surrounding the moon, the expanding halo of stars.

Still feeling the tension in Phil's muscles, she said "You need to meditate, sort of."

"Meditate?" He narrowed his eyes at her. "What are you, some kind of Zen master?"

"Well, I do have powers," she laughed. "A few, anyway."

"I noticed that. So, I'll meditate about *you*, then," he kidded. "That should be easy."

"No, this is *not* about me. You need to concentrate. You told me this lake is about twelve thousand years old, right?"

"Right."

"And that the Native Americans believed it had spiritual powers?"

He nodded.

"So maybe let your mind go in that direction. You need to find your inner poet. You don't know it yet, but he's hiding somewhere inside you."

"Okay, okay." Phil closed his eyes and let some random thoughts flow through his head. He imagined an ancient glacier, pushing the land into tall bluffs, then melting slowly and filling this circular bowl. It occurred to him that, right now, he was floating in the very same water that had melted from that ancient glacier. He pictured the water from this lake, evaporating high into cumulous clouds, then falling back to the earth as rain, then seeping down, down down until it reached the center of the earth. He imagined Mariah's depth, all the things he wanted to discover about her.

Sensing that he was finally relaxing, Mariah aimed Phil's body toward the center of the lake. Phil, eyes still closed, felt himself rotate slowly, like he could be a compass dial, finding true north. A few seconds passed. Mariah gave him a sudden push, launching him. "Swim!" she called after him.

"Swim!" he echoed. He glided on his back toward the deeper water, finning his arms and hands at his sides the way Mariah instructed him. He was surprised at how easily he stayed on the surface. Mariah was right.

In an instant, she was paralleling him, smiling, doing a graceful sidestroke, her long legs scissoring rhythmically, her lithe body parting the water, sending small waves lapping toward him. At that moment, he couldn't help but think: *water that touches her everyplace touches me everyplace.*

As those gentle waves caressed him, he felt himself gliding into the unknown. And he didn't fear it, because all those things—the net of starlight, the luminous moon, the deep heart of the lake, and especially her soft but strong hands—were buoying him up.

# CHAPTER 12

*Why isn't he back yet?* she wondered.

Frances parted the drapes and peered out the living room picture window, looking for Phil's headlights. She could always recognize his Rambler coming down the street, the left headlight bright, the right one dimmer. But she saw no sign of him, and it was almost midnight.

Francis had always been protective of Phil. Even when he was in junior high, enjoying a family outing at Bluff Lake beach, Frances would warn him about the drop-offs. When he'd wade in past his waist she would call out "Not too deep!" Frances, who her friends said looked slim and attractive in a swimsuit, never learned to swim. And she couldn't help feeling helpless if anything would happen to him out there. "Phil, not so deep," she'd repeat.

Lately, she worried about Phil for a different reason: his summer job at the Strongs plant. It was just a way to earn money for college, Frances rationalized, since she and Karl wouldn't be able to afford his college tuition. But still, she thought, it *is* a place that makes gunpowder. She hated to think of her dear, sensitive Phil, mowing so close to those buildings that stored explosives.

Karl never mentioned that part about the job—only how much money it would earn Phil, since the place paid wages that were better than any job in town.

But Frances couldn't say anything to Karl about her fears. She would just clam up when it came to talking about the plant and its dangers. She felt herself clamming up a lot lately, especially when it came to certain topics. What *about* that war? She'd asked herself at times. Some TV anchormen called it a conflict, while others called it a military action. So what *was* it, she wondered, and what about it? Then, like releasing small paper boats in a steadily-flowing river, she just let the questions drift away.

She knew what Karl felt about it. She always knew what Karl felt. It was America's duty to be there, to fight Communism. It was all about duty. Loyalty. America right or wrong. Those were his feelings, and no matter how much she might question on the inside, she nodded along with him.

That place called Vietnam was so far away, right? And the soldiers, boys who were almost Phil's age, were being sent over there each day. And some of them, like the Gruener boy, who enlisted in the Army, weren't coming back. Danny Gruener spent only 21 days in Vietnam, a neighbor woman told Frances, and that was it.

Frances occasionally played bridge with Mrs. Gruener, who lived in the neighborhood and, though Dolores didn't talk about it, Frances couldn't help but notice the small shrine on the desk. Inside a thin, gold-painted frame was the picture of eighteen-year-old Danny, beaming in an Army uniform. He was pressed beneath a layer of glass, as if he was holding his breath. Below his photo was written *Private First Class. D. Gruener, 1st Infantry Division, 2nd Battalion, 2nd Infantry, C Company.* His Gold Star and Purple Heart medals were arranged on velvet beneath the photo.

Frances checked the clock again, wondering when Phil would come home. She propped a pillow beneath her head, brushed back her hair with a slim hand, then lifted the family photo album from the coffee table. She glanced through the pictures, one with the three of them standing in the yard, shadows sharp and angled behind them. Each black and white photo was anchored onto the page, as if that could stop time. She noticed her face in another photo. It was Easter, she figured, a year or two before Phil was born, and she had smiled teasingly at the camera. She imagined her eyes were a vibrant, deep blue. She knew, from looking in the mirror, that her eyes were less vivid now; as years passed, eyes had a way of fading, losing their color.

She turned the page and looked fondly at photos of Phil as a boy. On his first day of third grade she had snapped a picture of him, a cute boy standing there in his blue and white striped shirt and tan slacks. He was holding a Lone Ranger lunch box. She still had the colors of his clothes in her memory. The flash from the Brownie caused a glare in the picture window behind him, but that didn't spoil the photo.

What happens to those little boys? she wondered. Why do they grow up too quickly, then get thrown into the world, and sometimes into a war?

She thought about that day when she was surprised to see the tender soft hairs on the side of Phil's cheek. He must have been twelve then. At the breakfast table, she reached up and touched his cheek with the back of her hand. "Phil," she exclaimed, "You're getting whiskers!" He had squirmed away, of course, embarrassed. He didn't say anything, just gave her that shrug she'd see a thousand times after that. She saw it often—that certain rise and fall of his shoulders, his way of blocking off a reply, and with it, his true feelings. Yet, she knew Phil had emotions, deep ones. She sensed they were somewhere inside him, like some underground stream you couldn't see beneath the land but always knew was there.

She turned from the window and sat the couch again. Her mind drifted back to the times, when Phil was ten or eleven, and he stayed home on Friday nights. They would watch the late reruns of old movies. One of them starring Esther Williams. Karl would already be asleep upstairs, and the two of them would sit on the purple floral couch. Phil would keep her company as they watched Esther, in a sequined swimsuit, glide across a rippling pool. Phil didn't have to talk to her—he just had to be there in the dim room with her, and that was enough. She knew he acted interested in the movies because *she* liked them. She'd glance, once in a while, at the bluish light flickering across his intent face.

"Wow," she had commented after they watched a dozen synchronized swimmers doing a graceful routine in a pool. "That was a nice scene, wasn't it?"

"Yeah," Phil had agreed. "Nice."

It bothered her that Karl never seemed to understand Phil at all. He didn't really try. Though Phil was already eighteen, Karl still gave him orders as though he didn't have a mind of his own: *You need to pick up your room. About time to get the lawn mowed. The car's low on oil. Better get out there and add a quart.* Frances noticed that lately, when Phil and Karl talked, their conversation was reserved for facts, the dry, practical things they could both agree on: what time they needed to leave for work, last night's ball game score, tomorrow's weather forecast. Or else they didn't speak at all, awkwardly turning sideways as they'd pass each other in the front doorway. She began to understand that it was the way of men and boys, fathers and sons, this clumsy dance of avoidance they seemed to perform every day. The way they just chewed their food at the dinner table, their jaws rising and falling steadily, and never made eye contact. She wished she could bridge the gap between Karl and Phil, but she just didn't know how to start.

She sometimes felt the same thing between Karl and her: that she, too was doing an awkward little dance and not saying what was on her mind. Frances noticed lately that Karl had begun giving orders, not just to Phil, but to her, too. She could hear his dry, mechanical voice now: *Launder my shirts. I need dinner on the table by five-thirty. Take off your clothes.* She sometimes thought: thirty years of marriage, and that's what it comes down to. Saying things, but not saying them.

So she continued to go through the motions. She just served her roast beef, her baked potatoes, and the carrots steamed until they were pale. She just served her rhubarb pie—her specialty, she called it—and placed it on the wire rack in the middle of the table, its steam rising as it cooled. "Want more of anything?" she asked the two of them with a washed-out smile, a large silver spoon clinking against the china dish. Sometimes she felt like her words were useless, bland as unsalted mashed potatoes.

She felt proud that Phil was already planning on college next year. He'd be the first from their family to attend, and she sometimes tried to envision him, a young man of 22 years, mature and handsome, standing on a commencement stage in his college cap and gown. She would focus an Instamatic camera on him as the flash cube went off. *How did it all happen so fast?* She wondered. *And when did the color of my eyes fade?*

"Have you noticed?" she remarked to Karl earlier this year. "The boy's growing up." She was hoping her comment might begin a conversation about him.

"No," Karl scoffed, "the boy's a boy."

Tonight, as the movie ended at midnight, the wavering credits rose slowly on the TV screen like bubbles rising to the surface of water. Frances rose from the couch, pulled the chord on the Venetian blinds, brushed away the pale green tendrils of the spider plant, and looked out again, hoping to see Phil. But there were no cars. Just the empty street. Just the glow of the streetlights, like the reflection of that dull flash when she took Phil's third grade picture. Tonight he was out with Tommy and his friends, she assumed, or maybe that girl he'd been mentioning a lot lately. He might not be back soon, she told herself. When you're eighteen, you're never back as soon as your mother expects you to be.

At midnight, a test pattern appeared on the screen. The movie credits were replaced by a circle in the middle of the screen, like a bull's eye in a target, with two lines crisscrossing through it. A man's baritone voice buzzed through the speakers, telling the viewers that Channel 27 would now cease its broadcast and would resume programming at six tomorrow morning.

After the announcer's voice stopped, there was a few second pause, and the screen went blank. Frances cringed as she thought of the morning news, and the images she might see. There'd be soldiers, walking through the jungle with rifles. Soldiers being carried on stretchers. Her faded eyes would stare at the clouds of smoke from rifles.

As she thought about this, a sensation of panic rose through her.

Just then, she heard the metallic sound of the back door unlocking. She looked to see Phil, stepping into the grainy light from the night light on the stove.

She looked toward the kitchen, and he called out, cheerily, "Hey Mom! You're still up?"

"I was watching…watching a movie," she said, trying not to admit she'd been waiting up for him. "Remember when we used to watch the late movie together? When you were in fifth grade?"

"Yeah, I guess." He tugged on the sleeve of his red and maroon madras shirt. His hair, falling slightly on his forehead, was a little longer lately, she had noticed. Though Karl didn't approve, it was a handsome look on him. Like that Beatle John Lennon. No more buzzed-to-the-scalp crewcuts, like Karl always used to give him with his electric razor.

"We'd always watch Esther Williams," she added.

"Who?"

Frances could tell he didn't really recall those movies. "Esther Williams. You know. She starred in those movies. The ones with the synchronized swimming. I always loved those."

"Oh," Phil replied, "Sure." An inquisitive look spread across his face, as if he wondered why she needed to talk about this at twelve-fifteen in the morning. Still he added, "Those were good movies, weren't they?"

"Yes. I think we saw *every one* of Esther Williams' pictures." She clasped her hands together in front of her. "She was always so graceful in the water."

As she stared at him, then took a step closer. She touched his hair, which was damp on the sides. Like he'd been out, deep, in some lake. "Have you been swimming? Your hair feels wet."

"Oh. It's just really warm and humid out," he explained. He didn't want to tell her about being at the lake in the dark with Mariah; he knew that would worry her. He glanced at his watch. "Well, um, I better get some sleep. G'night, Mom."

As he took a step to angle past her, she gently pressed her hand to the front of his chest, stopping him. She slipped both arms around him and hugged him tightly, his arms still at his sides. Then she pulled back and gazed at him intently.

"What, Mom?" he asked, confused. "What?"

"I'm going to miss you," she said, with a kind of gasp.

His face was a puzzle of light, shadow, whiskers, and stray strands of curling hair. "But I'm not going anywhere."

"Yes you are, Phil," she replied, her voice hushed and soft, "Yes you are."

# CHAPTER 13

After the late movie, Phil and Mariah drove up the narrow, winding dirt roads of the rising and falling hillsides. The chassis scraped against the scraggly weeds sprouting up between two tire tracks. When they reached the right fork in the road that led down to Bluff Lake, Phil turned left.

Mariah glanced over at him. "I thought we were heading back to town."

Phil tossed a playful smile her way. "Not yet. I'm taking you to a favorite spot."

The Rambler bumped over the rocky, uneven road for another half mile. At a wide spot, he pulled the car over and grabbed her hand. "We're taking a little hike."

"Here?" she questioned, though by the lilt in her voice he could tell that she liked the idea. "At midnight?"

"Why not?"

"So is this your impulsive side coming out?"

"I let my impulses guide my dullness," he joked.

They followed a narrow path through the woods. Twigs crackled beneath their feet. Lit by the milky moon, the branches of the small trees cast faint shadows, like lines on a map, on the path ahead of them. "I read that this used to be an old Indian trail," Phil said as the oaks gave way to a stand of small pine trees. "The Ho Chunk lived here. There were Native American mound builders, too, before them. They built effigy mounds out near the lake."

"Have you seen them?"

"Sure. I'll show you some time. There are all kinds of effigies. Animal shapes. A water spirit mound. And even a thunderbird."

"Wow. I'd really like to look at them."

"They're astounding. But I guess a lot of them were destroyed when settlers built homes or farmsteads. Anyway," he continued, sweeping his arm toward the ridge, "this whole area was formed by a glacier. It's a terminal moraine. Tommy refers to them as *the terminal morons*. A perfect description of the hills, he claims, and also the locals."

She laughed.

"Yeah, that's about all I remember from the regional history unit freshman year. Besides the scent of ol' Mrs. Rommel's perfume." He pretended to cough. "Almost choked me off in the front row."

He led her up the path that meandered between moss-covered fallen trees and ancient purplish-pink quartzite boulders. "These are pre-Cambrian," he said, pointing to the rocks. "About a billion and a half years old, and..." He stopped in the middle of his sentence. "Geeze, am I'm starting to sound like the town tour guide, or what?"

"I guess you are. But I don't mind."

They emerged in a clearing, and he led her to an outcrop of rocks, which they began to climb. Before they reached the lookout point, Phil put his hands over her eyes and led her the last few yards. He loved it that she let out a girlish giggle with each step.

"Voila!" he said, pulling his hands away. "Behold the kingdom."

There, in the distance of the valley below, were the lights of Bluff Lake, shimmering like jewels in a shallow pond. The streetlamps and lights of the late-night gas stations extended like tiny beads of a necklace, flowing east and west into the darkening folds of the rising hills. Beyond the town, and the lake, the hills on the other side of the valley raised their shoulders again toward the sky.

"Wow," she exclaimed. "What a view. Your town actually looks magical at night."

Phil nodded. "When I was a sophomore and first got my driver's license, I used to come up here all the time."

"With girlfriends?" she quizzed.

"No. Alone, I mean. Just to sit and think."

"About what?"

"Everything, I guess."

"About where you're headed in life?"

"No, not exactly. More about the *present*. Like where I fit in the world. All that."

"So what did you figure out?"

"Not much." He shook his head wryly. "That I was just a molecule among many. One blink of an eye in a billion years. One particle of dust in a great big dust storm."

"Wow, that's poetic." She studied him a few seconds. "You're deeper than you look, Phil Keyhoe."

"Nope. Not deep. Ordinary is a better word."

"Not at all," Mariah responded. "Though sometimes you try to hide the real you. Especially when you're with your buddies."

"Whatever you say," he said nonchalantly, though he knew she was getting at the truth.

"It's not whatever I say," she said tenderly. "It's whatever you *are*."

The moonlight brushed across her attractive features, making her face look like an artist's black and white charcoal drawing. He leaned over and gave her a quick kiss.

Then he grasped her hand and they strolled along the lookout to the place where the trail branched; one led back to his car, and the other sloped downward between rock outcroppings.

"So where does that path go?" she asked.

"Not sure. I never went past this lookout."

"Maybe now's the time," she said. They followed the trail that snaked downward along a small glistening stream and through pine trees. The end of the grove opened to a grassy hillside. "Well, what are you waiting for?" she asked.

When he gave her a questioning look, she grabbed his hand and pulled him into a run down the steep hillside. As he ran through the tall, swishing grass, Phil didn't know if she was pulling him, or if he was pulling her; he just liked the feeling of running, the freedom and reverie of just running, running with Mariah and not caring where he was going. He heard her laugh, and he felt a spontaneous laugh rise up through his chest and burst out. It felt good, that explosion of joy for its own sake, and for a few seconds—with the warm evening night air buffing against his face, the meadow's downward slant making him run faster, the gentle pulsing squeeze of her hand on his—he felt suddenly liberated, as free as he'd ever felt. At the base of the meadow, it felt as though the earth dropped out from under him and Phil fell forward, pulling her with him. Both of them tumbled to the ground, laughing. Arms around each other, they rolled over and over in the soft grass.

As they embraced, he felt her heartbeat in his own chest. He looked into the depths of her eyes and felt a current rushing through him. This girl, this woman, electrified him, made him feel things he never felt before. For some reason, she saw in him someone he never thought he could be.

Phil reached up and tucked a few strands of hair behind her ear. She lifted her hand and gently brushed a dry leaf from the side of his face. To Phil, the moment was perfect. Just the two of them, lifting their hands and touching each other silently. That was enough. "Now it's official," Phil finally whispered. "I'm falling for you."

Mariah parted her lips slightly, as if about to speak.

"Hey!" a gruff voice called, shattering the moment. "Who the hell's out there?" The beam of a flashlight swept toward them, and then stopped on Phil's face, blinding him.

The two of them jumped to their feet. Phil noticed, at the base of the slope, the cyclone fence with barbed wire on top. Suddenly he realized that this fence was part of the eastern border of the Strongs Plant, and that this man, his squat jeep parked on a dirt road, was a security guard, patrolling the perimeter. Phil recognized the black rectangle of the threatening warning sign wired to the fence. Though he couldn't make out the words in the darkness, he knew them by heart.

"What you two doin' out here?" the guard, a stocky man in a military helmet, asked with a suspicious voice. The flashlight beam searched them up and down from their toes to the tops of their heads. Phil noticed that the guard gave Mariah a twice-over, the beam lingering a few seconds on her tight T-shirt and the curves of her breasts.

"Um, nothing." Phil offered apologetically. Then he said, under his breath, "Let's get out of here." He turned toward the hillside and tugged at Mariah's hand, but she didn't move. She resisted his pull with surprising strength.

"We're just enjoying the night," Mariah clarified.

"Well, people ain't allowed in this area. So you two just better move along." Phil could see the silver glint of the man's badge pinned to his khaki shirt.

"We're not actually *in* the plant," Mariah countered, her voice suddenly defiant, confident. "We're not breaking any law."

Phil was surprised by her spunkiness, her determination to not be intimated.

The guard's expression pinched like putty being squeezed.

"C'mon, Mariah," Phil insisted.

The guard aimed the flashlight back at Phil. The light carved deep creases in his face. With a can of mace wobbling on one side of his belt and a pistol in a holster on the other side, the guard took a few steps closer. Squinting one eye, he said, "Say, you look kinda familiar. Do I know you or somethin'?"

Phil didn't answer at first. "I don't think so." He lowered his eyes.

The man tipped his head to one side and circled the light on Phil's face. Phil could feel the beam burning his cheeks. "Ain't you Karl Keyhoe's boy?"

"You're thinking of somebody else," Phil lied. At the same time, he felt guilty, denying his connection with his father.

"Thought maybe you was him." With that, the guard dropped the small talk and pointed at them menacingly. "Well, whatever. You two better get the hell outta here. This here's restricted territory."

Wanting to get out of this predicament as soon as possible, Phil started back up the hillside, pulling Mariah along with him. Behind them, Phil heard a voice squawk through the guard's walkie talkie. "You got trouble out there, Dick? Over."

"Naw," the guard replied. "Just a couple punk kids out for a hike, is all. Nothin' to worry about."

At the car, Mariah slammed the door hard behind her. "What the hell. We weren't trespassing. That damn plant. I hate it."

Hoping to calm her, Phil reached up to touch the side of Mariah's face again. But, still upset about the guard, and in no mood for another romantic moment, she just pushed his hand away. "What *do* you do out there, really?" she asked.

"Not much. Mow lawns, shovel gravel, replace railroad ties, unload boxcars. Whatever they tell me. It's just maintenance."

"So, you don't have anything to do with making gunpowder?"

"No. No, of course not."

They rode in silence as Phil drove back on the deserted Old Lake Road. Mariah sat, head turned toward the window, her knees pulled up to her chest.

As he drove, he couldn't help but think how the guard had interrupted his idyllic reverie with Mariah. *Was she about to confess how much she was falling for him, too?* he wondered. He hoped so. But lately, the damn plant seemed to be ever-present—it was on the front page of the *Bluff Lake Freedom,* in the conversations of the townspeople at the local cafes. It entered his own living room at dinner, when his father talked proudly about the wave of new hires. And now tonight, it intruded right in their middle of their tender moment.

*Karl Keyhoe's boy.* Phil heard the guard's words in his head again. He was sure the guard *did* recognize him from working there. He cringed at the thought of his father finding out that he'd caused a disturbance, minor as it was. He imagined Karl grilling him, saying "What the hell you *doing* out there at that time of night? And what's with that girl, anyway—smarting off to a guard like that?"

Phil stared straight ahead, where the two yellowed headlight beams seemed to pull the car along the blackness of the asphalt road. The beams were dim, and always a little off center. Still, Phil knew he'd follow them all the way back to town. He'd steer up the narrow gravel driveway and pull onto the lawn on the left side of the Chrysler, like usual, always leaving enough room for his dad to open the driver's side door.

But before that, he'd drop Mariah off at her trailer, give her a kiss, and hope she might finish the sentence he was waiting to hear. *But would she?* he wondered.

# CHAPTER 14

When she came home late, Mariah assumed, by the dimness inside the trailer, that her mother was already asleep in the back bedroom.

The trailer. It was a little depressing, compared to their house in Madison, and yet there was something more than homey about it. Framed Van Gogh and Monette posters—her mom's favorite artists—brightened the walls. A small French opalescent glass vase—a wedding gift from Janelle's mother—balanced on a small rosewood table. A tweed Sears couch with two slightly sagging but comfortable cushions centered itself beneath the small window. It was a Goodwill bargain at fifty bucks, so her mother bought it. "To get us by," she explained. "Just for now. Until something better comes along."

Mariah understood. These last few years, Janelle was always just getting by, just meeting basic needs, just scraping through. It was her way. Not that she was a low achiever or wanted to settle for less. It was just that life seemed to keep pushing her into a corner. When Mariah's father took off, he also evaded any child support by declaring bankruptcy in his realty business. And he sold their house, which turned out to be listed solely in his name, when he stashed the money in a hidden account. He had smart lawyer friends. When he walked out on them that day, he might as well have been wearing a mask over his face and holding a gun instead of his expensive suit. But the real crime, Mariah thought lately, was not cheating them out of the money; it was what her father did to the family, what he stole from the two of them. He stole their sense of self-worth. He stole the very ground beneath them.

The year her father left, Mariah was in junior high; she kept very first journal—labeled *Geometry*—in a notebook under her bed. A little storage closet for her thoughts, her doubts, her dreams. It was a graph paper notebook, and on those faint squares, Mariah wrote long rants about her dad written in scrawled blue ink:

*I'll always remember November 5. That day. That cold, awful day was the worst day of my life. And so was the next, and the next. You said you didn't love Mom anymore. I guess you didn't love me either. Whoever that woman is that you're with, I hate her. I really hate her. In fact, I think I hate you, too. And the sad thing is, though I really don't know why, I think I hate myself.*

Tonight, hoping to cross the living room to her bedroom as quietly as possible, Mariah heard a voice.

"How was your night?" Janelle asked from the back corner of the room.

"Mom?" Mariah was startled. "Why are you sitting in the dark?"

Janelle swiveled the overstuffed chair and faced Mariah.

Mariah noticed that the room smelled faintly of smoke. Without answering, Janelle rose from the chair, bumped the TV tray, scattering the cards from a game of solitaire. Ice cubes clinked as a glass tipped over and Janelle quickly tipped it back up. Brandy, Mariah figured. Her drink of choice lately. And she'd have it more and more often, which bothered Mariah.

Janelle straightened her wrinkled blouse and seemed unsteady as she took a step to the kitchen.

Mariah flipped the wall switch and the kitchen light flicked on. It was a double light bulb fixture that always cast a harsh light over the kitchen, sharpening the corners of the cabinets.

"Too bright," Janelle said, squinting and flipping the light switch off. Instead she clicked on a small table lamp that gave the room a pink glow. "The lamp's good enough. We all look better in soft lighting," she explained with a laugh. "So, tell me about the date."

"It was good. No, not good—great, actually."

Janelle leaned in. "I can tell you really like this boy."

"I do Mom." Mariah lowered herself onto a kitchen chair with the red plastic cushion and the stainless-steel frame. "Nothing's ever dull when I'm with him." Then she added, "In fact, it's just the opposite. Everything seems amazing." Mariah loved it that her mother was a confidante, a friend, almost. She could tell her just about anything. Whether it be about school, her friends, boys, or loneliness, her mother would always listen without judging.

"If somebody does that for you, that's important. Have you told him that?"

"Not exactly. Not in those words."

"Good," she said thoughtfully. "It's better to hold something back. Don't show all your cards." Her mom was always big on card analogies. It was her favorite parallel: life was a game of cards, and you did what you could with the one hand you were dealt. Some cards were bent, some were stuck together, others had creases in the middle, and some were even blank. But the point was, they were yours. Sappy, Mariah often thought, and she didn't really believe all that. You don't wait for things to be dealt. You had to go after your illusive dreams in order to catch up with them.

Her Mom's patented advice always sounded so easy to follow. But Mariah often wondered, where did it get *her*? A broken marriage. A husband who sailed away with a woman. A small trailer on the outskirts of a dingy town.

Janelle, noticing Mariah's low-cut tank top and her tight white Levis, questioned "You're not going too far with him, are you?"

"Mom!" Mariah snapped.

"I'm just asking, Mariah." She took a step closer. Mariah looked down at her mother's bare feet beneath her black stirrup pants. Her feet were small, especially for a woman who was five feet seven, an inch shorter than Mariah. "I know you're an emotional girl," Janelle continued. "Sometimes you let your feelings rule you. But you've got to let reason enter in, too. Especially if things get too heated. I know you'll have impulses, urges, and…"

"Don't worry," Mariah said blatantly, "we're not having sex. We're not going all the way. If that's what you mean." It was her usual manner with Janelle—just blurt it out, be honest, and take the consequences later. "Could we change the subject?" Mariah said emphatically, rotating toward the sink.

"I want to make sure you're not pushing things too far. I mean…"

"This is *really* embarrassing, Mom." Mariah lifted a plate from the counter and lowered it into the scratched aluminum sink. She wondered if too much brandy was making her mom go on and on. That was the very reason Mariah stayed away from alcohol.

Janelle took a step closer to her. "No, Mariah, this is important. You need to hear this. That's the way your father and I started out. It was mostly physical at first. I let all that happen. Then, well…I got pregnant, and we rushed into marriage. You know, sweetheart, I never regretting having you. But the truth is, I never knew your father very well. And that's a terrible feeling."

Mariah shifted her eyes above the sink to the small window, where she could see the silhouette of the hummingbird feeder her mother hung out there. The hummingbirds would appear at it with their fast-moving, invisible wings, then dart away just as quickly.

"Can you imagine it?" Janelle added, "Living in a house with someone that you don't really know?"

"I don't want to hear all this."

Her mother's face suddenly tightened, her cheekbones accentuated by her small pursed lips, and she grabbed Mariah by the wrists. "You *will* hear this," Janelle said. "I just don't want…." She didn't finish the sentence, just let it trail away. Her fingers squeezed on Mariah's wrist, then softened, then squeezed again. She began the sentence again: "I just don't want you to…."

In her mind, Mariah completed the sentence that was so hard for her mother to finish. *End up like me. End up like me.*

Mariah put her arm around her mother. "You know, Mom," she said, "I *do* want to be like you. You've been nothing but wonderful to me."

She felt her mother's shoulders tremble. "No I haven't," she said, voice catching in her throat. "Just look. Look where we are."

"It's not *your* fault, Mom." Mariah felt a sob rising in her, too, and she pushed it down. She had to be strong now. She had to, for the both of them. Maybe her mother had given up on the world, but Mariah couldn't do that. "Maybe things aren't perfect. But we're here, and we're fine. That's what counts. We'll make it through. The future's out there, right?

Janelle swallowed hard. "Thank you for saying that." She brushed Mariah's hair back from her face. "I just want to protect you, honey. The damn world can be cold, and uncaring…"

"Don't I *know*." Mariah tipped her head back and closed her eyes. "But I want to change it."

"I know." Janelle wiped her tears with the sleeve of her blouse. "You always were an idealist."

They stood in silence a few seconds, and then the corners of Janelle's mouth plied upward into a smile. "Okay," she said, her voice turning suddenly playful. She switched off the lamp. "It's star-gazing time."

"Oh, Mom… Not now."

"Yes, now. Like we did when you were little. Come on." She took Mariah's hand and pulled her to the living room. "Just humor me. Lie down next to me."

Mariah remembered this routine from when she was a small girl. If she was in a bad mood, or had a rough day at school, her mother would try to cheer her up with what Janelle called the star-gazing game.

"Mom, this is stupid," Mariah said, resisting, "I'm a little too old for that."

"No you're not," her Janelle insisted, tugging at her hand. "You're never too old for stargazing."

Mariah gave in and the two of them lay side by side on their backs on the green and gold carpet.

"All right," Janelle said, her voice light and encouraging like when Mariah was a six-year-old, "Close your eyes for a minute."

Mariah complied.

"Now open them and stare at the ceiling." Janelle waited a few seconds. "You see any stars?"

"Not really." Mariah said, looking up at the dim, low ceiling tiles. She knew what was coming next.

"Okay, then. Now *imagine* stars up there," Janelle said in a wistful, faraway voice. "Picture them." She let a pause sink in. "They're up there. Just believe in them. They're glistening. Dozens of them. Hundreds. Thousands. Millions, even. Can you see them now?"

"Yes," Mariah acquiesced, feeling herself relax. "I can."

"Okay, great. Don't take your eyes off them."

They lay there in the darkness for a moment, neither of them speaking. Finally Janelle asked, "Is he leading you somewhere?"

Mariah rolled her head toward her mother. "Is *who* leading me?"

"Phil. Is he doing that?"

"I'm not sure what you mean."

"I mean, will he take you places that will make you happy? Men are about potential, you know," she explained. "It's not what they are right now, it's what they *could be*, if they make the right choices. Is he like that?"

Mariah didn't have to think for more than a split second before she said "Sure." But she wasn't sure, exactly. Deep down she wasn't sure about as many things as she wanted to be: Phil, college, her future. Love, and its safety net below her.

There were stars on the ceiling, though, if she imagined them. There were always stars, because her mother had said so. Mariah believed. They were up there, glimmering slightly, always so close, and at the same time, so far away.

# CHAPTER 15

Before Phil even stopped his car, Mariah was already bounding down the porch steps of her trailer and running toward him. Her hair, spiraling behind her, lit up as she cut through an angled shaft of sunlight between the aluminum trailers.

"I'm so excited!" she exclaimed as she jumped into the passenger's seat. "So so so excited!"

"What's up?"

She pulled an envelope from the front pocket of her Levis, unfolded it, pulled out the contents and held it toward Phil. "I'm in! I got into the U!"

"That's awesome, Mariah!" Phil leaned over and gave her a quick hug. He stared at the letter. "Wow, a scholarship, too?"

"Yeah. Guess they thought I was smart enough."

"Smart enough? You made the national merit scholar list."

"This is such good news. Madison's my favorite town, and the U. was my first choice. They have a *great* political science department," she said, beaming. "Now it's all set, Phil."

He moved the Rambler's stick shift to neutral, took his foot off the clutch. "What's set?"

"*We're* set. We'll both be on campus. We can meet at the union and sit on the terrace by the lake. We can even take classes together."

"Only one thing," Phil said. He lowered his eyes to the keys in the ignition, tapped them with his finger, watched them sway back and forth. "I haven't heard from them yet."

"But you *will*. I'm sure you will," she said optimistically. "I saw your application. Your grades are way up there. There won't be a problem."

"If you say so," he said hesitantly. For some reason, he couldn't be as certain as she was.

She leaned over and gave him a kiss on the cheek. He could feel the intensity of her warm lips against his skin. "I say so," she whispered. "I *know* so."

"Burning grounds? What's that?" Phil asked the next day at the plant when he was told they'd be mowing that area.

Tommy filled the locker room with his cackle. "That's where you get sent when you're burnt out, like me."

"Seriously, Milk. What is it?"

"Seriously, Key. Don't you know? It's the place where they pile all the waste powder. And just before quitting time, they have a little bonfire. It's super cool."

"Sounds lovely," said Phil, remembering that his father did an inspection out there. "Maybe we could bring some marshmallows to toast."

"Or weenies. But not mine," Tommy said, grabbing his crotch. He stood and tried to balance his safety helmet by its brim on his index finger. When it tumbled to the floor, he picked it up and balanced it again. "I oughta try out for the circus, man." He flipped his safety glasses into the air, caught them behind his back.

"You *are* in the circus. You're such a freak."

Tommy gave Phil a lopsided look. Then he clamped his helmet on top of his head, placed his safety glasses on the brim with a cavalier flair, hopped onto the bench and did a little tap dance. "So how's Mariah these days?" he quizzed.

"Good. Not good, great."

"Didja tell her she has very good skin, like I coached you? Girls really like that. It'll get you far with them."

"No, I neglected to do that."

"Then what's happening with you two? Care to extrapolate? Gimmie some steamy details?"

Phil wasn't anxious to mar his memory of last night's memorable date with her. They had parked by the river and watched the layer of fog, like a thin, flattened ghost, rising and falling above its surface. Engaged in serious, heartfelt and sometimes humorous discussions, their conversation circled for hours.

"So, she pregnant yet?"

"Man, you are twisted." Phil pulled on a leather, high-topped work boot and began to lace it.

"Jesus, Key. Give me at least *something* to think about. So my mind doesn't turn to oatmeal this morning."

"She got into Madison."

"Wouldn't expect any different. After all, she's a total female Einstein."

"What about you? Heard from any of those community colleges?"

"Not exactly." Tommy hopped from the bench to the concrete floor. "Still hopin' that damn football scholarship comes through." He pulled off his helmet and ran his hand through his sandy hair. "It's pretty much my best shot." As a 210-pound fullback, Tommy could bowl over most defenders. The only problem was, Tommy spent more time goofing around in classes and ended up with only a C average for his high school career.

"Maybe you'll know soon," Phil offered. "They're slow when it comes to applications, I heard…"

Sensing that the conversation was about to take a sobering turn, Tommy gave Phil's shoulder a shove. "Ah, shit, you and Mariah. You guys are such frickin" scholars. You make quite the pair." He curled up his right arm and flexed his muscle beneath the gray and gold T-Birds T-shirt he always wore beneath his coveralls. "But hey, I'm still the Charles Atlas around here. Plus," he added as he glanced at the small oval mirror on the inside door of his locker, dabbed his index finger with his tongue, then brushed back the sides of his hair, "Of the three of us, I got the looks. I mean, Mariah might be close second…"

That afternoon, near the burning grounds at the north quadrant of the plant, Phil mowed mindlessly for hours. He pushed his Briggs and Stratton close to the outbuildings and beneath the maze of silver pipes leading from building to building. The pipes, covered with a shiny silvery foil, were twelve inches in diameter, and they seemed to zig-zag everywhere across the plant. As he mowed under them, Phil often wondered what traveled through those pipes. What was so important that it had to be carried, above ground, from one end of the plant to the other?

Because of the roar of the motors, you couldn't talk to anyone on the grass crew. So, as Phil pushed his mower across an open area, idle observations occurred to him. He gazed out over the stretch of the plant that led to the prairie to the west. Grass and more grass, he thought. Millions of blades, waving their tiny arms into infinity. The future of grass, he thought, was to be cut down, then to grow again to its full height, only to be cut down again. He could write a whole damn book about it.

He mulled over what Mariah told him last night as they sat in the car by the river. "The future's waiting for us, Phil," she exclaimed. "I can't wait for it." She talked about the importance of change and quoted Bob Dylan's lyrics from "My Back Pages" and "The Times They Are a Changin'.

She talked about her majoring in political science, something Phil knew very little about. "I want to teach someday," she told him. "Or work in politics. Or government." She slipped her sandals off, put her bare feet, with crisscrossed tan lines, on the dash. "I'm not sure I'll change the world or anything. "But I'd sure try to."

"Hmm, changing the world. That's one lofty goal."

"Someone has to start somewhere, right?"

"How can you be so positive?"

"Because," she answered. "I just am. There are just things in life you just know you're going to do. Or at least you *hope* so."

"I guess I live in the moment, kind of," Phil had admitted to her, causing a disappointed look to cross her face.

"I understand," she had replied, "But you can't just *stay* in the moment."

"I don't have much choice, do I?" he asked. She frowned.

She could hold it in the palm of her hand like a precious stone and show him. "Here," she seemed to say each day as she held up. "Here it is. This is tomorrow."

He admired her, of course, for her ability to plan things out, and he envied her a little for that, too. Phil knew what he *probably* wanted, but he wasn't all that definite about it. He felt neutral sometimes, as if he couldn't really control what was about to happen to him. Life was like a huge, oncoming ocean wave, and like a beginning surfer, sometimes he rode on top of that wave, and sometimes it churned him under so he didn't know up from down.

That night, in the darkness of the car, before he was about to take her home, she held out her hand toward him, fingers outstretched. "Pretend my hand is fire," she said.

"Huh?"

"Just pretend it's fire. Now put your hand on top of mine."

He complied and lowered his hand—fingers outstretched like hers—on top of her hand.

"How does it feel?"

"Like a hand," he tried to joke.

She rotated her hand so their two hands were palm to palm. Then she threaded her fingers between his and squeezed, gently at first, then harder. He was surprised at her strength.

"And now?" she asked. "How does it feel now?"

"Like a hand," he said again, and for a few seconds, it felt like someone was holding a lit candle beneath his palm. "And like fire."

That afternoon, Phil cut a steady path along the base of a clapboard building. As he reached a corner where the weeds were thick, two grouse, startled, burst up into the air, a few beige feathers floating beneath them as they rose.

Phil's mind drifted to the hazards that lurked everywhere in the plant. He'd heard about the workers who were killed at this place over the years, and whenever he passed the nitroglycerine building, the image of the three men blown through a wall haunted him. Phil was thankful he didn't work in the acid refinery, a building where drops of sulfuric acid sometimes fell on you from the pipes that angled across the ceiling. The acid could eat a hole through your coveralls, or worse, land on exposed skin, where it would burn like a lit match. Over the years, workers were injured or maimed at this place: they were burned while leaning over a vat filled with a chemicals, they were crushed by off-balance loads tumbling from trucks, their skulls were broken when heavy crane hooks accidentally dropped on them. The images swirled in Phil's head, making it feel like his brain was filling with smoke.

Phil knew those incidents were exactly what his father tried to prevent. Karl's view of the future was a simple, narrow one: no deaths, no injuries, no disruptions. His daily activities revolved around those three basic goals. Unlike Mariah, who saw change—even a dramatic change—as a positive thing, Karl looked at the lack of change as a standard: Keep things steady. Follow the status quo. No incidents. Every healthy person who strides through the gates in the morning should march out the same way.

"Hey, Key!" Tommy's voice yelled, breaking into Phil's thoughts. Tommy slapped the throttle handle of Phil's mower, cutting the motor off. "You turn into a zombie when you mow, or what?"

"You guessed it."

"C'mon, man. It's almost four o'clock." Tommy said enthusiastically. "Time for the touch off. It should be a smokin' good time!"

What workers referred to as the *touch off* was the highlight of the burning grounds. For hours during the day, the waste powder was delivered to a large white asbestos pad about half the size of a football field. The foreman, a rotund, always sweaty Don Ott, was the overseer of the process, keeping the powder in a neat but growing pile. The touch off would take place at exactly 4:20, Ott had told Phil and Tommy during their lunch break. He invited them to climb up to his lookout tower.

"No earlier, no later," Ott had assured them. "Company policy. There's a three second delay after I press this here ignition button," he had explained to Tommy and Phil, pointing to a red button on a metal console. "Then thar she blows." He described the moment with reverence, stressing the importance of the timing as if this was a manned rocket launch at Cape Kennedy. "Yep. Four twenty. That's when we have take-off," Ott proclaimed. Ott, who looked, because of his extra pounds, like a guy in his fifties, was still a bachelor at 38. All afternoon, he guided the powder to the middle of the pad with his crew using wooden rakes and shovels. "All our tools are woodies here," Don told Phil and Tommy with a snicker. "We keep 'em hard."

Ott had a panoramic view of the whole operation from an asbestos-covered lookout tower set a few dozen yards from the pad. Phil noticed that he also had a view of Playboy pinups that were taped to the walls of his tower. The girls lay on the polished red enamel of cars, reclined on beaches, sprawled on zebra-striped bedspreads. Topless and glamorous, they held spray-cans of car wax and plastic beach balls and roses, and they always, according to Ott, looked straight into his eyes. "Sometimes," he admitted to Phil and Tommy as his walkie-talkie squawked with an incoming call, "It's a little tough to concentrate on my job."

"Yeah, I bet," Tommy agreed.

Ott opened up a new Playboy centerfold to show them the new Miss June. "Lookit her boobies. Those things just about burn a hole right through my coveralls," Ott confessed.

After lunch, Tommy snickered and said "The guy's a regular Hugh Hefner up there. With his perch and his pinups, who needs a girlfriend?"

At quarter after four, out of sight of Duke, Phil and Tommy wheeled their mowers to a slight ridge overlooking the asbestos platform and walked halfway down to watch. On cue, Ott stood in his observation tower, staring through the double windows at his kingdom of powder. His minions—the rest of the crew, dressed in white coverall flame-resistant suits and looking through the windows of their hooded headgear—were all safely hidden in a small shelter a few yards from the platform. The warning siren on top of his booth blared, rising and falling like a noon whistle at city hall. With that siren, everyone around knew the powder was about to go off. At 4:20, Don Ott—with all the centerfold girls watching him, their languid lips parted—leaned toward the control panel and slowly lowered a pudgy finger toward the red button. Phil could see Ott in the observation tower, leaning forward, pressing his hips against the control panel, coaxing it, hoping there'd be no misfire. The crew workers straightened their backs.

After a couple of seconds, the first of the waste pellets at the outer edge of the triangular mound ignited, and then, with the chain reaction, the rest of it erupted in flames.

Phil watched as an orange fireball expanded and rose above the platform, making a hissing sound. "Aw, yeah," Tommy exclaimed. "Burn, baby!"

It wasn't an explosion; instead, the sound got gradually louder and louder, like a whole cage of snakes, until it grew to a softened roar. Above it, a large white mushroom cloud rolled upward into the azure sky. The perfect mushroom shape reminded Phil of the bomb tests, like the photos of the Trinity test in the desert in his Dad's collection.

"Wow!" Tommy shouted, tipping his head back as the cloud rose higher and higher. "It's like a freakin' A-bomb! "It's kinda pretty, in a way. "Ain't it?"

"I wouldn't call it that," Phil said, though he couldn't take his eyes off it. *Ugly* would be a better word for it, he thought. *Terrifying.*

A gust of wind, blowing across the valley, caught the cloud and swept it toward the two of them. "Jesus," Tommy blurted, "The goddamn thing's coming right at us!"

They turned to run up the slope, but the stem, swirling and widening like an opaque tornado, glided steadily toward them from behind, overtaking them. Tommy let out a short barking cough as the scent of gunpowder smoke engulfed them. Phil took in a quick gulp of air and held his breath. "Hit the deck!" Tommy called, exaggerating the danger as if they were playing war like they did as kids; back then they'd dive to the grass on their stomachs, pretending to avoid an incoming rocket attack or bombing raid.

After a few seconds, the cloud drifted beyond them, and Phil lifted his safety helmet that had slipped down over his eyes.

"Holy shit," Tommy uttered as they stood. "You think that smoke has radiation in it, too?"

"Probably."

"So we're frickin' poisoned?" Tommy comically clutched his hands around his throat and stuck out his tongue. "Oh the horror!" He raised his voice. "I'll be impotent! Or sterile! I'll never have a kid to follow my footsteps and work here!"

"Let's face it. You're zapped, Milk."

Tommy burbled his lips. "Seriously, Key. What kind of crazy hell hole are we working in?"

Phil watched as the dissipating cloud lifted itself over the bluffs and drifted toward town. "I ask myself that every day lately."

# CHAPTER 16

What Karl heard about Phil during his lunch break kept bothering him.

But he pushed it out of his mind, knowing he had to get on with the tasks he needed to complete this afternoon.

Making his way toward the garage where the government-issued sedans and trucks were kept, Karl passed the buildings that stored equipment for repairing the plant's roads. The building was filled with five-gallon cans of tar, piles of fluorescent cones, stacked one inside each other, yellow *Caution: Men Working* signs secured to sturdy sawhorses. As Karl entered the garage he pulled a key from the brass rack and nodded at Roland, the foreman in charge of maintaining the plant's vehicles.

Though he was the supervisor and could send one of the newly hired guys out, Karl still insisted on personally making the daily rounds. Each morning, he'd hop into car USG#33, a '63 Rambler with pointed fins. The car was painted a dull Army green, as were all the vehicles in the plant; no one vehicle stood out from the next. The cars were stripped down, basic models—no radio, no AC or power equipment. Their American Motors six-cylinder engine had never been run over 30 miles per hour, the maximum speed limit within the plant. Those simple six-cylinder engines were the most efficient, and Karl admired the way they'd run forever without needing repair. Steadiness. That was the governing principle. Steadiness and prudence kept the plant running and the men without injury.

As he pulled onto the paved road, Karl watched the black needle rise toward the 30 MPH mark and then he held it there. It was what was asked of him; it was what he did. And it was what he asked of the other workers. It was simple: **Safety is No Accident.** Last week, he had those signs posted at the entries of all the buildings. Black letters on a bright white background, for clarity. His idea. His vision. *If there are no accidents, we get things done,* he thought. *We move forward.*

This morning, he decided to check on the powder houses in the outlying areas of the plant to make sure everything was up to code and running smoothly. In Karl's mind, each building, no matter how remote, no matter how small, had a contribution to make. Like links in a chain, like small cogs in a big, important wheel, he sometimes thought. Like states in the union. The individual buildings worked together as one unit, and each area of the plant relied on the next, and all were part of the whole. The oleum production relied on the acid and ether production, the cotton dry house relied on the nitrating house, which later relied on the wringer house and then the roll house. There was a large, laminated chart, with intersecting lines describing it, on Karl's office wall.

Eventually everything led to the finished product: smokeless powder. Ball powder, that fine-grained, spherical gunpowder coated in graphite, is easy to store and transport in any climate and is ideal for the M-16 semi-automatic weapons used in Vietnam.

As he mused about all of this, Karl felt a slight tug of pride in his chest. He thought of using some of these ideas in one of his morning safety lectures, maybe print it on a flier to distribute.

He pulled the car to a stop, seventy-five yards from to Powder Production Building 18 in the east quadrant. As per protocol, no one was allowed to pull a vehicle close to a production building due to the potential of the ignition causing an incident.

As Karl entered the double-hinged swinging saloon-type doors of the of the building, the foreman nodded. "Karl," he said, acknowledging him.

"Randall," Karl nodded back. Randall Mienke used to work at the hardware store in town.

Karl's eyes shifted left, then right. They were trained at spotting imperfections.

"That window broken?" he asked the foreman as he noticed a crack in one of the ventilation windows near the ceiling. Karl envisioned half of the glass pane dropping. It would land right on the bench where the workers had set their lunch boxes.

"I guess."

"And that plank looks warped," he said, glancing down at a curved board in entryway.

"Sure does."

"Okay then. We'll get somebody out here to fix that. And that window." With a black government pen, Karl scrawled a few thick lettered-words on a work order form, then looked back up at Randall. "Any accidents this week?"

"Nothing much. Some splinters in one worker's hand. A sprained ankle when one guy pushed too hard on a loaded dolly."

"Overenthusiastic, eh?"

"I guess," the foreman conceded.

"Nothing wrong with that."

Small as these incidents seemed, Karl still had to record them, and he made a few notes in a log book. "You doing something to remedy things?"

"You bet," the foreman said. "I'm telling Johnny to wear his damn safety gloves. And Earl has to stop pretending he's still a tackle on the high school football team. He's thirty-one, for crissakes!"

"Good. Good," Karl grinned. Satisfied that corrections had been implemented, he marked his log.

These injuries were incidental, run-of-the-mill, of course. The kinds of injuries Karl was trying to avoid out there were the major ones. Before Karl became supervisor, a worker had been killed when a powder bin he was leaning over ignited in his face. The incident, as printed in the old record book—was listed as "Unknown Cause." Those unknown causes were what Karl was trying to eliminate. Steel beams dropping from hoists. The pavement pulling itself out from under you. Sudden fires. The things that happened unexpectedly, beyond people's control. Karl had read somewhere—perhaps in one of his *Popular Science* magazines—about spontaneous combustion, and how a pile of oily rags might burst into flame. He always wondered what would cause it. Last week he even had a nightmare about it: in the dream, he was sitting in his living room, reading a newspaper, and when he looked up, a pile of rags in a corner burst into bright flame. He woke that night and couldn't fall back asleep, the flickering image of the flame still in the back of his brain.

This morning, pushing that bad dream out of his mind, Karl focused on what was ahead. And what was ahead was just fifty yards down the road. Each powder house was placed exactly fifty yards from the other one, a safe distance of separation. Part of the balance.

As he pulled to a stop, his mind listed the building's vital stats: Powder House 19, twelve laborers, one foreman, a thirty by forty-foot log-insulated, tarpaper-sided building to keep out the heat. Net production: between two and three thousand pounds of raw powder a day. Two breaks for the workers—one at 9:15 a.m. until 9:30, and from 2:15 to 2:30. Everything running like clockwork, each tick another second that builds to a minute, each minute contributing to the hour, each hour to the 24-hour day. Each day at the plant with its own individual goal reached: 12,400 pounds of raw powder produced, six tons of finished powder. There was a war going on, after all, and America had to fight it.

As he drove the circular perimeter road and returned to his office, Karl oftentimes thought that he was a little like the smooth second hand of a clock gliding steadily around. Without a clock's hands, he knew, there'd be no sense of time. There'd be no moving forward, only chaos.

And chaos was what happened in the world outside the ten-foot barbed wire-topped fence of the Strongs Plant. Every day outside that fence, things happened: cars rolling over in the ditch on Highway 12, tough kids fighting in back alleys, men with guns demanding money from a liquor store, hippies picketing in front of the court house, and an apartment blaze, like the one that happened last night, smoke from second story windows and rising and billowing in a layer above the town.

Inside the plant, the goal was order, and commitment, and production. That's the way Karl saw it. **It's Been 0 Days Since the Last Accident.**

That's why, an hour ago at lunch, what Fred Delaney said bothered Karl as he sat there eating with the other fellows.

"Saw your son this morning," Delaney, a 30-something worker had said.

"Yeah?"

"He was out in the west quadrant. By the tracks."

"Yep," Karl said knowingly. "Shoveling gravel out there today."

"Yeah," Delaney smirked, "if you can call it that."

"What do *you* call it?" Karl swiveled toward the man.

"Well, it looked like the boys on the crew were kinda screwing around."

Karl studied his sandwich, the thin pink slice of bologna in the middle. Slightly curved from being packed against the stout thermos of coffee, it seemed to be frowning at him. "What's that supposed to mean?"

"Saw 'em dancing around on the tracks. Singing, it looked like. Playing their shovels like they was guitars." Delaney let out a wheezy laugh, as though it was funny. "Him and that Laudermilk kid."

Karl said nothing, just squeezed his sandwich, his thumbs sinking deep into the soft Wonder bread.

Right after his afternoon break, Karl veered the Rambler across the lot and drove toward the west quadrant. He usually stayed in his office in the afternoons, catching up on paperwork, but he told his secretary he'd be back in a few minutes and called it a "spot check."

He wasn't sure what speed he was going; his eyes just kept darting left and right, looking for that railroad crew as the road hummed beneath the tires. He passed a couple of riggers crews mowing the ditches, their mowers kicking out little puffs of bluish smoke. *Need to add more oil to those things,* he thought, and he made a mental note to stop and have a chat with the foreman on the way back. To his left, a small tram pulled a few open-air copper kettles of raw powder to the processing area. Six cars. The maximum number allowed for transport of powder.

As he spotted the railroad crew in the distance, he pulled to the shoulder and hit the brake. For some reason, the memory of his bad dream came back again: the oily rags in the corner of the living room, bursting into that bright orange flame. Him, rising from the La-Z-Boy and standing there, unable to move, like his arms and ankles were tied together by thick rope. He shook off those thoughts, pulled his binoculars from the glove box, got out from behind the wheel and watched the crew for a while. He recognized Phil's thin, lanky frame, saw him pushing a shovel into a small gravel pile, then depositing it between the railroad ties, then reaching back for another shovelful. Unexpectedly, Phil paused, rested his hands and chin on his shovel handle and teetered there. He seemed to be staring Karl's way, as if he could actually recognize his father, peering at him from five hundred yards away. Karl figured the boy was taking a breather, or just getting dreamy like he sometimes did. Maybe he was thinking about that girl he'd been dating. Puppy love, thought Karl—it'll never last. She was a girl Karl liked less and less the more he found out about her: She was overly emotional. And overly opinionated. A trailer court kid, runaway father—he had heard—and a mother drifting job to job. No stability.

Karl watched as Phil went back to work. He returned to his routine of bending, digging, lifting, then scattering the gravel between the evenly spaced ties of the narrow-gauge railroad track. Like the motion of a metronome, like clockwork.

And that was all Karl needed. He climbed back behind the wheel, stashed the binoculars into the glove box, dropped the stick shift into first. There was no trouble out here. Delaney must have imagined it, Karl reasoned, or maybe it wasn't even Phil, but some other goof-off on that crew. They were all kids, for crying out loud.

He refocused his mind to his next tasks; he had important things to deal with before he punched out this afternoon. After all, the war wasn't slowing down. And when you were in the powder production business, there could be no delays, no stalling. You moved forward, without hesitation. The boys over in Vietnam depended on you.

There was a work order to be filed, a cracked window to replace, a warped board to be straightened. Little things, sure, but they led to big things. He'd make a note to stop out at Powder House 19 next week to inspect, to make sure the clear glass was tightly in its frame, that the board was level again, so no one would lose their balance or stumble. No incidents. Not under his watch.

He veered the Rambler into a U-turn in the middle of the road. Before he accelerated toward headquarters, he glanced out at the railroad crew again. *Yup,* Karl thought, satisfied. Like everything else, the boy was there, right where he was supposed to be, doing his part.

# CHAPTER 17

"Can I drive?" Mariah asked on Sunday evening as they rode in the Chrysler. They were on their way back from a picnic in a state park a few miles from town. The question caught Phil off guard.

"Drive?" he asked tentatively.

"Come on," she insisted. "Just let me drive a mile or two."

"Okay," Phil relented. "I suppose."

He pulled the car to the shoulder, put it in neutral. Mariah stepped around to the driver's side, got behind the wheel, and adjusted the seat. "Hmm," she mused. "Power seats. And a leather steering wheel cover?"

"My dad's version of luxury."

"I like the feel of the wheel instead," she said as she slipped the cover off. It twisted around itself like a snakeskin as she dropped it to the carpeted floorboard. She slipped off her sandals and pressed on the clutch with her tanned bare foot. "And the feel of the pedals," she added.

"So, you can drive a stick shift?" Phil nodded to the three-speed shift on the floor.

"Sure. My mom has a stick on her Plymouth. Old as it is, it still torques out."

"Jeese," Phil joked. "Mariah, the Indy five-hundred driver."

"I wish," she replied. "Unfortunately, they don't allow women drivers."

She pushed in the clutch, shifted to first, and the 340-horsepower engine pulled the car forward with a lurch, the tires surprising the road with a sudden squeal.

She drove for a mile on the small county road, passing the broken-down resorts with cabins and a couple of farms, the leaning skeletons of windmills that seemed propped up by the moonlight. She accelerated to forty, fifty, sixty, then seventy as she passed the illuminated SPEED LIMIT 55 sign. The road crested to a slight incline, and a no-passing double yellow line striped the highway. Ahead, Phil could see they were catching up quickly to the taillights of a slow-moving car. When Mariah braked behind it, Phil could see a white-haired woman behind the wheel.

"Yep," Phil commented. "It's one of our faithful townspeople. Looks like Mrs. Schultz's ol' Desoto."

"Hmmm. Could she go any slower?" Mariah looked down at the speedometer, which read thirty-five. "I should just pass her."

"No passing zone," Phil warned. "You can pass in a quarter mile or so. The road'll even out again."

"I don't see any oncoming lights," she said. "So I can pass *right now*." She floored the car with her bare foot, the engine roared, and the car veered over the lines to the left lane. Caught off guard, Phil opened his mouth to say something but then held back. *If I cautioned her*, he thought, *it would sound just like my father, right?* Phil saw the speedometer jump from thirty-five to seventy and felt the force of the acceleration press his body into the velour seat. It was the same visceral thrill he got while riding with her on the whirling Twister or the Rock-O-Planes at the county fair. A part of him felt a little nervous about her, this chance-taking girl, and another part of him felt exhilarated, and loved it that she was so wild.

Mrs. Schultz gave them a startled look as they cruised past her.

Mariah veered back into the right lane. She glanced again at the speedometer, which now read ninety. "Wow," she said, and she continued driving at that speed for the next mile.

Phil gazed at the excited expression on her face. The air rushed through the open window, lifting her hair, then lowering it, then lifting it again in a rising and falling symphony.

"Yeah. Wow," he agreed.

At the plant the next morning, Phil didn't realize he was exhaling the word aloud.

"Wow?" Tommy questioned. "Wow *what?*"

"Just wow in general."

"Glad you're in such a state of euphoria," Tommy beamed. "What have you been smokin'? And do you care to share?"

"Um, no." Phil wanted to keep the memory to himself.

"Let me guess—might it have something to do with a female of the species named Mariah?"

Phil gave Tommy a smug smile.

"That confirms it. It's Mariah. You're such a goddamn dreamer, Key. And you're pussy whipped. She's all you think about lately, man."

"What better to think about?"

"Hmmm," Tommy conceded, rubbing his chin. "You've got a point there."

Phil hefted a forty-pound bag of lime from the railroad car, dropped it to the pallet, the puff of stinging white dust swirling into his face. Then he leaned over, picked up another bag, the dust caking onto the sweat on his arms. Tommy worked next to him, singing the Beatles "Ticket to Ride."

This morning, the hot, humid air of July seemed to cling to Phil. To escape the monotony and to lessen the ache in his arms, Phil let his mind wander. He pictured the calm waters of Bluff Lake at dusk. An evening sunset painted itself scarlet behind the bluffs. Mariah, smiling as she swam toward him. Her eyes: two cooling blue-green emeralds.

"We interrupt this program for an important announcement!" Tommy barked, pulling Phil from his fantasy. Tommy lifted his grandfather's stopwatch out of a deep pocket of his coveralls, studied it, and called out "It's nine thirty-two already, boys. Why is this day going so goddamned fast?" His grandpa had given him the watch. And although Tommy claimed he hated old stuff, he thought it was hip to carry the watch around at the plant rather than wear some cheap Timex. It also came in handy when he could plan a make out session with his new girlfriend Shirelle in his Falcon. When they stopped in front of Shirlelle's house, her dad, the stalwart Mr. Caluto, always came striding out to the car to investigate and break things up. The usual span of time—according to Tommy—was between eight-point-five and ten minutes.

"Nine thirty-two?" blurted Phil. "You've got to be kidding me." He was absolutely certain that half the morning had passed by during this rote, grueling job. He was absolutely certain that it was at least eleven, that he'd been working hours and hours, his spine aching as he lifted bag after bag of lime from the yawning mouth of the boxcar.

"I kid you not. Grandpa's watch doesn't frickin' lie. It's nine thirty-two. Oops, correct that. Nine thirty-three. Wow, Key. We've been working a whole hour and thirty-three minutes already." He smirked. "And oh, what luck! They just rolled up another loaded boxcar behind this one."

Phil didn't believe Tommy, but when he leaned over and checked the watch, he realized Tommy was telling the truth. Overhearing this, the rest of the new guys let out a collective moan. "Put that damn thing away!" called Schmitty from the far end of the boxcar. Another guy quickly echoed the sentiment.

From that moment on, there was an official ban on time-reporting. No one on the crew could ask about or report time, unless they were convinced that it was close enough to a break, or to lunch, or quitting time to make it bearable. By request, Tommy had to hide his cursed watch and not pull its Roman-numeral face into the light unless somebody asked. Which they didn't.

For Phil, the next few hours, time seemed to become a tangible thing. It covered you, like an armored suit. It told you when to move forward, when to stop, when to hesitate between the moving and the stopping. Phil understood this, and he followed the rules minute by minute. By afternoon, the clock's hands seemed to be stuck in hardening wax. Everything slowed down—his movements, his thoughts, even his words. "Damn. Got that one. Pallet's almost full. Two more. Shit, this sucks. Jesus, I'm tired."

One thing that did make time pass more quickly at the plant was when the guys talked. The repetitiveness of this tedious chore made even the quietest of the ten guys on the crew begin to chat: they jawed about football games, won and lost by the Thunderbirds, about classes they hated, bragged about wild parties, sneaking booze from their old man's liquor cabinets, about weekend plans with girlfriends, who set off firecrackers in the alley behind the theatre, about whose Plymouth Valiant broke down on the town square Saturday night. Tommy satirized the people he called "the lifers," who worked at the plant all year long, and he imitated them, distorting his face and stumbling around like those ghouls in *Night of the Living Dead*.

They talked about girls, about sex, about parking near the river and slipping their hands up a girlfriend's cashmere sweater. Some bragged, to skeptical ears, about how far they'd gotten, and with which girls. "Third base," one guy might say, and another might counter "No way. Not with her. That's bullshit." The lies and exaggerations piled up as high as the bags of lime on the pallets. During the morning break at 10:15, Tommy paced in front of the guys, who sat at the wide door of the boxcar. Like a visiting professor, he gave a lecture on the elaborate science of unhooking bra straps.

"Like you're the expert," Phil interrupted. "You wouldn't know Platex from latex."

"Expert?" Tommy shot back. "I happen to have a PhD in *bra-ing*, in case you don't know."

For the most part, the talk was mindless bull, but for Phil, this endless jawing was a shield from the boredom; it was a link, a connecting wire, an assurance that there was a real world beyond this rote, hum-drum existence of the plant. Sometimes, for fleeting moments near the end of a long day, they dropped their guard and even talked about things guys don't usually talk about: their dreams, their parents' divorces, their fears of being drafted into the Army, their own failures and hesitations.

At 11:30 they sat in a powder storage building, eating their lunches. "Okay," Tommy announced. "Let the game begin!" He had finished his liverwurst sandwich quickly and was about to instigate a game of name that tune, where he hummed a few bars of a song or sang a lyric and then waited for the first person on the crew to identify it, by title and artist. The first guy to slap his palm on the rubberized floor got the first guess. Using an elaborate scoring system for title, artist, and year, points were awarded to the winners and then tallied up each day. Sometimes Tommy was the moderator, sometimes the player. He gave extra points to the person who could guess what month the song was released, and even more points for how high it climbed on the *Billboard* charts. *Slap!* "Daytripper! Beatles!" a guy would shout. *Slap!* "I fought the Law! Bobby Fuller Four!" *Slap!* "Play With Fire! Rolling Stones!" *Slap!* "It's the Same old Song! Four Tops!" *Slap!* "We Gotta Get Out of this Place! Animals!" The answers were absorbed by the cool, thick log walls.

For Phil, what made time speed up a little, at least, was thinking about Mariah. When they sat on swings at the park and talked for hours, every topic was fair game, from parents to songs they loved to favorite poems to the injustice in society to the upcoming election. "I can't wait," she had said last weekend after Phil received his acceptance into the U. "I just can't wait for fall." She leaned toward him and pressed her lips to his cheek. Then she whispered "For everything. As soon as I step on that campus, my journey begins." They talked about classes they were excited to take. "Political science," she said, her voice sounding like a bright color. "Psychology," Phil would reply. "Then maybe sociology. Or, who knows—English or journalism."

He thought about sitting at the terrace behind the student union with Mariah, sipping cold strawberry sodas as they watched the white sails of sailboats drifting across Lake Mendota.

As he lifted another bag of lime, the heaviness of the bag was lessened by his daydream about seeing Mariah tonight. He pictured himself pulling his car in front of her trailer and seeing her lithe form crossing in front of the glow of the porch light. He closed his eyes and pictured Mariah, the fine blonde hairs on the back of her summer-tanned arm as she reached for him. Thought about her leaning toward him for a long, moist kiss; he loved the way that kiss made him feel like he was suddenly rushing backwards inside himself. A dizzying but euphoric feeling.

In the afternoon, as Phil and Tommy wandered along the tram tracks to unload another boxcar, Tommy discovered a new diversion. He picked up a round, smooth stone from the gravel track bed, nodded at a twelve-inch diameter aluminum pipe, which was braced by a scaffolding of ten-foot tall posts. He asked, "Hey, how much you give me if I hit that sucker?" The maze of above-ground pipes led everywhere across the plant, zigzagging from the refinery area to the acid area to the powder lines.

"Dunno. A quarter?"

"Quarter? Shit, you cheapskate. It's worth at least a buck."

"Okay," Phil conceded, "a dollar, then."

Tommy glanced around to make sure their foreman Duke wasn't in view, then reared back and gunned the stone toward the pipe, about thirty yards away. The stone met its mark, striking it with a sound like a dull *thunk*. The impact left a pockmark on the soft metallic wrapping of the pipe.

"Man, what a shot!" Tommy declared. "Just call me dead eye!" He extended his hand. "I'll take my buck, now, Key," he said, as if Phil had a roll of crisp Washingtons right there in his coveralls.

"Not unless I even it up." Phil reached down and found a smooth egg-shaped stone. He quickly glanced over his shoulder, feeling a sudden sensation of guilt for fooling around. It was as if his father, who he knew was probably miles away, was still somehow watching him from that distance, his harsh, leaden stare weighed on his shoulders. Phil shook off that feeling, took aim, and tossed the stone. It tumbled end over end in the air, then struck the pipe in its center.

"Shit, Key!" Tommy reached for more stones on the track bed. "Why'd you waste your talents in the outfield? Shoulda been a pitcher, like me." Then he whipped another rock, this one this one grazing the bottom edge of the pipe, leaving a crease-shaped dent.

Phil threw again and the rock thumped against the pipe.

"Okay, sports fans," Tommy announced, tossing his safety helmet to the gravel. "It's game on." With that, Tommy began a slow wind-up, twisting his arms into a pretzel, the way he did when he was an all-star pitcher for the Thunderbirds baseball team. He whipped his right arm down quickly, hitting the pipe square in the middle, making a deep dent. "Steee-rike!" he called gleefully.

As the game escalated, they threw more stones, some of them misses, some hits, and Tommy, as usual with all the games, kept the tally. "Seven to five, Key. You gotta catch up." He squinted at the pipes, which glared dully back at him. "So what do you think's in those damn pipes, anyway?"

"How should I know?"

"I figured your ol' man told you. He's the information expert, isn't he?"

"He doesn't talk to me, remember?"

"Shit, yeah. Almost forgot. Dads don't talk."

"But I'm guessing it's steam," Phil speculated. "Water, maybe." As he spoke, he heard the faint sound of a siren, rising and falling in the distance on Highway 12.

"Beer," declared Tommy with a grin, doing a little dance and pretending to play an air guitar. "Definitely beer. Schlitz, most likely. These pipes lead to the supervisor's building, you know. They've probably got spigots and a luxury bar in there. Gorgeous waitresses in low-cut coveralls, serving them." Tommy picked up a bigger stone. "Hey, think I can spring a leak in it?"

"I think your brain's already sprung a leak."

For the next few minutes, they threw stones again and again, until the score was 21 to 18, with Tommy leading. The pipe's smooth surface was quickly becoming pockmarked with craters. Phil grabbed a handful of stones for his next tosses.

The growl of an engine on the nearby dirt road startled them as Ray Duke's jeep emerged from between two outbuildings. Tommy quickly picked up his safety helmet, squashed it onto his head. "Uh-oh, we're in deep shit," Tommy said, wincing. Both of them turned and marched toward the boxcar further down the track, their original destination. "Keep walking," Tommy said, his voice low, as if Duke, in the jeep, could hear him from a hundred feet away. "Just keep walking, man. Like we've been working our asses off all day."

The jeep pulled up alongside them and stopped abruptly, the tires screeching. Phil couldn't help but think that Duke had seen them throwing the rocks. It was rumored that Duke kept a pair of binoculars under the seat, just to spy on his crew from a distance and see what they were up to.

"Keyhoe!" Duke shouted. "Keyhoe!"

Leaving the jeep idling in neutral, Duke jogged toward them.

*Damn,* Phil thought, cringing. *We're getting hauled to the front office. We're getting fired.*

"Keyhoe," Duke called again urgently, "Your Dad...!"

"Huh?"

"Your Dad," Duke gasped, out of breath. "He had a heart attack."

"What?" Phil blinked his eyes as though a cloud of stinging lime dust just billowed into them.

"Collapsed in his office. They're taking him to the hospital in an ambulance."

As the words sank in, time thickened and stopped, and Phil was caught in its paralyzing web, unable to move, unable to open his mouth and speak, unable to take a step, or not take a step.

"Don't just stand there, boy!" Duke ordered. "Get in the damn jeep. I'll get you a ride back to town."

When Duke grabbed Phil by the elbow, reality set in. Time lurched forward again. Phil opened his clenched fist, dropping the stones to the rusty tracks.

# PART
# TWO

# CHAPTER 18

Phil, elbows on his knees, sat on a card table chair and leaned toward his father's hospital bed. Thin silvery wires spiraled their way from Karl's chest to the heart monitor machine next to his bed. It had been a week since his father's heart attack, and Phil felt a sense of anticipation today, unsure about why his father insisted that he and Frances come in for a visit first thing this morning.

"So, um, you have a big bacon and egg breakfast today?" Phil asked, attempting a little humor.

"You should taste the bland porridge they serve here," Karl replied, his voice gravelly, but a little weak. His face looked sunken, as if you'd rubbed ashes on it. "Can hardly stand it." On the back wall, where the patient could see it, hung a gold-framed picture of Jesus pulling open his robe to expose his sacred heart, rays of yellow light spoking out from it.

"We'll get you back to home cooking soon enough," Frances assured him, trying to sound optimistic. "Won't be the same foods, though," she added tentatively, wringing her pale hands together as she often did, "but home cooking just the same." She stood from her chair, her frame small beneath her pink and purple house dress. "Let's let in some light," she said as pulled on a cord to open a blind. The sun angled across her face with parallel lines.

Phil knew it would be a long recovery for his father. He'd heard the doctor's reports, how Karl's heart was severely damaged in the attack, and he was lucky to survive. The emergency heart surgery pulled him through. His father wouldn't get out of the hospital for another week at least, and after that, there'd be therapy in the heart rehab unit, and visits by a nurse at their house. The bottom line—the surgeon told Phil and Frances—was he'd be out of work for quite some time. He was sure his dad knew about all this, too, and he wanted to lighten the mood a little. "I bet you'll be back in shape before you know it," Phil offered.

"That's not what they tell me." Karl let the words sit on his tongue like they were sour. "Guess I better get used to this dang powder blue," he said, lifting one arm to display his wrinkled hospital gown. "But I've dropped a few pounds, I suppose." He looked down at the pale sheet, rounded over his broad chest and neatly tucked into corners at the edge of the bed. "That I don't mind. I'm down to two-twenty-five at the last weigh-in, even."

"Oh Karl," Frances offered, "I'll fatten you up again once you get out."

"That's what I'm afraid of," he said under his breath, and when he did, her mouth melted into a frown, as though she'd said the wrong thing. Phil noticed that she often had that look when she was around Karl, as if she was testing things with the tentative, almost fragile webs of her words, and then waiting for Karl to tear at them.

"Look at all the pretty cards," Frances said lithely, changing the subject as she glanced at the row of get-well cards on the stainless-steel tray beside his bed. Frances had propped the cards open and stood them on end. "Such nice scenes on the covers.

Peaceful." The cards displayed watercolors of seagulls gliding over the ocean, of sprigs of roses, deer posing near streams, pastel meadows with bluebirds—all the optimistic images that assured the recipient they'd be getting well soon. Cards from friends, from his brother and sister in Iowa, from his bowling buddies. One, a cheap-looking card, depicting a misty meadow of flowers, was sent by the security office workers at the Strongs Plant. Signatures of his co-workers scrawled across the blank space like blue snakes. "Isn't it nice, how many people in town rallied around your father, Phil?"

"Yeah. Nice." Then Phil asked, a little impatiently, "So, um, you wanted to talk to us? About something?" Phil glanced at the red digital numbers, blinking in anticipation. 70. 72. 70.

"Yeah," Karl affirmed, "I do." His mouth moved to one side as though he was chewing on a piece of leather. For a few seconds, his eyes looked everywhere except at Phil. It was the way between them, Phil knew. Talk to the wall. To the faded light fixture. To anything. "The docs had a chat with me this morning...," he began.

"So, what'd they say?"

"They said he's improving, Phil," Frances interrupted, her voice lilting and musical in its optimism. "I mean, it will take a while, but..."

"Frances," Karl chided, pronouncing her name as though it was a cool stone. "I'm talking to the boy."

"I know, Karl," she said, eyelids fluttering. "I just...."

"I'm *talking* to the *boy*." His command flattened her lips together as if he'd squeezed them with between his thumb and index finger.

Phil could sense that his mother was trying to soften something, to ward off some unpleasantness, and he wondered what it was. He'd seen the pattern it all his life: his father, dominant and on the offensive, his mother, deflecting things with a fluttering hand, trying, somehow, to make the unpleasant things more bearable.

"As I was saying," Karl continued, taking quick breaths between the sentences, like a person who had been running, "I talked to the docs. They told me to take it easy. I'm going to be recovering a while. A big chunk of time, they said. Months. Half a year, even." Phil could see his father's face tightening, closing, as if some door had shut inside it.

Phil shifted uneasily on the chair, and glanced out the paned window where the power lines crisscrossed in the alley. A crow landed on one wire, and its feathers splayed out as a gust of wind rose up around it.

"So I have to take a leave from the plant." Karl reached over and winced a little. He slowly lifted the water glass from the tray, then took a sip and said, "It's a mandatory leave, actually. Or so they said, after a health issue like this. Hell, they've got somebody in my spot already." He let out in uncomfortable laugh that sounded more like a wheeze. "That's the way things are out there, what with all the expansion. New lines opening up. Nothing can slow it down."

Phil drew his eyes from the window back to his father's strong nose looming above his once full but now sallow cheeks. There was stubble on his chin that he always shaved clean each morning, leaning over the bathroom sink with a Schick razor, his face covered in a whipped-cream thick cloud.

"But you'll get back there eventually, right?" Phil asked.

"I will. I will. But that's not the point," Karl said. "Not the point at all." Karl rolled his head toward Phil, then rolled it back and seemed to focus on the beige ceiling tiles, the tiny holes like craters on the moon. "The thing is, my sick leave doesn't cover me for too long. And our health insurance only goes so far. We've got to pay a lot out of pocket." He sniffed at the air, a medicinal scent that filled the room. "I checked into workman's comp, but my ol' ticker attack doesn't qualify for that. And forget about getting some disability payments from the feds. You have to be out of work for a whole year for that to happen."

"We've had to look into a lot of options," Frances added.

"Then," Karl continued, "there's rehab for me, which, I hear, is going to cost a bundle. We're almost broke as it is. So, the point is…well," he hesitated. "We're not going to be able to afford your expenses at Madison."

"What?"

"You're going to have to stay on at the plant. You know—to earn enough money for your tuition, and all that."

"Stay on?" Phil said incredulously.

"Yeah. "Maybe for a few months," Karl let a deliberate pause drop like lead between them.

"Months?" The word was like dry paper in Phil's mouth.

"It's the only way you'll be able to pay for college. I mean, the tuition. And that damn room and board for the dorm. Guess you'll just have to postpone it."

*Postpone. Postpone.* Inside Phil's head, the word was a heavy rock, tied to his images of college, pulling them down to the bottom of some deep quarry pond.

"You can, you know, go next fall, maybe," Karl added.

To Phil, next fall sounded like a decade away. He rose from his chair, arms limp at his sides. "But Mariah…Mariah and I, we talked about…"

"Mariah?" Karl lifted himself to his elbows. "What's this got to do with that girl?"

"College. She's, she's going there, too," Phil stammered. "I mean, to the U… We, we made all kinds of plans…."

"*Plans,*" Karl scoffed. He pointed at Phil, and a tube, secured by white tape, swayed from one wrist. "Let me tell you something." He fixed his eyes directly on Phil for the first time since he entered the room. "I had plenty of plans. But I didn't plan on *this.*" He sat up in the bed. "I hope you wouldn't put your *damn plans* with some silly girlfriend ahead of this family!" The heart monitor beeped, the red number rapidly climbing: 74, 76, 80.

"Karl," Frances tried to interrupt, "Karl, don't get upset." She grabbed Phil by the shoulder, whispered to him: "He's got to stay calm. His…his blood pressure…."

Karl gulped a few wheezy breaths as if the air was too thick. "My blood pressure, my blood pressure," he snarled, pink blotches rising to the surface of his cheeks. "To hell with my blood pressure!" The monitor beeped even faster.

"Karl, please!" Frances pleaded, placing her palm on the center of his chest, as if she could slow his heartbeat. "Lie down. Lie down!"

"All right, Frances. For crimney sakes, all right," Karl said, lowering himself to the pillow again and taking a couple of deep breaths, his chest rising, falling beneath the pale tent of the sheet.

He squeezed his eyes shut a moment, then opened them again. "So here's the deal, Phil." Karl's voice lowered in pitch again. "The thing is, you've already got your foot in the door at the plant. And I can get you a better job out there," he said, trying to sound upbeat. "And it's not just some part-time thing. It's full time. With full pay."

Phil could feel the blood drain from his face. He felt suddenly dizzy.

"Yeah," Karl continued. "It'll earn you enough for college, eventually. And give us some extra income to support my rehab. You can get off that riggers' crew, and those maintenance jobs that bore you so damn much."

Phil didn't know what to say. "I'll...I'll think about it," he finally mumbled. He could almost see his words, flimsy and feathery, in front of his face as he said them.

"You can't just *think* about it," Karl said, rolling his eyes toward the door to the hallway, then back toward Phil. "The thing is, I made some calls this morning. Talked to a couple of my supervisor pals. I already set it up. There was an opening. Those openings fill up real quick, 'cause they're the highest-paying jobs out there." He nodded with himself. "So you've got a job on the lines."

Phil lowered his gaze to the morning sunlight, cut in orderly squares, that angled through a windowpane and fell flat on the hard-tiled floor.

Later, sleepless in bed, he would replay this conversation. He wished he had just resisted his father and said "No, I won't work on the powder lines. I'll take a full-time job out there, if I really need to. But *not* on the lines." Instead, his tongue had gone numb, as if it was stung by a dozen bees. And, feeling trapped, as though he was in handcuffs and a straight jacket, he lowered himself into silence, that pool of acquiescing silence he always seemed to submerge himself into when he was around his father. He sank deeper and deeper, felt himself drowning there.

After a long pause, Frances broke the impasse with a gentle voice. "All these cards. Aren't they pretty?" she exclaimed. She reached for the card with the meadow and flower scene from the plant workers. It leaned next to the row of plastic pill bottles, lined up like tiny cylindrical soldiers, each with their own set of orders printed in black ink on pale paper labels. She opened and closed the card in front of her face like a butterfly's wing, then held it out between Phil and Karl. "And just look at this scene," she said, trying to sound enthusiastic. "So peaceful, isn't it?"

# CHAPTER 19

Though Phil knew it wasn't really there, Mariah's room seemed filled with a hazy fog. It hung over Mariah's bookshelf, stacked with paperback classics: Shakespeare, Chaucer, *War and Peace*, *The Scarlett Letter*, T. S. Eliot's *The Waste Land*. A newer hardcover poetry book by Sylvia Plath rested sideways on top. The haze obscured her bulletin board, decorated with a collage of thumb-tacked pictures of James Dean in *Rebel Without a Cause*, The Beatles, John F. Kennedy, and Martin Luther King. Next to them, a Picasso calendar on which Mariah had penned black Xs on each of the days that had passed.

To Phil, everything seemed hazy, a little out of focus. He knew it wasn't really smoke, or fog; it was just a blurry film over everything caused last night's worrisome, sleepless night.

Whatever it was, Mariah moved through it, parting it. Obviously upset, she stepped to her desk, then back toward the window, then back to the desk again. She picked up a pen if she was about to write something, then snapped it back down, then picked it up again. She looked up at Phil. "I don't know what to say. I really don't."

Phil stared down at his feet. Pale beige converse tennis shoes. He counted the twelve shoelace holes on each. Laces tied in a double knot. "I don't know either," he said. Mariah's small Zenith radio played Dusty Springfield's "What the World Needs Now" in the background, and Phil thought *How fitting.*

During a long pause, Mariah stared at her fingernails and tugged on the hem of her pink gauze tank top, which seemed like the only bright thing in the room. Phil twisted the top button on his oxford shirt. He had never experienced this kind of awkwardness between them lately, but he felt it now. "So just say *some*thing," he pleaded.

"I feel terrible about all this," she finally said. "I'm so sorry about your dad. I feel really bad about it." Phil could see the pain crawl across her face. "This is going to be hard."

"Yeah, it is."

"And he doesn't have much insurance?"

"Guess not."

She turned, lifted the glossy page of the calendar and stared at the next month—September—as if she could see their future there. Phil figured she was seeing it clearer than he did. He couldn't see ahead to the next hour, let alone tomorrow. She turned toward him, glistening tears forming in her eyes. "I can't help but feel really upset. I mean, this changes everything. All our plans."

"I know. I…"

She tipped her face toward the ceiling, her hair falling over one eye. "Damn it all," she said, exasperated. "Why does life have to be like this?"

Phil helplessly stuffed his hands into his pockets.

"You know I love you," she said. She lifted her arms to his shoulders and pulled him close. "I do love you. And that's what matters. That's what will keep us together, even if you're here, and I'm in Madison."

He embraced her, felt the inhale and exhale of her breathing. "You're right. We still have *us*. Even if we're apart."

Phil knew that in just one week, she'd be leaving for college. In one week, she'd be packing the back seat of her Ford Fairlane with supplies. Phil had already envisioned the morning when he'd help her load the boxes, one of them containing an eight by ten of his senior picture. In it, he'd be half-smiling in a sport coat and tie, his eyes a little puffy that morning at the studio, his medium-length brown Beatle-style hair combed and shiny. Then there'd be the shoebox she'd enthusiastically marked *US!* with photos of the two of them reclining on the beach at the lake, laughing as they posed on opposite sides of a downtown parking meter, and waving as they rode the Scrambler at the county fair.

"I miss you already," she said sweetly. "So much. Too much." He felt her cheek against his, the supple flesh of her waist beneath his fingertips, the press of her bare thighs against his jeans. He held her tightly for minutes—minutes that he wished could stretch into hours, days, years. Felt her heart beating hard inside her as if it had wings and was trying to flutter its way out.

Just then Janelle pushed the bedroom door open. Phil pulled back from Mariah, a little embarrassed, as Janelle, holding a cigarette, gave them a knowing look.

Mariah wiped her tears with the back of her hand.

"Oh, you two…" Janelle said. "Don't look so tragic. You'll find a way. You're young. You have time." The wisps from her cigarette curled upward in a white spiral, then pooled against the low tiled ceiling. "And if what you feel is real, then there's always a way." She lifted her eyes to Mariah. "Right?"

Mariah nodded, opened her mouth slightly, as if to echo the word, but didn't reply.

That evening, Phil and Mariah stood on the beach, holding hands and facing the empty lake in the darkness. It was near midnight, and Bluff Lake Park was closed.

Families had packed up their kids and inflatable toys and beach towels and left, and the place was abandoned, quiet.

"So what's next?" Phil asked, his question skimming over the calm lake surface.

As if to answer him, she let go of his hand, unbuttoned her blouse, took it off, dropped it to the sand.

Phil watched her, surprised, as she slid her shorts and underpants off and took a few steps into the lake. They'd never been skinny dipping, and the thought didn't occur to him that she'd even consider it.

Knee deep, she whirled around and faced Phil. Silhouetted, she lifted her arms toward him, her body outlined by a thin silver coating of moonlight. He'd never seen her totally naked, and he couldn't get over how lovely she looked. "What are you waiting for?" she called flirtatiously.

"Here?" Phil asked, appreciating her sudden brazenness. "Now?"

"Yes. Here. Now."

Phil quickly pulled off his clothes and followed her.

When he reached her, they clasped hands and ran further into the lake until they were up to their waists, their shoulders.

"You're so beautiful," he said. "And crazy. And so amazing." He thought he saw her blush. "But you're not cold?" He could feel the chill of the spring-fed water.

"Of course not," she replied, though Phil suspected she was lying. "Are you?"

She cupped a handful of water and playfully splashed him. "Hey!" he said, and splashed her back. They splashed each other again, more frantically, each of them whipping the water back and forth at each other, laughing. The water fight ended with an embrace and a kiss, and as he kissed her, Phil felt her shoulders shuddering. When he pulled back slightly and looked into her face, he wasn't certain if the beads of liquid on her cheek were lake water or tears.

"Don't let go," she sighed as they embraced again, pulling each other close. For the next few minutes, he felt the warmth of her body radiating into him, though deep inside, he couldn't stop himself from shivering.

# CHAPTER 20

Frances glided from room to room, opening windows. She wanted to let the breeze in, so Karl, recuperating in the den, would have some fresh air. She always believed that fresh air healed you. Opening a window healed you. When Frances was a little girl with short-cropped page-boy hair, her mother always claimed that. Maybe it was just an old wives' tale, but Frances still believed it. The things you believe, Frances often thought, might just make them come to pass. Now, as she watched the cream embroidered drapes rise and fall with the breeze, it calmed her, and took her mind off Karl's condition. This morning she had thrown out all his packs of cigarettes, tossing the Luckys angrily into the garbage can on the side of the house. No more smoke in the air.

Those first few days after it happened, Karl's heart attack had frightened her so much she could barely sleep. She'd wake up five or six times a night and walk to the den and check on Karl, who would be sleeping in his day bed they'd bought from a hospital supply outlet. For a few minutes, until she went back to the bedroom, it would comfort her to see his broad chest rise and fall, rise and fall.

Last night, she checked on him before he slept and tucked the covers around his shoulders. As she turned to walk out, he grabbed her hand, surprising her. His charming smile surfaced. It was an expression she hadn't seen for a while. "I love you, Fran," he said.

"I love you, Karl," she replied. "And we'll get you better. I promise."

Frances believed Karl would heal steadily, that he'd eventually recover completely, and be himself again. Not this weak man lying in a day bed. Not this man who sometimes needed the nurse they'd hired to walk him to the bathroom. Not that man, but her strong and charismatic Karl that she used to know. She believed, and that would make it so. That was her role right now.

Her role was making a healthy breakfast for him. Bran flakes, skim milk, yogurt, toast with no butter. Oh, he'd complain, of course, and say things like "This? This is breakfast?" and she'd just nod and push the plate toward him and hope he would eat it. Then he'd relent, and the old Karl would return and his somber expression would be erased by a grin, and he'd say "Thank you, Frances. You're taking pretty darn good care of me. You know that?"

Her role was listening to him talk about some of the unfinished jobs at the plant. He'd muse, saying things like "I hope they overhauled the wiring on that south quadrant building." Or: "That nitroglycerine building, it needs maintenance. Scotty said he'd check on it. I filled out a fourteen-hundred form. Damn place has too many safety issues."

"Issues? What Issues?" Frances would ask, forcing herself to be interested.

"Not enough ventilation. I filled out a report, just a couple days before…."

Then he stopped short, not wanting to say the words *the attack.*

"I know, I know," Frances answered, though she really didn't know what went on in some of those buildings. It was out of her realm. Lately, with Karl home, her realm was arranging boxes of cereal and rice and instant mashed potatoes in the cupboard and checking the dates on the Tupperware containers in the freezer so she'd know when they should be used. Her realm was arranging the soup cans on the top shelf in alphabetical order. Asparagus. Cream of Mushroom. Vegetable Beef.

No more wearing her favorite navy blue or red dresses to dance club or a card club or a cocktail party. No need to dress up, no need for Audrey Hepburn or Jackie Kennedy lady-like elegance. Plain slacks and a sweatshirt were the fashion of the day. Not very feminine, she knew.

And lately her realm was knitting—a hobby she'd taken up. Doilies, socks, coasters. All with colorful red and orange patterns, little cloth flowers. Her realm was the needles clicking and clicking together like some kind of non-stop clock.

If she was tired, she knitted. If she was bored, she knitted. The process seemed to keep her focused and her hands occupied during the long day. Click, click, clicking with those needles—it seemed to keep her mind off her worries.

And her worries, if she allowed them to come in, were large, overwhelming ones. They were big, gaping holes in her life. First there was Karl, his terrifying heart attack. The doctors told her he nearly died at the plant, and on the operating table. Now there was his recovery—she wasn't sure at all how long it would take. Then there was Phil, working out there full time, and coming home so exhausted and seeming so down. But—different as each one's mission was—she could comfort both of them, right? That was her role, her realm. Her duty.

When Phil needed to talk about his boredom out there, she listened. When Karl called her name, she'd hurry in to see what he needed. She wasn't happy about it, but she'd do it.

He called her name now.

She entered the doorway to the den. "What, Karl?"

"You could turn the TV down."

"Okay." She turned down the volume dial on the Motorola. "Are you planning to sleep, then?"

"No. It's just a little too loud. And the reception's bad. Those damn rabbit ears don't really work."

Frances fiddled with the thin, slightly-bent rabbit-ear antennae on the top of the set. The delivery guy had bent them when he brought in the TV, she recalled. The picture—with The Newlywed Game—became fuzzy for a few seconds, then sharper, then fuzzy again. She finally got the image to come in clearer.

Karl turned his head toward the TV tray, filled with medications. "What time is it?"

"Ten fifteen."

"That's all?"

"You just asked me that a few minutes ago."

"Oh. I thought maybe I was asleep, and half the day passed already." He took a drink from the water glass next to the bed. "No such luck, I guess."

"Tomorrow will be here soon enough, Karl," she tried to say brightly. "And that means you'll be one day better."

"I wouldn't bet on it," he puffed, ending the conversation.

When the noon news came on the TV, she heard, from the other room, the latest report on Vietnam. Thinking that the war news might upset Karl, she stepped in front of him to change the channel.

"No," Karl said. "Leave it on. Leave it on."

"Oh, okay. I thought it might bother you."

"Bother me? We're winning over there, Frances. We're *winning*."

The anchorman reported the statistics for the week. The *body count*, people were starting to call it. It tallied how many Viet Cong soldiers and American troops were killed. Today the announcer reported that there were three times as many Viet Cong deaths as US casualties. He made it sound like a very positive thing. The screen switched to footage of a village being bombed, and a river boat aiming a napalm flame thrower at jungle foliage.

*Winning what?* Frances wondered, though she swallowed the words and didn't say them aloud. *What kind of win is that when we're losing boys over there?*

After lunch, she sat by the window, knitting and staring out at the yard.

"Frances?" Karl called from the other room.

"Yes?"

"What time is it?"

"Just half past one," she answered.

"Was I sleeping?"

"I don't know."

Soon it would be two o'clock, then three, then four. The seconds and minutes and hours marched slowly—like soldiers with leaden feet. They'd march tomorrow, too, and the day after that. They'd push her forward. She'd follow their orders. Tomorrow at eight, Karl would ask "This is breakfast?" Later, wondering if the morning had passed, he'd ask what time it was. Each time he asked, the clock in the den dragged slower, as if stones were attached to the black hands.

She picked up her knitting again. Her latest project, suggested by a craft magazine, was a starburst flower-patterned placemat. She didn't know what she'd do with this one, since they already had two sets of straw placemats for the dining table. Maybe she'd give it away to a neighbor woman. Still, she continued to work on it, inch by inch, the tips of the needles touching each other. Click click click. The clicking soothed her, calmed her nerves so they wouldn't be frayed to shreds.

She set the placemat on the TV tray, leaned over and raised the windowsill. A gust of wind wheezed through the rusted screen. Fresh air, she thought. Fresh air would cure things. When a sudden gust of wind swirled across the yard, the lacy curtains billowed, and she felt them brushing lightly against her cheek for a few seconds before they fell still again.

# CHAPTER 21

Tommy crossed the back yard of his house, swaying as he lugged a blue and white Coleman cooler. He tossed it into the trunk of Phil's car.

"What's with the big cooler?" Phil wondered.

"Supplies," Tommy stated. "Contraband."

"So where to? The lake?"

"Not the lake," Tommy replied. "The school."

"The high school?"

"Yeah. The goddamn high school. The ol' brick Pentagon."

Tommy's biting tone caught Phil off guard. Their usual Friday evening routine in summer included driving the old lake road or hanging out in front of Kluge's and jawing with a few buddies. After that, Tommy would meet up with his girlfriend Shirelle, and Phil would pick up Mariah—who worked at the library until nine.

"Why *there*?" Phil questioned.

"Dunno. I just want to see the ol' shithole. Do a little reminiscing, maybe. And in case you're wondering," he added, opening his backpack, exposing cluster of Hamms, the blue and gold cans jostling against each another, "I have loads of backup."

Phil could smell the alcohol on Tommy's breath and knew that he'd already had a beer or maybe even a smuggled shot of Jack Daniels or Southern Comfort from his dad's liquor cabinet. His face took on a wild look when he drank, his voice a little shriller, his eyes darting left, then right like ping-pong balls. And his high-energy personality became, if that were possible, even more energized.

"So I take it you started early?" Phil questioned.

"Earlier the better," Tommy laughed. "I always start early. And finish late."

"A true Wisconsin boy."

"True. Frickin' true. Frickin' loyal to Wisconsin, God and country."

They passed through the heart of Bluff Lake on the way to the school. Downtown two-story brick buildings gave way to the few large, well-kept, 1880s Victorian-style houses, built during the railroad boom. Faded vines spiraled up trellises. Those large houses gave way to smaller, shabby, 1940s structures with tin roofs that never seemed to have a glint, even on sunny days. Some leaned toward one another as if for comfort, and others had boarded windows, blinding them. On the edge of town, as they neared the high school, they passed yards decorated with fading wood piles, broken-down cars on blocks with their hoods tipped toward the sky, leaning sheds, and plastic kids' toys scattered here and there like red and yellow candy. Limp, slightly shredded American flags hung from posts on porches. Phil had noticed more flags flying around town lately. They passed a sign on someone's lawn that proclaimed *America. Love It or Leave It.*

"Screw that, eh?" Tommy snorted as they passed.

They reached the high school, a dreary, 1930s two-story red brick building with tall windows, their top halves covered in beige-painted plywood—for better insulation, the school board claimed. As Phil pulled to a stop in the gravel parking lot, dusk was settling, and the sky looked grainy.

"We've reached your chosen destination," Phil said. "Now what?"

"Now, a beer, perchance." Tommy had already pulled a can of Hamms from his canvas backpack and yanked at the pop top. Bubbly foam billowed out. He lifted another, tossed it to Phil. Tipping his head back, he chugged the contents, lowered the can and gasped for air. "Next one!" he barked.

"Hey," Phil said. "Slow down, Milk. It's early. We got a couple hours."

Tommy gave him an uncharacteristic frown, his lips curling downward, eyes half-mast. "I'm not slowing down," he replied. "Okay with you, *officer Keyhoe?*"

"Whatever," Phil replied, picking up on Tommy's sharp tone. "So what *are* we doing here?"

"What are we doing *any*where?" Tommy slipped from the car and faced the school.

Phil popped open his beer and by the time he did, Tommy, beer in one hand, was already climbing the fire-escape ladder to the second floor of the high school. He carried a plastic bag looped over his wrist. Phil got out and leaned against the fender, watching in wonder.

"Be my lookout, Key," Tommy called, taking another swig, "My wing man. "You always got my back. Are we clear?"

Phil swiveled his head. He could hear the swish of cars two blocks away on Broadway, all of them headed toward downtown or away from it. "Yeah, I guess," Phil called, unsure of what crazy plan his buddy had in mind.

Tommy pulled out a can of spray paint and drew the words **CLAS OF 67!!** on the side of the building in huge black letters. Finished, he began to climb down, his tennis shoe circling as he tried to locate the rungs of the iron ladder.

Phil pointed at the letters. "Hey honors student!" he called. "Might help to spell it right!"

"Huh?" Tommy uttered. His body swayed like a person losing balance at the edge of a cliff. Phil thought Tommy might fall from that height and crack his damn skull wide open.

"*C-L-A-S-S,*" Phil yelled. "Might help to spell the word right, dumb ass."

"Shit. Oh yeah," Tommy grimaced. "Never did good in English, did I? Hell, I got a D in it. Even though I've been speaking it all my life."

"Serves you right for throwing that book out the window," Phil chimed in, referring to the time Tommy threw his grammar book through an open window of Miss Tuttle's classroom. It smacked a frail freshman girl, heading out for gym class. Tuttle had spun around at that moment, and Tommy earned a week's detention.

Tommy climbed back up and sprayed another cramped **S** in the word **CLASs**. Then, with a flourish, he dropped the canister of spray paint. "Bombs away!" he called, and watched the can fall two stories to the sidewalk below. It exploded with a muffled *pfow*, leaving a black star of paint on the concrete.

When he reached the base of the ladder, Tommy jogged back to Phil's car.

"Reinforcements," he shouted, pointing to the cooler.

"C'mon, man." Phil finished his Hamms and crumpled the can, figuring they would head to the lake. He felt a little uneasy about the vandalism, knowing the town cops sometimes patrolled around the high school. "We should get out of here."

Tommy didn't seem to hear, or else he ignored him. He stood at the open trunk, lifted the cooler lid, and stared at the beer cans floating like aluminum fish in two inches of water. Cracking another beer, he chugged half of it, the rest spilling onto on the front of his blue and gold Thunderbirds T-shirt.

"Maybe you've had enough," Phil suggested. He noticed the cooler, leaking a little water into his trunk.

"Never enough." Tommy did a Heisman quarterback pose with his beer can, then pulled another one out and tossed it to Phil. "I see you still got that ol' Louisville Slugger back here." Tommy's eyes seemed to shift independently in their sockets.

"So?"

"So? I feel like hitting a goddamn home run!" Tommy pushed aside a blanket and a long-handled snow scraper, then reached to the back of the trunk and pulled out Phil's baseball bat. Phil, wondering what Tommy was up to next, slouched against the bumper. He could see the puddle in the trunk, spreading like an empty speech bubble. "I don't have any baseballs with me," Phil said.

Ignoring his comment, Tommy, with the Louisville Slugger in hand, staggered toward the school, then stood for a few seconds next to the shop window. In one motion, he reared back, then swung the bat hard, hitting the window and shattering the glass. "That's for the F I got in econ class!" he yelled, and he hit the window again, the glass shards flying. "And that's for the goddamn D in earth science!"

Phil heard an alarm blaring in the hallway. "Tommy! Jesus!" he called. "What the hell are you doing?" Phil knew this wasn't like Tommy at all. Sure, he was the world's best jokester and prankster, the king of hijinks, but he was never violent and destructive.

Phil ran toward him. "C'mon, man! Stop! Stop it!" He wrestled the bat from Tommy's hands and threw it aside, where it cartwheeled across the gravel and rolled to a stop. "What the *hell's* with you, anyway?"

Tommy glared at him a few long seconds with bloodshot eyes. "I graduated from this goddamn place," he said between his teeth. "And what *good* did it do me?"

"Damn it, Tommy! That doesn't mean we're smashing windows!" Phil glanced nervously back at the car. "Let's get out of here. Let's get to the lake."

Tommy seemed to sober up briefly, the drunkenness suddenly draining out of him. His spine straightened like it was filling with iron and he spoke numbly. "No lake. I'm, I'm not goin' to the lake." "I…I'm goin' somewhere else," he said with an uncharacteristic stutter.

"What the hell's up?"

Tommy's eyes went vacant. "My…draft…notice," he said slowly, his thick tongue lifting the words like the dumbbells he hefted in the football workout room. "That's, that's what's up."

Stunned, Phil didn't react for a few seconds. Then he asked "What about a deferment? What about college?"

"There is no frickin' college," Tommy said slurring, his voice bitter. "I got rejected at Blackhawk. A few weeks ago."

"You're kidding, right? Tell me you're shitting me."

"It's true, Key." Tommy wavered like a wobbling top on its last spin. "Got my goddamn draft notice this morning. I'm drafted, man. Goddamn drafted." His choked voice pushed out the words. "Gotta report in a couple weeks." A pained look crossed his face with sharp edges, as if the window he'd just broken was his own face. "Vietnam U., here I come."

# CHAPTER 22

Phil pulled his Rambler to the stoplight on fifth, turned right, then drove the block to the stop sign, turned right again. He was driving corner to corner, circling the town square in the middle of Bluff Lake as the faintly-illuminated courthouse clock read one o'clock a.m..

"Are we just going to drive *all night*?" Mariah questioned.

"What else is there to do?" Phil asked, realizing, after he said it, that the words sounded bitter. But that's how he felt tonight.

She glanced up at a flickering streetlight. "Come on, Phil. I need you to talk. Let's..."

"Talk?" Phil said, puffing his cheeks. "What good will that do? By tomorrow night, we'll be in two different towns, two-hundred miles apart." He pulled up to the stop sign on Oak where someone had spray-painted the word *War!* under the word *Stop*. "It might as well be a million miles."

"That's not true, Phil. We'll figure out how to meet. On weekends, maybe. We'll call each other. I know it's long distance, and our phone bills will be big, but still..."

"Yeah." But a part of him doubted it. He knew how preoccupied she'd probably be with the rush of classes and new friends and dorm life. He'd heard the stories of high school couples whose relationships were broken up when one of them went off to college.

Mariah gazed idly at the First National Bank clock, the broken hands on its dial always stuck at 5:21. They glided past the Civil War statue in the center of the square. A Yankee soldier in full uniform, with a blue stain on its chest, aimed a rifle. Tommy claimed that one night in junior high, he had thrown a bottle of ink at it as a prank. The statue's chest bled blue ink, and the city crew tried, unsuccessfully, to wash off the stain.

They drove, for the tenth time, past the old hangout—Kluge's soda fountain. No kids lingered in front like they usually did, chattering and goofing around as they leaned on the parking meters. At this time of night, the place was closed, and the storefront window was opaque; the tubes that pulsed with red neon were darkened and cooled. Friday nights when he stood in front of it, Phil sometimes noticed moths, dead, their wings dried on the sill. This night, the only activity on the street was Speedy, the assistant manager of the theatre that all the kids mocked. A half hour ago, he had locked the glass doors after the late movie and then turned the corner, swinging his arms in his oversized blue suit and striding too fast for a man that small.

"I guess I'm just frustrated," Phil sighed. "You'll be going to classes. And studying on the beach behind the student union. And I'll be working out there. Full time."

"You don't think it bothers me, too?" she said. "I feel really bad about it all—your dad, you…" she faltered a few seconds, tears clinging to her eyelids. "Just everything. *Every*thing." She wiped her cheek with the sleeve of her gauze blouse.

"And if something ever happens out there—at the plant, I mean—then just run."

"What's going to happen out there?"

"Anything. A fire. And accident. You told me you're practically knee-deep in gunpowder out there. I just want you to be safe. But right now," she added, "I just wish you'd just stop your damn driving."

Phil didn't reply. A *Freddie and the Dreamers* song played faintly on the radio, followed by *Herman's Hermits* singing, "I'm into Something Good." Irritated by the annoyingly upbeat voice, Phil reached down and flipped the radio off.

"Are we just going to drive all night?" Mariah asked.

The town's one stoplight glared red through the windshield. A yellowed front page of last week's *Bluff Lake Freedom* cartwheeled in front of his bumper. Phil tapped his fingers on the wheel, waiting for the flicker of green. "What else is there to do?" Phil finally replied, knowing he was repeating himself, a record needle stuck on the same lyric.

"This," she said. She leaned toward him, kissed him tenderly on the side of his cheek. He turned and their lips met. He felt the kiss deep down. He knew it was what he really needed, what he'd wanted to do all night, but just couldn't get himself to. It hurt. It hurt too much to kiss her like this, when he realized tonight was the last time he might kiss her for a long time.

The next thing he knew, the sound of a car horn startled them. It was the horn of the Rambler blaring. Without realizing it, Phil had pressed his shoulder against it. As they pulled apart, Mariah laughed. Phil joined in, and they both burst into laughter. It was the kind of spontaneous moment they'd shared at the beginning of summer when nothing and everything seemed to be funny.

Later, parked by the river behind the woolen mills, Phil pulled her hard to his chest and kissed her anxiously, insistently. She pulled back from him and he pulled her roughly toward him again.

"What is it?" she asked. "What are you feeling?"

"You *know* what I'm feeling." Darkness seemed to gather around the car and press against it. He felt the world, trying to crush the two of them. "I feel like I'm losing you."

"Well you're not," she said emphatically.

With that, he kissed the nape of her, her cheek, then her lips, the passion rising in him.

She leaned back on the seat in her embroidered ivory tank top. His hands touched her gently. She slipped his T-shirt over his head. As she pulled at him insistently, her hands on his bare back felt warm, and soft as moonlight.

He kissed her hard, harder; he didn't want his lips to ever pull away. Their two bodies intertwined. Phil felt the pulsing of his heart and the pulsing of the stars and the pulsing of the universe, all at once. All at once. At that instant, Mariah tipped her head back and gasped, making a sound that was almost like a cry. Phil gasped, too. Then their gasps turned to sobs as they lay there, and Phil couldn't help but feel his emotions moving through him like waves: love, then sadness, then love again. Though they embraced for long minutes, Phil couldn't stop the sensation that they were holding each other tightly and letting each other go at the same time.

An hour later, after he dropped Mariah off, Phil found himself driving aimlessly on the town square again. The courthouse clock seemed to stare at him disapprovingly. He wished he could reach up with a burning stick and poke out its glaring cyclops eye. He pulled up at the stoplight. He remembered a quiet night when he stood alone on this corner. He could hear the soft clicks, like distant insects, as the stoplight turned green to yellow to red, and then back again. He cranked the wheel to the left and accelerated. Maybe Mariah was right—maybe he did drive around too damn much. Maybe he was always stuck behind the wheel of a car, but not getting anywhere.

He pictured his dreams steadily draining from him. Pictured them sinking down beneath the floorboards, beneath the tarred street, deep into the cold soil.

He thought about how they laughed when the blaring horn startled them. But now, at 3:00 a.m., the only sounds were the steady purr of the engine, the slow, insistent thrum of his heart.

He didn't care if he drove all night, how late he got home, or how tired he'd be as he shuffled toward the plant's entry gates. Right now, the whole town seemed smothered and held still by the thick night. But still, it was *his* town. This was all he had.

So he kept driving around the square. And each time he passed it, the Civil War statue seemed to take aim at him but never fired.

# PART THREE

# CHAPTER 23

He could do this in his sleep.

Phil scraped the gunpowder from a copper bin with a paddle. Circling the paddle around and around, in a numbing motion, he eased the residue into a smaller bin. Sometimes he felt like he was steadily burying himself, inch by inch, beneath that layer of dry powder.

For a moment he recalled Tommy's satirical portrayal of the regulars. When Tommy heard about workers using paddles, he joked "When you work full time here, you're up shit creek without a paddle."

Then there were Tommy's comments on the metal slides attached to the second-floor doorways of the taller production buildings. In case of an incident, workers could push through the swinging doors and quickly slide to safety. "Man, I'd love to try one of those some time, wouldn't you, Key?" Tommy once exclaimed. "I mean, they're probably as much fun as the giant slide up at Big Chief Park in Wisconsin Dells. Think we could bribe somebody to let us slide down one?"

But here, in Powder House 121, there was no humor, no bantering.

Days like these, loneliness seemed like an actual, physical thing for Phil. Loneliness was thick, and tangible; he could feel it with his fingers; he could taste it on his tongue. Sometimes it was a net that tightened on him each time he trudged through the front gate. By the end of the day, it weighed him down, making him hunch as though, in a matter of weeks, he'd gone from a eighteen-year-old, just out of high school, to an aging man.

Each morning, dressed in his government-issue coveralls some anonymous worker had worn in the past, he'd report to Powder House 121 in the west quadrant of the plant. The powder house was a stained, dark log building. Its base was covered, on all sides, by piled dirt and a thick layer of sod. "The graves," the regulars called those mounds. Phil's days were nothing like the casual weekend and summer job where he mowed lawns and joked around with the crew. This was full-time work, with full-time lifers, somber guys in their forties and fifties, with wives and families, chalking up years of seniority on their belts. Phil couldn't relate to these blue-collar men who, mixing in expletives whenever they talked, discussed fixing carburetors, drinking Blatz at local taverns where Phil would never go, and cleaning their rain gutters. "Well, shit. I finally got them storm windows on yesterday," one guy mused, as if that was a major moment in his life. They complained how they didn't have much sex with their wives anymore, how thrilled they were by their new Skill-Saw in the garage.

"Keyhoe, eh?" Lester Statz, the building foreman, had said the first day Phil reported to the powder house. "Well got-damn," Statz exclaimed with his high nasal voice. "You Karl's boy?" There was his dad, a dense layer of fog looming over him again.

When Phil nodded, Statz presented Phil with a paddle that he'd use for scraping out the powder bins. The paddle, made of hardwood, insured that there'd be no static. "You don't want to ignite nothing," Statz advised, inhaling his lips. "The whole goddamn place would light up like a Christmas tree."

Phil had heard the stories about what happened at the plant last week at two a.m. During the graveyard shift, an incident occurred in a poorly-ventilated ether building, which produced ether and wood alcohol used for smokeless gunpowder. The explosion was apparently caused by static. Two men were seriously injured as the gas from the building's chemicals ignited. A thirty-yard tongue of fire burst through an open door and into the darkness like a huge flame thrower. According to the witnesses, before the men were shuttled to the hospital by the plant ambulance, they ran across a field, screaming, their safety glasses melted to their skin, their burned hands held high in the air to lessen the excruciating pain. Phil thought about how it must have looked like they were surrendering to a hostile enemy. He heard that the next day, at the local hospital, representatives from the Army appeared at the men's bedsides, trying to get them to confess that they were smoking a cigarette and caused the accident. Neither man was a smoker.

This humid morning, Phil tasted charcoal dust and his safety glasses fogged up, so the whole world turned cloudy. It seemed to take days for an hour to pass, to get to the mid-morning break. No Tommy beside him, singing "Wild Thing" by the Troggs, or jabbering about his freewheeling night out with Shirelle. No Tommy, gleefully tipping his lawn mower upside down so the oil seeped into the gas tank and sent out billowing bluish smoke when he started it. As the guys laughed, he'd stand inside that cloud with a mysterious expression, spread his arms, and proclaim, "It is I, the great and powerful Wizard of Oz!"

That was the thing about working at the plant: you were there, physically, raking powder, emptying bins, staring blankly at a conveyor belt, but mentally you could be a million miles away. And Phil usually was.

He was sitting with Mariah on the warm front fender of his Rambler in the high school parking lot. It was graduation day, last June. The lot was empty, except for his car. Their fellow classmates had all headed home, or to hang out in front of Delmonico's Pizza on the town square, or to graduation parties—those underage kegger and bonfire bashes—in a secluded campground near the north shore of the lake.

"Well, here we are." Phil said.

"Yes, here we are," Mariah echoed. Whenever he was silent, Phil was used to the way Mariah would fill up the spaces easily with words. But that afternoon she seemed hesitant to speak, and he hated the pauses that kept thickening between them. The silence seemed to ache. As the two of them watched, a small dust devil rose in the parking lot, swirling, its tan funnel lifting, a couple of pop cans scuttling around at its base. When it spun toward them, Phil said, "Uh Oh. Better close our eyes." The dust devil blew past them, whipping small particles into their faces. Then it glided away to the edge of the lot, then subsided and disappeared, candy wrappers and small sticks dropping to the gravel with a ticking sound. Phil opened his eyes. When he did, Mariah was staring at him, her face just inches from his.

"Look into my eyes," she said. "What do you see?"

"Eyes. Two of them," he said, trying to lighten the mood.

"That's all?"

"No," he admitted. "I see a lot more. So much that I can't even describe it."

"Try."

"Okay then. I see blue irises. Turquoise, almost. They're like rare gems. And they look lit from the inside." He waited a moment, then said "Now look into mine. What do *you* see?"

"Everything," she replied. "Galaxies. The future."

She slid off the fender, grabbed her yearbook from the front seat, then hopped next to him again. "You never signed this for me," she said. She handed him the book with the padded blue cover and the embossed gold words *Bluff Lake High, 1967* on the front.

"Oh. Yeah. I didn't." Phil didn't forget, he just kept putting it off all afternoon of this last day of Senior Week because he didn't know what to write, wasn't sure what would come out of his pen at this uncertain time. He didn't know how, in a few short sentences, to convey his love for Mariah, and how much she'd changed him, how lucky he felt to have met her. He couldn't find words for his plans and doubts and fears about everything that lay ahead. All those topics were just too real. No words seemed large enough or deep enough to contain all his emotions. He thought of her long message that filled the entire back page in his yearbook, her final flowingly scripted sentences that read, "The world is ours, Phil. All my love, Mariah." Her words weighed too much, and he couldn't begin to reply to them.

So instead, he tried to joke about her request. "I usually don't sign for strangers. But I'll make an exception this time." He opened her yearbook, lifted the pen to the blank page, but then the pen paused over the page like a speechless blue tongue. During the pause, he heard the town square clock sending out its loud, low-pitched chimes to signal four o'clock.

"What's wrong?"

"I can't," he answered. "How do I summarize everything in just a couple sentences?"

"You don't have to *summarize* it," she assured him, encouraging him. "Just write from your heart. Write what you *feel*." Mariah was always in touch with her feelings. She had empathy for a stray cat or a homeless woman on the street. She felt anger at injustice when she read about cops beating up nonviolent protestors in Selma, Alabama. She expressed sorrow about the Vietnam war casualties—not just American boys, but the North and South Vietnamese, too.

"That's just it." He lowered his eyes. "I *can't* explain what I feel. Here." He handed the pen back to her. "Maybe I'll write something later."

A car veered into the parking lot. The Falcon came roaring up to them and screeched to a stop in a cloud of gravel dust. Tommy leaped out, wearing his unbuttoned graduation gown, a brown paper bag under his arm.

"Hey, kids," he said, noticing their solemn expressions. Where's the goddamn funeral? Shit, school's finally out!" He pulled out three cans of Hamms from a 12-pack, tossed one to Phil and one to Mariah. "Okay, sports fans. Let the celebration commence!"

Phil and Mariah obliged and climbed off the fender. The three popped opened their cans. "To the tremendous trio!" Tommy proclaimed, the foam spilling onto his wrist. "To brains, brawn, and looks!" They toasted each other, clinking cans.

"Which one is which?" Phil asked, his gloominess beginning to lift.

"I'm the brawn, of course. And Mariah's the brains and the looks. I don't know what the hell *you* are, Key."

Phil gave Tommy a shove.

Tommy reached into his car and pulled out a football. "You ready, Key? You're going out for a pass. I want to show off my arm to Mariah."

Phil set his beer on the gravel, jogged out a few yards, and cut to the left.

"No! No, not on foot!" Tommy called, waving him back. "That's way too easy. I need you to do a square in. But with your *car*."

"My car?"

"You heard me. As of now, your Rambler is officially a wide receiver."

Mariah shook her head in disbelief.

"Milk always has a plan," Phil said to her. "Stupid ones, maybe, but still plans."

"So I see," she said.

Drawing carefully on the gravel with a stick, Tommy laid out instructions for the play. "Okay, Key. It's fourth and goal, with twenty yards to go. I'll roll out to my left, and hit you right about *here*." He jabbed the stick in the dirt. "Got it?"

"Got it, Bart Starr."

"Mariah," Tommy instructed, "You'll be the defensive lineman."

"What'll I do?" she asked.

"Just sort of stand in front of me, waving your arms. But please don't tackle me. I don't wanna get injured."

"Don't worry," she said.

"This'll be spectacular!" Tommy shouted, clapping his hands together. "Highlight reel material!"

When Tommy called "Hut one, hut two!" Phil floored his car and drove straight out for twenty yards. Then he cranked the wheel hard to the left, the tires skidding.

Tommy reared back and threw a perfect spiral that entered the Rambler through the open back window. The ball thumped against the interior and wobbled to a stop on the back seat.

"Complete!" Tommy shouted, dancing around with his arms in the air. "Complete! Touchdown! T-Birds win! T-Birds win!"

Phil stopped the car, ran back to them, and bowed down to Tommy. "Your highness," he uttered. When he straightened, he and Tommy jumped and did a high-five in the air.

"Oh, you two," Mariah chuckled. "You're unbelievable. It's like hanging out with Abbot and Costello."

"Our movie comes out next week," Tommy quipped. He quickly chugged the rest of his beer and announced "All right, folks. It's time for the flag ceremony."

"The what?" Phil quizzed.

Tommy took off his navy-blue graduation gown, exposing his wrinkled T-Birds T-shirt and plaid Bermuda shorts, tied the arm of the gown to the antenna of his Falcon. He hopped onto the hood, spread his arms out. "Ladies and gents, I present to you our flag of independence!" he yelled. "Magnificent, ain't it?"

"Oh for God's sakes," Mariah scoffed, though she was chuckling.

"I agree totally," Tommy shot back. "For God and country." He jumped to the ground, pulled his keys from the pocket of his baggy shorts. "Come on, you two lovebirds. Get in. The parade's about to begin!"

Five minutes later, they cruised around the town square, the windows rolled down, the radio turned up loud. Phil and Mariah laughed as Tommy honked the horn at the high school seniors who hung out on the sidewalk, and the kids chimed in by hooting and jeering at them. *Mony Mony* blared through the speakers, prompting Tommy to steer with his knees as he did a little boogaloo dance, his hands swinging less-than-gracefully in the air. At the red light, Tommy pulled three more beers from beneath the seat, cracked them open, and handed two to Phil and Mariah. "Keep 'em low, kids," he said, noticing the cop across the street.

"To our freedom!" Tommy exclaimed.

"Yes," Mariah echoed, "freedom."

"Freedom," Phil agreed, though he knew he was being a little ironic. He didn't really feel free; for some reason, he felt uncertainty. But he let the buzz from the beers wash that feeling away, and he managed a laugh as Tommy tipped his head back and sang, loudly but off-key, along with the radio.

The light turned green and Tommy floored the car, squealing the tires. Evan Woslowski, a town cop they all knew, eyed them from his squad car parked on the other side of the intersection. He just gave them a teens-will-be-teens shake of his head.

As the Falcon sped up, Phil watched the tattered graduation gown—Tommy's idea of a freedom flag. As they drove stop sign to stop sign, it inflated with air and fluttered, then fell limp, then rose again.

"That paddle workin' okay?" Lester Statz's voice cut into the memory. "You seem to be movin' it a little slow."

"Um, yeah," Phil replied.

Statz put his hands on his hips. "Yeah it's workin', or yeah it's slow?"

"Both," Phil said, trying to be slightly funny, though Statz, as usual, didn't get the humor.

As he returned to work, Phil's mind leaped to early September, the day Mariah left for college.

"We'll figure things out," she had said as the two stood by her trailer. "But you'll be okay here, right?" She spoke the words casually, yet the word "here" dropped on Phil like a boulder, crushing him. He knew exactly what Mariah meant by *here*. *Here* meant this echoing, two-story, four-bedroom house on Oak Street, *here* meant the dead-end, provincial town of Bluff Lake, *here* meant the Strongs Plant. *Here* was a powdery grave he was steadily digging himself into.

"So," Mariah said adjusting the leather shoulder strap of her woven purse. She seemed to shiver, though the afternoon was warm. "We'll see each other soon." Somehow, the words didn't seem convincing.

Mariah checked her watch and looked toward the waiting Fairlane. "Better go," she said. "I can't miss orientation."

"I guess this is it," Phil said. "So, um, goodbye."

"*Not* goodbye. I don't believe in saying goodbye."

"Then what?"

"We should say *to our future*. That sounds much better."

"Okay, then. To our future." The words sounded more tentative than he intended. Later, Phil would picture those words, falling from their lips and sinking down to some deep, dark place, like when they dropped pebbles into an old wishing well.

They whispered the word *love* to each other. She pressed against him and gave him one more kiss, a kiss that tasted like sunlight on his lips. It was a kiss he'd envision again and again in his mind, replaying it in a loop. Pulling back with a lingering gaze, she sighed. It was a deep, lingering sigh, a sigh he knew he'd hear later that night when he couldn't sleep, a sigh he'd hear in his dreams. A wistful sigh that would carry him on its wings for a long time.

Then she slipped from his embrace and opened her car door. In the back seat, her belongings—clothes, books, a burgundy Royal typewriter and a desk lamp, propped up by a pillow and a pink quilt with a paisley pattern—waited in boxes, the flaps open like cardboard mouths calling her name.

When she started the car, the sound of its six cylinders, stuttering and out of synch, grated in Phil's ears.

With tears etching her cheeks and a painful smile, Mariah drove slowly past him. Phil watched the car pull toward the faux Medieval-style archway at the entrance to Camelot Acres, which, from where he stood, appeared backwards as *sercA tolemaC*. The Fairlane hesitated slightly beneath arch, then accelerated, leaving behind it a small globe of exhaust.

Within seconds, she wasn't just at the end of the block; she was a thousand miles away.

"Dammit all!" a voice called, startling Phil. It was Lester Statz. "You just spilt powder on the goddamn floor." Statz—his eyebrows meeting in the middle of his forehead—pointed down at the small pile. "Gotta clean that shit up right away," he scolded. "That's a rule around here. You don't wanna upset The Colonel." Everyone knew that the front-office superintendent of this whole operation was a military big-shot named The Colonel, though no one Phil worked with had ever seen him.

"Oh," Phil replied. "Sorry. Sorry." Phil grabbed a broom, swept the powder into a dustpan, and poured it into the plastic bin labeled Waste Powder.

"After that, you can knock off for lunch. Unless you wanna keep working right through it." Statz pointed to his watch. "It's quarter after already."

"It is?" Phil realized his lunch break was half over.

"Jesus, kid," Statz scoffed. "It's like you're goddamn sleepwalking some days." Statz tipped his safety helmet back, exposing matted hair and a receding hairline that made him look much older than his thirty-five years.

"Yeah," Phil pushed out the word. "Sleepwalking."

As he ate his lunch outside on the grass, he daydreamed about that warm summer night when he lay on his back in a grassy field next to Mariah, watching in awe as the northern lights swayed, a rippling curtain of blue and red and violet. That night he wished he could reach up, pull the gorgeous, expansive sky down and tuck its edges in around them.

Phil lifted his sandwich. Bologna, on white. Iceberg lettuce. An exciting sandwich, he mused. A delectable gourmet meal polished off with a mouthful of soda that tasted like aluminum. He wondered: Isn't that exactly what his father used to eat each day? Then he thought about Tommy coming to work with his famous marshmallow crème sandwich. *Health food*, he always called it, and when he grinned, Phil could see the pale marshmallow stuck between his teeth. Now Tommy was in Da Nang Province, wherever that was.

By afternoon, when the hoarse, high-pitched 4:30 whistle cut through the air, Phil was finally done for the day. The asphalt path dragged him back to his change house.

Phil pulled off his safety goggles. When you worked in the lines, the plant required specialized goggles that cupped your face. As he stared into the mirror attached to the inside of his locker door, wired there by a previous worker, Phil wondered whose face he was looking at. He saw the charcoal dust that had darkened his skin except for a whiter shape around his eyes. *Raccoons!* He heard Tommy's voice joke about the powder line workers. *Those lifers are goddamn raccoons!*

"Say," a voice in the change house asked, replacing Tommy's voice. "Aren't you Karl's boy?" Phil hated the question, this time from a middle-aged man from town that he hardly knew. Phil nodded. "So you're out here now? Full time?" The questions echoed off the enameled dark green lockers and bounced from the corrugated tin ceiling. And all the way home, that question kept ricocheting back and forth inside Phil's head.

# CHAPTER 24

Sitting in his La-Z-boy chair, Karl studied his agate collection. He loved the beauty of the polished pink and red agates he kept in this velvet-lined box, the way their concentric rings circled around and around each other, leading toward their crystal center, their heart. He held one of the larger agates in front of his face and peered at it through half-shell glasses. Beneath a small cone-shaped overhead lamp that cast a triangular beam of light, the agate seemed to be lit from within. *A kind of flame*, he mused, *caught inside it.*

He tipped his head back in the chair, then unbuttoned his pajama top and glanced down at the scar on his chest from the bypass operation. Dark stitch marks, like a railroad track leading from his pectoral to his breastbone. It was a day he didn't want to remember, that deep, gnawing pain suddenly radiating outward from the center of his chest in waves until the world went black.

Shifting his focus, Karl lifted a pale beige agate to the light, noticing that it was almost translucent. He got Phil interested in agate collecting when he bought him boxes of agates from the Black Hills. Phil, a ten-year-old at the time, looked at them in wonder. But by his teen years, Phil's interests changed, and he never turned into much of a rockhound.

Karl, on the other hand, liked collecting rocks ever since he was young, ever since, as a kid, during a vacation, his parents stopped at the Agate Grotto in Iowa. The building was decorated with large agates, all of them polished to a sheen, all of them cut in half so you could see ring after ring all the way to the crystals at their centers. He was amazed at that place as a boy, and now, some forty years later, he's never forgotten it. He's never forgotten how his father, who worked at a shoe factory until his back was too bent and sore to work anymore, took him to the fields beyond town, where they searched the freshly plowed fields for agates. The old man knew heels, and rubber soles, and how to tack them securely to a shoe, but he also knew how to spot an agate in the field, even though it appeared to be nothing more than an ordinary brown rock.

Karl recalled taking Phil out to farmers' fields to look for agates. Those were fond memories. He and Phil were closer in those days, and they sometimes went on father-son hikes, or made a campfire together at the county park and cooked hot dogs and marshmallows. One day, Karl had spotted a brown stone at the edge of the field, held it up to Phil. "This one's a gem," Karl had said, "A keeper."

"How do you know?" young Phil had asked.

"All you have to do is polish it, and it'll look great." He handed it to Phil.

"It looks just like a plain rock," Phil remarked.

"But it's not. Sometimes you just know. You know there's something good inside."

Since the heart attack, Karl had time to reminisce; the days of recuperating stretched into weeks. Funny how a heart gives out when you least expect it, he thought. Funny how, when you're just riding around in a car at work, going to the next site for an inspection, your clipboard in hand, your damn ticker suddenly decides to squeeze its fist inside your chest. The sensation had begun with his right arm going numb on the steering wheel. At first, he thought his arm was just falling asleep, and he shook it a few times, figuring he could easily ignore it. Bud, his co-worker sitting in the passenger's seat asked "Hey, something wrong?"

"Nothing," Karl had replied. It's like there were hundreds of ants, digging their tiny pinchers into his skin. He shook his arm again.

"What the heck? Get stung by a bee?" Bud wondered.

"Dunno," Karl said, and that's when he started to feel the dull ache—a slow smoldering in his chest. Then it escalated, seeming to grow larger, like a fire flaring inside his rib cage. He jerked the car to the roadside and jammed the stick shift into neutral. Karl turned to Bud to try to say something, but when he opened his mouth it was like the wind was knocked out of him. That's when it happened—it was like a shotgun going off in his chest.

To get his mind off that, Karl focused again on the agates, his eyes following the rings around and around, around and around. He circled his thumb on the smooth stone. The Strongs plant had put him on an extended leave. With only a few weeks of sick leave stored up, Karl didn't want to be gone that long. But that was their decision. Someone already replaced him out there, he had heard from Bud. A former sergeant of some kind took over the reins to keep the security office running. They needed a full-time replacement right away, Bud said, not a temp. That's how fast the place was growing, what with the increased military contracts.

It would be a breeze for the new guy, Karl figured. They transferred some of Karl's files to the man's office, and each file contained notes on a different area of the plant. Important things, like repairing deteriorating fences, inspecting the newly opened powder production lines, beefing up the border patrols. A month ago, he heard that people were spotted out there, too close to the fence. Protestors, maybe, one co-worker said, some crazies from Madison scouting the border of the plant.

Strange, he thought, how the most dangerous thing out there would be an accident or an explosion, but what put me out of work is something inside my own chest. The doc explained to Karl that the layers in his constricted arteries were a little like the calcium deposits you might see in a water heater. A couple weeks ago, Karl—without Frances knowing—managed to slowly make his way down the sagging stairs to the basement, unscrewed the top lid of the water heater. He leaned close with a flashlight and peered in. Sure enough, inside were the calcium deposits—a series of dark rings. He shook his head, almost laughed, and thought *That's me, I guess. Damn it all to hell. That's me.*

With the furlough, he'd have a lot of time to rehab with a visiting nurse and then at the Heart Center in St. Cecilia's Hospital, where they'd put him on a slow-moving treadmill. He'd also have time to relax, and to focus on things: hobbies. Some woodworking in the basement, maybe. Catching up on books about antique guns and rifles that he'd kept for years but never read. Looking at his gun collection in the locked case in the den, the smooth iridescent blue-black stocks of vintage Remingtons and Winchesters. There were some good antique weapons in there, some keepers, their value going up year by year.

He leaned back and gazed around at the den: the oak paneling, which he hammered into place himself when he remodeled. The brass eagle wall decoration, hanging from a nail, its wings spread wide. Below it, framed in walnut and centered on red velvet, his WWII medals from when he was Lieutenant Colonel in the war. The Bronze Star, from the day he rescued Tiny McKenzie from their burning supply truck. *Now that was a day*, he thought. *That was really a day.*

Karl's mind drifted to the conversation with Phil last week. Karl had been napping in the La-Z-Boy. When Phil came home from work, he had bumped his work boot against a kitchen chair, and Karl jolted awake.

"So how was work out there today?" Karl had called to him from the living room.

"Work was work," Phil had replied indifferently, rubbing his fingers through his sweat-matted hair.

"You get your quota this week?" Karl was referring to the ideal powder quota—recommended by the plant commander—for each powder house, depending on its size and crew.

"Not quite," Phil called to the living room. He could hear his father but not see him, sitting in the chair backed up against the wall.

Karl leaned forward. "Well how short were you?"

"Just short, that's all."

A scowl crept across Karl's face. "You guys loafing out there?"

"Dunno." Phil took off his boots, dropped one with a clunk to the doormat in the entryway, then the other.

"Well then, what?"

"We just didn't finish, that's all." Phil sounded a little irritated. "It's not the end of the world."

"Well, you fellas better get going," Karl said admonishingly. "That's all I can say. You want the troops to run out of ammo over there?"

Phil dropped his silver lunch box on the counter. "Since when are you still supervisor?" Phil muttered to the half-open cabinet.

"What?" Karl said, craning his neck to see into the kitchen. He thought he caught part of Phil's sentence, but he wasn't sure. He was never sure what the boy was thinking lately. "What'd you say?"

Phil shuffled past in his soiled white T-shirt and jeans. "Didn't say anything," he mumbled, and he climbed upstairs to the shower.

No matter what the boy seemed to think, Karl felt proud that Phil was working out there. And he wasn't just doing busywork like mowing lawns or unloading freight, either. He felt a sense of satisfaction that Phil was right there in the production lines. The GIs needed it, after all, to defeat the Viet Cong marching by the thousands on the Ho Chi Minh trail. It was a step up for Phil, and though he didn't seem to realize it yet, Karl figured the responsibility would do him good. Not to mention that the government contract pay scale kept bread on the table at the Keyhoe household.

"Almost time for dinner," Frances called from the kitchen.

"Yup." He could already smell the pork roast in the oven, could hear the faint whistle from the pressure cooker steaming the string beans. As was her way lately, she'd boil some Minute Rice as a side, served without butter. Health food.

He lifted the agate collection from his lap, the rocks clinking together, wrapped a couple double-thick rubber-bands around it so nothing would spill out, and set it on a shelf. On the wall beside the shelf, a calendar, his next cardio appointment date circled in red pen. The doctors would access how much damage had been done to his heart, and how slowly or quickly it was repairing itself, and how much physical therapy he was capable of doing. A heart can always repair itself, the docs assured him; the cells know what to do. New cells replace old ones, layers of new tissues replace damaged ones. He heard that when something heals, like a broken bone, it can be even stronger than it was before. Karl wanted to believe that more than anything. He had to.

But when he stood from the Lay-z-Boy, he felt suddenly light-headed and weak. He hated that feeling.

"Karl?" Frances called again from the kitchen, "You need help getting to the table?"

"Nope. Thanks. I'm on my way," he said, covering up the dizziness.

He lingered by the calendar, flipping through the next months.

He considered what his first day back at work would be like. No circling in one place anymore. His day would fill with rectangular folders, lists, maps of the production areas, sectioned into grids. Issues followed by solutions. Straight lines, the way he liked it.

He yearned for that day: He pictured himself, striding briskly from his car. Not walking slowly on some goddamn treadmill, like the rehab he'd been doing every few days at the heart clinic. His first day back, there'd be a feeling in his chest— not aching, or cinders burning, but something else: a good feeling, a sensation that would make his wing tip shoes seem as though they were hardly touching the ground as he'd march toward the waiting administration building.

# CHAPTER 25

Tommy's letters from Vietnam never mentioned a single word about the war.

His first letter described the C-141 cargo plane that he flew on with the other draftees, saying "Shit, Key, that thing was huge. I mean, it can carry sixty-two thousand pounds of stuff. That's more than a few Jumbo the elephants. It's definitely a Jumbo Jet for sure! And, talk about perks—they served Cokes to us on the way, even. So how's everything back in Boomtown?"

His letters never referred to attacks by Charlie, or the aching pressure of the backpacks they wore each day, densely loaded with food rations and binoculars and canteens and good-luck charm stuffed animals from their girlfriends and rounds of ammunition for their M16s.

Instead of talking about guerrilla warfare, or slogged across rice paddies, his letters harkened back to the Bluff Lake High School football game highlights. "Remember that Portage game when I scored four touchdowns, Key? I carried the team that night. Remember when I faked that defensive back out of his jock? I head-faked left and then cut right, and he just fell on his keister and I hurdled over him for the winning touchdown. Man, that was one excellent day! Hey—do you know what they call the B-52s over here? They call them Thunderbirds. Just like the Bluff Lake team. Kinda crazy, eh? I wear my Thunderbirds T-shirt around the base and the guys marvel at it. Sunday afternoons I've actually gotten the guys in the platoon to toss a football around in a clearing—if we're not rained out, that is. Which is most days."

Phil heard from Tommy's mother that Tommy was in the infantry. But instead of writing about his patrols as they swept through villages, Tommy's letters focused on patrolling Bluff Lake in a vintage car: "As soon as I get back, I'm getting me a cherry '57 Chevy, all grooved out, white sidewalls, red and white paint, the real deal. I'm gonna drive around the square with a shit-ass grin and wave and honk at everybody. Can you picture it, Key?"

His letters described scenes from American movies shown in the mess hall. "This week," Tommy wrote, "I got to see *Gidget Goes Hawaiian*. Gidget on a surfboard is quite the babe, if you get my drift. And wow, that love scene on the beach in and *From Here to Eternity*. Cold outdoor shower, anyone? Oh, wait!—we have that every morning."

Instead of describing the sounds of machine-gun stutter or popping mortars, he described the latest records. "A few guys brought collections of cassettes, and we crank them up on a cassette player. All the big names: Beatles. Stones. The Hollies. The Supremes. Freddie and the Dreamers. Somebody even brought some old Elvis 45s, which we play on a small record player. I got to entertain the troops, greasing my hair back doing my Elvis voice impersonation. I've formed a Name That Tune club—Nam Chapter—and the guys here are wild about it. We chug some local pig-swill called 33 Beer while we play. It's a crappy rice beer—not even half as good as Hamms or Old Milwaukee. Fortunately, one guy managed to bring some Herman's Hermits 45s, so I'm really in the zone. I can name some songs just by the scratching sounds before the record starts. I win pretty much every time, unless they delegate me to being the MC. Still playing Name That Tune with the guys at the plant, Key? And by the way, you're so goddamn lucky to get a deferment for your employment at my former workplace, the Scenic Strongs House of Zombies."

The only reference Tommy made about the local Vietnamese culture was this: "Girls on the streets of the villages come up to me and say, 'You want hoochie-mama? I your hoochie mama.' Can you believe it? Some of the guys go for those girls, but I don't think Shirelle would approve of my adopting a hoochie mama. Do you? Ever see her, by the way? She hasn't been writing to me all that much lately. If you do see her, tell her hello, and tell her to get her sweet ass in gear and write more letters!"

Phil hated to tell Tommy that he had seen Shirelle around town, strolling arm in arm with a local guy, or hopping into a car full of guys and jumping onto somebody's lap. Loyalty to Tommy didn't seem like the first thing on her mind. "Okay," Phil wrote in reply, not wanting to mention any of that, "I'll tell her to write. Next time I see her."

If Phil judged solely by Tommy's letters, he'd say that his tour of duty in Southeast Asia was not much more than an extended high school. Typical Tommy, Phil thought—the classic screw-off, the ultimate escapist. He had a way of turning everything into a game and, no matter how dire, making it fun. There was no slogging from coordinate to coordinate, village to village, in sweat-dark fatigues during the humid afternoons, like other returning vets described. No red flowers of explosions. No clicks of triggers. No snipers. No bullets shattering chests. There was no shriek of incoming mortars, no water from rice paddies rippling around the floating bodies. It was all football games, driving around the town square, sipping cold Hamms on hot summer nights. It was the flicker of static when, in the back seat, you put your hand on your girlfriends' cashmere shoulder and leaned in for a kiss. There was no war, no Vietnam. Just hazy, nostalgic memories of a small Wisconsin town called Bluff Lake.

And Phil got to like it that way. He liked it that he didn't have to tell Tommy any details about the escalating war he saw each night on the nightly news.

Phil didn't have to tell Tommy about the weekly news articles about Vietnam, and how, at first, they were confined to the back pages of the *Bluff Lake Freedom*, like no one really wanted to read them anyway. They tallied the county's MIAs like a list of boys who were absent from school. Phil didn't have to explain that, week by week, month by month, the stories gradually made their way toward the front page. Associated Press articles described the Viet Cong and claimed U.S. troops were unprepared for the guerrilla warfare waiting for them in the jungles. Phil wouldn't have to mention LBJ's escalated bombing campaign, or the Viet Cong stepping up their offensives. He wasn't sure just how much Tommy knew about all that, though, Phil suspected, he knew a lot more than he was letting on.

Yet, each of Tommy's letters was a journey back into some safe, pleasant corner of the past, like sneaking a Kool or a beer when you were twelve, the way Phil and Tommy did behind the A & P store in eighth grade.

"I'll see your shit-faced grin again soon, Key," Tommy concluded in one of his letters. "I hate to admit it, but I'm really starting to miss ol' Bluff Lake, the armpit of Wisconsin. When I get back, we'll celebrate. We'll drink a *whole* goddamn case of Miller High Life—it's the champagne of bottle beer, you know! We'll go out with our girls and make out. We'll play Name That Tune all goddamn night! And that's an order from T. J. Laudermilk, your Commander in Chief. Your pal, Milk."

In his parent's *Life Magazine*, Phil saw a black-and-white photo of a young soldier in Vietnam. His muscular chest was bare, and dog tags dangled around his neck. He stood beside a tent, a trace of fear showing behind his just-out-of-high-school eyes. Though the soldier looked a little like Tommy, there would be no fear in Tommy's eyes. Instead, as he lay on his cot, Tommy's face would take on a nostalgic, faraway look, like he was envisioning the colored pinstripes on his Chevy.

Tommy would always close his letters with "Write back soon, you jerk." And Phil, the unwavering buddy, always *did* write back within a day or two. Mister Reliable, Tommy sometimes called him. No matter what, Phil took the time to compose some funny, entertaining, nostalgic letters that mentioned the Billboard top-40 list, the latest Beatles album. He wrote letters that pulled a thick blanket over his own doubts, smothering them. Loyalty was Phil's middle name. After all, his buddy was a soldier. In Vietnam. And Phil had a responsibility to shut up and support him, didn't he?

# CHAPTER 26

As she washed the breakfast dishes in the morning, her hands wrist-deep in the soap suds sloshing in the red dishpan, Frances thought about Karl's damaged heart. She pictured it as a red balloon, slightly deflated and wrinkled, but still pulsing. She knew it had to heal itself, the doctors told her. Its walls needed to become thick and strong; it needed to remember how to squeeze that rich blood through it without hesitating.

She knew she had to help Karl recover. And no matter what it took, she would do whatever was necessary. It was her duty and she accepted it. After all, it was what a wife did, wasn't it?

Then, unexpectedly, she started to question: *What about my feelings? My damaged heart? What about that?* Then, feeling guilty for her selfish thoughts, she quickly dismissed them.

Each day she woke, tired, but she supplied him with what he needed: Food, water, TV. In her mind, those three words followed each other, repeating themselves like a litany.

Karl needed her, now more than ever, she knew, but sometimes he seemed distant from her, a stranger who just moved into her house and made himself at home in the den adjacent to the living room. Mornings, he'd look at her from his adjustable day bed, his eyes a bit glazed, and it was as if he wasn't looking at her at all.

He spent hours gazing idly at quiz shows and soap operas on the small TV she had picked up at Goodwill. Sometimes he'd open the velvet-lined wooden box and for a long time, study his agates, their concentric rings hypnotizing him.

All the while, Frances gracefully went about her daily chores: preparing his food the way the doctors told her, bringing him glasses of water, tilting the TV at an angle so he could see it better, helping him to the bathroom, though his weight, on her arm, almost made her crumple. Those first weeks, it was a routine, an order she could follow. Food, water, TV. Life's basic supplies. The minimum daily requirement.

One day he called her to his bedside.

"Yes?" she said, figuring he needed more water, or the bed to be propped at a different angle. "What is it?"

He surprised her by saying, affectionately, "You know, you looked pretty cute this morning when you brought me breakfast."

"Oh?" she said, blushing.

"Yep," he said fondly. "I'm real sure I've got the best darn nurse in town."

But now, weeks after the heart attack, Karl's mood swings had become increasingly noticeable. The food wasn't hot enough, or cold enough. He claimed the broccoli tasted sour. Told her he craved steaks, buttered bread, a wedge of cheddar cheese rather than the healthier, vegetable-rich meals she was serving. He didn't like the hired nurse who came in every other day to check his vitals; he said she talked too much about nothing. He grumbled that he was getting bored with sitting around. The TV was less than entertaining. "It's nothing but quiz shows, quiz shows, quiz shows," he told her one afternoon. The weight of his words pressed on her, especially the way he growled her name with a guttural tone—

*Fran-ces*—as he demanded something.

She hated to see Phil like this, coming home each afternoon at five o'clock. He'd be so exhausted, his white T-shirt soiled, his hair matted from wearing that safety helmet in the heat. Phil had told her that those powder houses, with their open doorways, always pull in the heat from outside and trap it there, along with heat from the motorized conveyor belt. Sometimes he felt like he was gasping for breath, even if there was a chilly fall breeze blowing through. And she knew what he meant.

The only good part about the job was that it gave Phil a deferment from the draft. The county draft board decided that working full-time at a defense plant merited him an exemption.

As Frances lifted Phil's socks from the hamper, she noticed the gray half-moon shapes from the powder where his work boots didn't cover. On Saturday mornings, she would throw them into the Maytag and wash them on the hot cycle. But each time she lifted them out of the washer, she noticed the stains remained. She had tried everything: Tide, Cheer. Presoaking them in Clorox bleach. Frances would fold and lay the dried socks on Phil's dresser top for his next week of work. But as she set them down, she could still see the faint stains, like a smile or a frown, depending on which way it was facing. *What's in that powder, that it never comes out?* she wondered. The next day, Frances stopped at Sears and bought Phil a new package of six cotton socks.

This morning, she pulled a few pieces of silverware from the dishpan, rinsed them in the sink beneath the hot water faucet, then placed them with a clink in the dish rack. She recalled her conversation with Phil in the kitchen yesterday afternoon when he returned from work.

"I should be at college," he had told her as he grabbed a tall glass from the cupboard. "I should be in Madison."

"I know what you're feeling," she had said sympathetically, tipping her head sideways to look into his eyes. "It's Mariah, isn't it?" When he nodded with a pained expression, she assured him "This job's not forever."

He leaned against the yellow countertop. The Formica was chosen by Frances, decades ago to add a little brightness to the room. "It sure feels like it," he finally said under his breath.

"It might feel that way now. But you're young," she said, trying to add a lilt to her voice. "You've got a whole life ahead of you." She knew she had to be upbeat around her boy, knew she had to be the one who never got down, no matter what. It was her role.

"You don't understand, Mom. I feel like I'm in limbo. My life's on hold, and I don't know if I'll ever get to it."

"You will, Phil," she assured him. "Just have patience." She brushed a stray strand of hair behind one ear. "My whole life I've learned patience."

Phil turned, switched on the faucet, and watched the stream of water pour from the spout into the porcelain sink. A farm-style sink, Frances always thought. It was big and clumsy, like a trough, but it came with the older house when they bought it years ago, and it served its purpose.

Phil held the glass beneath the stream, filled it, then swirled the water. The evening sunlight, slanting through the window, circled around the rim. He took a long drink, his Adam's apple rising up and down. He always seemed to be thirsty since he started working full time.

"I just don't know how much longer I can take it out there," he said, pushing out the words like they were heavy.

"You can do it, Phil. You *have* to. For yourself. And for your father. For all of us." As she said this, she didn't know if she was smiling or frowning. She never was sure about the expressions on her face lately.

"Yeah," he acquiesced. "I have to."

"Frances," Karl called this morning as she finished the breakfast dishes. Her hands were still submerged in the red plastic dishpan. To save a little on the water bill, she had thought when she brought the dishpan home from the hardware store. The last couple of plates and glasses clunked beneath a layer of tiny soap bubbles from the Joy she added.

"*Fran*-ces!"

"What?" She entered the living room, drying her hands on a faded floral dish towel. "What do you want?" she asked again.

Propped up in his day bed, his bulging eyes stared at nothing. "I want to be back at the plant," he said gruffly. "That's what I want."

"You know I can't do anything about that." She tried to make her voice sound light.

He pushed a crocheted Afghan off his chest. "I hate it here."

She wanted to say *that makes two of us,* but she bit her tongue and squeezed the towel tightly. She always bit down on her feelings around Karl. Bite, bite bite. Eat the words. Let them crumble on her tongue, pulverize them to fine grains, swallow them, let them fill her body.

She went back into the kitchen, plunged her hands into the red dishpan, and as she did, she cut her finger on the sharp edge of a paring knife. "Damn!" she exclaimed, surprising herself with the word she almost never used. She pulled her hand out, saw the tiny scarlet river circle her finger a few seconds, a tributary gliding like a thread toward her gold wedding ring. "Damn!" she said again, raising her voice.

"What?" Karl called from the living room. "You say something, Frances?"

"No. I didn't." She closed off the words behind dry lips.

She turned on the cold-water tap, and held her hand under the stream, but each time she pulled it out, the small cut kept bleeding. She stared at the blood, the concentric red rings winding around her finger. She wrapped the fingertip with a paper towel, and still the red stain seeped faintly through it.

When the bleeding finally stopped, she put a band aid on it. When she lowered her hands back into the dishpan, the water sloshed left, then right, and the soap made the cut sting. The last of the silverware clinked against a glass plate as she finished her chore, the suds clinging to her pale wrists, the water pulsing back and forth, back and forth.

And for the rest of that day, she went about her usual activities like a gauze-winged moth fluttering around a light.

Food. Water. TV.

It was what he needed. It was what she did. It was what they had between them. And it would be enough, she told herself. For now, it would be enough.

# CHAPTER 27

Anticipating what she might hear, Mariah stood with the group on State Street in Madison. The students had gathered in front of a one-story storefront, its windows plastered with anti-war posters. The hand-written sign on the door read:

## STUDENTS FOR A DEMOCRATIC SOCIETY
## ORGANIZATIONAL RALLY HERE TODAY AT 2 P.M.!
## LISTEN AND LEARN!

She wasn't sure why she had come here today. She could have been in the library, studying, or could have been on the terrace of Lake Mendota sipping iced tea and enjoying the perfect late fall afternoon. However, she had seen a flier—slightly wrinkled—tacked to the bulletin board in the student union, and it piqued her curiosity.

A handsome young man—his curly black hair swirling onto the shoulders of his khaki green military jacket, a slight scruff of dark beard beneath his chiseled cheekbones—shouldered open the door of the store. He moved to the front of the crowd and paused there. For a few seconds, he bowed his head and stared at the sidewalk, as if composing himself. Mariah noticed a brown leather peace symbol inside the V of his partially unbuttoned shirt. He closed his eyes a few seconds, then started to speak.

"Most people…" he began with intensity, "Most people are tourists in life, man. They pass right through it, and don't give a damn." He waved one hand in the air. "As some people are starting to realize, middle class America doesn't give a crap about Vietnam. Reality is that the war is getting bigger and bigger every day. *Every* day. Thousands of eighteen-year-olds are being drafted against their will. Thousands more are in Vietnam, their fingers on the triggers of M16 rifles." He brushed back his wavy hair that spiraled in front of his left eye. His voice was deep, and full, and melodic. A Jim Morrison timbre to it. "We need to *do* something, people. The silent majority just sits quietly and lets it all happen. But silence is a cancer," he said, borrowing from a song by Simon and Garfunkle. "The more silent we are," he claimed, "the more it grows. We need to stand up against the establishment. Sit ins. Marches." He placed his hands thoughtfully on his hips. "And that's why I'm here. That's why I'm starting this new group on campus. It's called the Students for a Democratic Society." He gazed down at the sidewalk again, where someone had drawn peace symbols with pink and yellow chalk, then lifted his head. "Reciting slogans, wearing flowers in your hair, dropping out. Those things are frickin' useless. This war is *real*, people. Guys our age are dying over there every day. America is not a democratic society anymore. It's a militaristic one. It's totalitarian." He raised his voice. "America is eating her youth for breakfast. We need to take *action*, I'm telling you. Talk is for politicians. And losers." Then he added, his voice becoming softer and more intimate, "Take a stand, people. It's no time for neutrality. It's time to wake up." He spread his arms out, raised his voice again. "This country depends on us." His voice ascended to a shout. "You and me. *Us!* Are you with me?"

People in the crowd clapped and cheered in agreement. "Yeah, Daniel!" one guy shouted, and others began to chant "End the war! End the war!"

Daniel leaned his tall, muscular frame forward and scanned the crowd, then noticed Mariah standing near the back. The straps of his leather wristband dangled from his wrist as he pointed to her, then strode forward through the group. People parted on either side. "Now," he said, stopping in front of her. He stared at her, his eyes brown and captivating. Mariah looked down at the sidewalk, surprised and embarrassed that he had singled her out. "Imagine that you and I are in love," he said. "Imagine that the two of us are sitting across from each other. We're in the lotus position, legs crossed." He sat down on the concrete, then motioned her to sit down across from him, which she did. He leaned closer until his face was just an inch away from hers. "The two of us would stare at each other, just like this. Face to face. Slogans wouldn't matter. Small talk wouldn't matter. We'd drop our pretenses. All our barriers." He nodded slowly and spoke almost intimately. "Love. Not war. That's what it's all about. Right?" The people around them cheered again and applauded.

Captured by his hypnotic gaze and charismatic smile, she felt her face tingle as though a sudden warm breeze just blew against it. She was certain her cheeks were turning red. She wasn't sure if she nodded, or if she smiled back at him.

What she did feel was the sudden sensation of being drawn in by something—a current, maybe, a pull toward an unexpected shore. Maybe this was fate, she thought; maybe this was why she had noticed a random sign in the student union. Maybe this was the reason she was here, in Madison, on this street corner today. Maybe this was exactly what she needed. It was a feeling of urgency that, she sensed, might be more important than some of her uninspiring classes, her dull and trivial conversations in the dorm, her life that seemed so small these past weeks. And she liked that feeling. It felt powerful, and compelling, and right.

"So," he said, extending his open palm toward her. "Are you with us?" Mariah felt the world around her go silent except for his low, melodic voice. "Are you?"

"Yes," she finally replied impulsively. "Yes," she said again. It wasn't just a word—it was a choice. She reached out to him with her hand, and felt him curling his fingers around it.

# CHAPTER 28

In the living room, TV trays in front of each of them, the Keyhoe family gazed at the evening news on the black and white television. Tonight, Frances' meal consisted of roast chicken, mashed potatoes, and oval slices of jellied cranberries. With a soup spoon, she had made a crater in the middle of each helping of mashed potatoes, then filled it with gravy.

The three sat at their appointed places: Phil and Frances on the couch, Karl on the rust-colored plaid La-Z-Boy. After Walter Cronkite welcomed the audience, the broadcast began with a story of the Surveyor 3 probe landing on the moon. Karl, always fascinated by the space program, watched intently, a look of wonder on his face. "Wow," he said, "We're going to put a man on the moon soon," he mused. "Mark my words." He turned to Phil and Frances. "Just think of the technology it took to accomplish that. American ingenuity. Remarkable, isn't it?"

The two nodded.

"So what do you think's on the dark side of the moon?" Frances wondered.

"I don't know," Karl replied, "But I'm sure we'll find out."

The second feature focused on recent widespread protests across the country. A sea of black faces appeared in a march for fair housing in Milwaukee, led by a priest. The camera panned the crowd of black people, flanked by police with clubs and riot helmets. Some protestors wore NAACP T-shirts, and some waved signs that read **We Demand Fair Housing Now! Black Power!** The reporter estimated that eight thousand people joined in the march. As he watched, Karl's eyes squinted.

The National Guard had been called in, the newscaster said, and though the mayor issued a curfew for the city, the protestors planned to march every night. Police brutality was another issue for the marchers, the reporter added, and the video switched to a white policeman swinging a club at black protestors as they surged toward.

"At Columbia University..." the announcer said, and images of students taking over an administration building appeared on the screen.

Next was a women's rights rally in Washington. Thousands of women marched, blocking streets and carrying banners that shouted **Women Demand Equality! My Body, My Choice!** and **Sisterhood is Powerful—End the War!** Gloria Steinem appeared in front of the crowd as she gave a confident, defiant speech.

"What's happening?" Karl said aloud. He stopped chewing and poised his fork in the air.

Assuming the question wasn't directed at anyone in particular, Phil and Frances continued eating.

"What's happening in our country?" Karl asked, louder. "Phil? Frances?"

"They're activists, Dad," Phil finally offered. "It's about equal rights, and..."

"Equality my eye," Karl spat. "Blocking a street is not equality. Setting the

126

place on fire is not equality. People are breaking the law. And what do *you* know about it, anyway?"

"Mariah wrote about it," Phil blurted. "In a letter. She said society needs to change, and…"

"Mariah?" Karl cut Phil off. "You're quoting that Stiller girl? Since when is *she* an expert on society?"

Knowing it was time to back off, Phil went silent.

"Protests are erupting all across the country," the newscaster continued as more images appeared on the screen. "Ten-thousand people marched in Seattle. Anti-war activists are organizing marches this weekend in New York, Chicago, Madison, Ann Arbor…"

"I'm not watching this," Karl said, snapping his fork down on the edge of his plate. Red blotches forming on his cheeks, he stood quickly, bumping the TV tray with his knee. His glass of orange juice tipped over, spilling, and the cranberries slipped from the plate and landed in his lap.

"Damn!" he said, scooping the gel from his lap and tossing it back onto the plate.

"Karl…." Frances cautioned. "Don't get upset. Just sit down." She stood, picked up his overturned glass. "I'll get you some more juice. You need to…"

"I don't *need to* do anything, Frances." He brushed past her and turned the TV off. An image of a black female anti-war protestor—wearing a peace symbol T-shirt and raising her fist in the air—shrunk to a small pale dot.

The room went silent.

Karl picked up his plate and strode to the kitchen. He sat down hard on a chair at the kitchen table and, brooding, continued eating by himself.

Frances looked at Phil with a pained expression. "He's been real antsy lately," she said in a hushed tone. "Staying home doesn't agree with him, I guess. I know I should go out there and talk to him." Her face took on a determined look. "And I will. But first I'll give him a couple minutes. You know, to simmer down."

She soaked up the spill on his tray with a paper towel, then walked to the kitchen and refilled his juice glass.

When she set the glass in front of him, but he didn't look up. "Here's your juice, Karl." She tried to make her voice sound bright. He didn't acknowledge her, just kept eating slowly, while, on his plate, the red liquid from the cranberries bled into the edge of the mashed potatoes.

# CHAPTER 29

Her cascading blue words were like mountain streams that he, an aimless hiker dying of thirst, could drink from. Tonight, Phil sat at the small desk in his bedroom, re-reading Mariah's letters from the past months.

At the beginning of fall, Frances commented, "Seems like you two are supporting the whole post office." And maybe she was right; they wrote to each other almost daily. As soon as Phil got back from the plant, he'd open the mailbox on the front porch and look for another letter from her.

Crème envelopes, pastel pink paper, blue ink.

Sometimes her letters were light, like a monarch butterfly's wings—gossamer pages he took flight on. Other times they held so much weight that Phil could hardly hold them as he read and re-read them. For him, those letters from Mariah were his nourishment, his sustenance; her words helped him survive his eight-to-four-thirty shifts at the plant. Some nights he lay in bed and imagined her pink lips, her tongue, as she carefully sealed the envelopes.

In September, her letters described her first days on campus. She wrote about how excited and yet sad she felt that day, having to say goodbye to Phil and her mother. She described the way her mother cried after parent-student orientation, the look on Janelle's face as though she'd never see Mariah again. Mariah's words painted a picture of the student union overlooking Lake Mendota and her dorm room at Elizabeth Waters Residence Hall. She wrote about anticipating her classes, and how, the Sunday before they began, she toured campus, peering excitedly into each of the classrooms. "This is going to be incredible!" she had written.

In one letter she described her first class—a freshman comp class in White Hall, where they had a long-haired hippie-style teaching assistant who encouraged them to write about political topics. "A great suggestion," she wrote. "Really great. I mean, why write about trees or your below-average summer vacation?"

Her letters described her longing for her future, her confusion, her passion to change things, her good and bad days, about how much she missed him. Mariah's world swirled with feelings; it was as if she lived in a mansion of emotions, and each day she would move from room to room. She wrote impassioned letters to congressmen pleading for the passage of the Civil Rights Bill, cuts in the space program, and more funds to fight poverty and the humanitarian crisis in Biafra. Without her around, Phil's life felt small and stagnant; he could go for days without ever experiencing any waves of highs or lows.

By October, Mariah started writing about her sense of isolation in the freshman dorm, where many of the girls on her floor were mostly into new hairdos and their latest purchases of hip hugger jeans, sweaters, and perfumes. It was nothing she could really relate to. "They're nice, and well-meaning," Mariah wrote, "but they just seem somewhat naïve and immature. Some girls on my wing pin cheap stuffed animals to their bulletin boards and hang up posters from when they were in junior high."

She wished there were more people in the dorm who listened to Buffalo Springfield, Jimi Hendrix, or Jefferson Airplane. The campus fraternities and sororities seemed like nothing more than snobbish social clubs that you could buy your way into. She expressed how much she hoped to find a friend on campus, someone she could really talk to or even confide in. On a positive note, in one letter, Mariah wrote about one of the student organizations on campus that seemed to be making a difference. She had ended the letter with, "So I'm definitely going to get involved."

Mariah wrote about the loneliness of her late nights, lying in the top bunk at two or three a.m., her brain burning like a flame as she stared at the ceiling and thought about Phil. "You should be here with me," she wrote and as usual expressed her love for him. In a few letters, she had asked Phil to describe his job at the plant. He never responded to her questions.

Phil thought about telling her *I scrape the excess powder from bins with a paddle. The paddle is wood and the bins are copper, of course, so there'll be no friction. Sparks can be deadly, and not allowed, you know.* But he never wrote that; instead, he'd enclose a couple of short poems, based on the view from his bedroom window. One was about the oak leaves changing from green to rust. Another described the overalls hanging on the clothesline, the arms and legs inflating with the wind as they rose into the air. He'd imply that he was like the laundry, pinned to the clotheslines, and the wind, trying to free those clothes, was a lot like her. He wrote about how much he wanted to be in that freshman comp class, sitting near her, taking notes on Keats and Shelley. His daydreams always took him to that class in Madison—a modern classroom with high, clear windows where he would sit so close to her that her thigh, bare below her short skirt, pressed lightly against his leg. He imagined lowering his hand onto her thigh, her head turning toward him with a look of mild but approving surprise. During his long, dry days at the plant, those thoughts circled around and around his mind like refreshing blue whirlpools.

Sometimes what he didn't write in those letters was more telling than what he did write. What he really wanted to tell her some days was *I hate it here, working with these lifers who are twice my age, men and women who have nothing more to talk about than last night's Jackie Gleason Show. They go on and on about the tomatoes in their gardens, their grocery list for Super Value. Lately I feel like I'm walking around, lobotomized. I feel dry and dimensionless. A paper-thin cadaver. The only thing that would bring me to life would be your touch.*

"Cauliflower," one middle-aged woman co-worker had said to Phil during break yesterday as she put Squeeze Cheese on a cracker. "Now that's real good for you. Ever eat cauliflower?" Later, he quoted the woman in one letter to Mariah, thinking it would sound funny. And he enclosed a poem entitled "Cauliflower," implying that the food was bland as his work at the plant, and the person who ate too much of it became like the cauliflower itself: pale, tasteless, a brain-like shape, but without any thoughts.

On his manual typewriter, he typed poems about jagged, distant mountains, cracked mirrors that didn't reflect, roads leading to the horizon, shimmering lakes he wished he could swim in. "Think the enchanting Miss Turtle would give me a B on this poem??" he had asked in one letter. Then added, "Remember lit class? Wow, every day I wish I was back there, sitting at ol' BLHS. I picture myself, leaning forward to the back of your head and smelling your hair. I picture the two of us, sitting on the back steps of the school, talking for hours about the assigned readings in history and lit.

In her return letter to him, she responded: "You have to think forward, Phil. Not about where you were last year in high school, but about where you'll be next year. About what's ahead. Where you're going."

"You're right," he had written back to her. "You're right, right as usual. I can't keep trying to grab onto what's already gone. But I guess that's what I end up doing, when I'm working out here in a suffocating building all day looking through stupid safety goggles that make indentations around my eyes. The dents stay in my skin a long time. Damn—they're even there when I look in the mirror before bed."

The second month of school, Mariah sent a thin, polished stone through the mail, a stone she said she found on the shore of Lake Mendota. Perfectly symmetrical and the size of a quarter, the stone was mottled pink and white and speckled with black flecks. She told him that when he missed her, he should just pick up the stone, hold it between his thumb and index finger, and remember. "This stone is me," she wrote, "this stone is *us*." He cherished it, held it between his fingertips some evenings as he sat in the half-light beneath his lamp, listening to the Beatles *Rubber Soul* album. The stone was intricate—so different from the dull powder he worked with each day. Sometimes he took the stone with him to the plant, keeping it in the pocket of his T-shirt beneath his coveralls. If he held it up to the light, he could see, in its translucence, pink veins branching out from its inside, and a tiny cluster of pink crystals at its very center. Sometimes he envisioned her finding this stone—colorful and surprising, and unlike all the other dull stones—and carrying it back to her dorm in the front pocket of her white Levis. Yearning for her, he imagined the stone pressing softly against her warm inner thigh. Though the stone was cool to the touch, he could heat it, just by squeezing it between his fingers, or putting it into his mouth for a few seconds. When he placed it on his tongue, he was certain that he tasted her.

For the first few weeks, she wrote Phil frequently, saying how much she wanted to visit him, if she only had the extra money for bus fare. She wrote about the depth she could see in his eyes, the afternoon they spent lying on a striped blanket by a rushing stream, reading Shakespeare and Walt Whitman out loud and talking about their dreams. She wrote sentimental, personal things—the things girlfriends write to their boyfriends.

Mariah would sign her letters, "I miss you. Write soon, Phil. (Like right now, in other words). Love, Mariah."

And he'd sign his letters, saying: "I miss you more than you know. I don't know who I am without you. All My Love, Phil."

Months later, Mariah's letters began to confused him. There were more and more questions, questions with thorns on them. "How much powder does the plant make?" she asked. "Does anyone ever talk about what it's used for?" In one letter, she wrote, "Do you ever really think about what you do there?" Those words bothered him, echoing in his head for days. In the next paragraph, she had switched back to a descriptive, touching thought: "I'm lying on the top bunk in the near-dark as I write this. I'm staring at the Armstrong ceiling tiles noticing the patterns of holes in them that look like they could be stars, but without light. I stare at those holes, and I want to see your face instead."

Though he didn't answer any of her questions about the plant, Phil always wrote back, echoing her thoughts with some of his poetic musings: "Tonight, as I look out my bedroom window, the stars are so far away. They look like pinholes in the blackness. Where do they lead? What's on the other side of that dark dome? You, Mariah. You're there. And I wish I could be there with you."

Then, for a brief moment, he thought about writing: In answer to your other questions: In a month, this place can produce 16 million pounds of single base propellant, 5 million pounds of rocket propellant and three million pounds of ball powder. I have powder stains on my cheeks and hands. After work, I try to wash them off with a bar of Lava soap. I turn the bar around and around and around, but the stains never seem to come completely off.

Some nights, when he sealed his envelope and took it to the corner mailbox, the thought would cross his mind that some microscopic bits of powder from the plant were still on his fingertips when he wrote the letter. He thought of adding this p.s. to the back of the envelope: If some specks of gunpowder have fallen into this envelope with your letter, then forgive me. Please forgive me. But, of course, he never wrote that.

Some nights after he mailed a letter, he stood at the sink, washing and re-washing his hands.

"You coming back to Bluff Lake for Christmas?" he inquired in one late November letter.

"I'm not sure yet," she replied, leaving it indefinite. "I'll have to see… Busy," she explained. "Busy lately, with everything."

She didn't come back for Christmas, as it turned out, and that evening Phil stood in the back yard, watching the snow slice across his vision. He would watch that snow falling on New Year's Eve, too, and the last weeks in January, when the Wisconsin winter pressed its icy palms to the windows.

Tonight, after he re-read a few of the letters, he sorted them, arranging each by date from the first to the most recent. He gathered them into a stack, circled them with a rubber band, then closed them in the darkness of a drawer.

He lay on his bed and gazed out his bedroom window. It seemed like he had so many questions lately about the world, and his place in it. The answers, he decided, were somewhere out there in the night sky, above the taut power lines and the zig-zagging branches of the oaks, beyond the arc of stars. Like a lot of other answers in his life that he yearned for, they were—for the time being—beyond reach.

He had to face the painful reality: as the months went on, Mariah's letters had become less and less frequent. Her diligent daily letters trailed off to one a week, then to every other week, then to one in two weeks.

And then, like a stream trickling toward a rocky cliff and then finally drying up, the letters inexplicably stopped.

# PART
# FOUR

# CHAPTER 30

Mariah lifted the worn acoustic guitar off the display shelf and strummed her fingertips over the steel strings. The sound filled the small music pawn shop with a dissonant chord. The guitar, though missing a string, had pieces of ivory embedded in the frets. The back was made of dark rosewood, its grains whorled with a swirling pattern. Impulsively, she knew she had to have it. She carried it to the front of the store and set it on the counter.

"I want this one," she said to the clerk, a young teen with long hair tied back.

"So, you in a folk group?" he asked.

"No. Actually, I don't know how to play," she admitted. "But I plan to learn."

The clerk looked down at the guitar. "Looks like you're gonna need new strings on that one." He pointed to a rack behind him. "I've got some back here."

"Okay, I'll take a set. On second thought, make that two."

As she left the store, the black case in hand, she felt good about her purchase. She thought about those strings—they were silent now, but she was confident that she'd teach them to sing. She didn't care if the strings would give her blisters on her fingers, like someone once told her. She'd trade blisters for music any day.

She wished she was a better singer. Her voice was okay, but nothing fantastic or distinct. She loved Janis Joplin's voice. She'd seen a film of her singing at the Monterey Pop festival, and was drawn in by her Joplin's raspy voice, and the way she sang with such wild abandon. "Ball and Chain" and "Piece of My Heart" were her favorites.

Stepping through a small whirlwind of scuttling yellow leaves, Mariah strolled along the sidewalk toward the head shop called The Kaleidoscope. The store featured an array of posters ranging from Joplin, Jimi Hendrix, Jefferson Airplane, to Che Guevara and Malcom X. The shop always soothed her with its lavender incense scent; its walls were cluttered with racks of beads and jewelry, tie-dyed T-shirts, scarves, and Guatemalan purses. Beneath the scratched glass of the countertop, was an array of small pipes and Zig Zag papers.

She passed a bookstore and a couple of coffee houses, but then a window display in a travel agency made her stop abruptly.

One travel flier in the corner read: **Visit Bluff Lake, and Scenic Bluff Lake State Park**.

*Bluff Lake*. She hadn't thought about the place in weeks. The photos made the town look like an ideal a tourist destination, with manicured lawns, flower beds on the town square, and the serene lake with families picnicking on the shore. But she knew nothing there was ever what it seemed. She knew that not far from those idyllic scenes was the Strongs Plant, its smokestacks belching out toxic yellow fumes twenty-four hours a day.

For a few seconds, she pictured Phil's face: his encouraging smile, his sincere gaze that made her feel important, that her thoughts mattered and were worth listening to. He was as reliable as that steady throbbing beneath the skin of her wrist. Still, there was something missing.

She couldn't explain exactly why she had stopped writing to Phil. She couldn't explain it to herself, really, much less to him.

One day last week, sitting at her desk, she had picked up the pen to write an everyday, pleasant letter to him. But then the pen just lingered there, hovering over the flowery stationery like a seagull that couldn't land in the gusty wind.

Three weeks ago, during a boring lecture on co-signs in Trig 234, her mind began to wander. She stared down at her wrist and noticed her faint bluish artery. Her pulse throbbed there, beneath her pale skin. She watched that relentless, rhythmic, insistent pulse a few seconds, watched the blue artery rising and falling slightly, imagined it feeding the liquid to her lungs and her brain and then back to her heart. She wondered how many times it would beat during a day, and how many more times it would beat during her lifetime. A million? Five million? And how many did she have left? Just one hundred or two hundred thousand?

In the middle of that class, her heartbeats were the only calculation, the only sum, the only answer she cared about. She wondered just how much time she had left, and how much she still had to do—not just do, but accomplish.

She stood from her desk and walked from of the classroom, leaving her open math text with its puzzle of numbers. No explanation, no hesitation. She just walked out, as the professor and the other students turned their heads toward her in surprise. She never went back.

Though she excelled in her classes and got As on the tests, she felt guilty about dropping out. She didn't want to tell her mother about it and disappoint her. Janelle had such high hopes for her, writing supportive handwritten letters to her each week, assuring Mariah that once she got her degree, things would be great. But Mariah just couldn't force herself to go back to classes that began to seem so banal, so irrelevant, so out of touch with everything that was happening the world.

She was changing, evolving, she told herself, and she knew, instinctively, that this detour was something she needed to do. She wanted to be relevant. To make a difference.

"Hey, Mariah," a voice startled her from behind. "Planning a trip?"

She turned from the window of the travel agency to see Daniel, the anti-war group leader, standing behind her. He was wearing his trademark purple tie-dyed T-shirt, leather vest, and ripped jeans. Black and white buttons, anchored to his shirt, read **NO WAR** and **PEACE NOW**.

"Daniel," she said in surprise. He looked at her with penetrating eyes, a smile surfacing from beneath his dark brown beard. "I'm just on the way to the center," she said, self-consciously pushing back her hair that she had let grow longer. She was a little nervous in the presence of someone who seemed so dynamic and magnetic.

"Awesome," he affirmed. "It's great you're volunteering. We need way more people like you."

She lowered her gaze modestly.

He glanced down at the guitar case in her hand. "You play guitar?"

"Yes, and no. I'm waiting for it to inspire me."

Her response made him grin. "I'm sure it will. So," he said, arching one eyebrow, "You going to be at The Underground tomorrow?"

"Of course," she replied without hesitation.

"Cool. See you there, then." He took a few steps, then spun around and strolled back to her. "I like your commitment, Mariah," he said. Then he added: "Really. I'm not just saying that. I *mean* it. And not just your commitment. There's a lot to like about *you*." Daniel reached toward her and grasped her hand.

"Oh. Um, thanks," she said humbly. With the touch of his hand, she couldn't help but feel something, though she wasn't exactly sure what it was. A connection. An attraction. A direction.

A grin bloomed on his face. "We've *got* to talk more later," he said. "You know— to get to know each other. But hey, right now I've got a few hundred leaflets to print. The damn war never takes a day off, you know."

"Don't I know."

He whirled around and strode down the street in his suede boots, his khaki backpack swaying side to side.

Lately she had been hanging out at The Underground, a small coffeehouse crammed between two college bars on State Street. There, on Wednesday nights, she'd meet with people, people who cared about the country and its future. This committed group, called the SDS, discussed the war in Vietnam, and what it was doing to America. The meetings became her whole focus lately—this growing group of people who questioned authority, the establishment, and the way things were, as Daniel said, "in the plastic supermarket imperialistic racist America." At one meeting he told the group, "There's an election coming up next November, people. And if Tricky Dick Nixon gets in office, he'll step up the bombing and ramp up the war. But guess what?" He pointed to a few members in the group. "All of you guys out there under the age of twenty-one don't have the right to vote. But you can damn well get drafted to the military. You can damn well die for your country."

After just one or two meetings, Mariah began to feel suddenly close to the people in the group, and just as suddenly, far from her humdrum classes and dorm life.

When Daniel convened the meetings, it was clear that he was extremely articulate, and intelligent. He always spoke eloquently about what was really going on in Vietnam, about the villages being destroyed, the government cover-ups. "The body count you see on TV is a hoax," he said in one talk. "An inflated statistic. To give the impression that we're winning over there. Walter Cronkite is a pawn, people. The media is a pawn." Another evening he began the meeting with four simple words, spoken dramatically. "The Dow Chemical Corporation," he said. "Sound familiar? They make napalm for 'Nam, in case you don't know it. And guess what? They're recruiting right here on campus. We're going to stop that. I'm planning a sit-in in the Commerce Building next week." He rubbed his forehead thoughtfully. "Just be prepared to cry a little. The tear gas will most likely be flying. But hey, a few tears will be worth it! Right?" Members of the group called out in agreement.

One evening, Mariah was surprised when Daniel told the group, "You know, there's a place that's integral to supplying powder for 'Nam." He brushed his fingertips through his beard. "And it's right here in Wisconsin. Right in our own damn back yard. It's a place called the Strongs Ammunition Plant. It's over in Bluff Lake." A couple of the group members groaned. Someone called out "Screw those war-mongers."

After a few of the meetings, Mariah would join some of the activists who lingered afterwards. They drank coffee and read poetry and talked in rap sessions. The discussions weren't just rhetoric to her; their opinions really meant something. Some nights, Shane, a hippie with long brown hair and steel-rimmed glasses, would pull out his folk guitar and start playing protest songs, including some by Phil Ochs. Everyone listened intently and nodded. The group was a mix—students from small towns in Wisconsin and others from large east coast cities, a woman from a reservation in North Dakota, and a Latino guy who grew up in south L.A. Enthusiastic young women, claiming that women in America were second-class citizens, would call for women's liberation and women's rights. And several black students described joining the Civil Rights marches mobilized in Milwaukee. "Once you take your first step in a march like that," James, a handsome black newcomer, told the group, "You're changed. And you'll never take a step back."

That night, as the meeting was breaking up, Mariah stepped up to James, shook his hand and said "Thanks. For what you're doing."

James nodded. "For what we're *all* doing," he replied.

During those evenings, Mariah would lose track of time; meetings that began at eight stretched until one or two in the morning. She began reading Allen Ginsberg's poems, with lines like "America, I've given you all, and now I'm nothing." She memorized the first few pages of "Howl," a rant about how our country destroys the best minds of our generation. She studied essays about nonviolent resistance and civil disobedience. After reading Martin Luther King's *Letter from Birmingham Jail*, she posted, over her dorm desk, her favorite quote by King about how you acquire true freedom. She listened intently to lyrics by Bob Dylan and Joan Baez. She began to realize that these people—these brave, anti-establishment rebels—spoke to the real heart of the country. They envisioned a *better* America.

Meeting after meeting, Daniel espoused the spirit and commitment of those rebels. His words filtered into Mariah, and she began, steadily, to understand them. To believe them. And they made her feel electrified, and more alive than she'd ever felt. Made her feel like a guitar, silent for so long, suddenly playing a melodic chord.

Whatever was happening, Mariah knew one thing for certain: For the first time in a long time, she felt herself committed and grounded to something. Something meaningful. She was no longer standing in the quicksand of her former life. Last summer she told Phil she had absolutely no doubt that their lives would drastically change with college. She remembered how he just gave her an uncertain look, as if he didn't quite understand. Now, for her at least, that prediction was coming true.

As she cut across the quad near the bookstore and back to her dorm, Daniel's words resounded in her head. *I like your commitment, Mariah.*

And she wanted, more than anything, to live up to his words.

# CHAPTER 31

Late at night, Mariah opened her journal to the section entitled **The Non-Father** and began to write. The words came out spontaneously, feverishly. She entitled this entry "The Sand Father."

*I was just ten years old when I heard them arguing, late at night, in the study. Their loud voices woke me, and I crept down the stairway and stood, out of sight, listening. I heard Mom crying. I heard a few words and got the drift of the argument. "Damn it all!" Dad shouted. "If you'd never gotten pregnant..."*

*In an instant, my father's words changed my world. I realized I was a mistake. The house I lived in suddenly transformed, and the rooms that once seemed filled with love became dark with doubt and regret.*

*Dad, I could say a thousand, million things to you now, if I could only find you. But where are you? On an island somewhere, someone once told mom. But what island—Barbados, St. Marten, St. Lucia, Grand Bahama? Or maybe one of the hundreds of islands off Malaysia, or Indonesia?*

*Let's face it, Dad. You're like one single grain of sand on a huge beach. You're hidden there, somewhere, among the billions of grains, and they all look alike. Some days, I find myself sifting through the same pile of sand, searching for you. I keep scooping up a handful of sand and sifting it through my fingers, thinking I'll find that one grain. But how long can I keep doing this?*

*Questions, questions, questions. And no answers. No answers. No answers.*

A half hour later, she lifted the pay phone in the dorm lounge, dropped in a handful of quarters, and called her mom. The call woke Janelle, who was surprised to hear from Mariah at one-fifteen a.m.. "I miss you, mom," she began, "and I'm sorry."

"Sorry for what, dear?" Janelle said with a groggy voice, not quite understanding what Mariah was getting at.

"Sorry for everything. Sorry about you and dad. And the way he left you. Sorry about..."

"You don't have to apologize for anything, Mariah."

"I felt like we had to talk." She coiled the black phone cord around her index finger. "I should really call you more often, I know."

"It's so good to hear from you," Janelle exclaimed. "Even if it *is* the middle of the night."

"So how is work going, and all that?"

"I got a couple more temp jobs," Janelle responded. "The latest one has lasted a month."

"That's great, Mom. Where is it?"

"A law office. Downtown."

"That would be perfect for you. Just don't get..."

"I know, I know. Just don't get mixed up with another slick lawyer. You don't have to worry," Janelle said wryly. "I've learned my lesson."

An awkward pause followed.

"So, is everything okay?" Janelle questioned, sensing the anxiety in her daughter's voice.

"Sure. I guess. I feel like everything's...I don't know, sort of in transition."

"What about you and Phil?" Janelle questioned. "Are you two in touch?"

She stared at the front window of the dorm, which, at this time of night, appeared black, except for one faint security light on the lawn. "Somewhat. Yes. I mean, not all that much lately..." she hesitated. "Things are a little different between us."

"In what way?"

"It's hard to explain. I've got so much on my mind, Mom. It's school, it's what's going on at campus, it's...it's all the new people I'm meeting. Lately I feel a million miles away from Bluff Lake. But I can't help feeling a little lost sometimes."

"That's understandable, Mariah," Janelle said soothingly. "That feeling comes with the territory, doesn't it?" She let out a throaty laugh. "I guess we both feel it. But you're in a whole new phase of your life. And it's wonderful phase. You have to enjoy it, take it all in. But still, you shouldn't forget about Phil."

"Well, no, I won't," Mariah replied. "In fact, *I can't.*"

# CHAPTER 32

Mariah pushed open the door of the Draft Counseling Center, a small, makeshift office with fliers and leaflets splayed on mismatched tables around the room. Red and white peace symbol posters, along with black power and women's rights posters, stretched from the floor to the ceiling. Jamal waved to Mariah as she entered. Jamal, an intelligent black student from New York City and a black rights activist, had opened the center. He had rented the cramped space using funds from an anti-war group's donations. His usual orientation introduction for new counselors began with: "Did you know that black males are way more likely to be drafted and sent to Nam than white males? That's called black genocide, people."

"Hey, Jamal. What's up today?" Mariah asked as she sat down at a chipped, darkly varnished table, a salvage store purchase.

"A guy called here a half hour ago," Jamal began. "Sounded pretty freaked out. Said he needed to come down right away. Can you talk to him?"

"Sure," she said, pulling out a small stack of fliers entitled *Options for Draftees.*

The young man rushed through the door, a panicked expression washing over his face.

He grabbed a chair and sat down hard, while blurting out "Got my goddamn draft notice yesterday." His eyes seemed desperate, vacant, like something had been torn from behind them. "What the hell am I gonna do? My life is frickin' *over.*"

As Mariah talked to him—her voice empathetic—about his options, she couldn't help but picture the faces of the boys in the *Wisconsin State Journal* obituaries she read earlier this morning. They were Madison-area boys killed in Vietnam, and they all seemed so young, their faces floating above their military uniforms like smoothed stones. She pressed her fingertip on each face, trying to pay tribute to each one.

Now, from across the table, sensing the young man's anxiety, Mariah reached across and firmly clasped the boy's wrist, calming his shaking.

"You don't have to do this," she assured the boy. "Do you understand?" He gulped hard. "You have choices," she continued. "You *don't* have to go."

After getting to bed late, she woke at two a.m. with her mind racing. Unable to go back to sleep, she lit a cigarette, thinking it might calm her nerves. She stood at the fourth-floor window of her dorm room and gazed out at the skyline of Madison. In the foreground, Lake Mendota was a dark disc, with a dimly lit veil of the Milky Way above it. She looked out in silence, and could sense the pulse in her wrist, its tiny steady, relentless throbbing.

At times when she woke at night like this—which was almost every night, lately—her thoughts were turbulent and whirling. Sometimes she felt small, like a bubble rising from the deep middle of a huge lake. Other times she felt large, as if she were the lake itself. Tonight, her mind was especially unsettled after counseling that boy at the center. Though she tried to be strong and optimistic about his choices, she wasn't sure she had really influenced him.

Before leaving, he had broken down in sobs, then dropped the fliers she had handed him. He gave her a confused look and walked out the door. His sudden exit, without reaching a solution, made her feel frustrated. She wished she could have done more, and she sat silently at the table, wiping the burning tears from her cheeks.

"Doesn't look good for him," Jamal had said, shaking his head somberly. "He'll probably show up at the induction center. Like all the others."

But at least she had tried, Mariah thought now in the dim dorm room. She didn't feel the same about some of her fellow freshmen, who seemed oblivious. *The treadmill students*, Daniel called them, who wandered through the days like they were anesthetized. They'd eat breakfast at the commons, a bland bowl of oatmeal or two fried eggs staring up at them, daze their way through Geography 101, then plod back to the dorm to do a little homework. Evenings, at the College Club, which was a beer-only bar off State Street, they'd chug just enough 16-ounce taps of Old Milwaukee to get themselves drunk. The next day, hung over, they would start the whole routine again.

She knew she was different than those students. She needed to stay in touch with her passion. In one of her poems she wrote that her passion was like an ember, an emerald always glowing—no, igniting inside her. No more **Poems in Invisible Ink** in her secret journal, she vowed. These new words would be bold, meaningful, and *very* visible. These new words would sing. Not just sing, but shout, and be heard.

Her latest journal was filled with poems and song lyrics with images of oppression and war, about the dark whirlpool of death in a faraway place. She showed a few poems to Daniel, reading one aloud to him as he stared at her, his chin propped on his hands, his eyes pensive. "Yeah," he exclaimed, giving her an approving nod, "Heavy. You got it. You really got it."

Tonight, she snuffed out the cigarette in an ash tray. She stood at the window and pictured, again, the eyes of that boy in the counseling center, his bewildered, fatalistic expression. Would he resist the draft, like she advised? Would he defect to Canada? After all, if he could get there, the border was less than 500 miles away, a seven-hour drive. Or would he just report dutifully for his induction, his shoulders slumped, and then climb aboard a bus, the billowing exhaust rolling up around it?

There were too many questions, all of them fluttering in the wind.

Those haunting questions made her wish she was back in high school in Bluff Lake again, talking to Phil, late at night, on the fire escape. The wrought iron fire escape zig-zagged in the narrow space between the two-story brick walls of the theatre and a former hotel. Phil would climb a few steps on the rusty stairway, then reach down and pull Mariah up to the grated platform, where they'd both recline and gaze up at the narrow rectangle of sky above them. Lying there, they would talk for hours. She'd stare through the black iron gratings that sliced the sky into even, parallel segments. Sometimes she'd count the pinpoints of stars that were visible in the rectangle, then challenge Phil to do the same, to see if they came up with the same answer. Once, as they watched in awe, a meteor with a spiraling silver trail streaked through the narrow opening. As she thought about him now, she hoped Phil was still the same person, hoped he hadn't been hardened by his time at the plant.

The telephone in her dorm room rang, startling her, and her roommate rolled over and groaned. Mariah lifted the receiver.

"Hey," the voice said. "Yeah, it's me." It was Daniel. "We're both up late, I see."

"Do you always call people at two-thirty in the morning?"

"I do now," he said. "I was cutting through the commons after a meeting," he explained. "Saw the light on in your dorm room. And there you were, standing in the window."

"Oh."

"I'm at a phone booth down on State. There's a new coffee shop near here. It's open all night. We could talk. You know—about the war, about life, and all that." He waited a few seconds. "So, you want to meet up?"

"Yes," she answered, surprising herself, "I do."

# CHAPTER 33

This morning, with Karl gone for physical therapy, Frances crocheted a star-shaped white doily, the needles clicking faintly. She felt the words, the questions that kept rising inside her. Every day, her anxiety appeared as something different. One day, it was a faint hissing sound, like sand pouring into a container, the next day, it felt like clouds, billowing inside her. The questions were getting louder, more insistent, nagging at her. Dark words, angry words, words like storm clouds. Today, there seemed to be a storm somewhere inside her ready to rain. But she couldn't acknowledge it, so she tried her best to push it back down.

She told herself to focus on the doily, the needles moving in unison, creating a pattern extending outward from the middle. There were dozens of patterns, she knew; she had looked through her crochet book. There was the Cluster Stitch, the Butterfly, the Forget Me Not, the Whirl-A-Way. She'd made a dozen or so doilies, and today she'd decided on this Wish Upon a Star pattern because it was intricate and lovely. Not perfect, she knew, like those machine-made ones, but still pretty in their own way. She watched the silent cream-colored linen threads extend themselves in outward circles, forming a web. She listened to the clicking needles. Over and under, under and through.

Curious thoughts ran through her mind: Maybe this doily is a lot like me, she mused. The threads are connected from one to another but there are spaces in between. I'm connected to Karl and to Phil, and Phil to Karl, yet there are still so many spaces between them. And what good is a doily, anyway, if it's just decorative? Or just something to place on an end table and set things on? You weigh it down with vases of flowers, potted plants.

She pictured, these past weeks, the way Karl and Phil had opposed each other, but without ever saying a word. It's the way, when they're together, Phil stuffs his hands in his Levi pockets while Karl studies the intricacies of his fingernails. Their talk is like a map without directions, lines that never quite touch. Sometimes she thought their conversations might as well be printed on sets of cue cards they could read to each other. "Where's the Chrysler?" "In front." "Work go okay today?" "I guess." "Going out after dinner?" "Yeah." "Where?" "Don't know. Somewhere." "What'd you say?" "Nothing."

It bothered Frances, this lack of saying what they felt, this escalating tension between them. But what could she do about it? How could she make peace between them? What could a mother do to fix what's gone wrong between father and son? It didn't seem possible, so she always remained neutral when it came to the two of them.

Out of nowhere, Francis started to feel the panic again, those storm clouds rising inside her. She set the doily on the TV tray and stepped quickly to the phone in the hallway.

She dialed Mrs. Gruener's number. When Dolores answered, Frances heard the words burst from her mouth. "I don't know what I'm going to do."

"About what?" a befuddled Mrs. Gruener asked.

"About everything. About Phil, and Karl. And…and," she said, almost breaking into a sob, "this whole war thing."

Mrs. Gruener was silent for a few seconds. Finally, speaking slowly, she said, "You know we have to be strong, Frances. When I lost my boy over there, I learned how to be strong. It takes time. A long time."

Frances pictured the round-shouldered and slightly overweight Mrs. Gruener, standing by her kitchen window in her usual blue house dress, holding the phone close to her short-cropped reddish hair.

"But being strong doesn't make things right," Frances said. "It doesn't make anything right, at all."

"No, it doesn't. But, I have to tell myself that it was God's will. Some things just happen, and we don't know why. I pray about that every day."

She wondered how the woman could be so strong, after losing her boy like that. Frances saw her bowing her head at Mass every Sunday, and she wondered how Dolores found such faith, how she could keep from being bitter.

"Yes," Frances finally replied. "Pray. We'll hope and pray. That should help, right?" Her words sounded hollow as soon as she uttered them.

"Right."

Out of nowhere, Frances asked: "Do you need any doilies at your house?"

"What?"

"Doilies. I'm crocheting some. I'm about to finish a real nice Wish Upon a Star pattern."

"Oh, thank you, but I think I have enough. My sister makes them. Gives them to me every Christmas. But, um, thanks anyway." Trying to end the conversation, she said, "Well, I was just about to head out for groceries. And there's always the laundry. Frank has a few shirts he needs cleaned. He never runs out of those," she added, trying to laugh. "So, maybe we'll talk later."

Before she hung up, Frances needed to say the words. She felt like she'd shatter if she didn't say those dark, churning questions, the words she could never say to Karl. So she let them burst out: "Dolores, do you agree with what's going on over there? I mean, kids being drafted? And sent over there by the thousands? Boys dying. And what about Johnson, stepping up the bombings? It's wrong. God damn, it's wrong!" Frances never swore, but the words just burst out of her now, surprising Dolores as much as herself.

Delores was silent. Finally, she said, her voice choked, "I just don't know what to think anymore, Frances. I just don't want Danny to have died in vain. I pray for that, more than anything."

"Yes," Frances replied, not sure what she was agreeing with, but feeling like she should. She'd already stepped over her bounds with what she just said, and she knew Delores didn't need to take on the weight of her questions. "Yes," she said, steadying her voice. "I understand. I think we all pray for that." She turned toward the window, touched the spider plant's dangling tendrils with her fingertips.

"Um…are you, are you okay, Frances?" Delores asked, sensing something was wrong.

"Yes. I'm fine. Fine."

"Will you be at the Women's Sodality tomorrow?" The women's group was part of St. Stanislaus church.

"I will. And I'll see you there," Frances said, but she suspected Dolores wouldn't chat with her much at the meeting. The two were never too close. She shouldn't have called her today.

As soon as she hung up the phone, the feeling rose up inside her again.

To calm herself, she sat down again and picked up the doily. The pattern was almost done. She'd put something on this doily when it was finished, right? She'd set it on the varnished end table and place something on it.

But what? What would she put on it?

The two ceramic lamps in the room already had doilies under them. The granite bookends on the shelf had doilies beneath them. Karl's boxed agate collection had one, too. So what would weigh this one down? What would keep it silenced?

And would she, tonight at dinner, burst out with her tirade about the war? Would she stand up from the table and shout at the two of them to just stop the way they were acting with each other?

Over and under, under and through. Click, click, click. The sharp needles sounded like a clock ticking.

The sound seemed to get louder and louder. When it did, she dropped the needles and stood suddenly, bumping the TV tray with her thighs, knocking it over on the living room floor.

The doily sprawled, its spiderweb pattern folded in half.

She scooped up the doily from the floor; it draped over her open hand as if it was embracing it. She stared at the star-shaped holes between the cream-colored threads.

In the kitchen, she pressed the foot pedal of the trash bin. The lid opened wide. She stared into the silent mouth of the bin for a moment, then dropped the doily into it.

# CHAPTER 34

At one in the morning, Phil looked out the living room picture window. A late March snowstorm was predicted for overnight, and the weatherman on the Madison channel warned that it might be a bad one, snarling traffic, closing schools. Phil saw the first sign of the storm, a few flakes falling steadily.

His mind wandered. He hadn't heard from Mariah for months. On his desk calendar, he had crossed off the days since her last letter. Had her feelings toward him changed, he wondered, had the embers cooled? Were they steadily drifting farther and farther apart, like two continents that would never touch again?

He had sent her at least three letters since she stopped writing. The last one asked pointedly "When will I hear from you? Write soon, please. I need to know how you're doing." He waited for days, but there was no reply. Just a silence, a growing vacuum that filled the empty mailbox on their porch.

He knew Mariah could probably explain her lack of communication. She was most likely overwhelmed with classes and clubs. He understood that; her time was precious, she always said. She had told him, with enthusiasm, that she was positive her life would change once she arrived at college. At the time, he just didn't realize that this change might not include him.

He watched the snow slant at a 45-degree angle. It intensified, coating the oak tree branches, the porch railing, the neighborhood rooftops.

"Eight to ten inches," the weatherman had cautioned. "Gusty winds. No travel advised in the area. Road conditions will be poor."

Phil imagined his drive to the plant tomorrow. He pictured the Chrysler, suddenly out of control, doing a three-sixty. Pictured the car plunging down a steep embankment, the deep snow cushioning it, bringing it to muffled, harmless stop. Then, with the car stuck and out of sight, the steadily falling snow would cover the windshield, his vision turning white. Inside, with the ignition still on, he'd be tuning the radio to fading stations as he waited for rescue. He pictured himself, after hours of waiting, finally falling asleep in the front seat. Days later, a rescue crew might find him motionless and stiff, like some Neanderthal frozen inside a block of glacial ice, his mouth slightly open as if he was singing, his fingers still diligently clutching the wheel.

The absurdity of that scenario almost made him smile. He knew he'd be on the road at dawn as usual. The rear of the car might fishtail slightly right and left, but the big, heavy Chrysler with its reliable snow tires would never slide off County Road 12. After all, that highway, a main lifeline to the plant, was always a first priority during winter storms. City crews would clear the road, their steel plows sparking on the uneven surface, and behind them, more trucks would scatter salt and sand.

Phil knew the Strongs Plant never cancelled a shift. The damn plant: It never slept. It always marched steadily into the future to meet its weekly powder quota.

He suspected that he wouldn't sleep this night, either. He stared at the window, watching it gradually turn opaque as snow plastered against it. And he couldn't stop the sensation that everything—not just the porch and the houses, and the window, but his whole life—was steadily being covered over in a layer of numbing white.

# CHAPTER 35

"Mariah," Daniel said her name. He and Mariah sat at a small table in the coffee house. He said her name again slowly, then added "It's a really great name." He took a sip from his mug. "Reminds me of the sound of wind, almost. Or a song."

Mariah smiled. She had once looked up her name to learn the meaning of it. It meant "bitter," and also "beloved." A third meaning was "one drop of water in the sea." All three descriptions, she decided, seemed to fit her.

Soft instrumental folk music wafted through the speakers of the small shop that served organic foods and fair-trade coffee. Stools clustered around wood tables made from repurposed cable spindles. "You know," Daniel continued, "I really like the way you think. The way you communicate."

"Oh. Thanks," Mariah said humbly.

"I mean, you've got a good head on your shoulders." He gave her a pleasant yet probing stare. "And I've got an idea for tomorrow's action at the courthouse."

At their latest meeting, the group had planned a large protest and sit-in on the federal courthouse steps. A couple of the federal judges were extreme hawks; they were pro-war and pro-bombing. And one of them was clearly racist, having made several decisions against some indigenous Native American tribes. He also opposed the fair housing movement that black Americans were marching for.

"Oh?" Mariah asked. "What's that?" She lifted her glazed pottery cup, took a sip of coffee.

He leaned closer to her. "I want you to be there."

"Of *course* I'll be there," Mariah replied. "We just printed a new batch of fliers." At demonstrations, she and a thin girl named Hailey meandered through the crowd of onlookers and media people, handing out leaflets.

"I don't mean that." He gave her a meaningful nod. "I want you to be *up front.*

"Up front?"

"Yeah. At the mic. With me." Daniel always spoke to the crowd through a microphone connected to a speaker. At other rallies, he used a megaphone. Either way, his speeches could be heard for blocks.

When she gave him a slightly skeptical look, he continued. "I mean, I've heard you speak at our meetings. Let's face it. You're eloquent. You're articulate. And I want you right there on the front line with me. Not in the background."

"Thank you for thinking of me that way, Daniel," she said humbly. "But I don't know…"

"Yes, you *do know,*" he insisted. "The movement needs a woman's perspective." He spread his arms to his sides grandly. "The *world* needs a woman's perspective."

"Okay. But I'm not sure what I'd say," she confided, not completely confident that she could deliver a motivational speech to a large and diverse group.

"Just speak from the heart. Let your passion guide you. You know—like you always do." He gave her his patented charismatic grin. "Like you *always* do."

Mariah nodded. Of course, she was flattered. But it was much more than that. She couldn't help that sudden feeling from surging through her. She felt empowered. For the first time in her life, she felt really empowered.

# CHAPTER 36

Pulling a letter from the front porch mail slot, Phil saw the postmark from Madison and immediately recognized the swirling flow of the handwriting. He tore the envelope open and anxiously began to read:

*Dear Phil,*

*It's been quite a while since we've communicated, I know. Months, actually. And I haven't written or returned your calls. Well, I don't have to tell you that. I'm really sorry about being out of touch and I apologize. I do miss you, Phil.*

*Now, about what I've been doing lately…I've been so busy here that I've lost track of things. I won't bore you with details about my classes and how I've been attending them less frequently (yes, it's true—me, Mariah the scholar, skipping classes!) I won't tell you about the inane dorm antics I witnessed, like who short-sheeted whose bunk bed, or where the latest panty raid or beer kegger took place, or who won the bed race in front of the student union. I just don't relate to all that (sigh…).*

*Okay, back to my point…what I do want to tell you, Phil, is that my outlook on life is different now. I feel like I'm riding a wave of some kind and it's a big wave, too powerful to stop. My outlook has opened wide, thanks to the campus group I've joined. It's called Students for a Democratic Society. I'm amazed at how many great and committed people I've met in the group. They've intelligent, and have broad life experiences, coming from places like New York City and Berkeley and Boulder. We've organized marches and teach-ins and rallies on campus. Voter registration drives, too. The group's leader worked with the Free Speech Movement in Berkeley. To be honest, at times, the people in the group make me feel just average. The main point is, we're trying to change attitudes about this awful war.*

*Last night I had a nightmare of a soldier—I couldn't tell if he was U.S. or Vietnamese— standing next to my bed. He held his arms out to me. When I looked down, he had no legs—only bloody stumps. Lately, I feel some of those soldiers' blood on my hands. Did you ever think about those soldiers' blood on your hands? I feel like I should—no, have to—do something.*

*Yeah, I know what you're probably thinking—Mariah can't get off her soapbox. She's off on another of her philosophical tangents. If this were a Freshman comp essay, I'd probably get a C for preaching and a D+ for rambling. Sorry, Phil. Wish I had more pleasant things to write about. Sometimes I feel like my brain is on fire, and I just have to let those thoughts ignite.*

*Okay…I'll get to the point. What I'm asking is that you help us. What I'm hoping is that you can give us something we need. I can't really say more about it right now.*

*I'll try to be in contact with you—soon. It's important, Phil, and I hope you can do it. Maybe we can arrange a phone call this weekend where we can talk (in private, that is…)?*

*Hi to your mom and I hope your dad is recovering. How is he doing?*

*Love from Madison,*

*Mariah*

"Got a letter?" Karl's gravelly voice startled Phil.

"Yeah." Phil turned to see his dad standing behind him, one arm propping the paint-chipped screen door open.

"Who from?"

"Mariah."

"Oh," he said, his voice falling. "The girl."

"Um-hum." Phil folded the letter in half, in half again, held it between his thumb and index finger.

"What'd she have to say?"

"Not much," Phil responded automatically, and his dad seemed satisfied with that. Phil knew any of a half-dozen standard replies would do.

"Your mother's got dinner on the table. Time to come in."

"Sure. In a couple minutes."

"Make it thirty seconds," Karl countered, turning and letting the screen door clack behind him.

Phil unfolded the letter and re-read it. He was a little dismayed at the tone. He had hoped her words would have more to do with their relationship than rhetoric about politics. He wished there was more sentimentality—some kind, reminiscent words about their time together in Bluff Lake, some hints about seeing each other again. He wished she had written something like *Remember those nights when we sat near the river and traced circles on each other's cheeks with our fingertips, like we were trying to memorize each other's faces?* He skimmed her words again, looking for something he might have missed. He savored the words "I do miss you, Phil." Then he focused on her closing, "Love from Madison." Was it love from the town of Madison, he wondered, or love from Mariah? The words could be taken either way, he figured. Still, it was love, right?

His eyes stopped on the question "Did you ever think about those soldiers' blood on your hands?" The words haunted him. It was something he never really let himself think about. But now he recalled Tommy's cackle, and his words from last summer: "At least we're not working on the goddamn powder lines, Key. At least we're not making that shit for bullets that blast people in 'Nam."

He slipped the letter back into the envelope, then stuffed it into the pocket of his jeans.

What did she mean by that mysterious request to help her?

Then he looked down at his open hands. His palms weren't stained with blood. But they were covered with lines. How did they get so creased? he wondered. Why, in this harsh outdoor light, did they suddenly look so old? Was it the rough leather gloves he wore at work? Was it from gripping the paddle that he circled and circled for hours each day? He brought his hands closer to his face and stared at the tiny, creased roads, roads that led north, south, east, west, and crisscrossed all the directions between.

# CHAPTER 37

Mariah glanced around the room, wondering what she was doing here.

She hadn't planned it. She just let it happen. And now here she was, at one in the morning, feeling high from a joint and sitting in an unfamiliar room on the edge of a tie-dyed bedspread.

She looked around. An **END THE IMMORAL WAR** poster shouted at her from one wall, a clenched black fist rising through the words. Jim Morrison stared at her from the other wall, a thin beaded necklace sweeping across his bare chest, his outstretched arms reaching to touch the curled edges of the poster. On the desk: a few stubs of joints in twisted beige papers. Stacks of anti-war and fliers and leaflets shuffled themselves like a pile of fallen leaves. Words shouted from their pulp: **No More Vietnam!** and **Stop**! and **Resist!** In a wall mirror on the back of the door, her own reflection: disheveled hair, a sleeveless aqua blouse, tattered jeans and bare feet. What was that expression was on her face? She wondered. Why didn't she recognize it?

She shifted her eyes to the bulletin board riddled with pinholes. In its center was a picture from *Time Magazine* of a napalmed Vietnamese child, running on a dirt road and screaming. It was hard to pull her gaze away from it; the pain in that young girl's face made Mariah feel like the floor was shifting a little, as if it the room was afloat, and a tide was moving in. She was feeling the effects of the joint she'd smoked, but that horrifying image made her feel even more off balance.

She wondered why she had agreed to stop at this tawdry student apartment building on State Street. She had vowed, before she came to college, that she'd allow herself to experiment, to discover new experiences, and maybe this was one of them. Still, she wasn't sure, and she felt nervous, and guilty for being here.

"Wanna stop over?" Daniel had said, casually, an hour before. The meeting at The Underground had just ended, and Mariah and Daniel had lingered there, sitting on an overstuffed lime green sofa.

"Not sure," Mariah had replied, leaving it up in the air. Then she heard herself speak with a voice that sounded like it was far away. "Maybe." She let it ride that way, as if not deciding was a way of deciding.

"Maybe? *Maybe* is a word for procrastinators, you know."

"Oh?"

"Yeah. I hate that word." Daniel clenched his strong jaw shut a few seconds. "It's the reason things don't get done. The reason Congress tables motions to end the bombing. The reason things get delayed, get postponed. *Maybe* is the reason people *die*."

"I don't think it's quite that dramatic," she replied. "It's just a word." She took a sip, finishing her coffee, stared at the dark brown grounds at the bottom of the cup.

"Hey, words have power. When too many people say *maybe*, instead of yes or no, the world falls apart. Listen," he continued. His hair fell across his left eye, and he pushed it away with the sleeve of his tattered Army jacket. "Forget maybes. What our country needs is commitment. It's all about making a choice, and going with your choices. Right? A word like *maybe* postpones. It drops you off on a frickin" roadside at night with no place to go." He leaned close to her. His magnetic smile pulled her in. "So, you wanna stop over, or not?"

The door swung open, interrupting her thoughts. Daniel strode in and sat down close to her, his penetrating eyes staring at her.

"Hey," his voice slid through a grin.

"Hey," Mariah replied.

"I got a few more for us," he said, and held up four reefers in his hand. "This stuff is guaranteed to be good, so hang on. You ready?"

She didn't answer with a yes, or a no. She just watched the moment happen. *Indecision again,* a voice in her head cautioned. *But where had indecision ever gotten her? Where would it get her if she let her whole life continue to be stuck in neutral?*

He lit up one reefer with a Bic lighter, took a drag, held it toward Mariah and touched it to her lips. Though she was already high from an earlier joint and some wine, she inhaled the stinging smoke. She inhaled again. The smoke entered her and sent a massaging sensation throughout her body.

She held her breath and lifted her eyes to the four-paned window. Each pane was painted with a different peace symbol. One was painted white, with a small dove in the center, another was black, a third one was green, for the environment, she figured, and the fourth was red, the paint dripping below it like blood.

Daniel strolled to the stereo, dropped the needle onto a *Doors* album. As the first notes played—a deep base and a keyboard—he bobbed his head to a few beats. He whirled around toward her. "These *Doors* can really open doors," he said. "Their songs can fly. Really fly. *Fly.* That word tastes good on the tongue. I like that word. Don't you?"

"Sure," she said, though she didn't know exactly what she was agreeing to.

She knew she was taking a chance by being here. A dangerous one. Alone in this apartment. This guy who, though he was fascinating, she didn't know all that well. But she knew a part of her was testing boundaries. She was making choices, and not making them at the same time. That way, she avoided the guilt.

"I would be really great to fly with you," Daniel said, strolling back to her like he was walking in syrup. "You know that, babe?" He touched the joint to her lips again. She inhaled it and it seemed like purple smoke entered her lungs. She held her breath. It felt like sparklers were igniting inside them. In seconds, a swirling euphoria surrounded her. Strong stuff. Daniel mentioned once that he got the best dope from a guy on Mifflin Street. Imported from Colombia. As she exhaled, her brain seemed to separate from her head for a few seconds. She looked up at the clock's second hand, which seemed to be slipping forward, then backward, then forward again. She began to see things in colors: sounds, her feelings. She felt coherent one moment, then totally spaced out the next. Daniel had once told her he had contacts who would get him acid, hashish, whatever he wanted. Maybe the reefers were laced with something, a part of her thought. Maybe yes, maybe no.

She noticed the cracks on the ceiling branching like a map. They spread further, branches upon branches until they seemed to become a map. A map of America. A country she would change, make better.

When Jim Morrison's voice tunneled boldly through the black cloth speakers, she pulled her gaze from the ceiling. She saw one speaker tear apart for an instant as Morrison crooned the word *fire,* and then it sealed itself back again. As he sang "Light My Fire," she could see his voice, and his voice was blue. Midnight blue. Then, as it spiraled out of the speakers again, it turned to violet, then scarlet.

"You're far out," Daniel said as he paced, "Not to mention sexy." His pupils were wide, black. Two pools of shiny tar.

"Oh. Thanks." Her voice sounded like it was coming from somewhere down an echoing hallway.

"I mean, you're too fabulous, though you don't know you are. But still," he said, pausing in front of her, "I can see your doubts. I can read them. Your conservative Catholic upbringing, and all that shit. Plus, you've got issues. Baggage."

"Not really baggage." She was certain he was testing her with that comment. "It's just…just the past."

"You know…" he said dreamily, "The past is over and dead, Mariah. It's *gone.*" He didn't slur. Stoned as he was, he didn't slur, and though he was high, he seemed in perfect control. Always impassioned. Always tuned in. He lowered himself next to her on the bed. "Whatever's in your past, I don't care about it. Doesn't matter. What matters is right now. Right frickin' *now.*"

She felt high, higher than she'd ever been. She was in control for a few seconds, then wasn't sure what was happening, then back in control again. The room became a tilt-a-whirl at the fair, and then it stopped and was level again. The room felt like a train boxcar, moving quickly toward a pinhole in the horizon. Then it was stationary again.

Her thoughts were pink and lavender. She felt herself drift on top of those thoughts for a few seconds as if they were an inflated air mattress on a lake, and then they evaporated as she pinched her eyes shut and felt a rush, and she was being propelled backwards at a fast rate.

His soft voice stopped her from moving. His voice stopped her in the present. "What matters is us," he said. "You and me. Right now." His words sounded close, and still a long way away. A smile creeped onto his handsome face and then stretched itself into fullness. That smile was mesmerizing.

He placed his hand on the back of her neck, pulled her close, and kissed her. She knew the kiss would happen. She didn't say yes, she didn't say no. It just happened. His kiss was deep, and smoky. It was, like him, direct and intense, and it seemed to fill her, as if she was hollow and needed that filling. She felt a part of herself rise off the bed to the ceiling as the rest of her stayed there, her arms around his shoulders.

She felt the urgency of his lips, his tongue. As they kissed, he pressed her to the bed. She felt his hand gliding up her wrinkled blouse. She felt her passion rise, and she allowed it to rise.

A part of her let it happen. A part of her wanted to find out what the two of them were about, after these weeks of dancing around it. Another part of her, like an echo of herself, watched her in wonder—or was it disapproval? —from a far corner.

She felt his beard, soft and scratchy at the same time, as he kissed the bare skin at the nape of her neck. She felt guilty for a few seconds, but then let the passion spiraling inside her push it away. Because she decided not to resist, and didn't say *maybe*. Because the ceiling was a map of the America, the roads branching and branching outward like arteries, capillaries. Laced with something. Morrison's voice, like an echo in a distant tunnel. One word became two, two became four as the words bounced off each other. *Light light my my fire fire.*

Daniel lowered his body on top of her. But he was heavy. Too heavy, she thought. The weight of the whole world.

She felt like she was suffocating, everything twice as loud and twice as heavy. The ceiling too close to her. The second hand, too black and thick, weighing her down. The layers of the music and the dead soldiers in Vietnam and her own fears that she couldn't stop the war and her anger at her father for leaving without saying goodbye and Phil's face making her feel guilty. Her image in the mirror, the reflection she hardly recognized. All those things pressed down on her at once. All those things pushed her into the hard springs of the mattress. Daniel's hands, echoing, doubling in size and pressure as they touched her. She felt flattened, thin as a dry piece of paper. A flier pressed beneath a lead paperweight.

"C'mon," he said, his voice urgent. "C'mon!"

She felt like some layers were being peeled off her and she was suddenly herself again. "No!" she finally said, pulling the word from her nearly collapsed lungs. The word ricocheted off a corner of the ceiling and seemed to bounce back to her. "Stop!" she shouted. "Stop!"

He looked at her in surprise, his eyes wide. She pushed him off her and he sat up, slapping his bare feet to the tile floor. Daniel's face was red, flushed, sweaty. "Jesus Christ. What's wrong?" Tendrils of angry smoke curled from his mouth as he spoke the words.

Her high seemed to wash away in waves, then come back to her again. She stood from the bed and wavered. "I'm just... I'm just..." she couldn't come up with the words. They were somewhere out there like her mind was a vacuous gymnasium and they were helium balloons, bouncing in an upper corner of it. "Out... Out of breath, that's all. I can't breathe."

He shook his head admonishingly. "I thought you were—you know—about freedom." She stared at his pupils: large black ponds. The trickle of sweat on his forehead, meandering like salty streams leading to those ponds.

"I, I *am* free..." She could barely put together a sentence, her tongue thick, numb. "Light My Fire" was still playing. The song was only halfway through, though it seemed like a half hour had passed. She was stoned, then sober, then stoned. She didn't know which moment would be which. "I mean, I'm trying to be…"

"No you're not. You're a little hung up." His back arched like steel was filling his spine. He stood and paced the floor of the room, walking from one corner to the next. The sound of a guitar solo rushed from the speakers and spilled out like a violet stream, and with each step, it splashed around his feet. He took another hit of a joint, paused, and offered it to her.

"No." She pushed his hand away. "I've had enough."

When his frustration subsided, and he sat down on the bed, gave her a long stare that she could feel, like a heat lamp, on her face. His row of straight teeth lit up through his beard. He brushed back the strands of hair that had fallen over her face. "But hey," he said, his voice softening, "I can't be angry with you. You seem so *in tune*. You know, with the universe. And I like you at lot, Mariah. I like what you're *going to* be."

"Going to be?"

"Yeah. You're going to be *you*, that's what," he said, as if it was obvious. He grabbed her hand and caressed it. His eyelids lowered halfway; he tilted his head toward her. "You're gonna be *something else*. You're gonna fly. And I can wait for you, I guess." His voice was clear and strong as he said "Tomorrow, we march on the capitol, right?"

"Right," she replied.

"We're going to change things, you know. It's up to us. Nobody else. It's up to you and me. Together. No *maybes*."

"No maybes," she echoed.

Self-pleased, he tipped his head back against the dark paneling of the wall, a laugh erupting from his lips. He raised his arms and lifted his voice in a near-shout, as if he was speaking at a rally to a large group. "We're going to change the frickin" world, I'm telling you! The whole goddamn world!"

"Yes. That's just what I want," she agreed. She believed her words expanded and filled the whole room. "That's *all* I want."

# CHAPTER 38

At the corner of Second and Elm on a Saturday evening, Phil closed the glass panels of the phone booth behind him and waited. Ten minutes until he'd call. Mariah had sent him a brief letter, giving him her number and the best time to try to reach her. His heart sped up as he filled with a mixture of emotions. He was anxious to talk to Mariah, yet nervous about how they'd connect after not conversing for months. Also, there was that mysterious *something* she planned to ask him. Yet he wanted, not just wanted, but yearned, to talk to her again.

As he waited, Phil was acutely aware that the night seemed uncharacteristically silent. No nighthawks overhead, no doves cooing from eaves. No cars on the street, just a traffic light in the distance on Main, blinking at nothing. Through the foggy glass the lone streetlight looked frayed and hazy. Someone had scrawled *Diane + Jack, '66* with a marking pen on the glass. Other names and numbers were scratched into the aluminum base of the pay phone.

At ten o'clock, he dropped a few dollars' worth of coins into the phone, hoping for at least a fifteen-minute conversation.

"Mariah?" Phil exhaled her name as though he'd been holding his breath. It was hard to pull the air back into his lungs.

"Hi Phil," Mariah said. "So, how are you doing?"

"I'm doing. It's…it's good…" His words seemed to trip over themselves before he could say them. "To hear your voice, I mean. I really missed it. I mean *you*, I missed." His stumbling responses sounded like someone who could only spit out a few simple words at a time. *Like some cave man*, he thought, chiding himself.

"Me, too."

"So, um, how's Madison?" He hadn't intended to fall into small talk with her, but the conversation already seemed to be heading that direction.

"Great," she replied. "Really great. And things in Bluff Lake?"

"Well, um, you know Bluff Lake…"

"Do I ever." She stifled a laugh.

"How are classes going?" he asked. He hated the stiffness of this conversation that seemed to be dancing around what he really wanted to talk about, what he really felt. *Dammit, I love you*, he wanted to blurt, *and I hate it that you're so far away*.

"I'm not going to classes anymore," she admitted.

This didn't sound like the Mariah he knew, the honor roll student who was so committed to learning, to getting her degree. "Jeeze, Mariah. That sounds like a mistake." The comment came off as scolding, and he regretted saying it.

"There are other things besides attending general ed classes, Phil. A world of other things." Her voice intensified. "You heard about Robert Kennedy being shot. And Martin Luther King, two months ago."

"Of course I heard," Phil said. "It's really sad."

"Not just *sad*. It's awful. It's terrible." Her voice cracked. "People are thrilled about a space capsule orbiting the goddamn moon. And meanwhile we're sending thousands of boys to Vietnam to die. What's happening to our country, Phil?"

"I wish I knew," Phil sighed.

He could hear her take a deep breath as she seemed to collect herself. "I don't have much time," she said. "I need to ask you about something. Something *really* important."

"What is it?"

"I'm hoping you'll be able to get us some information."

"Information? About what?"

"Yes. About the plant."

"The plant?"

"We just need some details about the layout of the place. You know—like what buildings are where. Actually, some maps would be great. I mean, if you can get them."

"Maps?"

"We have inside information that there are maps in the security building. In your dad's office, to be exact." After a pause, she added, "And your dad's not using his office now, right?"

"So what are you saying?" Phil asked incredulously.

"Well, we're thinking, I mean, I'm thinking you might have access to his office."

Phil stared ahead. One radio tower in the distance, its red light blinking. "Oh," he said, getting her drift. "Oh."

"I wouldn't ask except it's for a big protest we're planning. Our group president needs them. We're just organizing it right now, and those maps would really, I mean *really* help. We'd figure out a way to pick them up."

"Oh," he repeated. The only word he could come up with at this point.

"Just so you know, this won't be just *any* protest," she said, her words rushing out faster and with sudden enthusiasm. "We're planning a major demonstration. It'll be peaceful, and it's going to be great. We're recruiting lots of people from campus." Her voice got louder. "We'll notify the TV stations so they'll cover it. We're contacting all the newspapers. The national media, too." Then she added "People are dying every day, Phil."

*I'm dying,* Phil wanted to say, but he didn't. *I'm goddamn dying here, and you don't even seem to care.*

"So, what do you think?" she asked again. "Can you help?"

Phil didn't answer for a few seconds. His silence joined the silence of the stuffy air inside the booth, the silence of the shade-pulled neighborhood, the silence of the whole town.

"I'll tell you what I think," Phil finally said, "I can't believe you called me to ask for something like this. *That*'s what I think." He rubbed a smear on the glass with his thumb. "I thought you called to *talk*."

When she didn't respond, he could hear, on the other end of the line, noises in the background. A door slammed, a voice called out. He recognized the chords of an acoustic guitar, and Bob Dylan's voice singing "A Hard Rain's a Gonna Fall."

Phil heard a low male voice call her name. Then the background became muffled as though she had put her palm over the receiver.

"So where *are* you, anyway?" Phil asked, sounding irritated.

"Off-campus. In a house."

"You at a party, or what?"

"Sort of. But not exactly. It's the group. We're just hanging out."

"What group?"

"I already told you about them. It's a group of activists. They're bright, intelligent. Committed to peace." Her voice was suddenly lilting again. "We're planning a sit-in tomorrow at the ROTC recruitment office."

When Phil didn't respond, she continued. "You know, the protest is going to happen, *with* or *without* maps. I imagine some people might even scale the fence and take the protest inside."

"They'll get thrown in jail," Phil responded, but then wished he hadn't—his comment sounding so cautionary.

"*Of course* they will," Mariah said as if that was obvious. "They might block entryways or doorways. Or take some other peaceful action. It'll raise awareness. That's the *point*, Phil." She took a deep breath. "When you really believe in something, you want it to happen. When you truly have passion, you don't wait for it to happen. You *make* it happen."

Phil heard the song in the background fade with a few high-pitched harmonica notes. There was a tense pause, and long seconds passed.

"Are you listening?" Mariah asked.

"Yeah, I'm listening."

"You just sound so…I don't know, flat. Sort of emotionless."

"Excuse me," he said, the words coming out sarcastically, "for sounding flat. But I'm working in a factory while my girlfriend is off at Madison, hanging out at houses and planning protests. Now she calls for the first time in months and talks to me like it's some kind of business meeting. Then she asks me to do something outrageous, like stealing. Pardon me for being just a little *numb*."

"Sorry if I came off like that, Phil. This *isn't* a business conversation. This is about life," she said emphatically. "You have to understand. This is the most important thing I've ever been involved in. It's…"

"It sounds like your plans are more important than anything else," he said, cutting her off. He swallowed; it felt like a ball of crepe paper inside his throat. "And I'm sorry I didn't go to Madison like we planned. I'm so *goddamn* sorry."

"I understand what you're feeling, Phil. But that's not what this is about." The connection crackled with static. The voices in the background got louder. "It's about this war. We've *got* to stop this whole damn thing…"

He leaned close to the glass, his breath fogging a circle on it. "And I suppose I'm a part of *this whole damn thing*. Is that what you're implying?"

"Well, Phil, the fact is…," she said, her voice sounding suddenly thinner, and farther away than the two-hundred miles it was traveling. "You *are* working for a war plant."

"I didn't have a choice," he said, raising his voice. "And you know it." Frustrated, he squeezed the receiver hard, his knuckles turning pale.

Phil heard the male voice say something to her again. He wasn't sure, but it sounded like *Let's go, Babe*.

"So who's that?" Phil asked.

"Um, the club president," she said, sounding flustered, "Our meeting starts soon. Can't talk much longer."

Sensing the conversation was about to end, he wanted, desperately, to veer their talk back to more personal things. He wanted to keep listening to her melodic voice that spiraled through those black wires and deep into his brain. "So," he wondered, "when are you coming back to Bluff Lake? For a weekend, I mean. And what about the summer?"

She was silent. He counted the seconds. *Three, four, five.* "Mariah," he asked again, "Did you hear me?" *Six, seven, eight.*

Finally, she said "I heard you. And the answer is, I don't know, Phil." There was sadness in her soft voice, but the words still stung. "I can't answer that. I can only say maybe."

"Why not?"

"I just…I just…." She faltered. Then, momentarily, the old Mariah surfaced again. She laughed and said "It's so hard to figure out the future, isn't it? It's so damn hard. And confusing." Then she added tenderly, "I do miss you, Phil. I really do. And I wish we could figure out how to see each other."

"You wish?" he questioned.

In the background, the male voice, sounding impatient, called her name again. "Okay, okay," she said, away from the phone. Then back to Phil: "I have to cut this short, Phil. I'm sorry."

"So am I."


After she hung up, he stood there a few seconds, listening to the hollow buzz of the dial tone. The ten holes in the rotary dial stared at him, empty metallic eyes.

As he pressed the phone back on its cradle, a beat-up red and crème Chevy, its muffler skimming on the street, skidded to a halt at the stop sign. Inside, a group of high school guys and girls he didn't recognize were out for the night. One of them drank from a quart bottle, passed it to the person next to them. Phil heard the cranked-up music as The Kinks' "You Really Got Me" thrummed through the rolled-down windows. The teens swayed to the song, their hands in the air.

Phil pushed at the folding door of the booth, and it jammed. He tried to step out, but got stuck halfway, one leg inside, one leg out. When he jostled there a few seconds, a guy in the car mocked him, yelling "Hey man! You having fun?" The kids' guffawed as the tires squealed and they sped off.

Phil rammed his fist hard against the door of the booth, springing it open. He thought, for an instant, of Clark Kent in those Superman shows he had watched on TV as a kid. But he knew he was no hero, no Superman.

He stepped from the phone booth as himself. Just himself, Phil Keyhoe. No red cape and no tight blue jersey gripping his rippling muscles—just a thin guy in a plain tan jacket and a faded pale blue button-down shirt. Just a guy, feeling alone right now, an ordinary guy who couldn't fly, caught here in the middle of a little town in the middle of a night sky that seemed so dark and vast that he'd be lost beneath it forever.

# CHAPTER 39

A few weeks later, on a warm early spring Saturday afternoon, Phil picked up the phone in his living room.

"Phil," a voice said. It was Tommy's mother.

"Hey Mrs. Laudermilk," Phil said pleasantly.

"Can you stop over?" she asked abruptly, her voice shaky. "We have something to…to tell you."

"Well sure, I guess," he said, wondering what this was about.

Phil drove to the Laudermilk house, a modest brick ranch-style home with a painted white fence in the side yard and trimmed shrubs in front. Tommy's dad worked at the post office and was big on upkeep and home maintenance.

Tommy's mom, dressed in tan slacks and a white blouse, was standing in the front doorway, waiting for Phil. Anguish filled the face of the usually jovial and smiling Mrs. Laudermilk.

"I thought I should tell you in person," she said. "I mean, because you're his best friend, and all," she began.

Phil blinked at her in anticipation.

"Tommy's been wounded."

"What?" Phil said, stunned, the words slowly sinking in.

"In Vietnam. We…we just got this today." She held out a telegram with a quivering hand.

*We regret to inform you that your son PFC Thomas J. Laudermilk, 2nd Battalion, 2nd Infantry, C Company, has been wounded in action in the performance of his duty and service of his country. I realize your great anxiety but nature of wounds not reported and delay in receipt of details must be expected. You will be promptly furnished any additional details received.*

"Oh," Phil felt like his breath was punched out of him. "Oh, that's terrible. I'm…I'm sorry…"

Tommy's dad Duane appeared behind his wife, his face solemn and blank. He put his hands on her shoulders as if to steady her.

"Duane and I are still hoping to find out more, though," she said. "I mean, we don't know how bad he's injured. Duane's been trying to call the Army headquarters. And the Defense Department. But…but he keeps getting a runaround. Nobody has any information." She broke down in a sob, and Phil gave her a hug.

As he walked slowly toward his car, he couldn't describe the emotions that raced through him. He was upset, and that feeling turned to anger, and anger to frustration. Pausing by the Rambler, he glared at the plant's ID numbers that showed faintly through the paint on the car's front door panel. *Govt. Issue 3350.* Tommy had often made fun of those numbers once, calling Phil's car "The thirty-three fifty-mobile." Suddenly Phil couldn't bear having those numbers on his car, a vehicle which was used at the Strongs Plant for a few years. The car was decommissioned, put up for auction, and Karl had bought it and gave it a makeshift paint job.

Right now, Phil hated those numbers, hated them.

A few minutes later, Phil exited Henry's Hardware with a can of black spray paint. Reaching the car, he aimed the nozzle at the door, then circled the can around and around, covering the numbers until they were gone. He never wanted to see those damn government numbers again.

*Nature of wounds not reported,* Phil thought as he drove aimlessly on a county road. *What the hell did that mean? How badly wounded was he?* Then more thoughts entered his head: *Would the Laudermilks receive a second telegram, one they couldn't imagine, even in their darkest nightmares?*

A few miles outside town, Phil recognized the familiar slant of the trees, the narrow road that led to the small park and a water-filled quarry where he used to hang out. He pressed his foot hard on the brake and the worn tires grabbed, skidding on the hard-packed dirt.

Phil thought of the hot summer days, freshman year, when he and Tommy swam in this deep, spring-filled quarry. Its clear water was surrounded by a shoreline of quartzite rocks. Tommy loved to do the cannonball and send up a big crown-shaped splash.

"I heard this thing is spring fed," Tommy once commented as he swam. "Everybody in town claims it's like a frikkin' fountain of youth. Damn, I feel younger already. In fact, I think I'm just reaching puberty," he chuckled. "How about you, Key?"

After swimming, they sat on the sun-warmed rocks, talked about school, girls, music, and, sometimes, the hazy horizon of what was ahead in their lives.

Today, a shiver rushed through Phil as he thought about Tommy being wounded. More disturbing thoughts followed: *Would Tommy survive? Would he ever see him again?*

He picked up a round stone, then pictured that day at the plant when he and Tommy threw rocks at that foil-wrapped pipe. *What was in those pipes?* Phil wondered again. *Water? Blood? Tears?*

Phil threw the rock into the middle of the pond, then picked up another one and threw it, hard. *God damn the Army,* he thought. *God damn the draft, and Uncle Sam.* He threw stone after stone, and then he just kept throwing them until it felt like his arm was being pulled out of its socket.

He lifted the receiver, and with shaking fingers, he dropped a few quarters into the slot. He heard the metallic clinking as they cascaded into the pay phone.

He listened to the phone ring—once, twice, three times.

The only person he could talk to right now.

He heard her answer. When she did, all he could exhale was "Tommy." He was out of breath, like wires were wrapped around his throat. "Tommy...."

"Phil, is that you?" Mariah asked.

He nodded as if she could see him, then pushed out a "Yeah."

"What? What's wrong?"

He swallowed hard. Then the words rose up from the back of his throat. "Tommy," he rasped, "He….he…" He stuttered over the heavy, metallic-tasting words. "He's been wounded. In Vietnam."

Mariah's cry of disbelief poured from the receiver and filled the booth. "Oh no, Phil," she cried, "Oh God! How bad is he hurt?"

"We don't know. Nobody knows."

Neither one spoke for a time, but Phil could tell, by the whimpering sound traveling through the thin black telephone lines, that she was sobbing.

"This war," Mariah finally said with a quivering but harsh voice. "This *goddamn war*. I hate what it's doing to our country."

He knew exactly what he needed to say next.

"I've decided to help."

"Help?"

"The maps. You said you needed those maps. For a protest. I'll do it. I'll do whatever it takes to get them for you."

# CHAPTER 40

It was the middle of the night, and Phil couldn't sleep. He stared out at the neighborhood from the small second-story window in the hallway.

The whole town was asleep, unmoving, as if it was an image etched in tin: the silvery power lines, the tall oaks and elms, the streets, flattened with fresh coats of tar, the tin rooftops and gables of the houses, vapor frozen above a few chimneys. Tacked high in the background was the quarter moon's bright white crescent, its tips so sharp it looked like they could puncture the sky. Even the few pale clouds seemed to be motionless, as if they, too, were asleep.

Everything seemed to be asleep, except Phil.

For hours, he'd been wrestling with his conscience. He knew what he was about to do was wrong. He also knew that, it in some ways, he could justify it. Then there were all those gray areas, whirling in his mind. Tonight, questions filled his brain like leaden weights, and he didn't know if he could go through with his plan. Right, wrong, right, wrong: the words circled him, and he felt paralyzed, holding his breath.

The thought of Mariah helped, making him feel like he could breathe again. Mariah, giving him answers. She was the sunrise, splitting the darkness. He imagined that she might be up at this late hour, as she often said she was. Perhaps she was thinking about him and staring at this same sky. He imagined that, somewhere out there, their vision intersected.

"You're up." His dad's voice startled him. It was three in the morning, and his father was on the way to the bathroom. Karl, barefoot in striped pajamas, walked closer.

"Um, I guess." Phil fidgeted.

"You're never up in the middle of the night," Karl said, keeping his voice low, so he wouldn't wake Frances. "So, is it Tommy, then?" Karl asked.

"Yeah," Phil agreed. It *was* about Tommy, of course, along with everything else.

"We all feel bad about him," Karl said. "Wounded in battle. But damn, that's the chance you take."

Phil nodded.

"Okay," Karl advised, "Better try to get some shut eye. So you're in shape for work tomorrow."

Crunching across the parking lot, Phil punched in early and angled toward the supervisor's building. At the entryway, the double steel doors blocked him. Above it, a large white sign with black lettering: **All Visitors Must Check In At Security Desk. Absolutely No Unauthorized Personnel Allowed.** A thick, scratched glass pane, like a drive-up window at a bank. A slightly pudgy middle-aged woman, dressed in a white blouse and a black skirt, looked up from her typewriter. Her round face was framed by reddish-brown chin-length hair.

"Can I help you?" she asked through a metallic speaker.

"Um, sure. I need to get some things. From my dad's office, I mean."

"Your dad?"

"Oh, yeah. Keyhoe," Phil said, backtracking, trying not to sound so nervous. "Karl Keyhoe. I'm his son, I mean."

She nodded and stood from her desk. Her name tag read *Midge*. "Oh, of course. Karl. How's he doing these days?"

"He's doing okay," Phil replied stiffly. "Yeah, okay."

She peered at Phil's ID badge, just to make sure: in the faded color photo, Phil was caught in a drowsy morning half-smile, his first day at the plant. She read his name aloud. "Yep. You're who you say you are, all right."

Midge, grabbing the key to Karl's office, reached up and pressed a black button on the wall. Phil stared at the second door, security-locked from the inside. *Everything sealed in this place,* he thought, *so nothing can get in, or out.* He heard a wavering buzz, the bolt slid back with a clunk, and she pulled on the handle.

Inside, the two of them passed a guard, who gave Phil a stony nod. Midge led him down a narrow hallway. Above them, suspended by metal brackets, were pastel green painted pipes and 1940's ductwork. As Phil trailed behind, he started to wonder if he could really do this. He wondered if he should just mutter *never mind* and walk back out, letting the thick doors seal behind him.

"So what things does he need?" Midge asked.

"I've got kind of a list," Phil said, pulling a piece of paper out of his coveralls. On the paper was written a bogus list Phil compiled last night when he couldn't sleep. *Safety Manual. Stapler. Backup eyeglasses from right desk drawer.*

"How nice that you're helping out," she beamed. "You're quite the good son."

"Um-hum."

She unlocked the office door with a large square frosted window. Above it the sign read **Karl Keyhoe, Security Supervisor.**

"Let me know when you're done," she chirped, walking away, "and we'll buzz you out." Phil was relieved she didn't follow him in or hover in the doorway.

Inside, Phil glanced at his father's desk. Papers stacked in orderly piles. A dark brown blotter, centered in the middle. A desk calendar in one corner and a small porcelain military tank decorating the other. Sealed inside a glass bubble paperweight was a picture of the family, with Phil as a newborn.

He pulled open the desk drawers and found the usual stuff: tape, plant stationery, black pens with **Property of US Govt** written on them, clusters of paper clips. Packs of Wrigley's Spearmint gum—which his father chewed daily to ward off the nervous urge to smoke. The middle drawer contained rubber-banded stacks of public relations fliers about the plant. The vintage ones, in the bottom, dated back to World War II, and featured corny cartoon images of men and women, their mouths proclaiming: **We Make the Best Powder in the World. Keep 'Em Shooting!** Another flier depicted a drawing of a tough-looking, strong cheek boned GI in full military gear standing proudly next to a Strongs Plant worker, exclaiming **Work for Victory, Shoulder to Shoulder!**

In the bottom drawer were empty manila folders, waiting for labels. Phil wondered: *How the hell am I going to find maps?* He could feel the sweat forming and trickling down his forehead, despite the building being air conditioned. He glanced up at the wall, noticed a framed family portrait of the three of them. Phil was a sixth grader, and they had posed in front of the quarried limestones of St. Stanislaus Catholic church. Frances stood behind Phil, beaming, her hands pressed firmly on Phil's shoulders as if he might rise from the earth. A thinner Karl posed rigidly, leaning slightly to the right in his white shirt and blue tie. In his hand, a thin, blurred white shape: a cigarette he was about to light. It was Phil's confirmation day, the day he was purified, his soul cleansed, the day he vowed to know the difference between right and wrong.

He turned to the file cabinets along the wall. Pressing on a latch, he pulled out a long drawer, bulging with stuffed folders, their tags slightly faded. Just as he had expected from his father, everything in alphabetical order: *Accident Reports. Building and Grounds Reports. Construction plans. Directory of Foremen's Names. Emergency Procedures. Fire Hazards.* In that way, his father had the whole plant categorized and placed into the dry open mouths of manilla folders.

But nothing under M for Maps. He flipped nervously through the files, and the only tab with an M was *Maintenance.* His Dad's favorite word. Anything that's not maintained falls apart, he always said. Phil pushed the drawer and it closed with a loud thump. He was sure someone could hear it. He pulled out another drawer. Nothing under M in this one, either. Anxiety began to fill him, as his eyes scanned the tabs. Then he spotted one that read **East Quadrant Maps**. He quickly lifted the file. Why didn't he figure his father would, like everything else in his life, have them divided that way? Why didn't he figure that everything—the whole world, even— would fit into four easy categories: East, West, North, South?

He pulled out the **West Quadrant Map** folder, and inside were individual blow-up maps of the buildings in that area. Seeing a shadow move across the opaque, frosted window of the office door, Phil froze. What would he say, he wondered, if a supervisor opened the door and discovered him there? "Just going through my old man's files, that's all," Phil would say with a nervous grin. "Just checking up on him. Y'know?"

As the shadow disappeared, Phil pulled the maps from each of the folders, folded them into thirds, unbuttoned his coveralls and slipped them inside, stuffing their sharp edges under his belt.

Then, his pulse throbbing in his temples, he hurried back to the desk and hastily grabbed a few pens and the glass paperweight. When he bumped a logbook, and it fell behind the desk. "Damn," he said under his breath as he knelt behind the desk to pull it up. As he reached for it, he brushed against a tangle of extension cords and spider webs. Lifting the logbook, he noticed something else: A book of matches, covered with dust. On it was printed an American flag with the heading **Freedom Lights the Way.** On the back was written **Support Our Boys** and an image of a World War II soldier. Inside, one pink-tipped match was missing from the book. Phil dropped the matches back where he found them.

Phil glanced toward the window, where outside, the American flag was whipping in the wind. He could hear the chain clanking against the aluminum pole. At the same time, he was certain he could hear his own heart, clanking against the inside of his ribs. Right and wrong and everything in between struggled there, inside that hollow space.

On his way out, Midge sidled up to him. "So, find everything you were looking for?"

"Yep," he said, his voice tight, "Sure."

"Hey, who's this?" the front door guard asked. The man was about six feet four, with a square-shaped head and a close-shaved crew cut. Most of the guards Phil had encountered here were paunchy and middle aged, but not this man, who looked about thirty, and was bulked up like a weightlifter. This guy was in prime military shape. Front-line security.

"Keyhoe," the woman answered. "It's Phil, right?"

Phil nodded.

"He's picking up a few incidentals," Midge continued. "For his dad."

Phil clutched the notebook and pens in one hand, the paperweight in the other, the little family staring up at him.

The guard gave Phil a suspicious look. His muscular arms crossed, he stood between Phil and the door. "We always check visitors on their way out," the man said severely, eyeing Phil up and down. "You know—so no government secrets are leaked or nothin'. So I'm gonna have to frisk you, then." The guard took a step closer to him. "Arms out to your sides," he commanded.

Phil froze, and felt the thickness of the maps stuffed beneath his T-shirt.

"Hey," the guard finally said, leaning back with a laugh, "Just kidding. I ain't frisking Karl Keyhoe's kid." Chuckling, the man turned, pressed the red button on the wall. Phil pushed through the door and hurried out.

"Tell the old man to heal up real soon," Midge called after him. "We need him back here. More than ever."

Outside, Phil tipped his shoulders against a splintered utility pole. He leaned there as long as it took for the tremors from the earthquake inside his body to subside.

Then a question he couldn't ignore surfaced: *What, exactly,* he wondered, *was Mariah and her group planning to do with these maps?*

# PART
FIVE

# CHAPTER 41

It was almost like a ceremony, he thought.

Karl snapped the ignition on the Chrysler and the engine started quickly, letting out a low-pitched whirr. He placed his palms on the steering wheel and at that very instant, he felt it—a powerful sensation that began in the engine, then glided to the dash, then right up through the vibrating steering wheel and into his wrists, where his pulse beat its steady rhythm.

And it felt good.

Backing out in the darkness, Karl thought about the inside of his heart. He pictured the layers of plaque chipped free and made harmless as the blood-thinner meds dissolved them little by little. Or so he liked to think. Whether it was scientific or not didn't matter. It was the way he pictured it this morning, and that's the way it was.

A newly installed One-Way sign pointed down Main toward the resurfaced County Road 12. His dashboard compass, bobbing in the thick liquid, aimed east. Everything pointing in one direction this morning, he thought. Everything smooth.

He glanced at the passenger's side. Phil, in his typical morning daze.

No need for conversation. The hum of the tires on the pavement was like a song, rising steadily in pitch as they passed the city limits sign. Karl was focused, already planning what he would accomplish this morning.

Halfway there, a sudden rain shower started, and Karl flipped on the wipers. The rain poured down harder for a minute, but then, in another mile, they drove out from under it. The shower stopped abruptly, and the rising sun carved its way through the dense clouds. Karl spotted a rainbow, its base touching the top of the bluff. Perfect, he thought. A little rain, and then the clearing.

Earlier that morning, Francis had hovered around him at breakfast, saying things like "It's so good you're starting again," and warning him not to do anything strenuous out there. "No lifting," she cautioned, her lips pursed like prunes. She had insisted on packing some health foods for his lunch—extra fruit and granola. "And you've got those meds with you, right?" she asked.

She was referring to the tiny, rice-sized nitroglycerin pills he was told to take if he had any sudden pains. Weird, and funny—the plant had a nitroglycerin area that produced rocket propellants. Damn, he thought, chuckling—it fixes the heart, and helps the war effort at the same time.

On the steady descent to the plant, the tires hit tar strips with a thump-thump-thumping sound, like a low-pitched drum. Karl felt the soft vibrations through the floorboards and he liked the sound. It reminded him of a steady heartbeat—rhythmic, never quitting. He believed his own heart was beating in synch with the tar strips on the road, beating in synch with all the other men who were headed to the plant, with all the workers across America who were, like him, on the way to do an honest day's work

Today, Phil strolled next to Karl as they made their way toward check-in. Not like that first summer, when the boy always insisted on lingering in the car to play the damn radio until the last minute. Phil was right there beside him, the way it should be: father and son, shoulder to shoulder. Maybe the boy was finally growing up a little, Karl thought.

Karl glanced at the oversized forty by seventy-foot flag at the entry to the plant. As it fluttered in slow motion, the two of them strode right through its huge ripping shadow.

Sure enough, he thought. A ceremony.

"Hey, Karl," a voice called from across the lot. It was Al Kreske, who sold his restaurant downtown and now worked in the admin offices. "You're back!"

Karl beamed and nodded.

Karl Keyhoe was back. Definitely back. And this time he was even stronger than ever.

# CHAPTER 42

This morning, the hissing began again.

Francis had heard it before, that faint sound that always put her on edge. Was it a city crew truck, pouring sand or gravel onto the street outside? She wondered. Or something else?

With Karl and Phil both gone to work for the first time in months, she was here in the house by herself, surrounded by the soft quilt of the morning. She should be happy with this time to herself, she told herself. Instead, as she cleared the dishes from the rack and stared at the lilac bushes, their bare branches scratching at the cracked kitchen window, it made her feel uneasy. To her, the house felt hollow—every small sound echoed off the corners of the high ceiling plaster.

But what was that odd hissing sound that seemed to magnify, louder than before? It seemed to begin in the cupboards, fill the empty sink. The neighbor's dog, barking from its wire kennel, didn't drown it out. Today, she had lots of things to do, of course—a backlog of laundry to wash, a grocery list to cross off, and begonias by the side of the house that need watering before they wilt. But still, the hissing was distracting her. That irritating sound, like sand sifting through an hourglass.

It was just in her head, she told herself. It must be tinnitus or something.

Her mind flashed to the morning news. An image of a wounded GI in Vietnam appeared on the screen. A red flower seeped through the white bandage tied around his forehead. Then body bags were being unloaded at an airport. Those black plastic cocoons, with name tags, held someone's son, she knew. Someone's *son*. She could almost hear the bags hiss as soldiers slid them down the ramps from the cargo planes. She could almost hear the sound of those long zippers on the bags. The disturbing footage was followed by an upbeat commercial for Palmolive Soap, a woman giddily washing her hands.

How long could she keep silent about things? she wondered. How long before all these thoughts made her crumble from the inside out? And who could she talk to about what she's feeling? Not Phil—it would trouble him too much. Certainly not Karl. Not Mrs. Zanslow, next door, who has a boy over there in Vietnam right now. Not the ladies in her card club. Who would ever listen to me? she wondered—I'm just a housewife, a fill-in secretary, a woman you see each week at Super Valu, mumbling to myself as I read my weekly shopping list.

That evening, with Karl reading in the den and Phil in his room, Frances sat on the couch, watching the Ed Sullivan Show.

Ed introduced a magician in a black cape and top hat. As the orchestra music played, his female assistant, wearing a pink sequined outfit, laid down in a rectangular box on a table at center stage. The magician lifted a large metal saw above his head so that it gleamed in the spotlights, tapped it twice with a hammer, and then began sawing the woman in half. The saw cut all the way through the box and the table and then, with a flourish, the magician rolled the two halves of the table away from each other. The woman's head turned toward the audience and beamed as her feet—ten yards away—wiggled from the other half of the box.

The audience gasped, and Frances felt herself gasp, too, there, alone in the living room. As her fingertips touched her stomach, she felt an empathetic, searing pain, and she pictured her midsection, sliced perfectly in half as if you'd cut a melon.

Later, she couldn't sleep. It was already past two a.m., and she couldn't stop thinking about that magician. She sat up suddenly in bed. Is that me? she wondered. Am I that woman? Cut in half just like her? It was as if she was being pulled apart, half of her on one side of the stage, half on the other side. This war, doing the cutting, she thought. This war. It's like some dark magician, cutting me right down the middle.

She heard, again, that sound begin in her head. She tried to stop it by thinking of the songs she loved as a girl, the crooning voices of Perry Como, Frank Sinatra.

But she couldn't push the sound out of her head. It was a dark, hissing sound, like a saw sliding back and forth, back and forth, cutting through something.

The sound became steadily louder, louder, louder.

She eased out of bed without waking Karl, then rushed down the darkened stairway and fumbled for her purse. Flipping on the desk lamp on, she grabbed the phone from its cradle and, even though it was the middle of the night, dialed the number. It was a contact number for a group—Women Against the War—organized by university women from Madison. She had noticed their small flier tacked to the corner of the Want Ads bulletin board at Super Value.

The phone rang once, twice, three times.

A voice on an answering machine said to leave a message after the tone.

The moment she spoke, Frances' voice finally made the hissing stop. "Um, hello. I'm…I'm Frances, Francis Keyhoe," she said haltingly. "I'd…I'd like to talk to someone. Or join one of your meetings. Maybe I'll…I'll call back tomorrow."

# CHAPTER 43

Leaning over his desk, Karl sorted through a stack of safety reports, alphabetizing the thin carbon-paper copies. A, B, C, D. Able, Baker, Charlie, Dog—those were the code words for the alphabet he learned in the Army. *Focus*, he kept telling himself this morning, though something else was on his mind: Today was Wes Brennan's first day back after the funeral. His son was killed three weeks ago. Somewhere outside Hanoi. Enemy artillery fire took him.

Brennan worked two offices down from Karl, and as he walked past the doorway, Karl called out "Hey there, Wes."

Brennan gave him a stoic nod, the usual pleasant expression missing from his face, then paused in the doorway. Always diligent, Wes spent most of his days writing orders for building repair crews and filing reports that were passed on to Karl for approval. Karl admired the way Wes filled out the orders quietly, but reliably, his face intent. By the end of the day, his thumb and index fingers were a bluish color from the carbon paper.

"I heard, you know," Karl said, after a few seconds of trying to come up with the right words. "About the boy." He shifted his eyes briefly to the ceiling light bulb in the hallway, inside a metal cage so it wouldn't get broken if someone hauled ladders or equipment. The light made Karl squint. "I'm sorry." He stood, walked over to Brennan and extended his hand. "Real sorry."

Wes made a sound as he shook Karl's hand. It wasn't "Thanks," or "Sure," but a muffled, guttural sound from inside his chest. His eyes looked glazed, and a pained expression filled his face, deepening the wrinkles on his forehead.

Neither of them spoke for a few seconds. Karl couldn't imagine the depth of the man's grief. And he couldn't stop a thought from entering his mind: his own son, Phil, being drafted, sent to Vietnam, then coming back in a body bag. HR bags, the airmen who flew the C130 transports called them. Human Remains.

To push the thoughts away, Karl picked up a stack of safety reports from a drop box, tapped them a few times, straightening their corners, then changed the subject. "So, how's everything been going since I've been out? At the plant, I mean." The place had hired almost five-hundred new workers in the months since Karl had been gone.

"You know the plant," Wes said. "It's steady out here. I took two weeks off, though. After it happened."

"Sure," Karl said empathetically. "I can understand that."

"When I got back, stuff was piled sky high on my desk," Wes added, lifting his hand to eye-level. "Sky high..." he repeated. He lowered his hand.

"Yeah," Karl said, trying to fill in. "Everything goes on, doesn't it. It just keeps going. Life, I mean."

"I guess." During an awkward pause, Brennan bowed his head, seemed to be studying the wood grains in the worn floor of Karl's office.

"So, how *you* feeling?" Wes inquired. "The heart, and all. You heal up okay?"

"Slow. But sure." Karl tapped his chest with his fingers. "A little better each day, I guess. That's the most you can ask for."

"So, how about you?" Karl inquired, knowing this must be a tough time for both Brennan and his spouse. "You and the wife all right, then? Need anything?" He was always happy to help out when he could. Maybe he'd bring in a fruit basket or something tomorrow and leave it on Wes' desk.

Brennan's mouth pinched to a line. Karl recognized his expression: those upwardly slanted eyebrows, like a person who was always pondering something. "Nope," he said, his voice soft. "I'm okay. Same old guy, I s'pose."

"Well, good to see you, then."

"Yup," Wes said, turning to walk back to his office.

Then Karl called after him, "The boy died for America, you know."

Wes turned around slowly.

"Your boy," Karl reiterated. "It's really sad news, I know." Then he added, "But he's a hero. He died serving his country. And that says a lot."

Wes just nodded solemnly, his shoulders wavering a little.


Karl went back to his own work, leaning over the backlog of waiting forms. Karl knew there was a lot to get done at the plant, and that the best thing they could do for those boys, and for everybody in Vietnam, was to go ahead with their daily work.

Last night, following the progress report on Vietnam, he had clicked off the evening news. The images shrunk to a small pinpoint of light in the center of the screen. *That's us,* he had thought as he stared at that point of light. *That's Bluff Lake, right there in the center of things.*

The military operation in Vietnam could be unpleasant, he knew. There would be sacrifices, hardships. But it had to be done. Just like WWII, the enemy had to be dealt with. Otherwise, everything would begin to fall, one by one. If Vietnam was taken over by the Communists, then all of Southeast Asia would tumble, Karl knew. A chain reaction. One little weak country after another would fall, like dominoes leading down the sidewalk and right to our front doors.

*Stack the reports in order,* he thought as he thumbed through them. *Be decisive. Be strong. Don't leave anything out. Able, Baker, Charlie, Dog.* Everything back in its place. Everything where it needed to be.

"Hey, Karl," a voice entered his thoughts. It was Midge, the security office secretary, poking her head through his office door. "You see the second set of files I put on your desk?"

"Couldn't miss 'em." He'd have to go through the monthly reports, one by one. Darrel Scharnke, in the office next door, was an assistant supervisor who took over some of Karl's duties when he was on leave. But he was inexperienced and not all that efficient.

"Saved 'em just for you," Midge replied pleasantly, her lips smudging into a smile. Her hair was always a little too red. Dyed a little, maybe, Karl always thought, for a woman of forty-five or fifty. Then, before she returned to her office in her squat black heels, she added, "Saw your boy here a while ago."

"Oh?" Karl gave her a questioning squint. "He was *here?*"

"Yeah. Your boy stopped to say hi. Told us know how you were doing, and all. Seems like a nice kid."

"Oh." Karl was a little confused about why Phil would stop at the security offices.

The conversation was interrupted as Warren Benke, a field supervisor, rushed in.

"Karl!" Benke said, his voice raised to a near shout. "We just had a fire on a tram."

Karl stood quickly from his desk chair. "Damn it all! What happened?"

"Guess one of the bins in the back caught a spark. It went up in flames." Benke puffed his cheeks. "The driver thought the fire might jump from bin to bin. So he bailed out."

"Jesus H. Christ. *Did* it jump?"

"Nope. Guess it burned just the one bin. The tram rolled to a stop before it got to the next powder house. Then it sorta fizzled out."

"Where?" Karl barked.

"The west quadrant."

"Cripes, that's the worst place for a fire. Who the hell's the driver?"

"Clifford Phillips, I guess."

"I want him in here, ASAP," Karl ordered. Karl knew every accident that occurred at the plant came back to his office. And to him, specifically, as supervisor, to review. The plant's Superintendent, Colonel Digby, chewing an unlit cigar, would be on all over him about it. Karl knew he had to be strong, to not buckle under the pressure of these incidents, no matter what.

"I want all the info on this," Karl added authoritatively. "Every goddamn detail. Got it?"

"Yes sir," Benke said, and he hurried back to his office.

Karl wondered just how close that tram was passing to the production houses in the west quadrant when it ignited. He hated to think about what would have happened if the burning tram had rolled too near one of those buildings.

He opened the file cabinet drawer, scanned the tabs of the manila envelopes. He lifted the one marked **West Quadrant,** but it was empty. Befuddled, he narrowed his eyes noticing that the **East Quadrant** map was gone. And the other two, too. Four empty manila folders, marked N, S, E, W, their dry mouths open.

"Huh," Karl muttered.

The thought occurred to him that maybe he moved them before the heart attack and then forgot about it. He had blacked out half of that day, and part of the next two days, for that matter. Missing days, missing tissue, missing brain cells. He'd have to get them all back.

He rummaged through a couple of file drawers. He checked a box in the corner. Nothing. Karl knew he couldn't spend much more time looking. The Colonel was always impatient when there was an incident and would want a full written report by the end of the workday by 1630 hours. Karl pushed away from his desk and stalked down the uneven linoleum hallway.

"Where are the quadrant maps?" he asked Midge. "I can't locate them."

"Hmmm," Midge replied. "Let me think. Maybe Darrel moved them. He stopped at your office once in a while to pick things up. He's a little disorganized, if you know what I mean," Midge smirked.

Karl winked at her. "Roger that."

She rolled her cushioned orange office chair to the wall of cabinets behind her. "But I've got the masters back here, as always." She opened a locked drawer, pulled them out. She strolled toward him and handed them to him, her usual wave of Revlon perfume following her.

"Thanks, Midge." Holding the maps again made Karl feel a little calmer. "You're a lifesaver, as usual."

"Takes one to know one."

A half hour later, with the west quadrant map spread out on his desk, Karl located the stretch of narrow-gauge railroad tracks near Powder House 121. He slid a form—with three carbon copies beneath it—into his black Underwood typewriter, and began filling out his report, clacking the words out steadily with his index fingers.

As he looked at the letterhead—**From the Office of Karl Keyhoe, Security Supervisor**—he felt a rush of satisfaction, and he finally calmed down. It was up to him to get this whole mishap straightened out. The driver would be called in, and Karl would chew him out for bailing from a moving powder tram and thus endangering others. Then he'd place a citation on the man's employment record. One more screw-up and Phillips would be fired.

Karl would have the full report turned in to the Colonel on schedule.

Action would be taken. Procedures would be followed. Carbon copies retained. As usual, he'd move step by step from cause to effect to solution. A, B, C, D. He'd solve this problem, like the others, he told himself. He'd extinguish this flare-up.

Then, a question pushed its way in, briefly detouring his focus. *Those quadrant maps. What did happen to those damn maps, anyway?*

# CHAPTER 44

During his morning break, Phil leaned his paddle against the copper bin and stepped outside. Overhead, he noticed a large bird—an eagle or a hawk—its wings wide, its feathers splayed. It circled slowly and gracefully, hovering over the east section of the plant, seeming to ride the warm updrafts from the valley.

Phil's momentary meditation was interrupted when a middle-aged co-worker standing next to him tore off his goggles and squinted toward the parking lot. "What the hell's goin' on?" the man said.

Phil followed the man's gaze and that's when he spotted them. Busses. First one. Then two, then three of them veering into the plant from the highway. As it reached the entrance of the plant, the first one, which looked like a repainted school bus, slowed. When the entrance guard stalked up to the driver's side, it lurched forward and accelerated past him. The guard ran after it, waving his arms. The bus braked abruptly near the gates and protesters carrying signs spilled out in a stream. Then the second bus pulled next to it. Then the third arrived. The last bus one was painted with swirling reds and greens and purples and sported a white, sloppily drawn peace symbol on its hood. People exited the buses, shouting "End the War in Vietnam! Shut down the Strongs Plant!" Soon almost three-hundred protestors had spilled into the lot, their voices rising like brightly colored banners in the air.

He had envisioned this moment hundreds of times in his mind during the past weeks, and now it was finally happening.

He listened intently to their voices that carried across the wavering heat of the parking lot; some were chanting "Stop the bombing!" and others called "No more war!"

The next thing Phil knew, he was walking hypnotically—no, not walking, but jogging—the three-hundred yards to the front of the plant.

By the time he reached the ten-foot cyclone fence, other workers had exited their buildings to view the commotion. The protesters chanted louder and louder, interwoven with those who continued to sing. They waved hand-lettered signs mounted on sticks, the cardboard fluttering like wings in the breeze. The signs declared **BRING THE TROOPS HOME NOW!** and **MAKE LOVE, NOT WAR!**

Roy Duke parked his pickup truck on the axis road and stalked toward the spectacle. "Well holy shit," Phil heard him snarl from behind. "Just look at those damn idiots!"

As Phil watched the scene unfold, he spotted someone pausing on the top stair of the bus. She took a graceful step to the lot, long legs clad in worn, embroidered bell-bottom jeans. Thick permed strands of reddish-blonde hair spiraled around the woman's face, obscuring it as she leaned over to pick up a sign. Then she raised the sign high above her head. Phil squinted and gasped as he recognized her.

It was Mariah. Of course—it was Mariah.

Phil saw her get in line with the other protesters who marched in a circle. Her hair was longer now and kinky. Small red and purple braided ribbons spiraled down from the headband she wore. He saw her singing along with "Blowin' in the Wind," a song filled with questions about wars and cannonballs and deaths and white doves.

The gathering workers began to shout angrily. "Get the hell out of here!" one man called. "Take your placards and go home! You assholes!" The checkpoint guards in blue uniforms rushed out and stood shoulder to shoulder, nightsticks in their hands as they blocked the entryways.

Ray Duke picked up a handful of mud and formed it into a baseball-sized shape. He hurled it at the circling marchers, hitting one protester on the back of his blue tie-dyed T-shirt. With a tight smile, the long-haired man turned and flashed the peace symbol with his two fingers. "Peace to you, too, man!" he called. Reaching down, Duke formed another ball of mud, and threw again. It splattered, making a brown star in the center of a sign that read "**Close the Strongs Now!**" A few workers let out mocking cheers of approval.

When one tall man with an afro began waving a peace banner in front of two guards, the guards pulled out their clubs and shoved at him. The tall man shoved back at them. "Hey, keep it peaceful, man!" a fellow protestor reminded him, and the guy backed away. Meanwhile, squad cars from the Bluff Lake sheriff's office—their lights flashing, sirens clashing—appeared on the ridge and sped down toward the plant. More guards spilled into the lot, formed a line, and approached the protestors.

Meanwhile, Mariah and another girl with feather earrings broke off from the circling group and approached the far end of the cyclone fence.

Phil watched as Mariah stepped along the perimeter of the fence, pushing leaflets through the wires toward the workers. The fliers fluttered to the mud. One worker picked one up, tore it to shreds, then threw it back at the girls with a scoff and a curse. Mariah's lips were moving, but Phil couldn't hear what she was repeating each time she calmly slid a curled leaflet through the diamond shapes of the fence.

He strained to hear her. Mariah's melodic voice was like a physical touch, and he was convinced that the very sound of it would wake him, bring him back to life again.

When Mariah finally reached Phil, she stopped. Her eyelashes fluttered in surprise. Her face—with a small mud splatter on one cheek—flushed pink and softened for a few seconds. Noticing that Mariah had paused, her friend gave her a puzzled look.

"Mariah," Phil said. He lifted his trembling hand and pressed his palm against the fence, his fingers outstretched like the feathers of a bird in flight. He repeated her name, louder. "Mariah?" He wanted, more than anything, for Mariah to lift her hand from the other side of the aluminum wires and gently press her palm against his. He wanted to feel the pulse beneath her skin, to feel that familiar rush he got when he touched her. As he held his hand there, the wires seemed cold and burning at the same time.

Then, as if he were nothing more than another production line lifer in stiff, iron-gray coveralls, she thrust a rolled-up leaflet toward his chest. With a sad but determined look, she said the same five words she'd been repeating to the rest of the men: "How can you work here?"

A tall guard sauntered up to Mariah and the other girl. "Step back from the fence!" he commanded.

"We have every right to be here," Mariah countered.

"The hell you do," the guard said. Holding his night stick with two hands, he extended it toward her.

Mariah pushed the night stick away. The guard shoved her harder, and, off-balance, she took a few steps backward.

"Hey!" Phil called out to the guard. "Leave her alone!" Phil's fingers curled tightly in the wires and his voice rose to a shout. "Leave her *alone!*"

The guard glared at Phil as Mariah's friend grabbed her by the arm, pulled her away from the scuffle, and the two of them returned to the main group of protestors.

Phil turned around, and that's when he saw Karl. His father had been standing there all along, watching him from behind.

Karl shook his head, a disapproving scowl carved into his chiseled face. Without a word, Karl pivoted, and stalked back to an idling jeep. He took a sharp U-turn and accelerated toward the administration building.

"Freak show's over, boys," Duke called to the gawking workers as the demonstrators gathered near the busses and regrouped. "Get back to work." He swiveled his head toward Phil. "That means, you, Keyhoe."

As Phil passed him, Duke sneered "What the hell? You *know* that damn hippie girl?"

Phil slowly made his way back toward his work station. He glanced occasionally over his shoulder at the demonstrators, who had gathered in a large circle at the center of the lot. A line of guards, their black clubs, approached them from one side, and a few policemen from the other. Though he was too far away to know for sure, Phil thought he could hear Mariah's voice, chanting through a megaphone.

When Phil reached Powder House 121, an angry supervisor confronted him. "God damn, Keyhoe," Lester Statz growled. "Where in hell did you go? I should frickin' dock you for that half hour." He pointed toward the copper bins. "Get your ass in gear."

Phil absently began to scrape the powder from a bin, circling a paddle around and around. As he did, a question kept circling in his mind. *Did he know her, after all?*

There was no clear answer, just silence.

But then that silence was broken by the deafening but unmistakable sound of an explosion.

Running to the doorway, Phil saw a black cloud billowing above a powder house. Circling above was a low-flying Cessna plane, its wings wobbling. He had heard rumors that a plane might fly over the plant, pulling an anti-war banner and dropping leaflets. But this plane, its whirring propeller cutting through the morning air like a buzz-saw slicing through metal, had no streaming banner. And instead of leaflets, an object—ablaze like a meteor—dropped from it. The object tumbled silently, in slow motion, until it struck a powder storage building and detonated, an angry orange flower surrounded by a ring of black and gray smoke. The shock wave hit Phil hard, and he felt it deep in his chest, like a fist pummeling him from the inside. He froze in the doorway, unable to move in or out, his legs and arms turning to concrete.

In seconds, a few co-workers rushed past Phil, bumping him against the door frame as they ran from the building.

"What the hell?" one man screamed, "Someone's bombin' the plant!"

Phil stood there, unable to move as more frantic workers rushed from the buildings and ran toward the exit gates. One man, shouting "God damn!" dashed a few feet from a building, then dove to the ground, his hands clasped on top of his yellow safety helmet as if he were expecting a grenade to go off.

A third explosion erupted about a hundred yards away, launching a confetti of splintered, burning wood and bits of sod into the sky.

But Phil still couldn't move.

It was as if his feet were fused to the floor. A numbness rose in him, the sensation climbing from his toes to his forehead. All he could do was stare, in open-mouthed shock, as smoke from the explosion rose and gathered itself into a mushroom cloud, a dark tornado-like stem dangling from it. The plane banked above it, a black cross silhouetted in the harsh glare of the morning sun.

Remembering Mariah's warnings about the plant's dangers, Phil finally lunged into a run toward the exit gate. He sprinted with a group of panicking workers, their faces distorted with fear.

As Phil raced through a gate and into the parking lot, he had to zig-zag through a kaleidoscope of scattering protestors, frantic guards, and terrified workers. The smoky air was filled with the ear-piercing sounds of police sirens, screams, and gunshots as guards fired pistols at the divebombing plane. This was no longer a peaceful demonstration. This was war.

Finally reaching the far corner of the parking lot, Phil stopped, panting for breath, and crouched down in a fetal position as if to protect himself. He lifted his head and stared, horrified, at the chaotic scene.

Shivering and dizzy, he felt sick, not just from the trauma of the explosions, or the caustic, metallic taste of the sulfuric smoke that burned his throat and clawed deep into his lungs. What sickened him most was, the thought, the terrifying realization that he had something—not just something, but *a lot*—to do with what was happening.

Wiping his watery eyes with his sleeve, Phil wondered if his father was out of danger. He looked to see that the supervisor's building was intact; the only fires were on the far east and west quadrants of the plant. Karl never made his rounds to storage houses until late afternoon, so Phil was convinced he'd be okay. Karl had once told him that in case of an emergency, there was a concrete World War II bunker beneath the supervisor's building. Phil pictured him down there now, huddled in the dank underbelly of the plant with other supervisors and staff. Phil couldn't even begin to imagine what was going through his father's head, or what he was feeling. He didn't want to know.

"Well, look at that!" a voice interrupted his thought. "The Strongs finally got a dose of its own medicine." Phil realized he was standing next to a couple of familiar protestors the workers referred to as "the daily weirdos." The two showed up each morning to stand silently outside the plant entrance, holding signs that demanded **Peace Now!** and **No More Ammo!** The bearded man, in his late twenties, eyed Phil's work clothes, then scoffed "So, you're one of *them*? You're part of this goddamn place?"

Phil didn't acknowledge them. In front of him was a white tagboard sign, face down, that someone had dropped during the clash with the guards. He lifted it from the ground. Turning it over, he read the words, hand-lettered in red paint: **STOP THE WAR!**

He had always understood those words. But now he felt himself truly beginning to believe them. As the message resonated deep inside him, he closed his eyes. He opened them again and he methodically he tossed his helmet and safety glasses aside, removed his work gear, and stood in his worn jeans, Thunderbirds T-shirt, and bare feet.

He wondered if Mariah was safe. Still in a state of shock, he began wandering numbly across the parking lot, hoping to find her. Some workers, still evacuating from the far end of the plant, jogged toward him, parting around him like a stream around a boulder. Scanning the blurry faces of the crowd, he couldn't spot her anywhere.

Across the lot, some protestors scattered and dashed back to the busses, while a few others clustered together and locked arms to protect themselves from the guards.

The next instant, another explosion detonated.

Phil's head filled with a searing pain and a sudden starburst of orange and yellow.

Then everything went black.

# CHAPTER 45

Somewhere in all that blackness, Mariah's face appeared. The two were circling on opposite sides of a strong, inky whirlpool. As they revolved around each other, Phil tried to swim toward her, but the whirlpool's current was too powerful. Her eyes were blank, and her face looked flat, like a pale leaf being pushed across the surface of a dark pond by the wind. The whirlpool began to drain into a pinpoint of light. Phil felt himself being pulled down, down, down. A few seconds passed. An hour, a year. Then the pinpoint steadily widened into bright daylight.

Opening his eyes, Phil realized was being dragged across the lot by two sheriff's department deputies.

"No!" Phil shouted to the cops. "No!" His skull ached, and he felt something trickling down the back of his head. He could see blood spatters on the shoulder of his T-shirt. As they pulled him toward a police van, its flashing lights stabbing the air, he pleaded, "What are you doing? I work here! I *work* at this plant!"

"Sure you do, you son of a bitch," one burly cop, a nightstick stuffed in his leather belt, growled with sarcasm. "That's why yer carryin' this goddamn sign." The cop nodded at the crumpled sign he had pinned under one arm.

When they reached the van, they shoved Phil against the side of it, and yanked his hands behind his back. Phil heard a metallic sound, felt a pair of cold handcuffs snapping their jaws around his wrists. An officer turned him around and, in a rote voice, began to recite the Miranda rights to him. "You have the right to remain silent…" Phil ignored the cop and stared into the distance, where clear arcs of water from the fire trucks sprayed one of the buildings. He was relieved when he spotted Mariah, climbing into one of the painted buses.

The deputies shoved him into the back of the van with several others and latched the double doors behind him. Surrounded by the dark steel walls, his view of the world was reduced to a single small square through a scratched, barred window.

At the Bluff Lake County jail, Phil sat on a hard bed that smelled like a mixture of mold and a strong disinfectant. He studied the faint, smudged handprints on the back wall that were left by previous offenders. In a moment of irony, he wondered if his hand would fit into any of them.

Phil's cellmate was a man in his twenties, also arrested at the protest. He was tall and skinny with a Fu Manchu moustache. Agitated, he kept pacing back. and forth in front of the barred door. The man smelled like hemp, or wet wool, and his long, stringy brown hair covered both sides of his face.

A headache gnawed at Phil, and he reached up to feel the lump on the back of his head. The blood had dried into a scab. He noticed a few expletives scratched into the concrete by Bluff Lake's hardened criminals, who were probably locked up for petty theft or drunk and disorderly. Above him, a high, thin rectangular air vent let in the diffused light from the hallway.

His cellmate stopped pacing and eyed Phil. "How long you think we'll be here?" he asked.

"Dunno. It already feels like years."

"Yeah," the guy agreed, "But, hell, I'm used to this shit." He began pacing again, looking down at his feet as if he was counting his steps, or tightrope walking. "Fifth time we've been busted," he bragged.

"Oh?"

"Yeah. Ann Arbor. Then Milwaukee, when I was at UWM. Two times in Madison. At the capitol."

"Did you get fined?"

"Just once. The other times they let me out. My uncle's an attorney in Mad City. So that helps. Lawyers have strings, you know," he said smugly. "They'll let me outta this rat hole, too, after I call him." His hair swayed on his shoulders as he paced. "Shit—small town cops don't know what to do with student activists," he scoffed. He squinted one eye. "Wonder where they ended up putting my girlfriend?"

"Your girlfriend's here?"

"Yeah. Somewhere. We got separated by the pigs." He stared at the wall a moment. "Her name's April, but goes by Lotus. We go to all the protests together. She's a veteran," he said proudly. "She has a PhD in disturbing the peace. And she writes angry letters to LBJ." He arched his back proudly in his rainbow tie-dyed t-shirt. "Yeah, we're in this together. It's all about make love, not war, if you get my drift," he added with a smirk.

The guy's full-of-himself attitude was grating, and it added to Phil's headache.

"Lotus reads the black activist poets out loud at sit-ins," the guy continued. "Leroi Jones. Nikki Giovanni. Langston Hughes. Ever read them?"

"No, guess not," Phil admitted.

"My name's Shane." The man stuck out his hand and scrutinized Phil, noticing his medium-length hair, his high school T-shirt and conservative jeans. "Damn, you seem kinda straight. How many times you been busted?"

"My first time."

"Congratulations, man! You hate that goddamn war factory as much as I do?"

Without replying, Phil stood from the bed and looked out at the empty hallway through the small window.

A half hour later, the outer security door creaked, then clanked shut. Phil heard footsteps coming toward their cell, hard soles grinding on the grit.

A chubby deputy stopped in front of the cell and unlocked the door. "Right here, I guess."

A shadow loomed up behind the deputy. Then Karl stepped into the light from the caged overhead fixture.

Karl pivoted toward Phil. His eyes narrowed slightly and he looked not at Phil, but beyond him, as if he was staring to see something across a wide valley.

Phil expected his father's face to be scowling. He expected his father's heat-lamp glare.

Instead, Karl tipped his head slightly to the side and his lips gathered into a patronizing smile. "Yep," Karl said, almost brightly. "That's him all right. My boy." Karl turned to the guard and said, confidentially, "Guess he got mixed up with the wrong crowd." He forced a laugh.

"Shoot, you can say that again," the deputy agreed.

"Thanks, Dwight," Karl said. "I'll take over from here."

"Yeah. Better keep him close to home, Karl," the deputy cautioned. "It's bad, you know. To have to arrest hometown boys, and all."

"I know what you mean," Karl agreed. He motioned Phil out of the cell with a casual wag of his head.

Seeing Karl's white shirt, blue and red tie, and Strongs Plant ID badge on his pocket, Phil's cellmate opened his mouth in surprise. "Dude!" he said. "*That's* your frickin' dad?"

Ignoring the comment, Phil followed Karl and the guard back to the front desk.

Karl signed Phil out, and the deputy handed over a clear plastic bag. Karl watched as Phil pulled out a thin brown leather wallet, a black Ace pocket comb, a set of keys on a Bluff Lake Motors keychain, two dollars and twenty-seven cents in change. Phil stuffed the items back into his pockets.

The deputy lifted the anti-war sign Phil had been carrying. "There's this, too."

Karl's eyes lowered to the sign, then rose back up to Phil.

"Had it at the time of the arrest, I guess," the deputy explained.

"Oh." Karl's word came out flat. He pulled out his wallet. "So, Dwight. Am I posting some kind of bail, then? Or paying a fine?"

"Naw." The deputy motioned to the exit door. "The boy's free to go. See you around town, Karl."

"You sure?" Karl quizzed, understanding that the deputy was letting them off without a penalty.

"Hey, maybe just buy me a beer at the next Kiwanis meeting."

"Yeah, sure. Deal." Karl tipped his head back. "So, when's this place going to get a new paint job?" he asked, noticing the faded wall behind the deputy's desk. "Looks like it hasn't had a coat since World War II."

"Dunno," the deputy smirked. "Maybe when the city council decides to cough up some funds. In about the year two-thousand one."

Karl laughed. His oddly nonchalant demeanor puzzled Phil. It was if he was picking up Phil in fifth grade after pee wee football practice and chatting with another dad.

Karl noticed Phil's bare feet. "What about your boots?"

"Don't have them."

"And where might they be?" Karl asked, glancing at the row of framed sepia photos on the wall—a dreary lineup of Bluff Lake's past chiefs of police. Since he arrived at jail, Karl had never once looked directly at Phil.

Phil's shoulders climbed into a shrug.

"Huh." Karl turned toward the deputy, tipped his head to one side, and managed a chuckle. "Kids these days, eh?"

Phil followed behind Karl as he pushed through the heavy frosted glass doors of the station. The two walked in silence to the Chrysler, which Karl had carefully parallel parked between the bumpers of two squad cars.

# CHAPTER 46

When Phil and Karl returned that evening, the whole house seemed to be holding its breath. Thick silence filled the rooms of the big, 1930s two-story house, from the den to the living room to the upstairs bedrooms. In the darkened den, Karl's Bronze Star glimmered faintly as headlights from passing cars shined through the windows.

Frances had dabbed some salve and bandaged the wound on the back of Phil's head. Not a concussion, she concluded after she talked to him a while.

After returning from the jail, Karl quickly slipped back into his angry mood and refused to speak to Phil or Frances. Instead, for the next hour, he sat in the den with a notebook, outlining the emergency meeting he would call tomorrow morning to discuss the incidents at the plant.

Frances prepared a chicken dinner for the three of them, but Phil sequestered himself in his upstairs room. Frances carried a plate of food up for him and set it on the small table outside his closed door.

Downstairs, Karl ate somberly, wordlessly, not looking at Frances, who sat across from him at the dining room table. Frances adjusted and readjusted the cloth napkin on her lap. Karl slid the plate, the meal half eaten, away from him, then pushed himself from the table and stood. His chair, teetering on two legs, clunked against the table.

"What, Karl?" Frances questioned. "What?"

Karl's eyes looked as if he were staring off at something a hundred miles away.

"The chicken's over done?" she asked, though she knew this had nothing to do with the meal.

"It's done," Karl said, his words bumping against hers.

"Then why don't you just stay and finish?"

Karl clenched and unclenched his fists.

"Karl, answer me," Frances insisted, though she knew the confrontation with Phil was inevitable, that it was going to happen, sooner or later, no matter how much she tried to deter it. She knew Karl's dark seething silence could only end in an eruption, and she didn't want to see that outburst aimed at Phil. She hurried around the table and put one hand on Karl's shoulder. "Why don't you sit back down, Karl. Just eat. Just finish your meal."

"I need to talk to the boy," he announced. Slipping out from under her hand, Karl stalked through the living room. As he passed Frances' mahogany spoon collection rack, some of the tiny, tarnished spoons vibrated. He began climbing the stairs toward Phil's room, his heavy frame taking slow, methodical steps, as if he was counting each one.

Frances followed to the stairway. "Karl," she said, her voice rising in pitch, like a strained singing. "Karl, please. I know you're upset, but let's just talk about this tomorrow…"

"Stay out of this, Frances," he growled, "It has nothing to do with you."

His command made her freeze at the bottom of the stairway.

He pushed at the closed door of Phil's room, and it swung all the way open, the doorknob bumping hard against the plaster. His eyes fixed on Phil, who sat with a book on his bed.

"I should have let you sit there in that damn jail," Karl began. "That's what I should have done. Should have let you stay there overnight. Just to see what it's like."

Pretending to read his book, Phil didn't look up, just kept his eyes focused on the jumbled letters of a worn copy of *A Farewell to Arms*.

"So tell me. Why in hell did you *join* them out there?" Karl demanded.

Phil turned toward his father. "I didn't, really."

"Don't lie to me. You spoke up for that protestor girl. You carried a sign in the parking lot with the rest of those lamebrains."

"I wasn't really *with* them, Dad. I just picked the sign up and..." he fumbled for words, trying to explain. "But I do sympathize with their cause."

"I think you just sympathize with that damn Mariah. That's what. It's the girl you're all starry-eyed about, not some cause."

Phil wanted to get out from under the bright lamp of his father's inquisition. He stood, dropped the book to the bed, where it bounced softly, and stepped toward the door. Karl lifted his thick arm to the door frame, blocking Phil's exit.

"Where do you think you're going?"

Phil ducked under his arm, hurried down the stairs, and Karl followed. When they reached the middle of the living room, Karl called: "I hope you feel good, turning your back on the plant like that!"

Phil paused and faced Karl. He didn't study the drapes, or the swirling purple pattern on the carpeting, as he usually did when he spoke to his father. This time he looked straight in his father's eyes, hardened stones that glared back at him. "I didn't turn my back on anything, Dad," Phil said, his words tight like wires. "Maybe I'm taking a stand *for* something."

"I can't believe you're saying this." Karl's anger smoldered.

"Karl..." Frances called from behind. "Karl, please," she implored, wringing her hands. "Be...be reasonable."

Karl whirled around toward her. "Reasonable? My own son, he joins some damn protest, then gets himself arrested. I have to bail him out of a damn jail. I have to face those deputies, guys I've known for *years* in Kiwanis Club. Do you know how humiliating that was?" He tossed his arms into the air. "And you're asking *me* to be reasonable?"

She shrunk a little, as if his glare was melting her. "Just cool down a little, Karl. Let's talk about all this later..."

As Phil turned toward the kitchen doorway, Karl lunged, grabbed him by his denim shirt. Phil tried to twist away, his shirt ripping at the sleeve. "I'm not done talking to you yet!" Karl snarled. "You stop right there, dammit. And that's an order!"

Phil spun around and faced him. "Do you have to give *orders* all the time? Do you always have to control someone?"

"I'm not controlling you. I'm just keeping you from screwing up. That's when I step in."

"And when," Phil rasped, "When do I get to make my own choices?" Phil let the rhetorical question hang in the air. The TV, its volume turned too low to hear, flickered weakly in the corner, casting a pale bluish-white light on Karl's broad forehead. "When, Dad? Tell me that?"

"When your choices make sense. When they're not ridiculous. That's when."

"Ridiculous?" Phil had never shouted at his father, never let the years of silence break open, never said what he really felt deep down, but he was saying it now. He was shouting it now. "Who decides they're ridiculous?" The words poured out, a sudden surge of dammed-up floodwaters. "Who decides?"

"*I* do. That's who. I do. Don't you get it? I'm keeping you on the right path."

"Whose path is it Dad? *Your* path?" Phil circled his hands in frustration. "Your own narrow little path about what's right and what's wrong?"

Karl tipped his chin forward. "You're goddamn right."

Adrenaline rushed through Phil's veins like electricity. "All you want to do is pin me down, isn't it? To...to hold me in place. All you want is to stop me from changing, from being who I want to be. Well guess what? That's not going to happen anymore. It's my life. And to be honest, I *did* want to join the protestors. I really *did.*"

"You have no idea what you're saying. People could have been killed out there today, with that idiot dropping firebombs."

"Nobody told us there'd be a plane..." Phil blurted without thinking. "It was all supposed to be peaceful. That wasn't in the plan. It... "

Karl's jaw fell open in shock. "Wait a minute. Wait a minute." Karl moved closer to Phil. "*Plan?* You mean you *knew* something about this beforehand? You were *in* on it? And you didn't say anything? You didn't tell anybody?" Karl inhaled a quick gasp, as if someone had just punched his chest. "Jesus Christ, tell me this isn't true!" His thick neck turned fire red, and the redness climbed up through his jaw, to his cheekbones and the top of his balding head.

Phil stood there, unable to call up any words. Beneath the bronze eagle, mounted on the wall, the ticking clock dropped hard seconds onto the living room floor. Phil felt as if the whole house—all this oak and plaster—was about to tip to one side and tumble down the hill.

Karl clenched his jaw as if he was biting down on steel. "Were you in my office?" he demanded. "Did you go in there while I was on sick leave?"

Phil lowered his head. "I did," he admitted.

"And I hope you didn't take those maps of the quadrants. I hope to God you didn't. Please tell me you didn't do that."

Phil's face contorted. He fixed his eyes on the cracks in the plaster of the back wall of the living room. Lines, crisscrossing. Branching. Widening, opening like canyons he wished he could fall into.

"You didn't answer my question," Karl probed. "Did you *take* those maps?"

"Dad, honestly, I, I feel bad about all this. I never knew anyone intended to... I mean, they told me the maps would only be used..."

Phil's words were cut off when Karl drew his arm back and, with one quick, mechanical motion, he slapped Phil hard across his face. It was the same kind of sudden slap he gave Phil when he was nine or ten and he disobeyed, but this blow was faster, harder.

Phil's face stung. The blow left the red imprint of Karl's fingers on his cheek.

Karl lifted his arm in the air to hit him again. Reaching up to protect himself, Phil grabbed Karl's arm. For a few seconds, their arms wavered in the air as they battled against each other, arm-wrestling in an even match.

"Stop it. Stop it, you two!" Francis shouted as she reached up and grabbed Karl's wrist. "I won't have this in my house!" The three of them struggled, their raised arms wavering, pushing back and forth. It was as though the three were doing some awkward dance, without music, in the middle of the living room.

Suddenly, Karl's muscles relaxed, and he gradually lowered his arm. He closed his eyes, and they rolled behind their lids, as if he was looking at something in the back of his skull. Then he opened them. "There's the door," he said to Phil in a level, modulated voice. He nodded toward the back entryway. "I want you out of this house."

"If he leaves," Frances said, her face surfacing between them, "then I'm leaving, too."

Karl's head swiveled toward her as if it was on ball bearings. "Huh?" he said incredulously.

"Just what I said, Karl. If Phil leaves, then I'm going, too." Her dry lips seemed to be fighting themselves as she spoke, and tears welled up in her eyes.

Karl's mouth opened in surprise. He peered at her like a person trying to recognize someone they haven't seen for a long time. "I don't think you mean that, Frances."

"I do. If this is what it comes down to," Frances said shrilly, her hands fluttering like startled birds bursting from a tree. "I...I understand why people are protesting."

Karl leveled a puzzled look at her. "What in hell are you saying?"

"Karl, I'm upset about the war," she said, her words pouring out. "About what it's doing to our town. And to the boys they keep sending over there. I don't agree with everything the protestors say. And yes, that bombing today was a terrible thing." She lowered her eyes to the floor, then lifted them back to Karl. "But at the same time, I can't stop wondering why we keep fighting this war."

"I can't believe you're saying this, Frances."

Phil could see Frances, composing herself, holding strong. "Maybe I'm on Phil's side. Maybe we're just..." She hesitated. "Maybe we're just wondering what's right anymore. And I've...I've been talking to some women who feel the same way."

"Women? What women?"

"There's a group in town. They don't agree with the war. I've been going to their meetings on Tuesday mornings, and, and..."

"Oh," Karl scoffed. "So you're disloyal, too. Is that it?"

"I'm *not* disloyal," Frances countered, tears skimming down her cheeks. "I'm being true, for once. Maybe Phil and I are just being true to what we feel."

None of them spoke for a few seconds, and to Phil it seemed like the corners of the walls were creaking against each other, and that the slightly off-kilter windows were about to shatter from the inside out.

"What in the hell is happening here?" Karl questioned, shaking his head. "I just wanted the best for you two, that's all. And now it's like you've both gone crazy. Has this whole house has gone crazy?"

"This house hasn't gone crazy," Frances said, raising her voice. "It's finally come to its senses, Karl. Maybe, for once, *we've* come to our senses!"

"Fine." Karl took a slow, uneven breath, as if his chest was constricted, chains tightening around it. "Fine, Frances," he said. "You can do what you want." He turned back toward Phil. "And you. You turned your back against the plant today. And against your country. Against your own family. Against *me*." His voice lowered in pitch. "You know what that makes you, don't you?" He dabbed his finger hard into Phil's chest and paused for emphasis. "A traitor, that's what. How can I call you my son anymore? You're, you're a damn *traitor*!"

The words stung Phil, and his head snapped back slightly.

"You heard what I said before," Karl continued. "I want you out of the house. Now."

Phil hung his head, knowing his father was right. He had made an irrational decision, and he was ready to accept the punishment.

None of the three spoke. Karl adjusted his blue and red striped tie that he'd worn at the plant that day. Then he turned to the glass door of his gun collection case on the wall, and pointed to the rifle he had placed as a centerpiece among the others. "You see this beautiful rifle?" he asked, his voice becoming surprisingly calm.

Phil and Frances listened.

"This is an M1903 Springfield," he said, his words slow and deliberate. "From World War II. It's a precision instrument, made from the finest materials. By American workers. Tiny and I kept one in the supply truck when we drove the Burma Road. The GIs carried these in Europe." He tilted his head sideways, closed his eyes, and spoke solemnly. "Thousands of them died over there for America, you know. They helped to win the war. They were patriots. They were loyal. They were heroes." He looked up at the two of them. "I don't think either of you know the significance of this rifle, do you?"

"No, we don't," Frances said, her words barely audible.

"No, you don't," Karl echoed. "But maybe it's time you thought about it."

He arched his back as if standing at attention, pivoted, and strode from the dining room. At the base of the stairway, he hesitated, his body half in the light from the desk lamp, half in shadow. He turned toward Frances and Phil. His jaw slowly opened, then slowly closed, as if he was about to say something else, as if a few more words, still caught deep inside, were trying to push their way out. Instead, he continued up the stairway to the bedroom. As he climbed, Phil could hear the intermittent creaking of the third and fifth stairs, the aching sound of those warped floorboards his father always meant to fix but never did.

# CHAPTER 47

North, south, east, west.

Sitting in his car in front of the high school, Phil felt like none of the directions seemed right. Was there a fifth direction? After everything that just had happened, he felt lost, just plain goddamn lost.

He envisioned tomorrow's front-page article about the catastrophic events at the plant.

**Strongs Plant Bombed by SDS Protestors**
**Protest Shut Down, Many Arrested**

Bluff Lake couldn't be preoccupied with local features about the Lady's Club Bake Sale or the upcoming Rotary Club picnic anymore. The war was closer, and right on everyone's doorstep. Then another thought worried him: would the article include a list of who got arrested? Would his name appear there? By choosing to steal those maps, he was connected to the horrific events at the plant. There'd be no going back.

He walked along the side of the high school next to the lunchroom. As he did, the innocent, romantic songs he used to dance to at BluffTeen played faintly in his head again. He heard the lyrics of "Blue Velvet" and "Everyone's Gone to the Moon"—songs that, like so many others, were deeply embedded in the folds of his brain. Those nights, as he and Mariah slow danced beneath it, the pastel pink and blue crepe paper ceiling rose and fell as if it was breathing. How far away those moments seemed to him now. A hundred years.

He passed a row of windows, including the one that Tommy had broken. The window was replaced by a new pane of glass. A faint reflection of himself appeared in that pane, and he studied it. His T-shirt, untucked and wrinkled. A rip on one sleeve where Karl had grabbed him hard, the fabric torn open like a jagged mouth. His usually combed hair disheveled, sticking out at angles. His eyes narrow and bloodshot, his face drained and desperate.

*Who is that person?* he wondered. And if he kept staring at himself, could see through his reflection to who he really was? Or who he had become?

He turned and jogged toward the empty football field. The concession stand was boarded up. He strolled onto the field that, in the darkness, appeared gray. Everything around him was gray—the storage equipment shed, the sagging rows of bleachers. He, too, felt gray—a cardboard cutout, exhaling gray air.

At the fifty-yard line, he posed in his wide receiver's stance, then sprinted full speed toward the end zone where the yellow goal posts held their arms to the low layer of clouds.

He crossed the goal line, a chalk line faded and partially washed away by the late summer rains. He jogged back to the fifty, then ran again. He sprinted again and again, running wind sprints like he used to at the end of football practice. Though the night air was chilly and damp, it burned like hot ashes in his chest, making him wheeze. He wanted to run all night long, run from this town, run from himself, and just keep running. He panted, feeling as though he was inhaling the whole night sky, and all the planets and the Milky Way with it. Or else the sky was inhaling him, and he was suddenly gone from this field, gone from this world.

Finally, exhausted, he knelt down at the goal line.

He imagined Tommy, dancing around in his prized blue and gold number 36 jersey. Imagined him giving his comic Heisman Trophy speech to his teammates before a game. Damn it, Phil thought—that guy was always in perpetual motion; he could jump a mile to catch an almost-out-of-reach spiraling pass. Phil replayed the end of that conference championship game again. He saw Tommy faking left, the right, then hurdling into the air over a crouched defender as the flashbulbs exploded along the sidelines. And every time, Tommy scored that touchdown; every damn time, he leaped high, high, high into the air in slow motion and then landed safely on the home turf.

And where was he now? Phil wondered. How badly was he injured? Why hadn't anyone heard from him? Was he recuperating, or...? He stopped himself, not wanting to consider the other options.

*Mr. and Mrs. Duane Laudermilk report that PFC Thomas J. Laudermilk, 2nd Battalion, 2nd Infantry, C Company, has been wounded in Bihn Long Province, Vietnam, in the Vietnam conflict. No further details are available.*

That's what the brief article on the back page of the *Bluff Lake Freedom* told the townspeople. Phil had torn it out of the paper and kept it in his wallet.

*Vietnam conflict?* Phil had questioned when he read it. *Just call it a goddamn war. After all, that's what it is.*

An hour before, as he was leaving his house, Phil had paused in the back doorway. Frances stood there with him. She leaned forward, kissed him on the forehead, then said, "Go, Phil. Just go."

"But what about *you*, Mom?"

"Don't worry about me," she had said, "I might leave, too, like I threatened." She looked down. "But then again, I might..." she hesitated. "I just might be staying here, like always. But at least I made my point."

Phil wrapped his arms around her in a hug. "I feel awful about all this." Then he added, his voice faltering, "And Dad should know that, too."

"I know, I know," Frances said. "But don't just tell me. You better tell *him*."

Phil stood in the doorway to his parent's upstairs bedroom. He looked into the dark room where Karl, fully dressed, lay on his back on the bedspread. His gaze seemed to be fixed on the ceiling.

"Dad, um..."I'm sorry," Phil said in a shaky voice. "I never meant for any of that to happen..."

Karl was silent.

"Did you hear me, Dad?" No response. Phil lingered there another minute, waiting for his father to say something. Anything. Instead, Karl didn't take his eyes off the ceiling.

Phil started his car and looked back sadly at his mother. Behind the screen door, she appeared like she did in those old black and white 16-millimeter films that Phil used to watch as a kid. Kept for years in tin canisters, the home movies preserved important scenes of Frances and Karl's lives: a Black Hills honeymoon, Sunday picnics, fourth of July parades. In one, Phil, a toddler, rode on Frances' lap on a swing as a younger, thinner, Karl was frozen in a laugh as he pushed them.

As Phil backed out of the driveway, Frances lifted her hand and waved as if nothing was wrong.

Phil saw a light on inside, so he rapped on the door.

Opening the door, Janelle Stiller was surprised to see him.

"I saw Mariah today," Phil began.

Janelle waved him in, and they sat at the kitchen table.

"So you saw her?" she asked anxiously. "Where?"

"At the demonstration. At the plant."

"What?" she stood from her chair, shocked. "Oh my God. She was out there? Is, is she okay?"

"She's safe," Phil assured her. "I saw her getting back on a bus. After the explosions, I mean."

"God, Phil." She lowered herself to the chair again. "Did you talk to her?"

"No. I only saw her for a few seconds. Then everything went crazy. The plane, and…"

"Yes," she gasped. "I saw the report on TV. They said some workers had minor injuries. But still, it was terrible. And I never even imagined *Mariah* would be out there. What was she *doing* there?"

"Passing out leaflets."

Janelle stood, then started pacing. "We're out of touch, you know. Lately, she doesn't write all that often. In fact, I haven't heard from her for weeks."

"Me, either."

Janelle leaned against the kitchen cabinet. "I don't know what's happened between us. She called me several times, but she sounded different. Preoccupied. Sort of distant." Tears started to form as she added "I feel like I've lost her, Phil."

"But maybe you didn't lose her. Maybe she's just trying to *find herself*," Phil offered.

Janelle looked up at him. "You really know my daughter, don't you?"

"I thought I did."

"No. You *do*," Janelle insisted. "You two have something special. Something real. I've always sensed it."

Phil nodded. He checked his watch and stood. "Well, I better go. I didn't mean to barge in on you."

"I'm glad you did." She lifted her arms and gave him a brief hug. "You know,

Phil, if you truly care about Mariah...."

"Stiller," Phil gasped to the girl behind the front desk of the Elizabeth Waters Residence Hall. "Mariah Stiller." Phil held one of Mariah's letters in his hand, though he knew the address by heart. "Room 334. Can you call her?"

Smacking on gum, the girl, in a motion that seemed to take forever, lifted her head from the biology textbook in her lap and finally pressed a button on the wall and spoke into an intercom.

"Mariah Stiller there?" the girl asked.

A long pause. The intercom speaker crackled. "Um, nope," a female voice finally answered. Phil assumed it was her roommate. "Hasn't been here for weeks. I think she kinda moved out."

"Moved out?" Phil repeated anxiously. "Does she know where?" he asked the desk attendant.

"Off-campus, I guess," the roommate replied. The roommate's voice buzzed through the speakers, describing the big green house next to the Sigma Phi Epsilon frat house, over on East Washington. Knowing he could find the house, Phil hurried out the double glass doors.

# CHAPTER 48

Phil climbed the steps to the front porch of the large, run-down house on East Washington Avenue. He tugged at the screen door. The door, locked from the inside with a corroded hook, didn't budge. He knocked hard on the paint-peeled frame and the warped door wobbled beneath his knuckles. As he waited, he glanced around at the large front porch. A few **PEACE NOW!** protest signs—their cardboard bent and creased, stacked themselves in the corner. Pairs of sandals, a single tennis shoe, someone's flattened lavender canvas backpack with anti-war buttons and pink and yellow flowers drawn with a marker pen. He knocked again. One, two, three times.

No one answered. But he could see a dim light inside. A face appeared for an instant from behind a thick drape, then disappeared.

Thoughts ran through his brain: *Maybe she's not even here. Stupid idea to drive all the way to Madison. Stupid.* He waited, hearing faint music and muffled voices inside.

Phil turned to leave just as a barefoot girl wearing a light blue peasant dress appeared behind the locked screen. Her braided hair dangled down to her waist. Her face was pale, except for a few freckles dotting her cheeks.

"Is Mariah Stiller here?" Phil asked.

"Oh," she said, "Um, who are you?"

"Friend of Mariah's"

"Me, too. I'm Alicia." She eyed him, her thick lids lifting a little. "You, um, with the group, then," she quizzed, "at the protest?"

"Yeah, I was," Phil lied.

"Far out," she cooed.

"I really need to see Mariah. She here?"

"Yeah," the girl's voice was wispy. "She's, like, here. In the back bedroom. Asleep, I think. Everybody's kinda holed up."

"I really need to talk to her."

"Um, okay. I'll check. Wait a minute." The girl turned, leaving the door slightly ajar.

Phil peered into the living room, lit by the hazy glow of a red lava lamp. A record spun on a turntable, its coiled wires leading to knee-high veneer speakers. Bluesy psychedelic guitar music played until someone pulled the needle off mid-song, and then *In A Gadda Da Vida* blared. Posters, masking-taped to the windows, were shielded by faded purple floral drapes. Two unlit candles rose from the tops of wine bottles, the wax dripping in frozen beads down the sides. An overturned crate, doubling as a coffee table, was strewn with fliers, newspapers, and topped with a few plates, ceramic coffee cups, and a couple of Boone's Farm bottles. One long-haired man lay, dozing on a sagging lime green sofa.

As Phil waited, he felt the months of silence mounting inside him, stacks of doubts like bricks he could barely lift any more.

The girl reappeared behind the screen. "No outsiders allowed, I guess. Sorry."

She quickly pushed the door shut, and Phil heard it lock from the inside.

Feeling desperate, Phil followed a cinder-covered driveway alongside the house. At the back of the house, he cupped his hands, peered through a partially opened window, and saw Mariah, lying on a bed beneath the covers. He pushed up the window sash another few inches, and smelled a wave of musky smoke, mixed with the sickly-sweet fragrance of incense. Strawberry or raspberry. Besides those scents was the scent of his own sweat that permeated his T-shirt, and beneath that, something else—the scent of his own uncertainty about what he was doing here. Determined, he pushed the window the rest of the way up and crawled inside.

"Phil?" Mariah said with a near-whisper, her voice husky from sleep. She sat up in bed. "Phil?" she said again. She untangled the covers and the two of them stood on opposite sides of the room in near darkness.

There was no welcoming hug, like he had expected. No smile, either, just that neutral repeating of his name. "How'd you get in here?" she asked. "And what... what are you *doing* here?"

Mariah's eyes looked tired, her face seemed thinner, drained and pale. She tugged self-consciously on the neckline of her wrinkled orange and red gauze top, then tugged at it again.

"Mariah, I, I left my house," he stammered. "And Bluff Lake. I'm..." Words, thousands of them, ached in his lungs, and he could hardly take in a breath. "A lot has happened. I didn't know what to do. So I came here. To see you."

"Oh." Her eyes flinched.

"Oh? That's all you can say?"

She didn't respond. "We've got to talk," Phil said urgently. "Let's go someplace. State Street. Let's find a cafe or something."

"I don't think I can do that, Phil. And you shouldn't *be* here. Her voice sounded raspy, as if it had been sandpapered. "I mean, this is a bad time... No one's allowed to leave. The headquarters, I mean."

"Headquarters?"

"Yes. This is the *SDS house*, Phil," she said emphatically, stepping toward him. "The police and the FBI are looking for Daniel, and some other organizers. Daniel...," she hesitated a little, then said, in a hushed voice, "Someone he knew was flying that plane."

"The plane that bombed the plant?" Phil asked incredulously, raising his voice. "What the hell...?"

Mariah put her index finger over his lips, shushing him. "I guess he was a friend of Daniel's," she said. "From Berkeley. The guy stole the plane from the Middleton airport."

"Unbelievable," Phil said.

"I...I didn't know...I didn't know that would happen. But...but now, I'm... I'm caught up, caught up in all of it," she said with a stutter that Phil had never heard before.

Phil closed his eyes. "Jesus, Mariah. How could you get...."

"We could all end up in jail," she interrupted, her voice panicky. "We're all tied to this thing. We're, we're regrouping. We might have to relocate."

"You claimed…I mean, you *assured* me that the protest was going to be peaceful," Phil said.

"I know. I *know*. That's what I thought, too." Phil could see the anguish on her face. "The media was at the demonstration. Someone from a Madison channel panned a camera toward me. The FBI's been called in. And the CIA. They're trying to identify people who were at the protest. They're questioning everybody they can find. We're all implicated." She pinched her eyes shut, took a long breath, exhaled. "I'm so strung out right now. I'm feeling a thousand things at once lately."

"God, Mariah. You *have* to get out of here. Just jump in the car with me and leave." He grabbed at her hand, but she drew it back.

"You don't understand. It's just not that simple, Phil. I can't just do that right now…"

"Why not?"

"I have a commitment here. I have…"

Phil's expression cooled. "You've changed. What happened to you, Mariah?"

"*I* did," a gruff voice declared. The bedroom door opened slowly and someone stepped into the dim room. It was Daniel, who had been eavesdropping on the other side of the door. "Of course she's changed," Daniel said. "She's evolved. She's been radicalized. And she's amazing." he said, smiling at her. "*Amazing.*" Daniel, wearing a faded military green jacket over a worn silkscreen T-shirt depicting blood dripping from LBJ's face, put his hands on his hips defiantly. "So, Riah," Daniel said, glaring at Phil. "Who's the hell is *this*? And how'd he get in here?"

"Daniel, it's, um, Phil," Mariah spilled the words out awkwardly. "Phil Keyhoe. He's, um, my friend from back at Bluff Lake." Her eyes shifted to Phil. "From high school, I mean." Phil didn't like the vague and casual way she described their relationship.

Daniel arched his back and scowled. "No outsiders are allowed in the house, Riah. We agreed on that."

"I just need to talk to her," Phil interjected.

Daniel crossed his arms and stepped in front of Mariah. "Riah can't talk right now," he announced.

"Since when do you speak for her?"

"Since now." Daniel glared at Phil. "Wait a minute, wait a minute," he said, looking at Mariah, "You said he's from Bluff Lake?"

Mariah nodded.

"Is this the dude who works at the Strongs? And his dad's some big-shot supervisor?"

"Well, yeah, he…" Mariah began.

"You work in a goddamn death factory, man," Daniel snarled, tipping his chin toward Phil. "Your famous powder kills babies, you know!" He pointed his finger toward Phil. "I want your ass out of here!"

"I came to talk to my girlfriend," Phil countered.

"Girlfriend?" A smug laugh emerged through Daniel's thick beard. "Ha," he scoffed. "She's been hanging out with *me*, man." Daniel reached with one arm and pulled Mariah close to him.

Phil felt a hollow, sinking sensation in his gut.

"Come on, Riah." Daniel steered Mariah toward the door.

Phil felt jealous, more jealous than he'd ever been in his life, and the sensation filled every cell of his body.

"Wait," Mariah said. "Let us talk, Daniel. Just for a minute."

"Huh?" Daniel's voice was laced with irritation. "I said come *on*. Meeting's starting soon." He tugged harshly on her shoulders, and she pulled away from him.

"Leave her alone!" Phil yelled, taking a step toward him. White lights flashed behind Phil's eyes.

Fists clenched, Daniel charged Phil and took a quick swing, hitting him on the side of his face. The punch sent needles through Phil's jaw. Phil had never been in a fight in his life, but at that moment he couldn't stop himself. Anger coiled inside him, then uncoiled.

He dove hard into Daniel's midsection and slammed him to the floor.

As Mariah pleaded with them from behind, Daniel rolled out from under Phil and struck him in the face and chest. "God damn fuckin' war monger!" Daniel shouted. Phil wrestled him to his back again, a maneuver that Tommy jokingly taught him once in gym class. He pinned his arms with his knees so Daniel couldn't move and punched him hard in the face. Phil lifted his fist to hit him again. Seeing Daniel flinch, and the blood on his face, Phil didn't strike him a second time.

"Stop it! Stop it, both of you!" Mariah screamed as she pulled Phil off Daniel.

Daniel jumped to his feet, his lip bleeding, one hand clutching his jaw. "Get the fuck out of here! Right now!" he shouted, pointing menacingly at Phil. Daniel motioned to a couple of tall hippie guys who, hearing the argument, appeared in the entryway, their arms crossed. "Or my pals and I are throwing you out!"

"Okay," Phil said, raising his hands and backing toward the window. The metallic taste of blood filled his mouth.

"We're boarding that damn window shut," Daniel said as he wiped the blood from his lip. "We're boarding *all* the goddamn windows. No one gets in or out without my say so." He tipped his chin toward Mariah and announced, in his lecture voice, "Meeting starts in five minutes, Riah. I'll see you in there." He shouldered through the door.

"You need to leave, Phil," Mariah stated in a shaky voice.

"I'm going," he said. He lunged and grabbed Mariah's hand. "But you're coming with me."

After climbing through the window, the two of them ran down the cinder-covered alley adjacent to the house, Phil pulling Mariah behind him. Halfway to Phil's car, she let go of his hand and stopped abruptly.

"I can't! I just can't!" she said, her voice filled with anguish. "I'm sorry, Phil, but I just have to stay here."

"What? Stay in the house with *that* guy?" Phil picked up a handful of cinders, threw them down hard.

"I...I don't have a choice. I'm just too involved right now. It's the cause. It's everything I worked for. Then you show up out of nowhere. I'm...I'm sorry about all this..."

"You're sorry for what?" he shouted. "Sorry to see me? Sorry I came here?" He took a step toward her. "You know, I had so much to talk to you about tonight. But I guess I came all the way here for nothing!" He leaned toward her. "So, tell me," he demanded, "Am I just some *friend,* like you said inside? Am I just some piece of your past you left behind?"

There was a long silence as Mariah just stared back at him.

Phil turned away from her, a whirlwind of anger and hurt and confusion swirling inside him.

Mariah put her hand on his shoulder and he spun around and faced her. "Phil," she said, her voice quivering, "Please. You just don't understand...."

"*What* don't I understand?"

"Things change. I'm not that innocent teenage girl I used to be."

"Well, I *loved* that girl," Phil said, his voice choked. He looked her in the eye and said, "And I *still* love her."

"So do I, in a way," Mariah said softly. "But she wasn't who I needed to be. I can't be her anymore, and she can't be me." She crossed her arms tightly in front of her, like she was caught in a net. "I just need time...time to figure everything out."

"By everything, you mean *Daniel?*"

Her lips tightened into a firm line. They parted slightly as if to reply, then closed again.

"Is that what you mean?" Phil demanded.

She still didn't answer.

"Okay then," Phil finally said. "Just go back to your goddamn group. Go back to your goddamn Daniel."

Phil strode to the curb, jumped behind the wheel, and sped away. He thought he heard Mariah call his name again, but because of the rage pounding in his ears he couldn't be sure. It was as if she was miles away, across a wide canyon, her words like pebbles dropping five-thousand feet to a river below.

# CHAPTER 49

When Phil returned to Bluff Lake at four a.m., he felt exhausted, emotionally drained, angry. A thousand things at once, like Mariah said. Beyond that, he felt more aimless than he'd ever felt in his life.

So he had only one place left to go.

He eased his car into the driveway on the left side of the Chrysler. Not too close, not too far away.

Then he tipped his seat back, closed his eyes, and fell asleep. It was an almost dreamless sleep, though a few scenes flickered through his head like a black and white film. He was dogpaddling in a swimming pool that had no water. He saw his father, pointing at his chest. Saw Mariah's confused, shattered expression as she faced him in the alley. Saw Tommy laughing as he clicked the fasteners of his lunch box.

That click jolted him awake.

Phil sat up, seeing that it was daylight, and his father was opening the car door.

"So," Karl said matter-of-factly. "I see you're back."

"Um, yeah," Phil managed with a sleepy voice.

Karl checked his watch. "It's almost seven o'clock. I'm headed to the plant. Are you coming along, or what?"

Karl didn't say the words harshly, but instead with an uncharacteristic, almost apologetic tenderness. He lowered his weight behind the wheel of the Chrysler, then sat there, not starting it. He lifted his work gloves from the dash, set them on the seat, then reached up and adjusted the rear-view mirror.

Phil slowly got out of the Rambler and stepped to the Chrysler. He pulled on the passenger side door handle, but it was locked. He stood there, arms at his sides. Karl pressed the power button, unlocking the door, and Phil finally climbed in. Leaning back in the seat, Phil noticed his mother, watching them from behind the screen door, a hopeful smile on her face.

Though neither he nor his father spoke, to Phil, things felt somehow almost normal.

Phil knew what both of them would see at the Strongs today. The aftermath of the protest and the bombing would be painfully evident. The burned buildings, their timbers blackened, would be surrounded by yellow caution tapes. Reporters would want eyewitness reports. Television station vans would be clustered in the lot. FBI agents would sift through rubble with protective gloves for clues and evidence. Army inspectors would demand answers.

There would be no answers today, only questions.

Phil knew the plant would not shut down, not even for an hour.

At the stop light, Karl opened his lunch box, lifted a sandwich in a plastic bag, and tossed it to Phil. Phil fumbled with it, dropping it to the floor mat. He picked it up and stared at it. A slice of deli turkey and a leaf of green lettuce, pressed between two pieces of wheat bread, carefully cut in half.

"I made this for you," Karl said, "Just in case." He kept his eyes fixed on the road ahead. "I figured my son would need some lunch."

# CHAPTER 50

The ball spiraled toward Phil and when he reached for it, it tipped off his fingers and bounced to the sand. He and Schmitty, the former high school quarterback, were playing catch at dusk on the abandoned beach on the north shore of Bluff Lake.

Just two days after the bombing at the plant, this spontaneous football outing was an escape that Phil needed.

Phil retrieved the dropped ball and shouted, "Now you see why I was second string."

"Hey," Schmitty returned, "You had your moments. In practice, anyway."

Phil threw the ball back to him, a wobbly pass. Then he did a square-in pattern, and Schmitty's perfect spiral landed just out of reach.

"Guess I'm used to faster receivers," Schmitty apologized.

"Guess you're used to *real* receivers, Phil countered.

A little winded, Phil trudged back to Schmitty. "How the hell do you throw a perfect spiral like that?" he asked. "I could never do that."

"Laudermilk taught me."

"Tommy?"

"You bet. When we were about thirteen, I was throwing lame ducks on the junior high playground. Tommy showed me how to place my hand on the ball. Showed me how to put my fingertips on the laces, and how much pressure to put on them." He clapped the ball in his hand a few times. "He claimed that's how he got his girlfriend to make out with him."

"Huh. Sounds just like him. Everything in life led to making out with a girl. Or sex," Phil joked. " So, you made out with a lot of girls?"

Schmitty tipped his head back and laughed. "Nope. But I made starting quarterback on the junior high team."

"Tommy was like that," Phil mused.

"Yeah," Schmitty said. "A genius in disguise. Always kind of dumb, but kind of smart." Schmitty hesitated, then asked, "Heard any more about him?"

"No. Nothing new about him being wounded. His parents keep trying to find out more details. It's frustrating."

"Ah, shit," Schmitty said. "The son of a bitch'll come back in one piece, I bet. Right?"

"Right," Phil echoed, though he really had no idea. "Okay," he said, changing the subject, "I'll go out for one more. And then I'm calling it quits. How about a post pattern? Long as you can throw it."

"Gotcha. One for Milk?"

"Sure," Phil said solemnly. "One for Milk."

He put his hands on his hips as if he was waiting for the signal at the line of scrimmage.

"Hut one, hut two, hut three!" Schmitty called, taking the hike from an imaginary center.

Phil dug in and ran. Looking over his shoulder, he saw the ball rise high, arcing across the beach, saw it spinning so perfectly that it looked like it wasn't spinning at all. As it began to drop from the sky, like a small, aimless, odd-shaped planet in space, he sprinted hard to get under it, to make this one a completion. As he ran, all he could hear was the sound of his own gasping breath, the soft hush of his footsteps in the thick sand. At the last second, he leaped as high as he could, stretching his arms until his muscles and tendons screamed. This time the ball didn't skim off the tips of his index fingers. This time he snagged it with both hands and pulled it home.

"Decent catch," Schmitty said afterwards as they strolled back toward their cars. "More than decent. I should have thrown to you more often last season."

Phil just smiled modestly.

"Wanna go out for a beer?" Schmitty asked. "O'Brien's Pour House is probably just revving up."

Phil pondered the idea, then said "Yeah. Okay."

It was after eleven p.m. when Phil drove back from the Pour House on the outskirts of Bluff Lake. He noticed, in the distance, red lights flashing near the center of town. He wondered if some speeder was picked up on the street. Driving closer, he realized that the red lights were jabbing the darkness on 5th Street. It was a squad car. And the squad was parked directly in front of his house.

His first thought was that someone found out about his involvement with the protest and stealing the maps.

He pictured the cop, and maybe even an FBI investigator inside their high-ceilinged kitchen, tossing questions at his numb mother and father about Phil's activities and whereabouts. An investigator might even be going through Phil's things in his room. He pictured his parents—his mother, worried and pacing, his father standing stone-still.

A part of him wanted to do a quick U-turn and floor the car out of town. But he couldn't do that. Instead, he let the Rambler coast to a stop directly behind the squad car.

He knew he had to face it, whatever was about to happen. The questioning. The painful admission of guilt. The punishment, whatever it would be. He had to accept it all.

When he first agreed to Mariah's plan, he had pushed all those scenarios out of his mind, and never considered the consequences. Passion was more important than reason. After all, it was love that had motivated him. Just love, and nothing else.

He got out of the car, the red lights stabbing his eyes. Walking slowly up the driveway, he spotted his mother, standing in the middle of the yard beneath the spreading branches of the oak. Motionless in the glow of the back porch light, her hands slightly raised, she looked like a plaster statue in a fountain. An officer stood by the back door, jotting something in a note pad.

"Mom?" Phil called as he jogged up the driveway.

"Phil. Oh Phil. Thank God you're back." She approached him unsteadily, as if she was stepping across a layer of ice.

"What's going on?"

She grasped him by the arms and spoke in a voice that sounded frantic, and, at the same time, oddly distant. "Downstairs. I was downstairs," she stammered. "Watching TV. A movie. Karl went to bed early. I should have gone upstairs, Phil. Oh God, why *didn't* I go upstairs?"

"Mom, what is it?"

"It's your father. It's Karl."

Phil put his hands on her shoulders. "What Mom? What?"

"Karl." She struggled for words, tears burning her cheeks. "Your father. He had….he had another heart attack," she rasped.

"Oh no…"

"I was there, in the living room. Right below him. Watching TV… I didn't know," she said. "How could I know?" She put her head on Phil's shoulder, and he could feel her whole body quivering. "When I finally went upstairs…he was already gone."

"Gone?" Phil gasped.

"The rescue squad, they tried to revive him. But it was too late." She burst into a sob. "Too late."

As the reality sunk in, Phil's mouth opened and closed on silent words. He embraced his mother and held her tightly. Suddenly, the whole night sky seemed to drop down on him. First the inky darkness, then the burning white stars, then the shattering moon all collapsed on him and weighed him down. He let out an anguished cry and wanted to fall to his knees, but instead he just stood there, holding it, holding it all up.

# PART
# SIX

# CHAPTER 51

In the full-length hallway mirror, Phil watched as the tie slowly looped around his neck. It was his father's tie from his closet, a blue and red striped one that his mother handed to him. When Phil hesitated, his mother insisted, saying "Just wear it." Phil couldn't quite get the knot right; each time he tried, the tie was a little too short, or too long.

He remembered that morning when he was fourteen, and late for church. Karl, noticing him standing in front of the oval bathroom mirror and struggling with his tie, stepped behind him. Karl's thick arms encircled Phil's chest. As Karl maneuvered the tie, he pressed his cheek next to Phil's. The awkward embrace made Phil uneasy as he felt his dad's rough whiskers and smelled his Old Spice aftershave. "Over and under, then back through," Karl instructed as he glided the silk fabric in a pattern that was mysterious to Phil. "There you go," Karl proclaimed as he finished, "A perfect knot." *Too tight, too tight,* Phil thought at the time. "Just right," his father had said.

"Phil," a voice from behind startled him. It was his mother. "We're almost late." She held out a set of keys. He knew he'd feel uncomfortable in the Chrysler, but his mother said they should take it.

When Phil entered the driver's seat, he couldn't help but notice his father's leather work gloves, folded on the dash, ready for the next workday. In the cup holder, a half-empty twenty-ounce root beer from the local Standard station, where Karl always stopped because it was a few cents cheaper than at Mobil. In the ashtray, an empty pack of Lucky Strike cigarettes, its red, target-shaped logo crumpled in half.

After the church ceremony, leading a line of cars with their headlights on, Phil drove to Elm Hill cemetery. As they passed beneath the archway at the entry, the tires hit a pothole, rocking the car and jolting the dashboard compass. East, West—the directions bobbed and swayed in the liquid, as if they couldn't decide which way they were headed. Angling into a parking stall behind the hearse, Phil pressed on the brake, the pedal worn by his father's large shoe. The brakes wheezed a little, and the tires crackled over some acorns before they lurched to a stop. Phil and Frances sat in silence, waiting for the priest and the rest of the funeral procession to arrive.

"It's not your fault, you know," Frances said.

"I *feel* like it is, Mom," Phil said to the blue padded dash.

"No. Don't blame yourself. Don't ever think that." Her black hat with the veil bobbed slightly on her head. "It's Karl's own fault, in a way. His damn cigarettes," she said, nodding at the ashtray. "His weight. And his heart." Then, breaking into a sob, she added, "Oh, maybe it's nobody's fault. And everyone's." She dabbed the handkerchief at her pug nose, closed her eyelids, and Phil could see her eyes moving beneath the lids, as though she was seeing something on the back of them. She opened her eyes again and looked at Phil for the first time since they left the church. "You look nice in that tie," she said. She lifted the tie with her fingertips. "Real nice." Phil felt the silk cloth constricting his windpipe, even though he had loosened it a little.

"He cared about you, you know," Frances said, her voice sad and slow. "Though you two didn't always agree on things. He was trying to guide you the best he knew how. Sometimes he didn't know how to show it, but he *loved* you. Deep down he did."

"I know, Mom," Phil replied softly.

The pallbearers arrived one by one, dressed in Army or Navy uniforms. They were Karl's friends from the plant and from the Kiwanis Club, all World War II vets that Karl had, over the years, worked and volunteered and drank whiskey sours and played cards with.

"Okay. It's time," Frances said. "We better go out there."

But Phil didn't move, just gripped the steering wheel. He didn't want to go through with this agonizing ceremony. He had served as an altar boy with Tommy a few times in in grade school. On those mornings, though they never knew the deceased person, he always hated the sound of the cloth belts and the winch as the casket was lowered into the freshly dug grave. He could always see the small roots, like pale snakes cut in half, on the wall of dark brown soil.

Today, Phil didn't want to see any of it. Not the priest, dressed in his black cassock embroidered with the word PAX, reciting the prayers. Not the incense burner, swinging three times toward the casket, the pale white smoke twisting up from it. Not the holy water, sprinkling on the draped American flag. Phil dreaded hearing the inevitable sound of his mother's sobs intertwined with the creak of those belts and the frail tenor voice of a man from the church choir singing, "God Bless America."

Phil stared at the dashboard clock. He wished he could stare at it until he could bend the clock hands backwards and reverse time.

The back doors of the hearse opened, and Phil walked over. Phil was the only young person in the group; several of Karl's friends had volunteered before the funeral Mass, but Frances insisted that Phil be one of the eight pallbearers. Phil grabbed a bronze handle at the back corner of the casket and one man rasped "Okay, fellas. One, two, three." The eight pallbearers hefted the weight up the hillside to the waiting gravesite.

*Heavier than I expected,* Phil couldn't help but think, though he tried not to.

He was carrying the physical weight of his father, but there was much more than that. There were other, heavier weights: He was carrying his father's past, his World War II service, his tenure at the Strongs, making the place safe for his co-workers, his years of trying to be a conscientious husband to Frances and a father to young Phil. And there was more: Phil carried his father's strengths and his weaknesses. But most of all, he was carrying his dad's unwavering commitment, and his pride. He was carrying that. All that. And it was almost too much to bear.

On the way up the steep hillside, Phil was certain he felt his father's carefully arranged body shift inside the casket, his weight sliding toward the corner where he stood.

At the graveside, Phil tipped his head back. Above him, silhouetted limbs of oak trees, like black arteries, arched over the gravesite. Nine, ten, eleven, twelve branches spoked outward from the limbs. Phil kept counting them over and over.

Phil wanted to utter some words of comfort to his mother. But the right words wouldn't come out; he felt panes of glass shattering inside his chest, cutting his vocal chords. The best he could do was put his arm around her shoulders. She felt soft, as if her bones were ready to crumble.

She wasn't that way at the funeral home visitation, though, when he stood in the back entryway, out of sight of the casket. He didn't know if he could walk in there, so he just lingered in the foyer, putting off the inevitable. She turned to him, grabbed his hand firmly with hers, and said, with a command that startled him, "Come on. Let's do this." Then she grabbed him by the arm and led him through the veneer doors. The rest of the mourners followed, parting the floral scent of the visitation room where the silver casket waited.

Up close, you couldn't even see any signs of his final pain on his face; somehow, the anguish of the heart attack had been repaired, erased. Nothing showing, just a passive, peaceful smile, the tips of Karl's lips pulled upward, sewed into a pleasant sleeping pose. The thought struck Phil that it was that easy to keep the idea of death away. The satin cloth beneath Karl's head was bunched up, a soft cumulous cloud on both sides of his face.

Phil could barely look at him, just gave him one quick glance as he approached. Then he shifted his eyes beyond the casket and fixed them on the gallery of enlarged photos propped on a small table. The photos, freezing each stage of Karl's life, skipped through the years: A thin, fresh-faced Karl, sat on a jeep on the Burma Road in 1944. The inscription read "To my stateside doll, Frances. Love, Karl." Karl, in a newly pressed Army uniform with a young and attractive Frances on their wedding day. Frances and Karl at the hospital entryway with a newborn Phil. An older Karl leaned against the fender of his new Chrysler in the front driveway. Next he was smiling proudly at his desk at the Strongs Plant.

Behind the open lid of the casket, Phil focused on the flowers sprayed into the air like the vapor trails of rockets turning red and orange.

Frances stood there a few long moments, staring at Karl, the fingers of her hand curled on the rounded edge of the casket as Phil held her by the arm. "Oh Karl, why...?" she moaned. Then she waited, staring into his face, as if expecting Karl to answer her question, right then and there. Finally, she leaned over the open casket and kissed Karl on the left cheek, as if she were just saying good night.

Now, at the cemetery, the service concluded with the color guard lifting their rifles. The drill sergeant issued the commands, though in a hushed voice. "Present arms." The six men from the VFW raised rifles to their shoulders. "Ready." The men aimed their weapons upward. "Fire!"

As they fired their rounds, the sound jolted Phil's body, both inside and out. He sobbed with each shot. His arm around his mother's shoulder, he felt her flinch with the explosions, too.

The six rifles fired again in unison again, white smoke bursting from the long, blue-black barrels. *Will those bullets land harmlessly in a field somewhere?* Phil wondered, *Or will they drop in someone's back alley, or on a house, or a kid's playground?* Then, for an absurd moment, he pictured those bullets flying for miles, arcing steadily, and finally dropping through the air and landing somewhere within the confines of the Strongs Plant. He pictured those dull pieces of lead, embedding themselves in the thick sod roof of a powder storage building.

Bluish clouds of smoke drifted from the barrels of the rifles and surrounded Phil and Frances. It was the caustic scent of ball powder, a precise mixture Phil knew all too well: 74.8 percent potassium nitrate, 13.3 per cent charcoal, 11.9 per cent sulfur. A perfect mixture, but deadly. A mixture not for healing, but for destroying. It was that scent that made Phil's nostrils burn and his eyes water.

The color guard fired again. Each round drove the pain deeper inside Phil. This much he knew: He loved his father. Despite everything, he really did love him.

As they walked slowly toward the car, Frances carried the folded, three-cornered flag the color guard captain had presented to her. Phil opened the passenger's side for her, and said, "I'll help you get through this, Mom. Whatever you need."

"Thank you, Phil." she assured him. "It won't be easy, but I'll survive."

And, judging by her sad but determined expression, he knew she would.

Then she turned to Phil and said "He's a hero, you know. Sure, there was what he did in World War II, saving his buddy. But all his life, he did what he thought was right. And he did it with all his heart. That makes you a hero, doesn't it?"

Phil nodded solemnly.

Minutes later, as Phil leaned against the fender, pondering his mother's words, he noticed someone slowly making their way down the hillside toward him. Her black dress fluttered in the wind and her hair blew across her face like wisps of blonde smoke. When the wind changed direction, her face was unveiled.

Mariah walked up to him, an empathetic expression on her face.

# CHAPTER 52

Mariah embraced Phil in a consoling hug. For months, he had longed for her touch, and now, as she held him, it seemed to ease some of his grief.

"Oh Phil, I feel so bad for you," she sighed, "And for your mother."

After checking with Frances, Phil and Mariah climbed the hillside, the highest point in the cemetery, and sat down in an open area.

Mariah adjusted her black dress around her knees. "I know it's not the same situation," she began, "and I know it's not the same pain you're feeling right now. But I know what it's like to lose a father." She kept her eyes fixed on her black sandals. "Unfortunately, it's something that you don't just get over." The lush grass circled, stirred by the wind. "I watched the whole ceremony from the hillside and when they lowered the casket, I could see you shuddering." She choked, then steadied her voice. "And I cried along with you." She wiped her tears with the silk sleeve of her dress. "You know, Phil, it's strange, but I think, as I watched, a part of me started letting go of my father, too." Knowing Phil's past struggles with Karl and her own struggles, she added "We both need to forgive. There's just too much resentment and anger and holding grudges. Those things just eat away at your insides."

"Yeah, I know what you mean."

"Life isn't about hate," she added. Then she asked, "Have you heard any more about Tommy?"

"No. It's really hard to get any more information. That's what his mom tells me."

"Typical of the military," Mariah scoffed.

"So," Phil said, changing the subject, "what about us?" It was a question that had been aching inside him ever since their conversation in Madison, and he had to confront her with it now.

"What do you mean?"

"Is there an *us* anymore?"

"I'm not sure how to answer that, Phil," she replied, her voice shrinking to a whisper. Soft as they were, her words still stung.

"I mean, there's still a war going on," she said. "I don't know how else to say it, except it's bigger than the two of us."

"Yeah. Tell me about it." The words came out more sarcastic than he intended. But it was what he felt: there definitely *was* a war going on, not just in faraway Vietnam, but right here, deep inside his gut.

"So," Phil wondered, "are you back in Bluff Lake, then?"

"No. I have to head back to Madison this afternoon. I've got a lot to do there. I have to… "

"And what about Daniel?" Phil interrupted. An image of the two them entered his mind, and he tried to push it away.

211

Neither of them spoke for a full minute. She gazed into the distance, where the shadowed bluffs hunkered, rounded and dark, as if the earth itself had lifted its broad shoulders in doubt.

"So is he your new boyfriend?" Phil persisted. He felt like something dry was stuck in his throat. "Is that it?" As he waited for her answer, she seemed so close to him, and yet, still a thousand miles away, like a blazing meteor that you're never able to touch.

"I...I just need to sort out my feelings," she finally stated. "To process everything."

"Everything?" he repeated.

"Yes. And part of what I'm processing has to do with *you*," she said. "There's something that's eating away at me." She looked at him intensely.

"What do you mean?"

"You're working for a *war plant*, Phil. You're supporting an immoral military action." A tear trickled down one cheek, then was absorbed by a dark fold of her dress. "I just can't be in a relationship with someone who works at a place like the Strongs. I just *can't*." She lowered her gaze, plucked a blade of grass, twirled it between her index finger and thumb, then let it fall to the ground. "You can understand the way I feel, right?" When he didn't reply, she asked again, "Right, Phil?"

Phil stood abruptly and started toward the car. "Mom's waiting. She needs me. I've really got to get back to her."

# CHAPTER 53

Phil quickly opened the envelope.

*Ten-hut!!! This is an official missive from one Thomas J. Laudermilk, PFC.*

*Hey, Key! It's me. Tommy. Or at least what's left of me. I know I didn't write for a while, but I had a damn good excuse. I'm sure that by now my parents have let you know that I'm okay. But I wanted to give you all the steamy details.*

*Let me proceed to tell you about my million-dollar war wound. The sad and happy tale begins with a Bouncing Betty. No, that's not a girl I'm dating—it's a goddamn land mine that I stepped on while on patrol. My boots were made for walking, so to speak (watch out, Nancy Sinatra!), and that got me in trouble. I thought I was stepping on solid ground, but it was a frickin' booby trap.*

*So, you remember my left leg? That's the other one, besides my right leg. Anyway, it got cut up pretty bad by shrapnel. I won't go into the ugly details, but I also got some shrapnel in my ass.*

*Anyway, it earned me an exciting free ride on a medivac Huey, and I had a delightful trip to a base hospital. After that ride, I ask you: Why go to Disney World?*

*Okay. Permit me to tell you a few things about hospital life, where I have holed up for quite a while, thanks to an infection. One—the food is damn good, compared to the crappy rations we got in a cardboard box at base camp. (Ham and lima beans in a can?—please permit me to puke!). Two—the beds are better than those stiff canvas cots. And three—the scenery around here is much lovelier. Speaking of which, I've met a nurse who stops to talk to me every day. She's part Vietnamese, and part French. As you might guess, I like the French part the best. Can you say Ooo la la? Anyway, Key, the bottom line is: I think I'm in love. And I think it's vice-versa. It's way different than when I was going with Shirelle, who, I guess, has forgotten about me. Me and Celine have even made some plans together, for later. So we'll see how that all plays out. Sounds kinda like a soap opera, doesn't it? As the World Turns…*

*But meanwhile, the other good news is that when I get out of here, I've earned a free trip home on a C-141 Jumbo plane they call the Starlifter. And, believe me—on the way back, I shall enjoy all the Coca-Cola I can drink! I expect to be served by Raquel Welch in her fur bikini. And also—as pursuant to Executive Order 11016 by the President—I have earned a Purple Heart. It's a little overboard, considering I just stepped in the wrong spot, but, what the hell, I will accept it anyway.*

*So look for my ugly face back in town in a few weeks. I might be limping a little, but I'm betting I can still beat you in a footrace! So get ready!*

*Your half-assed pal,*

*(Soon to be Honorable) Tommy (AKA Milk)*

As Phil re-read Tommy's last few sentences, he couldn't stop himself from tipping his head back and laughing, and laughing, and laughing.

# CHAPTER 54

A week later, Mariah sat on the shore of Lake Mendota a windy afternoon. She stared out at the water, her thoughts rushing through her mind like the waves washing, one after the other, onto the sand beach. Everything seemed to be in motion: the whitecaps, lifting their heads and then disappearing, the flickering lime-green leaves on the trees above her, the gulls banking on the wind. The world was alive, too alive today. Everything seemed to be calling her, pushing her, telling her to move in one direction or another. But she couldn't help but feel trapped and immobile.

"What's with the backpack, babe?" Daniel had asked her this morning when he saw her placing a paisley blouse and her journals into her lavender backpack.

"Daniel. I..." She lifted another blouse from the closet. "I've got a lot to think about."

"Huh? Like what?"

"Like everything. I just need some space."

"Space?" He laughed and held up a newly-rolled joint. "If you want space, I can give you that. This is some *really good* shit." He smelled strongly of the weed he'd been smoking; the pungent scent had filled her small bedroom in the SDS house. He seemed stoned already, and it was only eleven a.m.

"I don't mean that kind of space." She opened a drawer, pulled out a pair of worn bell-bottom jeans with torn knees. She turned and tossed them toward the backpack.

Daniel lunged, caught the jeans in mid-air, and held them out to her. "Hey, you look always look real sexy in these," he exclaimed. "So what's going on?"

"Daniel, please leave me alone," she said curtly.

He tipped his chin toward her. "No way. Not 'til you tell me what the hell's up."

She turned to him and finally said what was on her mind. "You didn't bother to tell me or anyone, for that matter, what was up. I mean with the plane. I've been thinking about what happened out there."

"What happened out there? he interrupted. I'll tell you what happened. We really shook things up. Shit, we even made the national news."

"Yeah, it made the news alright," Mariah said under her breath. She looked up at him. "But come on, Daniel, the truth is you never really leveled with us. About the bombing."

Daniel didn't respond. He stood looking out the back window, his eyes glazed.

"I thought," Mariah continued, "in fact, we *all* thought some guy from Berkeley was going to fly over the plant and drop leaflets. But last night I found out it was *you* who stole a plane. It was *you* who was actually flying it. Is that true?"

"Hey, hey, cool it, babe." He tossed her a cynical squint. "That was all part of the plan."

"Well you didn't let *me* in on the plan. You know, it took a lot for me to get you those maps. Nobody said any of that would happen..."

"It had to be done, Mariah," he interrupted, nodding with himself. He finished the reefer, snuffed it out in a pottery ashtray, lit another one with a Bic lighter, took a long drag. "Some things just *have* to be done."

"Do they?" She shook her head, pushed the dresser drawer hard, and it thumped shut. "You're stinking up the room with that smoke."

"Yeah, I cause smoke wherever I go. Somebody has to." He smirked.

"It's not funny, Daniel. When you see the damage you caused. People could have been killed." Her voice tightened.

"Listen," he said, leaning toward her. "Sometimes you've gotta take action. You know—to get your point across to those fuckin' idiots."

"Take action? Like flying a stolen plane and bombing a factory? Isn't that a little extreme?"

He scowled, and, lifting his arm and pointing at her, he assumed his lofty I'm-the-SDS-President voice. "Is blowing the hell out of Vietnamese villages *a little extreme*? Is killing innocent women and children in Da Nang *a little extreme*? You don't know what extreme is until you've been torched by fuckin' napalm. Ever see the pictures of those little kids, burned and running for their lives?"

She pushed his pointing finger aside. "So you fight fire with fire? Violence with violence? Is that it? Whatever happened to peace and love?"

"I do what I have to do." He tipped his chin toward her. "Maybe people will realize we're serious about all this. I've been talking to this new group called the Weathermen. They get things done. The military industrial complex has to be stopped, you know. It *has* to be stopped." Hands on his hips, he leaned forward, the way he sometimes did at the podium during a rally to look authoritative. "And I want to be the one who helps to shut it down." His eyes took on a dreamy look. "I want us to get noticed. I want all the SDS chapters, even on the west coast, to know we're out here. That *I'm* out here. That we're kicking ass. I want 'em to say *Wow, man, look what they're fuckin' doin' in Mad City*!"

"I get that. But there are better ways to do things. A right way."

"Right?" His mouth opened as if the word was heavy and hanging from his jaw. "What the hell is *right*?"

"I thought you knew," she said, her voice rising. "I really did. When I first met you, I admired you. You planned teach-ins and discussion sessions. You organized peaceful demonstrations and sit-ins. And now..."

He lifted his palm in the air like a stop sign, the way he did at rallies to silence the chanting crowd. He finished the reefer, smudged it out, then stalked closer to her. "Come on, Mariah," he said condescendingly. "I thought you were—you know—one of us. I thought you were trying to make a difference." His arms were suddenly circling her waist.

She peeled his hands away. "I *do* want to make a difference. I plan to. I just have to figure out *my* way of doing it. Not yours." Her voice quivered a moment, then became strong again. "Let's face it. You deceived me, Daniel. You lied to me. To all of us, really. And I can't stand liars."

"You've got it all wrong, babe. It's the pigs in Washington who are lying to *us*. It's that bomb-happy LBJ, and McNamara's morons, and..." He lifted his hands again and cupped her bare shoulders. "Hey," he said, his voice turning softer, "we're in this together, you know? We've got a frickin'' world to change. Remember?" He kissed the side of her face; his thick beard—stiff like steel wool—scraped her skin.

Mariah tried to pull away. With a sudden motion, he shoved her toward the bed. She fell backwards and Daniel lunged on top of her.

As she struggled to get out from under him, he growled "Come on, babe!" Digging his fingernails into her wrists, he pinned her arms down. "You've shut me down before," he said through clenched teeth. "But not this time."

"Stop!" she shouted, "Get off me!" Freeing one arm, she slapped him in the face. When he didn't stop, she grabbed the ashtray from the nightstand and hit him, hard, on the side of his head.

"God damn!" he howled, clutching his head and jumping back up. "You goddamn bitch!"

He pointed at her. "Okay, if that's the way you're going to be." His face was flushed, and his hair fell over his glaring, bloodshot eyes.

"Yes," she shouted angrily, "That's the way I'm going to be." Brushing past him, she lifted her backpack with shaking hands. Her wrists stung.

"You know what?" he snarled, his voice crawling from his throat in a harsh, low tone. "I see exactly what you are now. You're not *with* us, like I thought. You're just a goddamn conservative Midwest girl with hang ups. Little miss middle class. Too bad I misjudged you."

"No, I misjudged *you*. And I'm out of here!"

"Hey," he said, "Wait a minute. Wait just a frickin" minute. There's one little goddamn problem."

She turned.

"Nobody just leaves the organization. Nobody quits. Not without my permission." He ran his hand through his greasy hair. "I mean, for all I know, you could rat on me. You could go to the feds."

"I wouldn't do that," she replied. "You know I wouldn't, Daniel."

"I have to be sure." He turned to a closet in the back of the room, opened a metal box.

Mariah looked on with disbelief as Daniel pulled out a handgun.

"What are you doing?" she gasped.

"I said I have to be sure. Real sure. The feds have been nosing around here." His eyes fixed on her with a hostile stare. Mariah knew he was high and wasn't sure what to expect next. "I hope you're not a turncoat, babe," he continued, stepping closer to her. Tell me you're still loyal to the people. To the cause. And to me. To *me*." He stared at her without blinking, his smiling mouth contorted, a burning craziness showing through the embers of his eyes.

She was silent, her vocal chords numb.

"I need your word that you won't tell anybody who was flying that plane," he raised the gun slowly to her chest, pushed it between the buttons of her top. She could feel the cold touch of the bluish metal barrel on her bare skin. "Tell me you're loyal." He waited. "Just say it."

Fear rushed through her. "Okay," she finally managed. "Okay, I won't say anything."

"You know," he reminded her, nudging the barrel into her skin, "You're tied to all this. Everything that happened at the Strongs plant." She could smell the acrid  smoke on his breath. "You're part of it, Mariah."

For the first time since she had met Daniel, she felt terrified of him, of what he was capable of doing. She knew now this wasn't the Daniel she had met few months ago. This wasn't Daniel, the idealistic leader who organized peaceful marches and swayed the crowd with enlightening speeches. This was Daniel the egomaniac, a madman on a power trip. Daniel the womanizer.

"Would you please please please put that gun away?" she asked.

He finally lowered the pistol slowly to his side. He glanced down at it and smirked. "Huh," he uttered casually. "I'd never use this thing, would I? I mean, hey, I'm all about nonviolence." With a raspy laugh, he set the gun on the end table.

Mariah flung one strap of her backpack over her shoulder and turned. "Goodbye, Daniel."

"Yeah, go ahead." He pulled another reefer from the pocket of his vest, lit it. "I guess I'll let you go. It's cool with me," he uttered, his voice sounding suddenly cavalier, the reefer wiggling between his lips as he spoke. "You know," he said to her back, "there's a lot of chicks in this house that are anxious to have sex with me. A lot. I hope you realize that. I mean, love is free, right?" His face filled with a sarcastic sneer as he inhaled a long drag of the reefer.

Mariah spun around and glared at him. "You're such an asshole, you know that?"

He held up two fingers in a V. Through a haze of pale smoke, he exhaled the word "Peace."

Now, on the shore, Mariah gazed out over the water, the low afternoon sun turning its surface silvery and blinding. Her backpack, stuffed with her clothes and a few belongings, was heavier than she thought. She set it next to her on the beach, glanced at the peace symbol buttons attached to it, studied the swirling pink and yellow flowers, drawn with a marking pen. What idealistic but gullible girl drew those flowers last fall? She wondered. She glanced down at her wrists, noticing the bluish bruises on them where Daniel had grabbed her.

She knew she couldn't go back to the SDS house. Nor could she stop at her former roommate's dorm room, asking to crash there, maybe sleep on the floor. Besides, why would she go back there? She hadn't talked to her roommate in months, and she knew she didn't really didn't fit in.

In fact, she didn't fit in any world right now.

She knew she couldn't drive anywhere. Her broken-down Fairlane—a car that hadn't started for weeks—was abandoned in the alley behind the SDS house. She had a fleeting thought that maybe she could hitchhike somewhere like Bob Dylan once did, to New York City. But which direction would she go? And then what? she asked herself.

She leaned over, picked up a few flat stones at the edge of the beach, then tried to skip them over the water. She threw one, two, three stones. None of them skipped. The mute stones just slapped against the oncoming waves with a small splash, flipped awkwardly into the air, then sunk to the bottom. A lyric from Dylan's "The Times They Are a Changin'" played briefly through her head. Something about sinking if you don't try to swim. How damn true, she thought.

Impulsively, she slipped off her sandals and waded into the lake in her cut-off jeans and blouse. She kept walking, feeling the cool water rise up to her thighs, her waist, her chest.

She took a couple more steps, the water rising, lapping at her neck. Then she opened her arms wide, like wings, and plunged forward, leaning into a crawl stroke. She kept her eyes focused on the other shore. Though she hadn't swum any distance for a while, she knew she was always an accomplished swimmer, the captain of the high school swim team. It was only about a mile to the far shore, wasn't it? she thought. An easy goal for her. She used to swim twice that far during swimming practice.

She cupped the water gracefully with her palms, arching her body and gliding across its surface. She kept going, pulling the water rhythmically with her left hand, her right, her left. Soon she was fifty yards from the beach. Then one hundred. But the longer she swam, the more the far shore seemed to be pulling away from her. Was it just an illusion, she wondered? She really *was* getting closer, wasn't she?

A few yards further, the wind picked up and larger waves rose and sloshed against her face. She inhaled a mouthful of water. Pausing and treading water, she coughed it out. She swam forward again, but she felt like she was losing her rhythm, her strong stroke. She began to tire, and it seemed like she was hardly moving; the more she tried to pull at the waves, the heavier and slower she began to feel. She wasn't swimming any more—just fighting the water, swinging at it, slapping it, fighting it. Slapping Daniel's face, with that vacuous glare. Slapping away his controlling, ugly personality, his deceit.

For an instant, through her blurred vision, she thought she saw someone on the other shore. A figure standing on the beach beneath those tall pines.

Halfway across, the water was much colder, and panicked thoughts raced through her head: Should she turn around and go back to shore where she started? Or was she too far out already? Did she still have some stones in her pockets, and were they pulling her down? Her limbs were turning numb; her legs felt stiff, her feet like blocks of pink marble.

Her backpack on the beach, her father's heavy shadow, her guilt for leaving Phil for a person who turned out to be a liar and a con-man—all those heavy things were pulling her down. She felt like, any second, she could just let go, and it would all be over. She could just sink under and slip down, down, down into the water's blue embrace. Into the peaceful darkness.

But she had to be strong. Strong. She imagined that figure on the other shore, waving her forward, encouraging her. So she kept going, though she was panting for air, though the thick water seemed to keep trying to pull her under.

Minutes later, her fingertips touched the mud of the lake bottom, and she knew she had finally made it across.

As she stood in the waist-deep water, gasping and exhausted, she wondered: Was that lake water trickling down her numb cheeks, or were those tears?

If they were tears, she decided, they were tears of joy, because she just swam all the way to the far shore. She just swam all the way to that person she needed so desperately to reach, to know again, to reunite with. The one person who could save her.

She looked down at the surface of the water and her rippling reflection smiled back at her. And she knew, then, that she just swam all the way back to herself.

# CHAPTER 55

*Thump thump thump.* Janelle was awakened from a deep sleep by the sound. She fumbled for her alarm clock on the nightstand, saw that it was quarter to twelve. She heard the sound again. *Thump thump thump.*

She sat up in bed, switched on the bedroom light, grabbed a robe and slipped it on.

Uneasy, she wondered who'd be knocking urgently on the door at nearly midnight. Drunks coming back from the Pair-a-Dice Bar, maybe? She crossed the kitchen in bare feet. Leaning close to the door, she called out "Who's there?"

She recognized the voice that called back. "It's me. It's me!"

"Mariah!" When Janelle opened the door, she was shocked at her daughter's appearance: Her face was sallow, and thinner; her hair was unwashed and stringy, and strands of it drooped over her face. Her saggy T-shirt was wrinkled, and her cutoffs looked soiled. But what bothered her the most was the forlorn expression that painted itself across her daughter's face.

"I thought you might like some company," Mariah said.

As Mariah stepped in and they hugged, Janelle could feel her daughter's shoulders shaking. "I'm home," Mariah whispered. "I'm finally home."

"It's so good to see you," Janelle said. "But…I thought you were in Madison."

"It's a long story, Mom," Mariah said, wiping a tear away. "Very long. Right now I need some sleep. But I promise I'll explain it all tomorrow. So what time do you get up?"

"Seven. And I'm at work by eight." Janelle noticed the dark lines etching themselves under her daughter's hooded, bloodshot eyes. "But don't you want to sleep in? You look really tired."

Mariah placed her backpack on a hook beside the door. "Wake me at seven."

In the morning, as Mariah exited her bedroom, she glanced around at the living room. The comfortable furniture looked slightly rearranged. A few decorations, but no clutter. The t.v. was in a different corner, its rabbit ear antennae rising in a V toward the ceiling. The ceiling where, last year, she and Janelle imagined the night sky when they played the stargazing game. Mariah wondered if the stars might still be there, if she looked hard enough for them.

"The place looks nice," Mariah commented, entering the kitchen where her mom was reaching for some cereal. Janelle was already dressed for work in a navy skirt and a white blouse with a lacy collar. "It's cozy, in fact."

"This cramped little space? It's…"

"Homey," Mariah said, filling in the word. Noticing a framed painting on the living room wall, she walked back to it and studied it up close. Inside a black frame was an impressionistic watercolor, the animated brush strokes depicting a woman with a parasol in the field, the blue and white background shimmering behind her. "New painting?" she asked.

"Yes. It's *Woman with a Parasol.* I always loved that painting. It's a Monet."

"Dreamy colors. So it's an original oil, then?" Mariah joked.

"Of course. For five bucks at a garage sale, it was quite a steal."

Mariah returned to the kitchen and began making coffee for the two of them. She filled the coffeemaker with water, scooped some grounds into the filter basket. "You want it strong, right? she asked.

"My daughter knows me, alright," Janelle said. "Strong it is."

Mariah added an extra scoop. "So where are you working today?"

"Remember that legal office downtown?"

"Yeah?"

"They gave me a full-time position."

"That's awesome, mom," Mariah exclaimed. "And what's with the flowers?" She had noticed the bouquet of roses in a thin glass vase in the living room.

Janelle seemed to blush. "That's part of my good news. I've been seeing someone."

"Oh?" Mariah asked brightly.

"I don't want to say too much about it right now. It's early, and we've only dated a few times. But he's really nice. And considerate. And he makes me laugh."

"Sounds like a pretty good combination." Then, echoing what her mother had asked her more than a year ago, she asked "Is he *real*, mom?"

"I hope so," Janelle replied. "And what about Phil?"

Mariah looked down at the percolating coffee pot, the steam rising from it in swirling wisps. "It's complicated," she sighed. "By the time I explain it all, you'd be late for work. So I'll talk about it tonight."

"So, how long will you be staying?" Janelle asked.

"A while. Until I decompress, I guess. If that's okay."

"Of *course* it's okay."

"And then what?"

"And then…? Good question."

"What about college?"

"I'm planning to go back, of course. In fall. I have some classes to re-take. And my scholarship extends to next year."

"Good. Great."

Mariah strolled toward the cupboard to take out their coffee cups. At the same time, Janelle was gliding toward the silverware drawer. The two of them dodged each other, shuffling left, then right, then left, in synch. At that moment, they both broke out in spontaneous laughter.

"We could be dancing," Mariah said.

"We *are* dancing," Janelle replied.

# PART
# SEVEN

# CHAPTER 56

On this humid late August morning, Phil checked his watch. It was only seven a.m., but he was already headed to punch-in, as if he was some over-eager worker arriving way too early. But there were things he needed to accomplish today.

At the security gate, an iron-faced guard remarked "First one here. Can't wait to get started, eh?" He patted down the pockets of Phil's jeans in case he was carrying any flammable materials. He wasn't, of course. The only flammable things he carried with him today were those feelings inside him—a combustible mixture of conflicting emotions.

As he approached the change house, he could see, in the distance, the buildings that were damaged or burned during the bombing. Metal scaffolds climbed up their walls, and crews were already replacing their roofs and timbers. The maze of power lines, stretched like black snakes between the transformers and utility poles, still fed their energy to the hungry production buildings.

Reaching his locker, he climbed into the coveralls slowly, methodically, as if he was under water. Right leg. Left leg. Right arm. Left arm. He buttoned it to his neck. Always a little too tight.

He pushed his feet into his steel-toed boots, then turned and stared at himself in the cracked full-length mirror bolted to the wall. A slightly distorted image of a boy, a man, stared back at him.

He studied that reflection one more time. Minutes might have passed. Or hours. He wasn't sure.

Then, as if in a reverse slow-motion video, he unlaced his scuffed boots, pulled them off. Those boots dragged him down each day like anchors pulling him under. He unbuttoned the worn coveralls and peeled them off like a snake shedding its dead skin. Dropping to the floor, they gathered themselves into a rumpled pile. The stiff cotton didn't flicker with static. He slipped on his black Converse tennies, grabbed his work gear, and marched toward the door in his T-shirt and jeans.

The bundle of work clothes seemed to double in weight until he lowered it to the scratched counter and said "I need to sign out."

"Takin' a sick day?" the man quizzed.

"No. Signing out. For good."

"Oh. Quittin', then?"

"Yeah. Quitting."

The man tossed the coveralls into a bin and placed the helmet and glasses on a shelf. "You'll get your last check in the mail," the man said. "It'll take three, maybe four weeks, though. Gov'ment bureaucracy, y'know."

"Yeah. I know."

"I'll notify personnel." Scribbling on a clipboard, the man said "You can bet your job'll get filled pretty damn quick. They got a big waitin' list goin'."

Phil pulled the laminated ID badge still clipped to his T-shirt, placed it on the counter. He glanced down at the nervous-looking photo of himself on his first day of work. Beneath the photo was stamped **Keyhoe, Phillip K. Strongs Army Ammunition Plant. No. 12021.** Younger he was, then. Innocent. A kid mowing lawns on weekends in spring, a carefree high school senior, goofing off with Tommy and the crew, a part-timer just trying to earn some money for college. How could he have known what was ahead for that kid?

The man nodded at the badge. "When somebody's done, we just toss 'em. Unless you want it."

Phil hesitated. Then he thought that his father would want him to keep it. "I'll hang on to this," he said, slipping the badge into the breast pocket of his T-shirt.

Outside, he felt relieved.

He'd finally left this place for good, cutting the steel umbilical cord of the Strongs Plant. It had been easier to sever it than he thought, though its scar, he knew, would stay with him a long time.

A rumbling sound startled him. Phil looked up and noticed a storm cloud looming over the bluffs and moving steadily toward him. The sky had been threatening all morning, and now a scent of ozone filled the air as a silvery curtain of rain dropped on the far end of the plant, then swept over the Acid Area, then the refinery buildings. It reached the powder storage buildings—slumbering a safe distance from each other—then slanted against the change houses barracks with their dust-blinded windows. Though he didn't see any lightning, the claps of thunder, like booming explosions, reverberated between the buildings and echoed deep inside Phil's chest, making him shudder.

The first heavy drops fell around him, making dark splotches on the pavement. For a fleeting moment, he thought about jogging over to the car and grabbing the navy-blue rain jacket his dad always kept in the trunk. But he knew the jacket would be too large for him, and besides, he was carrying enough weights today.

Instead, he just tipped his head back, welcoming the downpour, letting it fall on his forehead and cheeks as if his face was an empty bowl and he was dying of thirst. If someone saw him from a distance, they'd never know that the clear rainwater, rolling down his face, was mixed with bitter tears. Still, Phil felt comforted as he imagined all that rainwater, soaking the powder spilled on the grass, making it soft and harmless as a kid's modeling clay.

It poured hard for another minute, and then just as suddenly the cloudburst stopped. As the wind began to gust, the wedge of dark clouds folded on itself and retreated steadily. A swath of sunlight moved in a wave toward Phil, its yellow fire flooding the parking lot and finally igniting in his upturned face.

As he turned and jogged through the puddles, he noticed an idling car, pulled nose-to-nose with his Chrysler. He squinted at the rain-splattered windshield, wondering who was inside.

# CHAPTER 57

Mariah motioned him into her car.

Phil, his T-shirt drenched, his hair wet and curling on his forehead, climbed into the passenger's side.

"So," Mariah asked, "do you always make a habit of standing in rainstorms?"

"Um, yeah," Phil answered. "Skipped my shower this morning. What about you? You make a habit of idling outside war plants?"

She brushed back her feathery hair. The red streaks she had added to it were fading. "Sometimes." She hesitated. "If it's for a good reason."

"And what's a good reason?"

She didn't reply. Recalling their impasse after his father's funeral, Phil wondered if their conversation was going to stall again. "Really, Mariah. What *are* you doing here?" he asked skeptically.

"I feel like we need to catch up," she said. "On...on everything."

"Well then, catch up," Phil said, a sharp edge in his voice.

"I'm...I'm not sure where to begin." Her voice sounded small and tentative. "So much has happened." She took in a long, slow breath as if it wasn't quite filling her lungs. "Ever hear 'For What It's Worth?' That Buffalo Springfield song?"

Phil nodded.

"Well, last night in my bedroom at mom's, I kept playing that song over and over." She began to speak more rapidly, the words spilling out. "I love the song, but its lyrics started to haunt me. Words about a man with a gun, telling you to beware, about battle lines, and thousands of people in the streets. About terrible things happening all around us, but nothing is clear. The more I played it, it was almost like the lyrics were entering me, all the way to my bones. I...I couldn't stand it anymore. But still, I kept playing it. I could have played it a million times."

"Then what?"

"I finally pulled the record from the turntable. And smashed it on the floor." She pinched her eyes shut, then opened them. "That's when I knew *I* was about to break into pieces, too. And I knew I had to talk to someone." She turned toward Phil, her pale blue eyes igniting. "Not just someone. *You.*"

"Why talk to me?" Phil said, keeping his eyes fixed straight ahead. "I mean, you've got all your friends in Madison. And, of course, Daniel." Simply saying the man's name caused a bitter taste in Phil's mouth.

"There is no Daniel," she blurted. "He's been arrested. And the SDS house is in chaos. Everybody left, and...."

"So, *that's* what you came here to tell me?" Phil interrupted. "That your other life in Madison is falling apart?" He opened the door and began to step out of the car.

"Phil, get back in. Please," Mariah pleaded. When he sat down again, she said "There is no *other life* in Madison."

"No? I thought...," he said tensely, "I thought you were in love with your great leader."

"That's over, Phil. And I realize now that I was naïve. And stupid. I can't believe I confused passion for a cause with passion for *someone*." Her lips pursed into a thin line. "I never really loved Daniel. I just loved what he stood for. Or what I *thought* he stood for. But now all that's changed." Her face pulled taut. "So no, I don't love him. In fact, I *hate* him."

Phil listened intently, wanting to believe her.

"These last months," she continued, "I was swept up in a movement." She spoke rapidly, her words pushing at a dam that couldn't hold them any longer. "It was all about peace and love. And fighting for a cause." She tipped her head back against the headrest. "The meetings, the protests, the marches. I was finally doing what I was meant to do. To fight injustice. To help change the world."

"That's always been your way," Phil agreed.

"But somehow…." Her voice trembled. "I got overwhelmed. I let the group take over my life." A tear rolled down her cheek and she wiped it away. "Somehow, I lost my*self*."

"Sometimes it's easy to lose ourselves," he agreed, looking at her for the first time since he got in the car.

"Yeah. And harder to find ourselves again." She lifted her gaze to Phil. "The point is," she continued, "I can't go back. But at the same time, I guess I'm having trouble moving forward."

"That doesn't sound like you, Mariah. You couldn't *wait* for the future."

She reached up and drew a circle in the steam on the window. Phil couldn't help but notice the fading bruises on the pale skin of her wrists. "Back in high school," she said, "I pictured my future as a map. Something I could follow. But the map's not so clear anymore."

"I know what you mean." He thought for a moment. "But maybe," he offered, "the future's made up of a whole series of *nows*. At least that's how I've been looking at it lately." He paused. "Maybe it's easier to deal with that way."

She nodded slightly. "I just want the world to be back to normal." She sighed, closing her eyes behind pink eyelids. Then she opened them again. "I still hate this war. I keep dreaming of the day it will finally be over. I'm never giving up on my commitment."

"I wouldn't expect you to." After a few seconds, Phil said, "I made a decision today. A big one."

"Oh?"

"I quit the plant. I'm done. I can't work for a place that supports the war."

A relieved expression filled her face, but it was quickly erased by a look of concern. "But Phil, what about the draft…?"

"Don't worry. I won't get drafted. I just got accepted into Madison. For the fall."

"I'm so glad to hear that."

"And back home," he continued, "Mom will be okay financially. There's Dad's insurance policy, and the government pension. It hasn't been easy, but she's slowly healing. She's a lot stronger than I thought."

Neither one spoke for a moment. Phil lifted his eyes to see the dome of sky was still divided: half a wedge of dark scalloped clouds, the other half an endless royal blue.

"You know," Phil said softly, intensely, "I feel like there's been a war inside me for a long time. But now that I'm with you, I finally feel peace."

"Yes," she agreed, "peace." She gazed at him expectantly. "And what about love?"

Phil leaned toward her, and at the same moment, she was leaning toward him. They met in the middle in a long kiss. The kiss made Phil feel as though light was filling him, pushing away the layers of gray he had felt inside himself for months.

When Mariah's elbow bumped a lever on the steering column, the windshield wipers suddenly swished back and forth, whisking the beads of rain from the glass.

Pulling back from the kiss, the two of them burst into laughter.

"Damn," Mariah exclaimed. "I wish I could wash away my mistakes that easily."

"Same here."

"So what's next?" Mariah asked, her voice suddenly flirtatious.

"How about we get away from this place?"

"So, are we in the middle of one of your famous *nows*?"

"We might be."

"Okay. But where are we going?"

"You'll see. But let's take the Chrysler. I'll drive us."

# CHAPTER 58

Mariah opened door of the Chrysler, leaned in, and echoed the words she had said that night after the high school dance. "Nice looking innards."

"Need a ride, stranger?" Phil asked, playing along with her. "Home, I mean?" Though it was a year and a half ago, it seemed like a decade since they said those words.

"I'd like that," she said, smiling as she jumped in. She glanced at the dash. "Where's the dashboard compass?"

"I took it out. Don't need it."

"Hmmm," she said wryly, "How will you know where you're going?"

He didn't answer her. Somehow, he just knew that there *was* a compass needle, deep inside, pointing him toward where he needed to go.

They drove down County 12, then branched off to a narrow dirt road that weaved back and forth between a patchwork of leaning pine trees and jagged quartzite outcroppings.

At the base of the bluff, Phil pulled the car to a stop.

"Here?" she said, her voice both expectant and excited.

"Yes," he replied, "Here."

They gazed at the lake in silence. Though there was a light breeze, the water looked perfectly calm, as though the circular shore had pulled its surface taut. To Phil, it seemed so small, yet somehow large and expansive at the same time, as if it might contain the whole ocean. It could have been any lake in the world, he thought, but it wasn't. He turned toward Mariah, noticing the sunlight, gathering softly around her face, the same way it did all those months ago. They could have been any two ordinary people in the world, but he knew they weren't.

There was so much he wanted to say to her. And he knew that he would, later.

For now, Phil took Mariah's hand and guided her down the embankment toward the fifteen-foot rock slab that jutted over the water. Then he pointed to one side of the rock. On it was written: *Phil + Mariah = ?*

Phil had painted the silver letters on the rock the day after Mariah left for college.

"So," she asked, "Do you have an answer to your equation yet?"

"Not yet. But I hope to find out." He turned toward the lake again. "I bet you forgot all about this place."

"How could I?"

"When you dove from this rock," he said, "I fell in love with you." He recalled the rush of emotion that had swept over him, and, looking at her now, he couldn't help but feel that same feeling.

On an impulse, he took off his T-shirt and tennis shoes, set his wallet, watch, and car keys on a rock, then stood there in his jeans with a wide grin.

She gave him an inquisitive look. "So what are we doing?"

"We're going swimming."

Obliging and laughing lightly, Mariah slipped off her sandals and placed her beaded peace-symbol necklace on his T-shirt.

She noticed Phil's Strongs plant badge that had slid halfway out of his T-shirt pocket. "You still have this?"

"Yeah. Guess it's just a reminder."

Phil grabbed her hand. "What are we waiting for?" he called. He lunged into a run across the rock platform, pulling her with him. Reaching the edge, Mariah let go of his hand and stopped there, watching with surprise as Phil leaped into a graceful dive. He arced into the lake, and a glistening silvery crown of water rose up as he disappeared.

When he surfaced and waved her in, she swam toward him. But before she reached him, he gulped a quick breath and ducked under. It was twenty feet deep, and he could see through the clear water all the way to the bottom. He swam down, down where the mosaic of large rock slabs fit together like puzzle pieces.

Seconds later, he burst through the surface directly in front of her.

Shaking the water from his hair, he let out a laugh that echoed off the rocks.

"I thought deep water scared you," Mariah questioned. "What's *with* you, Phil Keyhoe?"

"You," he replied. "That's what." Phil felt no panic, no panic at all.

As they faced each other, just inches apart, they treaded water gracefully, their legs moving in unison as if they were dancing. Suddenly Phil had the sensation that he could swim this way for hours, days, years. He could swim with her into his future without ever getting tired; he didn't care how deep the water.

He lifted his hand and reached toward her. She lifted hers, and their fingertips touched. Though it was impossible, Phil thought he felt a static spark.

Mariah was the spark, the fire. She always was. Phil understood that now. Love was the spark.

As they embraced and kissed again, Phil imagined the concentric ripples gliding out from them and carrying all the way to the far shore.

Back in the car, Mariah slid close to him. "Where to now?" she asked.

Phil didn't reply, just twisted the key. Then he reached down, grasped Mariah's hand and gave it a gentle squeeze. And when he placed his hands on the wheel, he was certain he could already feel it turning.

Minnesota writer and teacher Bill Meissner is the author of eleven books, including four books of short stories and five books of poems. His first novel, *Spirits in the Grass*, was awarded the Midwest Book Award. He has won numerous awards for his writing, including an NEA Creative Writing Fellowship, a Minnesota State Arts Board Fellowship, a Loft-McKnight Fellowship for Poetry, and a Loft-McKnight Award of Distinction in Fiction. For over a decade, Meissner taught a university course based on the culture, literature, and music of the late 1960s. Bill's interests include rock music, photography, baseball, pulp fiction magazines, American culture, vintage typewriters, and travel—especially to tropical/beach locations such as Mexico, Costa Rica, Puerto Rico and the U.S. Virgin Islands. He lives in Minnesota with his wife, Chris.

His Facebook author page is https://www.facebook.com/wjmeissner/